The River House

MARGARET LEROY

MIRA

All the characters in this book have no existence outside the imagination of the author, and have no relation whatsoever to anyone bearing the same name or names. They are not even distantly inspired by any individual known or unknown to the author, and all the incidents are pure invention.

Published in Great Britain 2011
MIRA Books, Eton House, 18-24 Paradise Road,
Richmond, Surrey, TW9 1SR

THE RIVER HOUSE © Margaret Leroy 2005

This is the revised text of a work first published in North America by Little, Brown and Company in 2005.

ISBN 978 0 7783 0409 8

59-0111

Printed in Great Britain
by CPI Mackays, Chatham, ME5 8TD

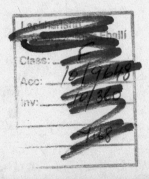

The River House

"In some ways *The River House* reads like a suspense novel written by Richard Yates. Leroy handles marriage and domestic life with the same graceful, precise, rueful style as the late novelist did, though with a warmer, more hopeful intelligence... Leroy elucidates Ginnie's moral conundrum beautifully. Although there is never much doubt as to what Ginnie will do, it's how she does it that provides considerable suspense."
—*Washington Post*

"Leroy delineates Ginnie's diffidence in a deliberately hypnotic, masterly fashion. Her quiet, self-assured narrative voice delivers tremendous psychological depth and emotional resonance."
—*Kirkus Reviews*

"Leroy's sensuously ethereal, subtly electric drama discerningly probes the affective fragility of a woman struggling to preserve all she holds dear, without losing herself in the process."
—*Booklist*

"Margaret Leroy, who also wrote the excellent *Postcards from Berlin*, makes you care about her characters, who feel so real that you know they must be out there leading the lives she talks about... Settle down in a deep armchair or hammock with *The River House*, and make sure you're comfortable—you won't want to get up for a while."
—*BookLoons*

"This gripping suspense novel by British author Margaret Leroy is more about the complex relationships between people than it is about crime... Leroy expertly draws a picture of a woman and a family in crisis and the moral questions one sometimes has to face."
—*Toronto Sun*

ACKNOWLEDGEMENTS

I am deeply grateful to my wonderful editor, Maddie West, for her intelligence and empathy; to the brilliant team at MIRA, especially Catherine Burke and Oliver Rhodes; to Judy Clain, my editor at Little, Brown and Company, New York; and to my marvellous agents, Kathleen Anderson and Laura Longrigg. Brian Hook very generously enlightened me about the workings of the Metropolitan Police—any errors are, of course, mine alone. My thanks also to Lucy Floyd and Vicki Tippet for contributing contacts and insights; and as always to Mick, Becky and Izzie for their love and understanding.

In researching this story, I found these books especially valuable: "*Men Who Batter Women*", by Adam Edward Jukes; "*A Celtic Miscellany: Translations from the Celtic Literatures*," by Kenneth Hurlstone Jackson; and Peter Ackroyd's "*London: A Biography*".

CHAPTER I

He's building a wall from Lego. There's no sound but the click as he slots the bricks together, and his rapid, fluttery breathing. His face is white as wax. I know he's very afraid.

'You're building something,' I say.

He doesn't respond.

He's seven, small for his age, like a little pot-bound plant. Blond hair and skin so pale you'd think the sun could hurt him, and wrists as thin as twigs. A freckled nose that would wrinkle if he smiled: but I've yet to see a smile.

I kneel on the floor, to one side of him, so as not to be intrusive. His fear infects me: the palms of my hands are clammy.

'Kyle, I'm wondering what kind of room you're building. I don't think it's a playroom, like this one.'

'It's the bedroom,' he says. Impatient, as though this should be obvious.

'Yes. You're building the bedroom.'

His building is complete now—four walls, no door.

It's a warm September afternoon, syrupy sunlight falling over everything. My consulting room seems welcoming in the lavish light, vivid with the primary colours of toys and paints and Play-Doh, and the animal puppets that children will use to speak for them, that will sometimes free them to say astonishing things. The walls are covered with drawings that children have given me, though there's nothing of my own life here—no traces of my family, of Greg or my daughters, no Christmas or holiday photos: for the children who come here, I want to be theirs alone for the time that they're with me. The mellow light falls across Kyle's face, but it doesn't brighten his pallor.

He digs around in the Lego box, looking for something. I don't reach out to help him: I don't want to distract him from his inner world. His movements are narrow, restricted; he will never reach out or make an expansive gesture. Even when he's drawing he confines himself to a corner of the page. Once I said, Could you do me a picture to fill up all this space? He drew the tiniest figures in the margin, his fingers scarcely moving.

He finds the people in the box. A boy, and an adult that could be a man or a woman: just the same as last time.

'The people are going into your building. I'm wondering what they're doing there.'

He's grasping the figures so tightly you can see his bones white through his skin.

I feel a slight chill as a shadow passes across us. Instinctively, I turn—thinking I might see someone behind me, peering in at the window. But of course there's nothing there—just a wind that stirs the leaves of the elms that grow at the edge of the car park.

There's a checklist in my mind. Violence, or sex abuse, or something he has seen—because I have learnt from years of working with these troubled children that it's not just about what is done to you, that what is seen also hurts you. I know so little. His foster parents say he's very withdrawn. His mother could have helped me—but she's on a psychiatric ward, profoundly depressed, not well enough to be talked to. The school were certainly worried. 'He seems so scared,' said the teacher who referred him to the clinic.

'Of anything in particular?' I said. 'Swimming lessons, storytime, male teachers?'

She had riotous, nut-brown hair and her eyes were puzzled. I liked her. She frowned and fiddled with her hair. 'Not really. Just afraid.'

'Perhaps a bad thing happened in the bedroom,' I say now, very gently. 'Perhaps the boy is unhappy because a bad thing happened.'

Noises from outside scratch at the stillness: the slam of a door in the car park, the harsh cries of rooks in the elms. He clicks the figures into place. The sounds are clear in the quiet, like the breaking of tiny bones.

'You can talk about anything here,' I tell him. 'Even bad things, Kyle. No one will tell you off, whatever you say. Sometimes children think that what happened was their fault, but no one will think that here...'

He doesn't respond. Nothing I say makes sense to him. Yet I know this must be significant, this room with the child and the adult, over and over. And no way out, no door.

Perhaps this is the detail that matters. I sit there, thinking of doors. Of going through into new, expectant spaces: of that image I love from *Alice in Wonderland*, the narrow door at the end of the hall that leads to the rose garden. Maybe he needs to experience here in the safety of my playroom the opening of that door. I feel a surge of hope. Briefly, I thrill to my imagery of liberation, of walking out of prison.

'Perhaps the boy feels trapped.' I keep my voice very casual. 'Like there's no way out for him. But there is a way. He doesn't know it yet, but there is a way out of the room for him. He could build a door and open it. All that he has to do is to open the door...'

He turns so his back is towards me, just a slight movement, but definite. He rips a few bricks from his building and dumps them back in the box, like he's throwing rubbish away. His face is blank. He stands by the sandpit and digs in the sand with his fingers and lets the grains fall through his hands. When I speak to him now, he doesn't seem to hear.

After Kyle has gone, I stand there for a moment, looking into the empty space outside my window, needing a moment of quiet to try and make sense of the session. I watch as Peter, my boss, the consultant in charge of the clinic, struggles to back his substantial BMW into rather too small a space. The roots of the elms have pushed to the surface and spread across the car park: the tarmac is cracked and uneven.

The things that have to be done tonight pass briefly through my mind. Something for dinner. The graduates' art exhibition at Molly's old school. Soy milk for Greg, and buckwheat flour for his bread. Has Amber finished her Graphics coursework? Fix up a drink with Eva... A little wind shivers the tops of the elms: a single bright leaf falls. I can still feel Kyle's fear: he's left something of it behind him, as people may leave the smell of their cigarettes or scent.

I sit at my desk and flick through his file, looking for anything that might help, a way of understanding him. A sense of futility moves through me. I wonder when this happened—when my certainty that I could help these children started to seep away.

I have half an hour before my next appointment. I take the file from my desk and go out into the corridor.

CHAPTER 2

Light from the high windows slants across the floor, and I can hear Brigid typing energetically in the secretaries' office. Clem's door is open: she doesn't have anyone with her. I go in, clutching the file.

'Clem, d'you have a moment? I need some help,' I tell her.

Her smile lights up her face.

Clem goes for a thrift-shop look. Today she looks delectable in a long russet skirt and a little leopardskin gilet. She has unruly, dirty-blonde hair: she pushes it out of her eyes. On her desk, there's a litter of files and psychology journals and last week's copy of *Bliss*, in which she gave some quotes for an article called My Best Friend Has Bulimia. We both get these calls from time to time, from journalists wanting a psychological opinion: we're on some database somewhere. She gets the anorexia ones, and I get the ones about female sexuality, because of a study I once did with teenage girls, to the lasting chagrin of my daughters. In a welcoming little gesture, Clem sweeps it all aside.

'It's Kyle McConville,' I tell her.

She nods. We're always consulting one another. Last week she came to me about an anorexic girl she's seeing, who has an obsession with purity and will only eat white food—cauliflower, egg white, an occasional piece of white fish.

'We'll have a coffee,' she says. 'I think you need a coffee.'

Clem refuses to drink the flavoured water that comes out of the drinks machine in the corridor: she has a percolator in her room. She gets up and hunts for a clean cup.

'When does Molly go?'

'On Sunday.'

'It's a big thing, Ginnie. It gets to people,' she says. 'When Brigid's daughter went off to college, Brigid wept for hours. Will you?'

'I don't expect to.'

'Neither did Brigid,' she says. She pours me a coffee and rifles through some papers on a side table. 'Bother,' she said. 'I thought I had some choc chip cookies left. I must have eaten them when I wasn't concentrating.'

She gives me the coffee and, just for a moment, rests her light hands on my arms. It's always so good to see her poised and happy. Her divorce last year was savage: there were weeks when she never smiled.

Gordon, her husband, was very possessive and prone to jealous outbursts. She finally found the courage to leave, and was briefly involved with an osteopath who lived in Wesley Street. Gordon sent her photos of herself with the eyes cut out. About this time last year, on just such a mellow autumn day, I took her to pick up some furniture from the home they'd shared, an antique inlaid cabinet that had belonged to her mother. Gordon was there, tense, white-lipped.

She looked at the cabinet. She was shaking. Something was going on between them, something I couldn't work out.

'I don't want it now,' she said.

'You asked for it, so you'll damn well take it,' he said.

As we loaded it into the back of my car I saw that he'd carved 'Clem fucks in Wesley Street' all down the side of the cabinet.

She sits behind her desk again, resting her chin on her hands. There are pigeons on her window sill, pressed against the glass: you can see their tiny pink eyes. The room is full of their throaty murmurings.

'Are you OK, Ginnie? You look kind of shattered,' she says.

'It's death by shopping. I've got this massive list of stuff that Molly seems to need...'

'You need to treat yourself,' says Clem. 'A bit of self-indulgence.'

I sip my coffee. Clem likes to eat organic food,

but the coffee she makes is satisfyingly toxic. I feel a surge of energy as it slides into my veins.

'I did,' I say. 'I really tried.'

I tell her about the boots I bought, in a reckless moment out buying bedding with Molly. How they caught my eye in a shop window—ankle boots the colour of claret with spindly improbable heels. How Molly urged me on: Go for it, Mum. You look fab in them: and for a moment I believed her: I felt a shiver of possibility, a sense of something shifting. And then the moment of doubt when I handed over my credit card, wondering why I was doing this.

'You haven't worn them yet,' says Clem sternly.

'No. Well, I probably never will.'

She shakes her head at me.

'Ginnie, you're hopeless,' she says, with affection. 'So tell me. Kyle McConville.'

'There's something I'm missing,' I tell her.

She waits, her fingers steepled in front of her face, like someone praying. She has bitten nails, and lots of silver rings engraved with runes, which she buys at Camden Market.

I take a breath.

'He makes me feel afraid. Like there's some threat there, something that's happened or might happen. It sounds silly now, but I found myself kind of looking over my shoulder… I don't know when I've had such a powerful feeling of dread—not even with kids we know have been abused. But there's nothing in his case-notes…'

She nods. I know she'll take my feeling seriously. We have a mantra, Clem and I: How someone makes you feel is information. We understand this differently. I'm more prosaic perhaps: I think we're all more sensitive than we realise and respond unconsciously to one another's signals; while Clem's quite mystical about it, believing we're all connected in ways we don't understand.

'He builds a bedroom from Lego,' I tell her. 'Over and over. I feel that he went through some trauma there. But maybe that's too simplistic.'

'So much *is* simple,' she says.

'I said that he wasn't trapped, he could escape from the room. He just closed up completely when I said that. But it felt so right to me—you know, to walk out of your prison…'

Her eyes are on me. She has brown, full eyes, always a little dilated, that give her a childlike look. Now they widen a little.

'Ginnie,' she says tentatively. 'Perhaps there was some other reason that it seemed to make so much sense…' Her voice fades.

I sip my coffee.

'I just can't tell if it's something to pursue. Given how he reacted.'

She leans towards me across the desk.

'Ginnie, you need the story,' she says. 'You're dancing in the dark here. You need a bit more background. Who else has been involved?'

'There's a note to say the police were called to the house.'

'Well, there you are, then.'

'But no one was charged. And no one told Social Services, so Kyle can't have been thought to have been in any danger.'

'So what?' she says. 'Maybe someone messed up. Go and talk to them, Ginnie.' There are lights in her eyes: this amuses her. 'Isn't it what we're all meant to be doing nowadays? I mean, it's all about interfacing, isn't it? Collaboration and interfacing and stuff. You need to go off and collaborate...'

She pulls the notes towards her, flicks open the cardboard cover. Her fingers with the runic rings move deftly through the file. I wait to see what she says. You can hear the murmuring of the pigeons, as though the air is breathing.

She pauses, her hand on the page. A shadow crosses her face.

'Oh,' she says. 'That's not what you'd choose exactly.'

'What do you mean?'

She looks up at me, a little frown stitched to her forehead. 'I've met this guy—the detective you need to talk to. He's at Fairfield Street, he runs the Community Safety Unit. DI Hampden. I know him.'

'You don't sound convinced.'

'Maybe it's nothing,' she says. 'I mean, I could have

got the wrong impression. He spoke at this conference I went to. Very energetic.'

'You mean difficult.'

'I didn't say that, Ginnie. A bit combative, perhaps— but there were some pretty crass questions from the floor. What the hell. I'll give you his number.'

She writes it down for me.

I feel tired suddenly. I know just how it will be, this encounter with Clem's rather combative detective. A meeting like all the others, hurried and inconclusive, both of us distracted and rushing on to the next thing, in a room that smells of warm vinyl: trying to find a way forward for yet another troubled, damaged child.

'I guess I could try him,' I say.

The reluctance is there in my voice. She looks up sharply.

'Ginnie, you are OK, aren't you? I mean, should I be worried?'

'I'm fine, Clem, really. Just shattered, like you said.'

She frowns at me with mock-severity.

'This isn't burnout, is it, Ginnie?'

'Nothing so glamorous.'

I can't quite tell her how I really feel. How I've lost the shiny hopefulness I used to have. How as you get older it changes. You learn how deep the scars go: you worry that healing is only temporary, if it happens at all. You know there's so much that cannot be mended.

I take the number and walk back to my office. The bars of sunlight falling from the windows seem almost opaque, like solid things: as though if you put out your hand you might touch something warm and real.

CHAPTER 3

My house is half hidden behind tall hedges. It's a house that belongs in the country—you'd never guess you were on the edge of London: a cottage, with a little sunken garden; and at night its crooked old walls and beams and banisters seem to stretch and creak as if they're living things that are shifting and turning over and settling down to sleep. Sometimes I think how we'd all have loved this house if we'd moved here earlier, when the girls were little and we lived in a forgettable thirties semi. How it would have preoccupied me in my domestic days, when I thrilled to fabric catalogues and those little pots of paint you can try out on your walls. How the girls would have relished its secrets and hiding places: and how Amber especially would have loved that the river was down the end of the road, the Thames that runs on through London, with its willows and islands

and waterbirds. Like in the poem she made me read
each night when she was three:

Grey goose and gander
Clap your hands together
And carry the good king's daughter
Over the one-strand river.

I don't know what it was about the poem. It made
her think perhaps of the walks we sometimes took
on weekend afternoons, when Greg was busy in his
study preparing his lectures: driving down to the
river, and parking on a patch of gravel where nobody
seemed to come, and walking along the river path
where in summer the balsam and meadowsweet grow
higher than your head. Amber especially loved those
walks, poking around with Molly in the tangle of
bushes beside the path, and coming upon some tiny
astonishing creature, a sepia moth with lacy wings,
a beetle like a jewel, black and emerald. Or maybe
it was just the sound of the words—maybe gander
sounded to her a little like Amber—for when children are greedy for poetry, it's often for the sound
as much as the sense. There was a picture that went
with the poem—the rush-fringed mudflats beside the
glinting river: the princess a teenage girl in a cloak
and a coronet with a look of perplexity: the soaring
goose, wide-winged. I'd read it endlessly, till it had no
meaning: but it always evoked a particular mood—
lonely, a little melancholic, with bulrushes whispering

and the smell of the river, the mingled scent of salt and rotting vegetation. This house would have been perfect for us in those days. But things don't always happen at the right time in our lives, and I think my daughters now scarcely notice the house they live in, as they move towards independence and their centre of gravity starts to shift away.

Molly has begun packing, ready for Sunday and the start of her first term at Oxford: the hall is cluttered with boxes. I check my voicemail for messages. Amber must be already home: she leaves a trail behind her— her shoes kicked off, her grubby pink school bag with books spilling out, her blazer, still inside out, flung down on the floor. I remember she had the afternoon off for an orthodontic appointment.

I call to her. She appears at the top of the stairs. The light from the landing window shines on her and glints in her long red hair. She is drinking something electric blue from a bottle.

'You shouldn't drink that stuff,' I say routinely. 'It leaches the calcium out of your bones. Girls of twenty are getting osteoporosis….'

With a stagy gesture, she hides the bottle behind her.

'You weren't meant to see it,' she says.

'Nice day?'

'OK,' she says.

She pushes back the soft heap of her hair, tossing her head a little. Stray flyaway bits turn gold.

'Have you finished your Graphics coursework?'

She shrugs. 'I'm waiting to get in the mood.'

There's a brief blare of music as she opens her door and goes back into her bedroom.

Molly, making the most of her last week of leisure, is sprawled on the sofa in the living room, her little pot of Vaseline lipsalve beside her. She's already dressed and made up for the art exhibition; she's put on lots of pink eyeshadow and she's wearing one of her many pairs of embroidered jeans. She glitters against the dark colours of my living room, the kelims and patchwork cushions. My daughters dazzle me, with their long limbs, bright hair, and that sudden startling shapeliness that seems to happen between one day and the next. Molly once told me she could remember the precise day—she was just thirteen, she said—when she first looked at herself in the mirror with interest.

She fixes me now with her eyes that are dark and glossy as liquorice.

'Hi, Mum. I don't suppose there's any food?'

I suppress a sigh. Molly is quite capable of complaining that there's never anything to eat while standing in front of a fridge containing a shepherd's pie, a cheesecake and six yogurts.

'I'll be cooking in a minute.'

'OK.' She turns to me then, her fingers tangled in the kelim on the sofa. Her lips are slick from the Vaseline. 'Dad *is* coming, isn't he?'

'Yes,' I say, a bit too emphatically. 'Of course.'

I remember her as a little girl, one time when I had

a case conference and couldn't make it to her Harvest Festival: What's the point of me learning all the words to these songs if *you* aren't there to hear me?

'Dad wouldn't miss it,' I tell her.

'I want him to see it.'

'Of course you do,' I say. 'Don't worry. He'll be there.'

I go to the kitchen to ring him, so that she won't be able to hear.

My kitchen soothes me, with its warm red walls and its silence. It's a jumble of things that don't quite fit together, that almost seem to belong in different houses. There's a clutter of mismatched flowered china on the dresser, and a mirror shaped like a crescent moon, and an apothecary cabinet that I loved the look of, though its many little drawers are really very impractical. I keep all sorts of oddments in the drawers, things that aren't much use but that I can't bear to get rid of—the wrist tags the girls were given in hospital just after they were born, and a piece of pink indeterminate knitting Molly did in infant school, and the tiny photos you get in the pack of assorted prints from the school photographer that are too small to frame but that I'd never throw away. On the wall by the sink, there's a copy of my sister Ursula's painting of the Little Mermaid, from one of the fairy-tale books she's illustrated, the mermaid diving down through the blue translucent water, with around her the dark drenched treasure and the seaweed like curling hair. When Molly was a toddler, the picture used to trouble her, and she'd stare at it with widening liquorice eyes: 'But won't she drown, Mum, under all that water?' On the window sill there are some leggy geraniums, and apples from the Anglican convent down the road. Passers-by were invited to help themselves to the apples: and I had some vague hope that, given their ecclesiastical origins, they might be specially nourishing. I see in the rich afternoon light that it all needs cleaning, that I haven't wiped my window sills for weeks.

He's slow to answer. I worry that he's in the middle of a tutorial.

'Greg, it's me. It was just to check you hadn't forgotten tonight.'

'What about tonight?'

'It's Molly's exhibition. The art show at the school.'

There's a brief silence. Something tenses in my chest.

'Hell,' he says then.

'I *did* tell you.' I hear the irritation edge into my voice: I try to control it. 'It matters, Greg.' It depresses me how familiar this is: me always wanting more from him than he is willing to give. 'She worked so hard,' I tell him. 'And she spent all yesterday stapling it up.'

'Look, I'll be there, OK? There's no need to go on about it. Though it's quite a pain, to be honest. I was hoping to get in a bit more work on my book.'

I sit there a moment longer. I should be making the

dinner, but I just wait for a while and let the quiet knit up the ravelled bits of me and ease away the disturbance of the day. I see that a tiny fern is growing out of the wall behind the sink: this shouldn't happen. An apple shoot once sprouted from a pip that had fallen behind my fridge. Sometimes I feel that if I relaxed my vigilance for too long, my house would rapidly revert to the wild.

I decide I will make a vegetable gratin, a concession to Amber's incipient vegetarianism. I cut up leeks and cauliflower. I'm just at the delicate stage, adding the milk to the roux, when the phone rings.

A woman's voice, bright and vivid. 'Am I speaking to Ginnie Holmes?'

'Yes.'

'Ginnie. *Great*. I'm so glad I managed to get hold of you.' She's too polite: she wants something. Behind her, there are ringing phones, a busy clattery office. 'I'm Suzie Draper,' she says, as though she's someone I should know.

'Hi, Suzie.' I brace myself.

She's ringing from *Cosmopolitan*, she says, and she'd be hugely grateful for my comments.

'I read that study you did on teenage sexuality—the one that was in *The Psychologist*,' she says. 'I thought you made some great points.'

'Right,' I say.

'I'd love to have your perceptions for something I'm writing,' she says. 'You know, as a psychologist. It's a piece on one-night stands. Would you have a few moments, perhaps, Ginnie?'

'Yes. Sure,' I tell her.

There's a smell of burning. I reach across to pull the pan off the heat.

'It's about a trend we've noticed, Ginnie. That more and more women are choosing one-night stands. You know, choosing just to have sex? A bit less concerned about commitment and so on.'

I'm distracted because the sauce is ruined and I don't think that there's enough milk to make any more.

'The thing is,' I say without thinking, 'you don't always know it's a one-night stand till afterwards.'

There's a little pause. This isn't what she wants.

'Ginnie, would you like me to ring you back?' she says then, rather anxiously. 'So you can have a bit of a think about it?'

'No. It's fine. Really.'

'OK. If you're sure.' She clears her throat. 'So, Ginnie, d'you agree that lots of women today can enjoy sex without strings? What I mean is—sex without love, I suppose. Without romance. Like men have always done?'

I take a deep breath and try to think up some intelligent insight. But I don't really have to say much: she puts the words in my mouth and I only have to agree.

'That's a good thing, surely—women taking initiatives, being clear in what they want? Rather than always fitting in with men?'

'Absolutely,' I say.

'I mean, to be honest, I've been there, Ginnie: I'm sure we've all been there—you know, letting men set the agenda. But what we have now is women saying, I really want that guy, and I'm going to have him…'

I agree that this is a good thing.

The door opens and Amber comes in. She's over-heard some of the conversation and makes a vomiting face. I gesture at her to go.

'Is it OK if I quote you on that, Ginnie? This idea that more and more women enjoy sex for itself and kind of keep it separate? I can quote you?'

I tell her, yes, she can quote me.

She thanks me profusely and seems to be happy enough.

I put down the phone with a flicker of guilt about the women who'll read the things I've said—thought up at the end of a tiring workday while the dinner was burning. They surely deserve better.

I open the window to let out the burnt smell. A blackbird is singing in the pear tree in my garden. I stand there for a moment, listening to the blackbird's lavish song, leaning on the window sill, thinking about the last time I had a one-night stand. Quite a long time ago now. It was just before I met Greg: an attractive paediatrician I met at a conference on attention deficit disorder seduced me by pretending to read my palm. I loved his touch as he made to trace out my life line, as if he'd discovered a new erogenous zone: that was the best bit really. The sex was pleasant enough—but

the next morning, when we made love again before
the plenary session, it took him for ever to come, and
afterwards he complained he was getting a cold and
sent me out to buy Lemsip. When we said goodbye, I
asked for his phone number—not really wanting to see
him again, just feeling it was only polite to ask—and
he said, It's in the phone book. I remember driving
home down the motorway, tired and rather hungover:
and noticing in the mirror in the motorway service
station that there were mascara smudges under my
eyes and I looked like I was crying.

I wonder if that was really why I married Greg—to
get away from all those complications, the unfamiliar beds, mismatched desires, awkwardness about
phone numbers. It was such a relief for everything
to be settled. And choosing Greg was surely a good
decision. I tell myself we have a solid marriage: that
it really doesn't matter that we haven't made love for
years.

I hunt in the fridge for milk. There's just an inch left
in the bottle. I top it up from the tap and start again
with the sauce.

CHAPTER 4

Greg is there already, parked outside the school. He gets out of his car. From a distance he seems the perfect academic—tall, thin, cerebral-looking, with little wire-rimmed glasses. He never seems to age, though his hair, which was reddish, is whitening.

'Are you OK?' I ask him.

'Not exactly,' he says. He has a crooked, rueful smile. 'It was the Standards and Provisions committee this morning.'

The exhibition is in the art suite, up at the top of the building. We go into the first room. The place is crowded already, and crammed with sculptures and paintings, the whole room fizzing with colour. I'm dazzled by this marvellous multiplicity of things—harsh cityscapes, bold abstracts, masks, pottery, flowers. Beside us a boy with a baseball cap and a laconic expression is standing in front of a painting, his arm wrapped round his girlfriend. 'Is this the one with me in?' he says: his face is pink and proud. I feel an instant, surprising surge of tenderness: like when I used to weep embarrassingly at infant school carol concerts. There are certain startling emotions—rage at whatever threatens your child, or this surging tenderness, or fear—that you only really feel when you have children. I talk about this sometimes with Max Sutton, my lawyer friend from university, when we meet up over a glass or two of Glenfiddich and compare lifestyles—mine, domestic, anxious, enmeshed: his, bold and coolly promiscuous. He's travelled widely, been to Haiti, Colombia—nothing seems to throw him.

'To be honest, Ginnie, I never feel fear,' he says.

'You don't know what fear is till you have children,' I tell him. 'It's your children who teach you fear.'

We're offered Chardonnay, and cheese straws made in Food Technology that crumble when you bite them. Mr Bates, Molly's art teacher, comes to congratulate her; he has a single earring and looks perpetually alarmed. Cameras whir and flash as embarrassed students are photographed.

Eva is there, in red crushed velvet from Monsoon.

'Molly! Your pictures are *wonderful*. Are you going to be like Ursula, do you think? You've certainly got the gene. Ginnie, I *love* Molly's stuff!'

We hug. I'm wrapped in her capacious arms and her musky cedarwood scent. We've been close since the time we first bonded, in a moment of delicious hysteria at antenatal class, when I was pregnant with Amber, and Eva was having Lauren and Josh, her twins. It was during the evening when you could bring your partner, and some of the men, seeking perhaps to assert a masculine presence in this too-female environment, were pronouncing on the benefits of eating the placenta: they claimed it was full of nutrients. I saw that Eva was shaking with barely suppressed laughter and I caught her eye and we had to leave the room.

I tell her about the *Cosmopolitan* journalist.

She grins. 'I used to love *Cosmo*,' she says. 'Now I buy those lifestyle magazines—you know, forty-nine things to do with problem windows.'

'But, Eva, you haven't got problem windows.'

'I'm working on it,' she says.

'Mum,' says Molly, 'you've got to see my stuff.'

Her display is in the second room: she pulls Amber and me towards it. I look round for Greg, but he's met a woman from his department, an earnest woman with wild grey hair who lectures in Nordic philology: she has a daughter here. They're having an urgent discussion about spreadsheets.

'I'll be right with you,' he tells me, but he shows no sign of following us.

'Mum, come *on*,' says Molly. 'I want you to see my canvas.' She has a look she sometimes had as a child, when she would tug at me, especially after Amber had arrived and she couldn't get enough of me: intent, with deep little lines between her eyes.

We go into the second room. Her display is in the corner, facing us as we enter—her sketchbooks and pottery heaped on the table, and behind them the canvas, nailed up on the wall. I stare at the painting. It's huge, taller than me, so the figures are more than life-size. I don't know how she controlled the proportions, how she made it so real. It's based on a photo from my childhood—me and Ursula and our mother and father, in the garden at Bridlington Road. I don't know who took it, perhaps a visiting aunt. It's a rare photo of all of us together, and we look just like a perfectly normal family. It was one of a heap of old photos that Molly found in the kitchen cabinet: she was hunting around for something to paint for her final A-level piece. 'It has to be about Change,' she said. 'I ask you. I think it's a freaky topic. Change is totally random. I mean, it could be *anything*.' She was pleased when she found the photos of me and Ursula: she loved our candy-striped summer frocks, our feet in shiny bar shoes. The two of us would stand to attention with neat cheerful smiles, every time anyone pointed a Kodak in our direction. 'Look, you've got parallel feet,' said Molly. 'Amber, look, it's so cute. In every picture their feet are kind of *arranged*.'

The photograph was black and white, but the painting is in the strong acrylic colours Molly loves; our skin in the picture has purple and tangerine in it. The photograph may have made her smile, but the picture she's painted has an intensity to it. She has quite a harsh style, like an etching, the lines and structure of people's faces exaggerated, so that they look older than they are: and she's seen so much that was only subtly there in the photograph, that was just a hint, a subtext. My mother, her forehead creased in spite of her smile. My father, a looming presence, his shadow falling across us: my father, who was a pillar of the community, a school governor, a churchwarden, a grower of fine lupins: and I think how shockingly glad I was when he died. Ursula and me, eight and six, with our parallel feet in their shiny shoes: not wanting to step out of line. I see myself then, my conscientious smile, my six-year-old hope that if I was good, stayed good, everything would be all right. I wonder if Molly has brought to this painting some knowledge she has of my family. Yet I've told them so little, really, even though in my work I always maintain that families shouldn't have secrets. Maybe Molly's gleaned something from the absolute rule I have that there's no hitting in our family: or from the things I've said about marriage, the advice I so often feel a compulsion to give. The very worst thing in a man is possessiveness… Don't ever imagine that you can change a man… Promise me—if he's cruel or hits you, that's it, it's over, you go straight out of that door. *Promise* me… Yeah, yeah, they'll say, glancing at one another, with a look of complicity, of 'There she goes again', indulging me: We *know*, Mum, you've *told* us.

Molly turns to me, unsure suddenly. She's never had Amber's certainty.

'Is it OK? D'you like it, Mum?'

I realise I've just been standing here, staring.

'Molly. I love it. It's wonderful.' Instinctively, I put my arm around her, then realise she will hate me doing this in public. But she tolerates it for a second or two before she slides away.

'Mr Bates asked if my grandparents were coming,' she says. 'He kind of blushed when I said that Grandad was dead. It was, like, really embarrassing... Mum, make sure Dad sees it.' She moves off with Amber towards a gang of her friends.

I go to find Greg.

'You have to come and see Molly's work,' I tell him.

He says goodbye to the earnest philologist. I take him to see the canvas.

He has an appraising look, one eyebrow raised, the look he has when he's reading a student's essay.

'Goodness,' he says. 'It's quite in your face, isn't it?'

'Don't you like it, though?'

But I see that he doesn't, that he wouldn't.

'It's rather raw,' he says.

'Yes. But isn't that good? All that emotion? I love it.'

'Her plant drawings are great,' he says. 'But it takes a bit of maturity to draw people. Maybe she should stick to plants for now.'

'For God's sake don't say that to her,' I tell him.

I feel a flicker of anger: why can't he just be generous?

I go to find the girls, to say it's time to leave. Amber has moved away from her friends, from Jamila and Katrine, and is talking to someone Molly knows, a boy about three years older: she's standing close with her head on one side and flicking back her hair. She mutters to me that she'll make her own way home.

'What about your Graphics?'

'Mum, for God's sake.'

It's dark in the street now. There's an edge to the air, a smell of autumn, a hint of frost and bonfires. We stand by Greg's car in a pool of apricot lamplight.

'Did you like it, Dad?' says Molly.

I'm worried what he'll say.

'Sure, it was great,' he tells her.

I remember her when she was little, thrusting some drawing she'd done at me: But d'you *really really* like it, Mum? Say it as though you mean it...

Now, she doesn't say anything.

'Mum, I'm coming with you,' she tells me.

We go to our separate cars. I notice how scruffy my Ford Escort looks beside all the other cars, and that moss is growing in the rubber round the passenger window. When I turn the ignition, there's a grinding sound from under the car and it's hard to get into gear.

I glance at Molly. The lamplight leaches all the colour from her face, so you can't see most of her make-up; her face looks rounder, more open, as though she is a child again. A bit of glittery eyeshadow has smudged under her eye.

'He didn't look at it, Mum,' she says.

'He did, sweetheart.'

She chews at a strand of her hair.

'Not properly,' she says. 'He didn't look through my sketchbooks or anything. I was watching. Well, why would he want to look at it anyway? It's a load of crap.'

'That's nonsense, Molly.'

'No, it's true,' she says. 'I don't know why I got such a good mark. It must have been a mistake.'

There's a tug at my heart.

'Don't say that.' I want to stop the car and reach out and hold her, but I know she'd hate it. 'Sweetheart, you've got to have faith in yourself: everyone loves what you've done.'

But the shine has gone from the day for her, and I know she isn't listening.

I wake in the night with a start, from some indeterminate dream, feeling the thickness of the dark against me. Greg is snoring quietly beside me: I can sense the sleep-warmth coming off his body. I press the button that illuminates the face of my alarm clock. 4.15. Shit. This happens over and over, this sudden waking at three or four, and the thoughts are always the same. Thoughts of dying, of endings, when death seems so real to me I almost believe that if I turned I would see him there behind me. Looking perhaps like the picture of Death in one of the girls' old storybooks: Death who played dice with a soldier in

The Storyteller, with green bulbous eyes and a sack and a look of cool composure. He lays it out before me, clinical, utterly rational. You're forty-six, you're over halfway through; even with luck, great blessings and longevity, you're more than halfway through; and you've certainly had the best bit… He fixes me with his cool green stare, knowing and expectant.

I slip out of bed carefully, so as not to wake Greg, though nothing seems to stir him. I go downstairs. I haven't drawn the curtains in my kitchen: outside, the yawn of a black night. I make myself some toast and flick through the heap of yesterday's post on the table, a catalogue full of cardigans with little satin trimmings, an offer of a new credit card: seeking to ground myself in these safe and trivial things.

CHAPTER 5

It's eight in the morning, and Amber isn't yet up. I go to her room.

'Amber, you ought to be dressed.'

I pull back the curtains. She groans and hides under the duvet.

'My braces hurt,' she says. 'I can't go in.'

'Amber, for God's sake, you can't stay home because your braces have been adjusted.'

'Sofia always has a day off after her orthodontic appointments,' she says, though without much hope, from under the bedclothes.

'I don't care what Sofia does,' I tell her. I suspect a hangover. She went to the pub last night with the boy that she met at the art show, and he probably bought her one too many Malibus. 'I'll bring you a Nurofen, but you are going in.'

Then I find I have no clean work clothes. All my trousers have paint and Play-Doh on them, and the only thing that's respectable is a short black skirt I hardly ever wear. It's velvet, shapely, too smart for work really. I'm keeping it for best, I suppose. I do that with clothes, I probably do it with everything. It's a pattern of mine—deferring gratification, saving things up for some brilliant future time. This is always thought to be a positive trait. There's an experiment where you sit a three-year-old at a table with a single marshmallow, and you ask them not to eat the sweet while you go out of the room. You promise that if they don't eat it, when you come back they can have two. The children who can wait do better at school and even later in life: there's something fundamental about being able to postpone the small, immediate pleasure, in hope of achieving a greater one further down the line. But perhaps you can carry this too far. Perhaps there's a time in life when you have to stop deferring. Sometimes I think that at forty-six I'm still waiting patiently for my two marshmallows.

I put on the skirt, but my usual flat boots look silly with it. My eyes fall on the wine-coloured boots I bought in a rash moment with Molly. I slip into them. High heels feel odd to me—it's only rarely that I wear them: in spite of their sophistication they make me feel somehow childlike, as though I'm just trying on grown-up things. Like when Ursula and I would borrow our mother's shoes and put a jazz record on the ancient wind-up gramophone she'd inherited from our grandmother and stomp around the living room. Conjuring up a life of unguessable glamour, of glasses of Martini with little umbrellas in them, and dancing under a pink-striped awning and the sound of the band.

I glance at myself in the mirror. I'm taller, thinner, more vivid. I look like somebody different.

Amber is dressed now, but she says her mouth is too painful to eat, and really she can only manage a can of Dr Pepper for breakfast: so she won't be able to concentrate, so what's the point of school... I don't respond.

I'm late: I hate being late. I have a case conference at the hospital and I'll only get there in time if there's hardly any traffic. I go out to the road, into a sodden world of thick brown water-laden light. The traffic is always slower in the rain. I start up the car. In my unfamiliar shoes, the pedals seem to be at the wrong angle: and then I realise the problem isn't the shoes. The grinding sound from under the car is louder than yesterday. I don't know enough about cars to guess what's wrong with the engine: perhaps the rain has got in.

Where the side road joins the main road, I pull out in front of a bus and press on the accelerator, and there's no response from the car—no power, nothing. The car creeps forward, the bus driver hoots aggressively. Panicked, I pull in to the side of the road and switch on my hazard flashers and crawl to the nearest garage, where a stooped and rather smug man who smells of engine oil informs me sombrely that my gearbox has gone.

I know my hair will be frizzing in the rain. My new red boots have mud on. I ask tentatively what kind of money we're talking about.

'I could do a reconditioned one for about five hundred quid,' he says. 'New, we'd be talking seven.' He casts a pitying eye over my car, taking in the rust marks and the moss round the passenger window. 'But, to be honest, love, there's no point putting a new one into this, now, is there?'

Briefly, I feel ashamed, as though my mossy car is a moral failing.

It will take two days, he tells me. I manage to get a taxi, but I am still late for my meeting. I arrive with mud on my legs, self-conscious in my new boots.

At lunchtime, looking through my To Do list, I see where I have written the number of Fairfield Street police station, and Will Hampden's name.

I ring.

A woman's voice, brisk and sibilant. 'Sorry, he's in a meeting. Can I take a message?'

I leave my number and say it's about a patient—nothing current, I just need some information.

At the corner shop I buy baguettes for Clem and for me. It's still raining. We eat in Clem's office.

'The boots are fab,' she says. 'You ought to wear things like that more often.'

Clem's in a rather mournful mood. She's just had a date with a rather hunky medical insurance broker who explained between the sorbet and the espresso that he really enjoys her company but she has to know commitment isn't his thing.

After lunch there is a team meeting. Peter lectures us on the vexed subject of the waiting list, and how cutting patient waiting times really has to be our priority. Brigid talks with passion about the coffee fund. Rain traces out its spider patterns on the windows: pigeons, plumped-up, pink-eyed, huddle on the sills. Bad temper has its claws in me.

The phone rings as I go back to my office and I hope it will be Will Hampden, but it's the man from the garage, saying he needs to revise his estimate upwards.

I try the police station again. It's the same woman.

'Like I said, he'll ring you back. You must understand, he has to prioritise, he's very busy,' she says.

There's an edge to her voice, but I know she's probably responding to some crossness in my own.

There are days that you can't make right or mend. I make more calls but no one is in. I have a desultory session with Kerry James, a ten-year-old girl who's been referred with suspected depression: she draws immaculate little pictures of cats, and nothing I say gets near her. In the end I just leave, rather early. The rain has stopped. I'll walk for part of the journey and pick up the bus when I'm tired. Perhaps the walk will calm me.

I need my street plan, I have to go down roads where I've never been. These streets are dreary, with bleak

terraced houses with grimy curtains and gardens full
of old motorbikes. I turn into Acton Street, where
there's an ugly purple-painted pub with advertisements for Sports Night and a wide-screen television.
I pass a grim tower block, where the playground has
a high wire fence, like an exercise yard in a prison.
But over all this there's a wide washed sky, and a light
that makes distant things seem near, so you feel you
could see for ever. Birds fly over, grey geese like in
Amber's poem, clapping their wings together: six of
them, in a black ragged V, against the shining sky. I
watch them till they're out of sight and their creaking cries have faded in the distance. I feel the day's
irritations start to seep away.

As I study my map on a street corner, I see that
my route will take me near to Fairfield Street. And
something perhaps can be retrieved from the general
mess of my day.

C H A P T E R 6

The desk sergeant is young and angular, with gelled hair.

'Is it possible to speak to Detective Inspector Hampden?'

'It should be. Who shall I say it is?'

I tell him. 'I did try ringing earlier. I just wanted some information about a case.'

'I'll see what I can do,' he says. He speaks into his phone. 'He isn't answering,' he says, 'but I know he's somewhere around.'

Suddenly I wonder why I'm here.

'Don't worry,' I tell him. 'Not if he's busy. I can ring him. I just dropped in on the off chance. You know, as I was passing…'

'You might as well see him now you're here,' he says. 'I'm sure I can get hold of him. Why don't you sit down for a moment, Mrs Holmes?'

In the waiting area there are metal seats fixed to

the wall. The only other person waiting is an elderly woman: a faint smell of urine hangs about her and she has three bulging Aldi bags and many large safety pins fixed to the front of her coat. A voice crackles over an intercom: it sounds like traffic information. The woman shuffles sideways towards me, catching her capacious skirts in the space at the back of the seats.

She reaches out and puts her hand on my arm. 'You're pretty, aren't you?' she says. Her voice is surprisingly cultured. There's a fierce scent of spirits on her breath.

'Mrs Holmes,' says the desk sergeant. I get up, go to him. 'Let me take you through,' he says. 'I'm sure he won't be long.'

He takes me down a corridor; through the open doors on either side, you can hear phones shrilling and cut-off scraps of conversation. He shows me into an empty office, which smells of tuna and of illicit cigarette smoke.

'I thought you might prefer to wait in here,' he says. 'Maureen does go on a bit.'

'Thanks,' I say.

He closes the door behind him.

It's a cluttered, disorderly office: on the desk a computer, a litter of papers, a heap of blue ring-binders: and the more personal stuff, framed photos, a mug with pens and highlighters in. My eye is drawn to the photographs. A little blond boy, rather serious: a woman with a fall of straight dark hair. I think idly of something I once read in a novel by Milan Kundera, which I thought to be rather wise: that women aren't essentially drawn to the most beautiful men—that the men we desire are the ones who have slept with beautiful women. There's a half-drunk cup of coffee on the desktop and discarded sandwich wrappings in the bin.

The phone on the desk rings, and I have a brief instinctive urge to answer it. The voice over the inter-com makes a new announcement, giving the number of a car that's been abandoned, and inside it the body of an unidentified male. Above the sounds of phones and footsteps from the corridor, I can hear shouting, a man's voice harsh with anger: I can only make out certain phrases—For fuck's sake, repeated several times—and then a softer voice, a woman, seeking to placate. The anger in the first voice makes my pulse race. I sit there for what feels like an age in the smells of smoke and tuna, hearing the distant shouting.

The shouting stops, there are rapid footsteps along the corridor. The door bangs as it is pushed back. He comes into the room, then stops quite suddenly when he sees me.

'What are *you* doing here?' he says, as though I'm someone he knows, and I shouldn't be there.

He's a little taller than me, with cropped greying hair and a lived-in face. Forty-something. I see in a theoretical kind of way that he is quite attractive: that other women may like the way he looks.

'I'm sorry.' I feel an acute, disproportionate

embarrassment about everything—hearing the quarrel, that I'm here at all.

He's staring at me still, as though he finds me perplexing.

'I'm Ginnie Holmes from the Westcotes Clinic,' I tell him.

'Hi, Ginnie,' he says. He reaches out, as though he's remembering how he ought to behave. I half get up, unsure what to do. He shakes my hand, and I notice the warmth of his skin.

'The desk sergeant showed me through,' I say.

'He could have told me,' he says.

I decide that Clem was right: that he is a difficult man.

He's restless, the energy of his anger still hanging around him. He sits at the desk and takes out his cufflinks and pushes up his sleeves.

'So, Ginnie, how can I help you?' His gaze is hard, puzzled.

'I've been trying to ring you,' I tell him. 'I couldn't get through.'

'That happens, I'm afraid,' he says. 'It's been crazy here. Tell me what I can do for you.'

I tell him I'm a psychologist, that I'm working with a child that I don't understand.

He's leaning forward across the desk, his hands loosely clasped in front of him. His hands are close to mine. I notice the pale skin, the dark hairs on the backs of his fingers, the lilac web of veins inside his wrists.

I tell him about Kyle, how I feel he's been through some trauma but I don't know what it was. Will Hampden has his eyes on me, dark eyes, with red flecks in. As I talk I'm very conscious of his intent, puzzled gaze. I decide he doesn't like me. I think how I must seem to him, prissy, bland, ineffectual; my skin reddened from walking here, my hair all messy from the morning's rain.

'I don't remember the name,' he says, 'but that doesn't mean a thing. I'll have a look on Crim Int. Let's see what we can find out for you…'

He searches on his computer and gives me the dates the police were called to the house. He says he'll have a word with the officer involved.

'Where can I find you, Ginnie?'

I give him my cell phone number.

'I'll see what I can do for you,' he says.

I know this means that our conversation is over. I get up, pull my jacket round my shoulders. I have an odd, incomplete feeling, but there's no reason to stay.

'OK, then. Thanks.'

'My pleasure,' he says. He sits there for a moment, looking me over. There's something unequal about this, the way he doesn't stand although I'm standing, as though he's breaking some unspoken rule.

'I like the shoes,' he says.

'Thanks.' I make a little dismissive gesture, unnerved by this, not knowing what to say. 'To be honest, I'm not sure they're really me,' I tell him. Then wonder why I said that.

His eyes hold mine.

'What *is* really you, Ginnie?' he says.

My stomach tightens. I don't say anything.

There's a little silence while he just sits there looking at me. I can hear my breathing.

'Well,' he says then. He pushes back his chair: he's brisk again, full of purpose. 'I'll show you out, Ginnie. Where did you leave your car?'

'I didn't,' I tell him. 'It's in the garage. They told me the gearbox had packed up. It's been one of those days.'

'For me too,' he says. He smiles at me, a sudden vivid smile.

He takes me out through the back of the station, down a long white corridor lit by harsh tubular lighting that shines into all the corners. The walls are scuffed in places, as though they have been kicked. We hear the shriek of a siren as a police car pulls away from the car park at the back of the building. I hunt around for something to say—some light appropriate comment—but my mind is blank, as though all thoughts have been erased.

'I'd give you a lift,' he tells me, 'but there's someone I've got to see. Some crap meeting that got set up and nobody bothered to tell me. I'd like to have given you a lift.'

'I'll be fine,' I tell him.

We come to the door that opens onto the car park.

The doorway is quite narrow and he's standing close to me: he smells of rain and smoky rooms, and some faint spicy cologne.

He looks at me in a serious way, unsmiling now.

'Sorry about the shouting,' he says. 'Someone messed up. Sorry. You shouldn't have heard that.'

'Don't worry,' I say blandly.

'I wouldn't like you to think I'm always shouting at people,' he says.

I put my hand on his arm. It's happened without thought, an instinctive gesture of reassurance. But his sleeve is rolled up and I touch his skin. It's inappropriate, far too intimate, and I know he likes it. He turns to me: his face is close to mine. It would be the easiest thing in the world to reach out and trail my finger down the side of his face. It enters my mind that this is how it will be. The thought astonishes me.

The voice comes on the intercom again: the registration number, the body they need to identify, repeated over and over. This is how it happens, with the news of a death, with someone's story ending.

I turn and walk across the car park between the lines of police cars, quickly, without looking back. I feel how his gaze follows me. In my new red shoes, the ground feels insubstantial under my feet, as though it could slide away from me.

That night I have a dream about Will Hampden. It's a sexual dream—which is not in itself unusual, I have such dreams quite often. But usually they're rather vague—as though my unconscious mind demurely follows the conventions of between-the-wars Hollywood movies. In these dreams, some indeterminate man, a stranger whose face I don't see, might hold me or kiss me, or stand behind me and run his hand through my hair. Or the sexual feeling might be allied to some entirely neutral image: I might simply be swimming in a sunlit sea. And these images will be transient, rapidly merging with some other blurry narrative.

This dream is different. A dream of penetration, first his fingers, then his cock, gentle, slow, insistent. And it's quite precise and vivid. I'm on top of him in the dream, I'm gazing down at him, seeing his face quite clearly, my eyes on his as he moves so deeply inside me: and it seems to go on for a very long time, though the end still comes too soon.

CHAPTER 7

We park near the restaurant in a wide mellow street. The girls extricate themselves from the back of the car: they have bags of clothes wedged round their feet, and boxes on their knees.

Honeyed autumn sunlight falls on Molly as she steps out onto the pavement. She's wearing her flimsiest top, her most flamboyantly embroidered jeans. Her face is creased with worry.

'What if someone nicks the car while we're having lunch?' she says. 'All my stuff's in there.'

She chews absently at a tendril of hair that's slipped out of her hairband.

'For God's sake, Molly, no one will steal it,' says Greg.

'We'll sit in the window,' I tell her. 'Then you can keep an eye on it.'

Greg raises his eyebrows.

Molly's nervousness is like a glittery sheen on her. She moves on to her next worry.

'Are you *sure* other people will have their parents with them?'

'Yes, of course,' I tell her. 'Everyone will have their parents.'

'They won't,' she says. 'I bet they'll all come with their mates in a van. They won't have their parents... And, Mum.' Her frown deepening as another fear comes rushing in. 'What if they all know each other already? What if half of them come from the same school and they've known each other for years?'

'Molly, stop freaking,' says Amber severely.

The restaurant is crowded, but we manage to get a table by the window. Molly takes out her lipsalve. When her chicken pie comes, she just dips a chip in the sauce and sucks at the end of the chip. I terribly want her to eat, as though I have some unexamined idea that we're feeding her up for weeks, as though this final family meal will magically sustain her.

She feels my gaze on her.

'Sorry, Mum, I'd normally like it. I just can't eat today.'

She's hunched in on herself, as though she's shrunk a little. I wonder how well I have prepared her for this moment of moving on, the ultimate test of my mothering. Maybe I should have pushed her more towards independence—right from when she was tiny and I used to go on feeding her, when I should perhaps have urged her to take the spoon. She was always rather too willing then to let me look after her. Whereas Amber would grab the spoon from the moment she could clasp it, mashed pears and custard flying exuberantly everywhere. Amber would grab whatever she wanted however much mess it made.

Another family comes to a table near us, two parents and a serious young man in a stylish denim shirt. He has a chiselled face and fine dark hairs on his arms. Amber glances at him, then away. She has an intent look.

She catches Molly's eye.

'Mmm,' she says, thoughtfully. 'I hope he's going to *your* college.'

'For Chrissake, shut up,' hisses Molly.

Amber's lips curve in a small secret smile.

We have crème brulée for pudding. Amber wolfs hers, then takes herself off to the cloakroom; and comes back by a devious route, brushing past the boy's table, catching his eye and smiling slightly, keeping her lips pressed together to hide her braces. I love it that it comes so easily to her, this intuitive choreography that I've always found so perplexing.

I murmur to Greg, 'Perhaps she'll work a bit harder now. Maybe she'll see the benefits.'

He shrugs. He gives me a puzzled look. Perhaps he didn't see.

'We need to get back to the car,' he says. 'We're out of time on the meter.'

He pays the bill.

'OK?' I say to Molly.

She nods. She puts on more lipsalve.

We park at Molly's college and she goes to the porter's lodge and is given her key. Two o'clock chimes across the city: we hear the hollow sounds of many clocks and bells. We're directed round the back; there's a patch of gravel to park on, a tangled herbaceous border, a decrepit potting shed. The plants in the border are drying out and dying back with autumn—shaggy heads of chrysanthemums, and tatty Michaelmas daisies, their colours fading as though they've been left too long in water. The thin white stalks of some of the flowers have a calcified look, like tiny bones. Rich sunlight lies over everything. Around us, other families are unpacking their cars.

We go through the open fire door, along a brown corridor with many photographs of academic women, who all have solemn expressions and mildly unkempt hair. White rose petals have blown in through the open door onto the carpet. Someone has drawn genitals in black felt tip on the figure on the door of the men's cloakroom.

Molly unlocks her door. The room has that immediate bleakness of all uninhabited student rooms; it's under-furnished and nothing matches, the purple curtains ugly against the mustard walls. The ceiling is high. Our voices echo.

A brief panic flickers over her face, now it's really happening.

'I like the view,' she says determinedly.

We go to the window. The gardens are spread

out before us: a velvet lawn, an ancient beech tree,
its massive limbs propped up with wooden struts, a
round flowerbed with a sundial in the middle. It all
has a subtle dishevelled loveliness, nothing too neat
or ordered, no gravel path without its casual edging
of lavender or sprawl of yellow daisies. Some autumn
cyclamen, frail as moth wings, are flowering in the
bare earth under the beech tree.

'God, Molly,' says Amber. 'I wish I was a geek.'

We bring the boxes in, while Molly starts to unpack.
I tip out cosmetics into a drawer, and the vitamins I
bought for her. Her bath oil isn't properly fastened
and spills as I unpack it. I bite back the urge to tell
her off. I go to the bathroom to wash the oil from my
hands. The basins are swarming with green gauzy
flies, and word-processed posters urge the ecological
advantages of showers: 'If you're gagging for a bath,
share one with a friend.'

The window is open, looking out over the gardens. I
linger there for a moment, resting my arms. Nostalgia
floods me. I'm eighteen again, walking a sepia corridor much like this one. Memories pass through
me, a kaleidoscope of images. Men I went out with,
tutors who scared me. The choir I used to sing in with
Max, performing very old music in some chill college chapel: and afterwards there'd be a party where
everyone got drunk because the medical students had
doctored the punch with ethanol. I think of a tight
black velvet dress I wore for one of those concerts,
and, at the party afterwards, a stranger who came

up behind me and ran his hands quite slowly down my sides, his palms curved into me, his fingers just missing my breasts. And I remember how I felt then that life was a quest or journey, a movement onwards towards some ultimate attainment: that at some point you'd get there, there'd be a kind of clarity. And here I am, years later: yet the present remains tentative, far too full of traffic jams and compromise: and the thing I thought I was moving towards continues to elude me.

I take the final suitcase to Molly's room. There are urgent lists in my head, things I need to tell her: This is how your heater works, and if you leave your radio there on the window sill somebody could steal it, and promise you'll take your vitamins… Amber is pinning Molly's postcard collection to the pinboard.

Molly unpacks an alarm clock. It's frivolously pink and was a present from a friend: she's never used it.

'I want to know you can set that thing,' I tell her.

'For God's sake, Mum, I'll manage.'

I insist. She tries, but it's complicated.

'I'll be OK,' she says. 'I can set the alarm on my phone.'

'But then you have to leave it on all night—and what if somebody rings and wakes you?' My voice is shrill: all my anxiety about her focused onto this clock.

She puts her hand on my arm.

'Mum, it's OK. Really.'

She comes to the car park with us. It's colder now.

The wind stirs the leaves of the beech tree: the leaves are drying though they haven't fallen yet, and there's a rattle to the sound, a harshness that makes you think of winter. Behind us a girl with a sleek black bob is weeping as her parents' car drives off. We stand there for a moment. Molly seems so small, suddenly. I put my arms all round her.

'I'll be fine, Mum,' she says.

I realise I am utterly unprepared for this moment. I hold her for a moment and then she pulls away.

Amber wraps herself round her sister.

'Go, girl,' she says.

Greg gives Molly a rare hug. She holds him a little stiffly.

We get into the car and Molly turns and walks away. As we crunch out over the gravel, past the borders where the flower stalks are pale and fine as bones, I turn to watch her. She's on the steps to the fire door, talking excitedly to the girl with the shiny bob, who a moment ago was crying and wanting her mother, and who is laughing now and flicking back her hair.

CHAPTER 8

We drive slowly out of the city, through heavy
traffic. The car feels lighter without all
Molly's stuff in it.

'I wonder how she'll get on,' I say to Greg.

'Don't worry, she'll be fine,' he says. 'Molly always
copes. Look, I don't suppose you could dig me out a
Milk of Magnesia, could you? I shouldn't have had
that crème brulée.'

There's a packet he keeps in the glove compartment.
I tip out a pill and hand it to him. The jasmine scent
of Molly's bath oil is still all over my hands. We have
to wait for a long time at the roundabout on the ring
road. I feel as if there's something lurking just round
the corner of my mind: some grief, skulking there,
waiting to grab me.

Amber is hunting in her bag for her iPod.

'It's weird,' she says. 'You feel you haven't said

goodbye properly—that there's something you should have said which you forgot to say.'

'I feel the same,' I tell her.

She takes out the iPod and chooses a song.

'I'll miss her,' she says, her voice a little husky.

'I know you will, sweetheart. We all will.'

She isn't listening any more; she has her earphones in.

'Greg, I'm worried Molly won't wake in time in the mornings,' I say. 'I thought I'd send her our alarm clock—you know, just to tide her over till she can get to the shops…'

'Ginnie, for God's sake.'

'She needs something.'

'Well, so do I. I mean, what will wake *me* up?' He turns slightly towards me; I smell the chalk on his breath.

'You could use the alarm on your watch.'

'OK, OK,' he says wearily.

We drive through the Chilterns, through the swoop and dip of the downs. The sky is blue as ash. I can just hear the faint tinny sound of the music on Amber's iPod.

'I wonder what it will be like without her,' I say.

'Well, not so very different, I imagine.'

'We could do more things together, I suppose.'

'Such as?'

'Oh, I don't know. Perhaps we could go out a bit.' My voice small, tentative. 'You know, when Amber stays with her friends. Perhaps we could go away together or something.'

'It's a possibility,' he says. 'Though to be honest I'd welcome a bit more time to get this book together. Fenella's very patient, but she's starting to make noises.'

I think of Fenella, his literary agent: her Sloaney clothes—the pearls, the velvet Alice bands—her immaculate vowels and limitless self-assurance. I try to push away the irritation I feel.

'But—I mean—things will be different now, won't they? It's a big change.'

'Ginnie, we only left Molly half an hour ago.'

'But we have to make it a positive thing. You know, a chance to do things differently…'

He's quiet as though he's thinking. I feel a flicker of hopefulness—that maybe he will agree.

'There *was* one thing I thought of,' he says. 'I thought I might move into Molly's bedroom. Just while she's away. I'm sure we'd both sleep better. Would that be OK with you?'

'Yes, of course,' I say. 'If you want to.' This jolts me. I swallow hard. 'I'd have to clear out her room first—it's a total tip in there.' Trying to be light about it. 'But I was thinking more of maybe doing things together…'

'Let's not go rushing into anything,' he says.

A dark mood washes through me.

The cars all have their headlights on now: bright beams from the oncoming traffic weave across us. We drive through a stand of birches, their slender trunks and branches pale and naked in the lights. I realise I had hoped for something in this moment—though the hope was never fully conscious, and certainly never expressed. That there'd be a kind of freedom or renewal. That we'd enter a new landscape, with glimmerings of what life might be like when Amber too goes, when it's just the two of us, and that it would be a place that I could live in. That there'd be a new intimacy—dinner sometimes in restaurants on the waterfront, trips to the theatre, winter weekends in Prague. A rediscovery of one another.

Yet in this moment I know the limits of what we have, what we are. I see that what is missing is not just something postponed or which can be recovered. Not something put aside for a while or safely stowed away—like a book you never quite finished but hoped one day to return to. Is this my fault? I wonder. Have I tried hard enough, done enough to mend it?

We went to a Marriage Guidance counsellor once. It was my idea, of course, but Greg agreed to come— unwillingly, but at least he agreed. I was so grateful to him. I remember this, as we drive along the motorway and the countryside darkens around us. I tell myself— at least I did what I could, at least I tried.

The counsellor had a room with walls the colour of mint toothpaste, and on the table an African violet that looked as though it was made from plastic, the leaves too clean and symmetrical to be real. She smelt

of anti-bacterial soap and she wore a polyester blouse
with a floppy bow at the collar.

We talked for three sessions before we reached what
we'd come for. She never seemed quite comfortable
with us: perhaps my being a psychologist made her
nervous. We talked about our children, the families
we grew up in, and what we did when we disagreed—
which seemed to be her speciality. The thing we had
really come to say hung there in the room with us.

Eventually I told her that sex was our problem. She
flushed a little when I said this, her neck blotching
with purple above the polyester bow. Her embarrassment seemed a serious flaw in a marriage counsellor.
She said, rather primly, that she thought the physical relationship between any two people would be
fine if the communication was right. And I thought,
No, that's not true: sex is about sex, it's not about
communication.

I remembered how it had happened. How after the
children I was always so tired; and we went on having
sex, though I didn't really want to, because it seemed
mean to say No: but an orgasm seemed to take more
energy than I had. There's a moment of decision,
of reaching out for pleasure, you have to focus, to
fantasise—well, it's like that for me anyway—and it
never seemed quite worth the effort. So I used to say,
Leave it, really, I don't mind… And sex had come
to seem pointless, even inappropriate—as though it
wasn't what our relationship was for. I'd tell myself this
didn't matter, that I could live without it. Yet always

with an awareness of something obscurely wrong, of an absence—some primary colour missing from my life, as though I were a picture painted without red. I couldn't begin to explain this to her.

She tried a different tack. She said how sex—just the physical thing—often isn't enough for women: we women need to feel we're *making love*. She said this with emphasis, as though it were a unique insight. I told her this was a distinction I'd never understood. My response seemed to perplex her. But romance was so important, she said, all those little gestures that make a woman feel special.

I tried again.

'But I mean—after having kids—sex does go sometimes, doesn't it? Don't you find that with other couples? What happens to them? Does it ever come back?' My voice was shrill, urgent. I really wanted to know this.

She said it was us she wanted to talk about now— not other couples.

She had some suggestions, some stratagems. I was to ring Greg at work and to make an appointment for sex. When she saw how we both responded to this, imagining me interrupting a semiotics tutorial with a lascivious proposition, she moved on down her list. I needed to pamper myself, she said—she was very keen on pampering, which seemed to involve the purchase of scented candles and expensive bath products. I muse on this now, as we drive on through the darkening landscape—because it's quite a common belief,

and yet so very strange. As though sex can be found
at a department store cosmetics counter, among the
flash balms and exfoliants, and purchased from one
of those pushy women with clinical white coats and
far too much mascara. Whereas desire is to be found
in other places entirely. At a party where a stranger
comes up behind you and runs his hands down your
sides. Or in an afternoon office, where a man who
smells of smoky rooms holds your eyes for a little too
long and pushes up his shirtsleeves. Yes, especially
that: just thinking of it.

And then Greg said, 'Ginnie's ever so tired, aren't
you, darling? Bringing up the girls—she has her hands
full. You know, life's very busy...'

And the counsellor said yes, that it would probably
all change when our daughters were older. I felt a kind
of despair then, as they both insisted that our problem
was not such an issue really and perfectly predictable.
I knew such bleakness, in the room with the African
violet and the toothpaste walls. Feeling that this was
beyond repair, that we'd reached the end of the line.

After that she retreated to safer ground—to our
relationship history and the story of how we'd met.
She sat back in her chair now, she seemed to be more
at ease. I understood what she was seeking to do—to
unearth or recover whatever had originally drawn us
together. I might well have done the same in her place.
Though I didn't see how this could help us. You can't
go back there.

I told her how we'd met at a dinner party—just

giving the outline of the evening. It was a Burns
Night dinner, held by some friends of Max's, who'd
wangled me an invite: and we were all told to bring
a song or a poem: and I fell in love with Greg when
he was reading aloud.

It was done with panache—a long refectory table, a
proper damask tablecloth, the whole place shimmering with candles. The men wore dinner jackets, the
women were in long dresses. I remember one woman
who had a dress of some slippery cloth that was tight
across her breasts, and a heap of blonde hair pinned
high up on her head. There was whisky that tasted
wonderfully of woodsmoke.

But even after the whisky, most of us were a little
embarrassed reading the poems we'd brought. Mostly
we chose comic poems, keeping the emotional tem-
perature down, so as not to seem pretentious. Max
read something by Craig Raine. I read a poem by
Wendy Cope, which was short and a little poignant.
The blonde woman didn't read anything, though toward
the end of the evening she pulled out her hair clip
and let down all her hair, shaking her head a little as
it fell, so it rippled and gleamed in the candle-light.
Max watched intently. Someone took out a guitar and
sang a Tom Lehrer song.

I didn't really notice Greg till he started to read. He
was rather too thin for my taste, and anyway seated
up at the other end of the table. But he had a beguiling speaking voice—a subtle, cultured baritone. He
read something obscure and Celtic, a strange tale of

enchantment, of four companions who were walking in their lands when a mist fell: and when it lifted the land was bright but everything they knew had disappeared, all their flocks and herds and houses and the people who were with them; there was no animal, no smoke, no fire, no man, no dwelling, so only the four of them remained alone. The narrative was disjointed, dreamlike, as though the storyteller had stitched together many different strands. There were curses and metamorphoses and one thing becoming another, and magical objects and animals—a shining white boar, a golden bowl. Greg read with complete confidence, expecting to be listened to. It was a bold thing to do, to read something so rich and elusive. We heard him in attentive silence. Afterwards, before we clapped, there was a little collective sigh of pleasure.

At the end of the evening, as people started to drift away, I went to him and asked about the story. I was warm with the wine, fluid, more forthcoming than usual. It was from the Mabinogion, a collection of medieval Welsh stories, he said. He lent me his copy, wrote his phone number in it, insisted that I had to give it back when I'd finished. I noticed that his cufflinks were little silver fish. He seemed quirky, cerebral, charming: but with a kind of reserve that made me feel at ease. Max gave me a quick knowing smile as he slid out of the room, his arm round the blonde woman, his fingers tracing the curve of her hip through the flimsy fabric of her frock, as though they were lovers already.

Yet I misread Greg, of course. The whole attraction was based on errors of interpretation. I saw his detachment as a kind of peacefulness, a safety I knew I needed. And he, I think, misunderstood me too— welcomed my shyness, my hesitancy, believing I would be happy to be a rather traditional wife, grounding him, keeping everything calm and stable: while life for him, the real thing, happened elsewhere. There's such readiness, at some points in your life, to move on to the next stage—the old world over, the new one not yet begun. You grasp at anything you feel might take you forward. There, it's all signed and sealed, the choices made, the path plotted out… And you find yourself in the middle way: your marriage empty, your children leaving, the mist falling over the land.

CHAPTER 9

I sit in the soft late afternoon sun that falls across my office, sipping a final coffee. I like to stay here sometimes before I head for home, letting the day and all its tensions fall from me.

The file of the last child I saw is on the desk in front of me. Gemma Westerley—a little waif in frilled socks, with hair the colour of straw and a naked, timid smile. She has special needs, though for years her teachers didn't realise; she was quiet in class and her exercise books were orderly with hearts drawn in the margins, and nobody saw how little she understood. Now her teacher is worried she might have been abused. Her confusion is still here in the room, like a trace of smoke or perfume. I make some notes, then put the file away.

I plan my evening. There's fish in my bag for tea. I went to the market at lunchtime and braved the fish stall with its glazed dead eyes: this made me feel like

a good mother. Amber is going out later, to the Blue
Hawaii for a birthday party, where they will drink
cocktails named after sex acts and laced with too
much vodka, and I want to make sure that at least
she's eaten properly. And when Amber has gone I
shall start to tidy Molly's room.

At the thought of Molly, I feel a little surge of anxiety.
I wonder whether she woke on time this morning, and
whether she has made friends with the girl with the
black shiny hair. I wonder when she will ring me.

I look through some post that wasn't urgent—courses
I could go on, and a catalogue from a firm I've used
before. They make hand puppets and therapeutic
games. The catalogue is glossy, full of colours. I flick
through. There's a crocodile with a zipper mouth, to
use with children who've been abused, to help them
tell the things they're keeping secret. There's a wolf
that's half as big as a child. 'A large scary wolf who
can also be afraid. Is he then so scary?' I think how
Amber would have adored him when she was little
and had a scheme to keep a wolf as a pet. And there's
a grey velvet caterpillar, with poppers you can undo
to hatch a yellow butterfly. I shall take the catalogue
home and see if there's anything useful. Perhaps I
should order the crocodile for Gemma. But I'm tempted
too by the chrysalis that turns into a butterfly. I'm
not sure which child I would use it with: but I love
its velvet wings.

My mobile rings. I scrabble in my handbag, thinking it's Molly.

It's a number I don't recognise.

'Now, am I speaking to Ginnie?'

My pulse has skittered off before I consciously recognise his voice.

'Yes.'

'Ginnie,' he says. 'It's Will.' I notice how he doesn't give his surname. 'Look, I've got some info on your little patient. Quite interesting.'

'Thanks so much,' I tell him.

There's a little pause, as though he's drawing breath or working out how to put something. The sun through the window is warm on the skin of my arms.

'Would you like to meet up to talk about it?' he says.

'That would be really helpful,' I tell him.

'I wondered about after work today,' he says. 'About six. I could do that if it suits you.'

I tell him, yes, it would suit me. We talk for a moment or two with enthusiasm about how useful this will be—to talk about it properly. Our voices are level, reasonable: we are two professionals planning a case discussion. I have a crazy fear that even over the phone he can hear the thud of my heart.

'There's a pub,' he says. 'In Acton Street. D'you know it?'

I explain, perhaps with rather too much emphasis, that it will be the easiest place in the world for me to find.

'I'll see you there,' he says.

I put down the phone but his voice is still inside me. Desire ambushes me, taking away my breath.

I ring Amber. It's her voicemail.

'Sweetheart, look, I'm going to be late, I have to go to a meeting. There's some lamb stew from yesterday in the fridge. It just needs heating through. Make sure you heat it for ten minutes, and be really careful to switch the ring off afterwards...' But I know she'll ignore my message, and go to the Co-op for crisps and a pack of Cherry Bakewells.

In the cloakroom I study myself in the mirror for a moment. I think of the dream I had of him. I hold my hands under the tap then pull wet fingers through my hair. At least I have a lipstick. My skin is still flushed from talking to him.

I take my coat from my office, and the bag with the fish in—though I'll probably have to throw it out, it needs to be cooked today—and the catalogue with all its therapeutic toys. I decide I shall order the butterfly.

CHAPTER 10

It's the pub that I passed when I walked home from work, a lumbering building with purple paintwork and advertisements for Sports Night. I get there too early and sit in my car round the corner, nervous, suddenly wondering why I'm here.

At exactly six I go in. At first I can't see him. I try to remember his face, but it eludes me, though I saw it so precisely in my dream. I worry, like a girl on a first date, that he's here and I haven't recognised him.

He's in the corner, by the fruit machine. I see him before he sees me. In that brief moment before he knows I'm there, he seems quite different from when we met before, his shoulders bowed, head lowered—as though something weighs on him and presses him down. As though there's a shadow on him. This surprises me.

He looks up.

'Ginnie.'

He's vivid, eager, again. I forget the shadow.

He stands and kisses me lightly, his mouth just brushing my skin. I breathe in his smell of smoke and cinnamon.

'I'll get you a drink,' he says.

'I'd love a whisky.' I wish that my voice didn't sound so girlish and high.

The pub looks as though it hasn't been decorated for years. The chairs have grubby corduroy seats, and there are curtains with heavy swags, and eighties ragrolled walls. You can smell hot chip oil. The place is filling up with workers from local offices, relaxing before their journey home—raucous men with florid ties, and women in crisp trouser suits and wearing lots of lip gloss. A teenage boy with an undernourished look and blue shadows round his mouth and eyes comes up to the fruit machine and starts to play.

I take off my coat, rather carefully: my body feels clumsy and ungainly. I watch all the glittering colours that chase across the fruit machine. I have a strong sense that I'm forgetting something important. Pictures of home move through my mind, a catalogue of possible disasters: Amber losing her keys and waiting on the doorstep in the cold, or starting a fire because she heats up the casserole after all and then gets sidetracked by an urgent text message. I take out my phone, I'm about to ring her again. But Will is coming back with my drink. I watch his easy grace as he weaves through the crowd towards me. Instead of ringing Amber, I turn off my phone.

He sits.

'So you're OK?' he asks. Just to fill in the silence. His eyes linger on my face for a moment, then flick away. I realise he too is nervous.

'I'm fine.'

He smiles at me rather earnestly, as though this is encouraging information.

'I hope this pub's all right,' he says. 'I thought it would be easier to talk here.'

'Of course, it's great,' I tell him.

I think of the dream I had about him, his warm slide into me, the shocking openness of it. Now, sitting here in this banal place with this man who's still a stranger, I'm embarrassed by the memory of my dream.

He sips his beer.

'Let me tell you,' he says. 'About young Kyle.'

'Yes. Please.'

'You were absolutely right,' he says. 'In what you suspected. The father's very violent.'

I nod.

'The mother called us a few times. I had a word with Naomi Yates, who's her liaison officer. Nasty stuff: he used to choke her, she said. It started when she was pregnant. As so often.' A kind of weariness seeps into his voice.

'Did he ever hurt Kyle directly?'

'Not so far as we know. That happens, doesn't it?

There are men who'll beat up their wives and not lay a hand on the kids.'

'Yes,' I say.

He takes a sip of his beer. I watch his hands, his long pale fingers curving round the glass.

'She'd leave and then go back to him. You know the story—these women who keep on leaving and then can't stay away. All it takes is some tears and a bunch of cut-price roses... It's one of the great mysteries, isn't it?' he says. 'Why women don't just give up on these psycho husbands.' When he frowns, there are hard lines etched in his face. 'There's fear, of course, but it isn't always fear. I don't want to buy into that whole hooked-on-violence thing, but you've got to wonder.'

'Perhaps it's remorse they get hooked on,' I say.

This interests him. Lights from the fruit machine with all their kaleidoscopic colours glitter in his eyes.

'You could be onto something,' he says. 'I imagine it's very seductive. He sobs and says he's sorry and it'll never happen again... We believe what we want to believe, I guess. About the people we love.' His gaze is on me, that intent look. 'I mean, we all do that, don't we?'

'Yes,' I say.

This hint of intimacy stirs something in me, a little shimmer of sex.

'You know about this stuff, then, Ginnie,' he says,

after a moment. 'Well, of course you would. You work with the kids who get caught up in it all.'

I have a sudden sharp impulse to uncover myself, to reveal something.

'It's not just that,' I tell him. 'It's in the family.'

His eyes widen. He's very still suddenly.

'Now, you mean?' He leans towards me, his voice is careful, slow. 'Or are we talking about the past here?'

'Not now. Now is OK. In the past. My childhood.'

'Your childhood,' he says gently.

He makes a little gesture, reaching his hand towards me as though to touch me. His hand just over mine. My breathing quickens—I don't know if he hears this.

There's a resonant clatter of coins from the fruit machine beside us. The noise intrudes and pushes us apart. Will leans back in his chair again. The teenage boy scoops up his winnings and stuffs his pockets with coins.

Will looks at me uncertainly, but the mood has changed, we can't get back there.

'Tell me more about Kyle,' I say.

'The last time was the worst,' says Will. 'Naomi reckons this is what triggered the mother's breakdown. She said she was going to leave, that this time she really meant it, and he threatened her with a pickaxe. Actually, threatened doesn't quite capture it. I think this could be the thing you need to know.'

'Kyle built a room with Lego,' I say, 'but he wouldn't open the door.'

Will nods.

'How Naomi told it—Kyle and his mother were in the bedroom, and she pushed the wardrobe over and barricaded them in. She'd got her phone, thank God, she managed to call us. We got there just as the father was breaking down the door... Afterwards he said he wanted to make her love him. Weird kind of loving.' He twists his mouth, as though he has a bitter taste.

I shake my head.

'I got it totally wrong,' I tell him.

'I'm sure you didn't,' he says.

'No, really. He's so terrified. And I thought the thing he was so scared of—I thought it was there in the room with him. That he'd been abused or something... He's always so afraid.'

'It's a pebble chucked in a pond,' he says. 'That kind of violence. It reaches out, it hurts a lot of people...'

'Yes,' I say.

A little silence falls.

He leans towards me again. His hands are close to mine on the table.

'Tell me about yourself, Ginnie,' he says lightly. 'You have a family of your own?'

I tell him about taking Molly to university. I feel uncertain though: it makes you seem so old, to have a child at college. I wonder if he's working out my age.

'It made me think how when I was just eighteen, I

was so sure that one day I'd have everything sorted,' I tell him. 'That I'd know where I was going.'

'I know just what you mean,' he says. 'And then you wake up and you find you're forty and all that's happened is that life just got more complicated...'

Forty, I think. Shit. Forty.

'My other one—Amber,' I tell him. 'She's sixteen. I worry about her. She drinks a lot and stays out late—I mean, she's quite pretty.'

'Well, she would be,' he says.

His eyes are on me. I realise I am flirting, running my hand through my hair, pushing it back from my forehead, as though it were the sleek glossy hair you can do that with. For a moment I feel I have that kind of hair.

'And you?' I ask.

'We've got a son. He's eight.'

He doesn't tell me his son's name, or anything else about him. I'm suddenly uneasy, as though everything is fragile. I don't know where this feeling comes from.

'So you've still got all that teenage stuff to look forward to,' I say lightly.

He nods. There's still a wariness about him.

'And your wife?' I ask tentatively, thinking of the photograph in his office, the woman with the long dark fall of hair. 'What does she do?'

'Megan's a photographer,' he says.

'That sounds so glamorous,' I say.

'She's good,' he says, with a thread of pride in

his voice. 'She doesn't work much now though. She's not happy with that really. But I guess we all compromise.'

I would like to hear more: I have a feverish, disproportionate curiosity about her. But Will is distracted, staring over my shoulder across the room.

'Great,' he says, very quietly, meaning the opposite.

I turn and follow his gaze. The man who walks towards us is shorter than Will, but authoritative, in a sharply cut linen jacket the colour of wheat. They greet each other with that slightly forced bonhomie men will sometimes use, when they know each other well but aren't at ease together. Will introduces us: the man's name is Roger Prior and he works in the murder squad.

'I'm helping Ginnie with a case,' Will tells him.

'Great to meet you, Ginnie,' says Roger. I'd guess he comes from a different background from Will, probably rather affluent, his voice deliberately roughened to fit in.

He leans in towards me: I can smell his aftershave, a bland, rather sweet smell, with vanilla in it. His skin against mine is cool, like some smooth fabric: his handshake seems to last a little too long. I see myself through his eyes, sitting here drinking whisky when I should be home with my family, too old to be holding a stranger's gaze and running my hand through my hair, my voice too eager, my shoes too bright and high.

'Will's helping out, then?' says Roger. 'Will's always pleased to help.'

'Ginnie's a psychologist at the Westcotes Clinic,' says Will.

'A psychologist?' says Roger, his cool grey gaze on me. 'So you can see straight into me, Ginnie?'

My laugh sounds forced and shrill. Roger has an affable look but his eyes are veiled.

'Well, I mustn't distract you both,' he says. 'I mean, from your case discussion. Good to meet you, Ginnie. Don't let Will take advantage.'

He goes to join someone the other side of the bar: but it's as if he's still with us—his scepticism and cool amusement and his vanilla smell. It's hard to talk, to recover the ease we had, as though Roger's pragmatism has undone something. I realise I had impossible hopes of this encounter—deluded, impossible fantasies. I know it's time to leave.

I pick up my bag.

'Well, thanks for the drink and the info. I guess I have to go.'

I'd like him to grasp my wrist and say, Don't go yet, Ginnie.

'Yes,' he says. 'We both should.'

As we get up the noise in the place breaks over me, all the talk and music and laughter. I can't believe how unaware of it I've been. Roger is at the bar, chatting to a very toned blonde woman, who smiles and nods subserviently at everything he says.

I follow Will to the door. I think how I'll never see him again, and a sense of loss tugs at me.

Outside it's getting dark and the street lamps are lit, casting pools of tawny light. There are smells of petrol and rotting fruit, and a dangerous, sulphurous smell where kids have been letting off fireworks. A chill wind stirs the litter on the pavements.

'God, what a dreary night,' he says. 'You're the only bright thing in the street.'

This charms me.

I point out where I've parked my car, thinking we'll say goodbye now and he'll leave me. But he walks beside me.

I stop by the car.

'That was a real help,' I tell him. I'm very polite and reserved. 'Thanks for taking the trouble.'

I'm fumbling in my bag for my keys, keeping my head down. I'm embarrassed at what he might read in my face, something too open and hungry.

'A pleasure,' he says.

I expect him to say goodbye but he just stands there. It's quiet on the pavement, just for the moment no traffic, no one passing. I feel the quiet in me everywhere. I am stilled, waiting.

'Would you like to meet again?' he says. 'Perhaps for lunch or something.'

'Yes. Yes, I'd like that. I'd like that very much,' I say. I manage not to say Please.

'We'll do that, then,' he says. 'If you'd like to.' But he doesn't move.

I can feel his eyes on me, but there's such a space between us: unbridgeable space.

'Ginnie,' he says.

My name in his mouth. The tenderness in his voice undoes me. I look up, meet his eyes: everything loose, fluid in me.

Slowly he moves his hand across the space between us, reaches his hand out to me, runs one finger slowly down the side of my face, tracing me out, watching me. I feel the astonishing warmth of his hand right through me: hear my quick in-breath.

He shakes his head, with that look he has, as though I puzzle him.

'I dream about you,' he says.

'Yes,' I say. I think of my own dream.

'I want to make love to you. You know that, don't you?'

I nod. I can't speak.

We stand there for a moment. He cups the side of my face in his hand. I press my mouth into his palm: there is an extraordinary pleasure in the feel of his skin against my mouth. I would like to feel his whole body against me. He says my name again.

But people are coming towards us along the pavement—people from the bar, with their harsh raised voices and laughter. He takes a step away from me, lowers his hand. I can understand that he doesn't want to be seen here with me: but I still feel a quick ache of rejection when he takes away his hand. I hate these people. I would like to stay here for ever on this pavement, his gaze on me, feeling his warmth on my skin.

He shrugs a little.

'We'll speak,' he says, and turns and walks away.

CHAPTER II

Thursday is my day off. I decide I shall clean out Molly's room so Greg can sleep there.

Greg is working at home today, in his study under the eaves. Before I start on the bedroom I take him a mug of coffee. He's intent on his work; he doesn't hear me come in. In the angled light from his desk lamp, the bones and lines of his face are etched in shadow; he looks older, more severe. The room feels cloistered, apart; up here you're scarcely conscious of the bustle of the street. You can see across the trees in people's gardens and down to the river, on this dull wet day a sullen dark surge.

He's checking through the editing of his latest book, an anthology of medieval Irish prose and poetry, aimed at a general readership. I glance at the page over his shoulder. There's a little poem called 'The Coming of Winter': it tells how the bracken is red and the wind high and cold, the wild goose crying, cold seizing the wings of the birds.

'I like that,' I say.

'It's Irish,' he says. 'Probably ninth century.'

'It makes me feel cold just to read it,' I say.

He smiles a little. This pleases him.

'We're calling the book *Our Celtic Heritage*,' he says. 'Fenella reckons that anything Celtic sells.'

'It's a good title,' I tell him.

'D'you think so? I'm really not sure,' he says. 'I thought I'd have a word with Mother about it.'

Greg's mother is a highly energetic woman, who likes to wear elegant layers of grey linen, and volunteers with the Citizens' Advice Bureau, work to which she seems admirably well suited. I don't doubt she'd have an opinion.

I put the coffee mug down on the desk beside him.

'Not there,' he says.

I put it on the floor.

Molly's room has purple walls and fairy lights and a feather boa draped across the mantelpiece. She used to say smugly, No one would think it's a lad's room, would they, Mum? But today her room smells troublingly of vinegar and everything is covered with a velvet bloom of dust. I fling the curtains wide. This hasn't been done for months: she lived a subterranean life, never let the day in. There are cobwebs where I've pushed back the curtains; I swipe at them with a duster and they break up, but the rags of web have an unnerving stickiness, lacy grey fragments clinging to my fingers. I feel a vague surge of guilt. There are certain feminine skills I've never really mastered—ironing, making your home gleam, straightening your hair. When the girls were small and I picked them up from school, there were women I used to notice at the gate who had clearly mastered these things, who knew what it means to be female: who were different from me, sleek and ironed and certain. I bet those women never find such cobwebs in their homes.

Molly is a hoarder. Her desk is littered with things she has no use for but can't quite throw away—earrings speckled with tarnish, dog-eared essays, karma bracelets. I come on a handmade birthday card from Else, her German penfriend: it's decorated with spangly stickers, and inside Else has written, in carefully looped handwriting, 'To your 18 birthday. I wish you health, good luck and a lot of effect in your life!'

I penetrate under the bed, where I find a collapsed heap of celebrity magazines and an apple core and an open bag of crisps—the source of the vinegar smell. I heap up all the glittery chaos from her desk into boxes, and dust and polish everywhere. The room comes into focus, as though its lines and edges are clearer, sharper, than before.

And as I do these things there's part of me that's somewhere else entirely—as though I'm living another life in parallel to this one. A life in which I'm with Will on the pavement in the dark of the evening:

and this time no one disturbs us, and he pulls me towards him and holds me to him, the whole warm length of his body pressing into mine. The sensation overwhelms me, and for a moment I sit on the bed and just let myself feel it: and the smell of his skin and the touch of his hands are almost as real as if these things are happening. As though it's this room and my life here that is imagined. But mixed in with the longing, I feel a kind of fear. Yet what is it I'm so afraid of? That something will happen between us, that I could imperil everything? Or do I fear that nothing at all will happen, that nothing will be imperilled, that my life will just carry on, quite calmly, like before?

I hoover under the bed, and the noise brings Greg downstairs.

'How long is this going to take?'

'I'm sorry,' I say. 'It'll just be a moment or two.'

Next to the fireplace there are bookshelves that stretch to the ceiling. It's a kind of archaeology, these layers of the past—A-level and GCSE textbooks, and, from further back, the books the girls liked as children. There have always been loud protests if I threatened to give them away. *The Storyteller* is here, and Death who played dice with a soldier, with his bulbous eyes and his sack, the drawing that haunts me; and Amber's book of nursery rhymes. I turn to 'Grey goose and gander', that I had to read each evening, feeling a mix of tenderness and tiredness, remembering the countless repetitions of early mothering, the things that always had to be done the same. Eva can get quite poignant about this sometimes, in the Cafe Matisse after one too many Bloody Marys, leaning towards me across the table, her splendid cleavage gleaming, the candle-flames reflecting in her eyes. 'What happened, Ginnie?' she'll say. 'D'you ever think—what happened to those children? The little children you bathed and read all those stories to? Don't you sometimes want to be back there? You know—when you could make them perfectly happy by buying a chocolate muffin… And you're so scared for them—you fear for them, that it's all so fragile, that something awful could happen, that they'll stick their fingers in an electric socket or something. But the thing is, you lose them anyway. You don't think about that, you think it'll go on for ever.' She'll look down into her wine glass and slowly shake her head. 'Sometimes I wonder—where have those little children gone?' I always tell her that I don't share her nostalgia—that I like the teenage years; but now as I pile these books into boxes, ready to go to the second-hand bookshop in Sunbury, it seizes me for a moment, that sense of something lost and irreplaceable.

Right at the top of the bookcase there's a shelf of Ursula's books. Leaves and tendrils from her drawings decorate the spines. Ursula draws such wonderful plants—extravagant, Italianate—that she sometimes gets letters from fans—Ursula, I would so love to see your garden… But the plot at her Southampton home is a few square yards of decking and a cactus: the enchanted gardens she draws are all from her imagination.

I run my finger along the spines, feeling a flicker of envy; it must be good to have achieved something as solid as this whole shelf of books. The one that made all the difference for her is there—the volume of Hans Anderson fairy tales she illustrated.

She wasn't always successful. She'd been struggling for years, largely living off Paul, her husband, wondering if it was worth it, or whether she should perhaps go back to primary teaching, when she did this book. I remember when she showed it to me— hesitant, self-deprecating—she used to be hesitant then. I could see at once it was special. There was something about these stories that suited her wayward imagination—these white-fleshed girls with their voluptuous deprivations: the mermaid trying to walk on her beautiful legs that cut her, the curve of Gerda's white throat and the scratch of the robber girl's knife. Everything was animate, full of sex or threat, every petal, every tree-root; tendrils of ivy clutched like greedy caressing fingers, the flowers had lascivious smiles.

Nothing much happened to start with—she sold the usual few thousand copies; and then it was chosen by children's BBC, to illustrate a series of fairy tales read by celebrities—and suddenly everyone was buying it. Not just children either, for her books inhabited that sought-after terrain—books for children that adults also enjoy. One drawing was even reproduced in *Vogue*, in a piece on the New Romantics—the picture of the Little Mermaid that I have in my kitchen, that

Molly found so troubling as a little girl. I remember when Ursula visited, just after the arrival of her first fat royalty cheque. She looked different. Still hardly any make-up, and her hair severely tied back, but with a new coat of the softest buttery suede. Though it wasn't just the money. There was a new certainty about her: she knew what she was for.

My phone rings. It's Molly.

'Sweetheart, how are you?'

'Well…my pimp beat me and then I got raped and I've started shooting up…' She can't quite suppress a giggle. 'Fine otherwise.'

'Tell me what's happening.'

The Freshers' Fair was great, she says, she's joined at least thirty societies. Even the Blonde Society—you don't have to be blonde, they just go round all the cocktail bars. And can she have a long denim skirt and some shots glasses for Christmas? And thanks for the alarm clock, but she didn't really need it, she's using the clock on her mobile.

'Molly, are you eating OK? Can you manage all right with the cooker?'

'I don't cook much really,' she says. 'If I miss a meal I have Pringles.'

I question whether Pringles are a satisfactory meal.

Molly sighs extravagantly over the phone.

'Mum, d'you ever listen to yourself? You been on one of those parenting courses or something? Look,

I'm fine, OK? I've just joined thirty societies and I'm fine.'

'Have you got everything you need? D'you want me to send you anything? I could send you some echinacea.'

'OK, Mum, if you want to…'

'Are you making plenty of friends?'

'They're really nice in my corridor. We're going out for corridor curry tomorrow.'

'Any men you like the look of?' I say tentatively.

'Just don't go there, Mum, OK? Anyway, half the guys in my college are gay—that's why they have such nice trainers… Look, my phone needs recharging,' she says. 'I've really got to go.'

I finish the room. I box up the books and dust everywhere. I strip the bed and heap up the linen to take to the kitchen to wash.

It's raining more heavily now: there's a thick brown light in my kitchen. I make a coffee and sit at my kitchen table. Suddenly, after talking to Molly, I feel ashamed; the things I've been thinking astound me. All the desire has left me. I can't believe I considered getting involved with this man, this stranger: took it seriously, half imagining it would actually happen. My family and their needs are all that seem real to me now: Amber, struggling with school work, needing stability: Molly just starting out, eager but brittle, tense with the newness of everything, joining thirty societies: Greg and the Celtic anthology that he works on with such diligence, for which he has such hopes. How could I have imagined I would put this life at risk?

I make plans. I shall put more energy into my home, my family. I shall get a private tutor to help with Amber's Maths and one of those French courses she can do on the computer. I shall hold a dinner party; if Greg won't take me out to dinner, then I shall ask people here: Clem and Max, perhaps—they might get on well together. I shall redecorate my kitchen, which looks so gloomy in this dull brown light. These colours I've loved—deep russet red, and the sort of green that has a lot of blue in it—are all too dark, too dreary. I shall paint this room a brisk cheerful colour, cream, or the yellow of marigolds. I shall have a lot of effect in my life.

I sip my coffee, hearing the rain on the gravel, like many people walking outside my window.

My phone rings and I jump. I take it out of my pocket, expecting Molly again.

'Ginnie, it's Will.'

My body changes when I hear his voice, something opening out in me.

'Oh. I mean, I wasn't expecting you...'

'It was good to see you,' he says.

'Yes, it was good,' I say.

There are moments when we choose. Maybe this is the moment: here in the silence, waiting, hearing his breathing the other end of the line.

'Will.' I hear how my voice is hushed now. 'Look, I'm at home at the moment, so...'

I leave the rest of the sentence unsaid. In that moment we become conspirators.

'OK,' he says evenly. 'We won't talk long. I only wanted to ask if you'd like to have lunch some time? There's a bar in Sheffield Street—it's a little further from where I work, we shouldn't be interrupted.'

He says we could meet at twelve-thirty. He tells me how to get there. We both know I have said yes already.

CHAPTER 12

The bar is empty. It has cream walls and big mirrors on the walls with elaborate gilt frames, like in an old-fashioned ballroom. As I walk in I am surrounded by reflections of reflections. There are hanging baskets full of ivies that curl and reach out like hands. The back wall is all glass, wide French windows that look out into the garden, letting in lots of light: but today the light is dull, thick, like in an old photograph. Soon it will rain again.

A barmaid is wiping glasses at a sink behind the bar: she's young, with sharp, pretty features, her hair tied up with string. There are baguettes in a glass case. I order a whisky and go to sit by the windows on a flimsy bentwood chair. There are only one or two other people drinking here. Outside there's a wet grey sky and eddies of starlings, and the lawn is covered in drifts of fallen leaves, soaked through and shiny as mahogany, everything fading, sifting down, except in the flowerbed where a random rose still clings to a blood-red stem. A saxophone is playing a song on the edge of memory, something I know but can't name.

I sip my drink and read my newspaper, the same paragraph over and over, none of it making sense. My other world doesn't exist—my children, my home, my husband: there's just here, now, the sepia garden, the saxophone, in my mouth the taste of whisky.

Half twelve passes and Will doesn't come. Perhaps he will never come. I was crazy, deluded, to think that he meant what he said. Undoubtedly, he has been prudent and thought better of it. What did I expect? I'm not the kind of woman men take risks for. I would like to be someone different, to be confident, at ease: a woman skilled in the way she moves her body, the way she touches a man. I would like to be balanced on one of the slender barstools, poised, rather louche, a woman who expects to be looked at: or leaning on my elbow at the bar, wearing a short black dress and vanilla-pale stockings and dazzlingly high heels, the sort of heels that make your pelvis tip and your body arch a little: a woman perhaps who has a vibrator discreet as a silvery lipstick hidden in her handbag.

The barmaid changes the CD. A lazy beat, a pensive muted trumpet. Maybe like me she only likes slow music.

I can see how it will happen, the whole thing spooling out in front of me, filmic, vivid, as though I am watching myself. How I sit here, drinking whisky, studying my paper, not looking up too often, and still he doesn't come: and then at last I shrug and gather up my things and walk away—not very embarrassed, because I'm too old for that, but a little: watched by the barmaid with string in her hair, who has seen this before, who immediately comprehends the whole scenario. Feeling a surge of shame—the shame of having so longed for something that I have no right to, no claim on.

The music stops and you can hear the squawk and clatter of starlings in the garden. The barmaid wipes some glasses, holding them up to the light to check for smears.

I look up and into the mirror on the wall in front of me: Will is there, his reflection as he walks down the street towards me. A sudden easy happiness warms me. Of course he would do what he said. I watch him in the mirror: intrigued to see him when he can't see me. He's serious, unsmiling: like someone heading for a work meeting, preoccupied, someone on whom things weigh heavily. Not someone coming to meet a woman. I watch him till he walks out of the mirror.

The door opens behind me and I turn. We smile, he kisses my cheek.

I eat him up eagerly with my eyes, his worn face, knowing hands.

'So. Was your morning OK?' I ask him.

He shrugs. He brings the dregs of work with him—the things that still have to be done, or that have been done, but badly. While I have given no thought to such things, coming here with reckless abandon, leaving my whole other world behind. I want to peel all this preoccupation from him, to say, Don't think about all that. Just be here with me, for a while, for this moment.

He doesn't take off his coat: I notice this. He sits in one of the bentwood chairs; he's too big for this feminine furniture. I sense his uncertainty. He's looking at me, trying to read me. It would be easy to keep it all ordinary and safe: to buy him a drink, to talk about our work. The easiest thing in the world.

'Are you hungry?' he says.

'Not especially.'

'Me neither,' he says.

I don't know what to say now. I don't know how to get from here to where we want to be.

I look at his face, his mouth, his dark eyes with the red flecks in, his jaw shadowed with stubble. I would like to move my hand on his face, to trace out the lines of him, to pull him towards me and press my mouth into his. I feel no guilt, just this wanting—clear, explicit, exact.

'Perhaps we could go off somewhere?' I say.

'Where would you like to go?' he says.

'We could go down to the river.' My voice hushed, questioning. 'There's a car park I know. It's quiet there. Perhaps we could walk by the river.'

'I'd like that,' he says.

I leave my whisky undrunk.

We drive there through the dull day. We talk about the traffic and the weather.

At the park by the river I stop the car. It's raining again. It seems a bleak, forsaken place in the rain: there are puddles on the gravel, holding the grey of the sky, and a starling pecks at a litter bin. When I turn off the engine, all you can hear is the water on the roof, like drumming fingers. A single dark leaf with a rim of white light is pressed against the windscreen. I turn to him as he undoes his seat belt: I hope he will kiss me properly, but he just gets out of the car. I put on my mac but I leave my umbrella—some calculation that there's something deeply unsexy about an umbrella. It's as though I'm drugged or in a dream.

'I'm sorry about the rain,' I say. Then think how silly this sounds.

There's one other car in the car park: a man sitting there, smoking, his newspaper propped against the steering-wheel. He stares at us, a cool unguarded stare. This makes me uneasy. I think how obvious we must be—a preoccupied man, a middle-aged woman in suede boots that are clearly all wrong for the weather, and both of us oblivious to the rain.

We walk to the left along the path by the river. Even on this dull day, the water has a faint shine, reflecting the opalescence of the sky. The river is running high and dimpled by the rain and full of movement, all its contrary surges and eddies and ripples. We can see Eel Pie Island to our right across the water, one of the biggest islands in the Thames. At either end there's a nature reserve, huge gold willows reaching down to the water, but there are houses too, and from this bank we can see the back gardens of some of them, ending abruptly in a steep drop to the river. On the flagstones at the end of one garden sits a terracotta boy, one leg dangled over the edge, his head turned as if he's looking down the river; he's so precisely the colour of sunburnt flesh that you think for a moment he's real. But there are no houses or gardens here on the bank where we walk—on one side of us the river, to the other side a tangle of bushes and trees.

Ahead there's a noise and chaos of geese and swans on the path: an old man in a tattered coat is scattering bread from a bag, undeterred by the rain. With the birds all clustering round he's a figure from an engraving, from one of Ursula's fairy tales, at once grotesque and beneficent, the sort of man who might give you three gifts or three wishes. Scattering crusts, paying us no attention, around him the flurry of wings.

The river path curves. We're out of sight of the car park and the old man. The trees hang low over the path here. A pigeon startles through the tree canopy above us, with a sound like something torn. Will takes my hand and pulls me after him, in under the trees. Bramble bushes catch at my legs. We go in a long way, so we're hidden from the path. There's a place where the bushes open out a bit, though the branches are low over our heads, catching at our hair. The rain doesn't penetrate here, but it's wet underfoot, a thick shiny mulch of dead bracken and earth and leaves.

He turns to face me. He puts his hands on my shoulders, lightly moving me to face him. I shiver at his touch. He keeps his hands on my shoulders, keeping me there, looking in my face, that hungry unsmiling look that stirs me. I feel my stomach harden. Then, so slowly, he reaches out and starts to unbutton my coat. I love the slow purposefulness of his hands. I can hear the loud sound of our mingled breathing. He undoes my coat, moves his hands under my T-shirt, pushing my T-shirt and my bra above my breasts. There's a catch in his breath as he does this. I feel exposed, but utterly without self-consciousness. My skin is cold in the chilly wet air: the warmth of his hands on me astonishes me. I would like him to touch me like this for a long time, just the slow turning and trail of his hands on my breasts, their roughness and gentleness. He kisses me, and slides his hand down my stomach between my clothes and my skin and into me. The sensation is so strong, it makes me shake, I cling to him.

He pushes my clothes down, moving his hand on me, gentle but very rapid. It feels good but it isn't in quite the right place, his movement constricted by the waistband of my skirt that is resting on my hips. I think, I must tell him: in a moment, I'll tell him. I feel a little surge of weariness, that there is always this moment, having to explain. Then before I can say anything, I find myself coming, my hands clutching at his shoulders, feeling I will collapse. I hear my voice cry out, and it sounds a long way away.

'Shh,' he says, holding me. 'Shh.'

There are slow footsteps on the gravel of the path. He pulls me close to him.

'Someone could see us here,' he says.

We stay quite still, pressed together under my coat. I feel a different kind of hunger, wanting to be filled with him. When the footsteps have faded, I move my hand down, struggling with his belt, wrapping my fingers round his cock, feeling him hot and silky against my palm. I feel his shudder. When I kneel I'm vaguely aware of the wetness of the ground under me. He tastes of salt: the way his breathing quickens excites me. He lifts me up, turning me round to rest against the trunk of a tree, peeling down my clothes. I hear the rustle as he unwraps the condom. He moves my legs apart, slides into me. When he comes he says my name.

We put on our clothes and inspect our coats for leaves and bits of mud. My legs are shaking so much it's hard to walk. I am full of a sense of astonishment. The old man is sitting on a bench now, his empty bag in his hand: the geese and swans have gone.

As we drive back, Will rests his hand on my thigh. I feel a light happiness, my body fluid, loose. I catch sight of myself in the rear-view mirror: my mascara is smudged, my hair messy, all the strain wiped out of my face.

I drive back to the pub where we met.

'Shall we have a drink?' I say. 'Before you go back to work?'

He hesitates. I'm suddenly anxious. His answer

matters so much. Will I see him again? Is this all there will be?

I put my hand on his wrist. I think how his hands still look unfamiliar to me.

'Just for a moment or two? I'd really like you to,' I say.

He looks at his watch. It's as if he's somewhere else already.

'I could do ten minutes,' he says.

He has a Coke, I have another whisky. As we stand at the bar and I reach across him to take my glass I let my hand brush his. I feel the warmth of his skin. I'd like to make love again.

He puts the change back into his wallet. There's a picture tucked in the photograph slot, the child I saw in the picture in his office.

'Is that your little boy?'

'Yes.'

He pulls it out so I can see it properly. My heart thuds. The sex all seeps away. I feel how the cold has got into me, all the cold from the river: I wrap my coat closer around me.

The child in the picture is beautiful—fair hair, delicate features, his face quite smooth and still. It's an unusual picture of a child because he isn't smiling.

'He's beautiful,' I say.

'That's Jake,' he says.

'How old is Jake?'

'Eight. I know you'll be thinking I'm far too old

to have a child of eight. But it took us a long time to have him.'

He puts the picture away. He picks up his glass and I follow him to a table.

'Tell me about him.'

He hesitates, as though he isn't expecting this.

'Well—he likes his Pikachu T-shirt,' he says. 'He always has to wear it.'

I smile. 'Mine had their share of obsessions too,' I say. Thinking of Amber, and the rhyme that always had to be read.

I expect him to say more, as parents always do, to talk about Jake's passion for Mario Kart or his loathing of broccoli. But he looks into his drink and doesn't say anything. His reluctance makes me uneasy, as though I have trodden in a place that's forbidden.

'How's young Kyle doing?' he says then. 'I'd been wondering how it's all going.'

'I feel I know how to approach it now,' I say. 'It helped a lot—what you told me.'

'I'm glad,' he says.

We are ordinary again, professionals discussing a case: we are back in the everyday world.

When he's finished his drink, we go out to my car together.

'I could give you a lift,' I say, wanting to hold onto him for a little longer.

But he shakes his head and says it's better if he walks.

He kisses me lightly on the lips.

'I enjoyed that,' he says. 'Very much.'

'It was wonderful,' I tell him.

But I know it's different for him, that he doesn't have my sense of astonishment.

'We could meet next week,' he says. 'If you'd like to.'

'Yes. I'd love that.'

He takes a scrap of paper from his pocket and writes down his mobile number.

'But you must absolutely promise not to ring me in the evening,' he says.

'Of course I won't,' I say. 'I'll be careful, I promise.'

We smile, happy for a moment, everything settled, arranged. He leaves me with tenderness, his hand lingering on mine.

The house is empty when I get back. I'm relieved, though there's no reason why Amber or Greg would be here. I put my T-shirt in the wash. I clean off all my make-up. I shower and meticulously shampoo my hair. I try to brush the mud from my boots, though because they're suede it doesn't come off easily, and there are stains on the toes, where I knelt in the mulch of leaves and earth on the river bank, that take a long time to remove. But even when I've done all these things, the smell of his skin seems still to hang around me, as shockingly real to me as the perfume of the gardenias that grow in a pot on my window sill.

I decide to make a casserole—something healthy,

with lots of olive oil and vegetables. It's perhaps some unthought-out notion of penance, of proving that I am still a dutiful mother and wife.

I'm frying tomatoes and peppers when Amber comes in.

She dumps her school-bag on the kitchen table.

'The police stopped the bus and they came and took somebody off,' she says. She's flushed, pleased, enjoying her story. 'He looked the dodgy type. I mean, I don't want to stereotype, he may do meals-on-wheels—but he had a shaved head and about nineteen earrings...' She hunts around in a cupboard, looking for crisps. 'Mum, you were singing,' she says.

I feel my face go hot.

'Oh. I didn't realise,' I tell her.

I keep my back to her.

'You were,' she says. 'You were singing when I came in.'

There's a question in her voice. I don't respond.

She pokes a spoon in the frying pan.

'That smells yummy,' she says. 'I hope you're not going to mess it up with any bits of dead animal.'

Greg is home at five o'clock.

'I thought I could come back early and get in some work on my book,' he says.

'Did you have a good day?' I ask him.

'So so,' he says. But he seems surprised by the question.

I'd worried that he would look at me and see it all written there in my face and immediately suspect me. But he's keen to get up to his study; he scarcely glances at me.

That night when I wake in the dark, as Greg stirs, breathing slowly beside me, I'm in the wet thicket with Will again. And we make love, from start to finish, every touch remembered, and Death with his bulbous eyes, his sack, his terrible rapaciousness, doesn't come near.

CHAPTER 13

I'm raking the leaves from my lawn. They've fallen quite suddenly, during the night. All my plants are dying back now, summer and its lavish muddle and disorder giving way to the clarity of winter—white sky, black branches, seeing so much further than before.

The phone startles me. I run in, wanting it to be Will.

It's Ursula.

'Ginnie. So how are things?'

Her intonation is like mine. Families are so strange—these things that mark you out as belonging together. She and I inhabit different universes, yet our voices are just the same.

'How's Molly?' she says. 'And Amber? Everyone OK?'

I tell her that everyone's fine.

'That's wonderful,' she says. But she's rather brisk

and formal and I know she isn't listening. All this politeness is just postponing the thing she's rung to say.

She clears her throat.

'Ginnie, it's Mother,' she says then. 'I'm a little bit
worried about her.'

There's a mouse-scurry of fear in the corner of my
mind.

'We were round there last week,' she says. 'It's hard
to put your finger on… When did you last see her?'

I try to remember: and realise, with a rush of the
guilt my mother has throughout my life called up in
me, that it's been several weeks at least.

'I've been busy with Molly going away,' I tell
her. And I think, There's been Will too—filling my
mind, so I've forgotten everything. 'I'll go down at
the weekend. She sounds OK on the phone. Is it her
arthritis?'

'No,' she says. 'It's not her arthritis. I mean, it
troubles her, of course, but she never makes a fuss.'

'No. Well, she wouldn't.'

'I don't know, Ginnie,' she says again. 'Sometimes
she just kind of sits there and keeps taking her glasses
off and putting them on again.' Her fear is circling,
darkly predatory, swimming just under the surface
of her words. 'It's not like her. She's just not quite
herself.'

There's silence between us for a moment. I sense
how our relationship shifts, to accommodate this new
possibility. Something we aren't ready for: something
you can never be ready for.

'It's not like it's stopped her from doing things,' says Ursula. 'She gets to her church service. Though she did say one day she fainted halfway through the Offertory and alarmed everybody. She was quite funny about it, but really I think she was scared.'

'What about the doctor?'

'I'm working on it. But you know how Mother is. She never complains. She doesn't like to trouble people. She's a very private person.'

'Yes,' I say. 'She is.'

The things we have been through and never talked about together hang over us, press down.

'Oh well, it's probably nothing,' says Ursula then.

I know she doesn't think that.

'I'll go to see her as soon as I possibly can,' I tell her. 'Probably Sunday.'

'And I'll keep on at her about going to the doctor,' says Ursula. 'There's nothing more we can do, is there, really?'

'No,' I say.

Perhaps there has never been anything more that we could do.

Our mother still lives in the house where we grew up, in Hampshire near the sea. She's kept it much the same. The bedroom I shared with Ursula still has the twin beds and the eiderdowns of magenta taffeta that were slippery and always fell off in the night, so however well you'd been tucked in you always woke up cold: and the mistily painted pictures of ballet dancers, and

the night light with the cut-outs of Enid Blyton elves
that threw fantastical shadows. And in the hall and the
sitting room, there are still the vivid colours, the tulip
prints, the spider plants, the wallpaper patterned with
violets: our mother has always loved cheerful things,
Gilbert and Sullivan, flowered fabric, letting these
things sustain her. Everywhere there are photographs,
in silver or stained wood frames. Photos from our
childhood and photos of our weddings, and of Molly
and Amber as children, and of Ursula and Paul on
their increasingly exotic holidays. Photographs have
always been important in our family; in childhood
they mapped out a separate world, a sunlit family life,
a place of celebrations, and cake and tea with relatives,
and shiny bar shoes. Now, Ursula and I always have
two prints made—one to give to our mother—and
there's a ritual to handing them over, every picture
examined and appraised.

Over the years the house has perhaps become even
more itself. Our mother is from the generation that
recycled without thinking; everything was kept because
it might come in useful. All our childhood possessions
are there—clothes, toys—carefully stashed away in
labelled boxes. It's hard to breathe in the house, as
though these many objects use up all the air. There
are runners down the middle of the carpet, and dust
sheets on the sofas, and when she isn't in a room she
draws the curtains to keep the sunlight out. She has
such a fear of things wearing out or fading, a fear
that goes beyond a need to preserve these things for

a purpose—for now she may leave on the dust sheets even when visitors come. As though the preservation of these things has become an end in itself. Or as though these things protect her.

The garden too is much as it always was, just a little more overgrown; there are lupins, and buddleia that in summer is bright with butterflies, and the little mossy lawn; and, in autumn, the ragged Michaelmas daisies under the sitting room window, their flowers of a purple so faded they look as though they're over even when they've only just opened out. At the bottom of the garden is a stream that's shadowed by a heavy hedge. Effluent from the dye factory in the village sometimes seeps out into the water, which was always a source of great fascination to our school friends: one day it might be red, another purple, another a viscous green. And further down the road, there are other houses and gardens, most of them too with their lawns and lupins and sometimes a loop of the stream: and the Freedom Hall with its urgently evangelical posters, promising a different kind of religion from the undemanding Anglicanism of the Norman church where we went every Sunday morning, where we'd kneel on the tapestry hassocks in the gorgeous stained light, our mother in her pillbox hat, and we'd mumble the stately words of the Anglican prayer book, words that stay with you always: 'We have done those things that we ought not to have done, and there is no health in us.'

Our mother knew a lot about the people who lived

in these houses. As her own circle grew ever more restricted, because our father didn't like her going out, these neighbours, these glimpsed and hinted-at households, became her life, her world. Like Mary Grayson next door, whose daughter had left her husband and gone to live with a woman: and the doctor had told Mary that once a woman had gone that way there was no going back. Or the Barkers who lived in the big mock-Tudor house next to the Freedom Hall. He was an executive at the Esso refinery, and they used to hold swinging parties there, said my mother, all the men putting their car keys into a salad bowl and being taken to bed by other people's wives.

But did our neighbours ever gossip about us? Did they wonder what happened in our house, behind the Michaelmas daisies and the little mossy lawn? Maybe the more astute women noticed the small things— an edge to his voice, or the way he always seemed to walk a few paces in front of her. But our father was always so charming, a pillar of the community, handing out the prayerbooks for the Family Service: and our mother had blouses that buttoned high at the collar.

They're vivid even now, the bad times. Waking in the bedroom I shared with Ursula, with the lamp with the Enid Blyton cut-outs throwing intricate shadows, shivering, my taffeta eiderdown slipping to the floor. Waking suddenly, pulses hammering everywhere in my body, hearing his voice from downstairs, rising, hardening. There are voices that can hurt you, that

can seem to tear into you: that make you want to hide,
to burrow under your blankets, clasping them to you,
bunched tight inside your fists.

'Don't start.' He would always say that. 'Don't start.'
But when he said that, his voice too loud for the house,
it had already begun. And then, 'Bitch. You fucking
stupid bitch. You fucking whore.' The torrent of in-
sults, the things he called her. I'd feel that everything
was breaking up around us, that there was too much
rage, too much hate for the house to contain.

Ursula always stayed in bed, deep down under the
bedcovers, her rapid breathing muffled by the blankets
that she pressed to her ears and her eyes. But sometimes I'd creep out onto the landing—frightened but
needing to know. I'd kneel by the banister, clasping
my hands tight around the posts, gripping so hard
that later I'd find the imprint of the carving on my
palms. Knowing I should go down, perhaps I could
do something, perhaps I could stop it happening. I
remember the violets on the landing wallpaper, and
the tiles downstairs on the floor of the hall, and the
stab of white light across the tiles from the half-open
kitchen door. Kneeling there on the landing among
the ordinary things: the spider plant, the flowered
walls, the gilt-framed mirror. And then the click as my
mother closed the door before he hit her. Knowing I
was there, perhaps, and trying to protect me: making
sure at least that I couldn't see.

Sometimes, the morning after, he'd be the one who
woke us. He would be white, with a muffled melancholy

look, an air of being sorry for himself: as though it was he who'd suffered. 'Your mother's not well,' he'd say. Those mornings he'd put out our breakfast cereal himself. It would be quiet in the house, a flat, dull feeling, as though the tension had been drained away. I would creep into their bedroom before I went to school, needing to be sure she was alive: she'd be asleep, or pretending to sleep, her back towards the doorway, but I'd be able to see the blankets moving with her breathing.

Afterwards, he'd buy her flowers. Once I came back from school earlier than Ursula—we normally walked home together but she must have stayed for Art Club—and there were flowers, great blowsy bouquets, roses, arum lilies, too many for the room: she'd put them in two vases, and she was sitting there between them surrounded by all these heavy, polleny blossoms, her face swollen, the bruises bright as the toxic stream in our garden. She held her head very still as though it were breakable, moving her whole body when she turned as I came in. Her bruised face frightened me, the fragile skin shiny, ugly, the paintbox of bruising. I hated the way the bloating distorted her face, as though she weren't the mother I knew any more. I wished that Ursula were there. The room was full of the sore-throat smell of Dettol and the clingy sweetness of roses.

'He's very sorry, Ginnie,' she said. 'You mustn't think too badly of him. He doesn't know what got into him.'

I didn't say anything. I should have gone and held her, but I hated her being so ugly and weak, so broken. I left her and went upstairs. I tidied my bedroom and got on with my homework. Doing it immaculately, all so neat and fastidious, measuring out the margin with absolute precision.

I think they tried to get help once. I was about thirteen. It was an odd day, everything out of shape, both of them wearing their Sunday best clothes on a Wednesday, our father in his churchwarden suit, our mother wearing her best Ponds coral lipstick and a blouse in oyster silk with buttons that looked like pearls. She kissed me when we said goodbye, holding my face in her hands to be sure she had my attention. Her voice was hushed and secret.

'It's going to be all right now,' she said. 'We're seeing a special doctor. We're going to get things sorted out.' Whispering to me: it made me feel so special. 'D'you mind not telling Ursula? I don't want her getting all worried.'

Auntie Carol picked us up from school. We had our tea in her kitchen. For dessert, there were tinned peach halves, rounded side up, in a pool of Carnation milk, which she said looked like poached eggs. She seemed very pleased with herself, she thought this might amuse us. Ursula and I ate diligently, though we'd never had Carnation before, and its sweetness made my teeth hurt. I was longing to be back home, for our happy new life to begin.

But that night our mother was quiet, with a grey look

in spite of the cheerful coral lipstick. She didn't tell me anything. A few weeks later, it all began again.

I don't think people did talk about us, I don't think anyone knew. I once heard Mary Grayson of the lesbian daughter say to my mother, I saw your Brian in the flower-shop. Those were lovely flowers he got you. He's so romantic, your Brian. You're lucky to have found yourself a man who's so romantic.

We grew up and went our separate ways, Ursula and I—we're very different people—yet each of us perhaps seeking to heal what happened, to recreate childhood as a gentle place—me within the containing walls of my clinic, Ursula between the covers of her fairy-tale books. I can see this clearly now, though at the time it was quite unconscious and our choices seemed to follow from quite other imperatives—Ursula's very evident talent, and my sudden infatuation with psychology, at the age of thirteen, after finding a tattered paperback on Jung's archetypes on the second-hand book stall at the Church Fayre. We never talked about our father's violence—not with one another, not with our mother, not with anyone—not even after he'd died.

Just once I raised it with her. It was when I was pregnant with Molly, towards the end of the pregnancy, when I was on maternity leave, too huge and tired to do anything. It was a hot summer, and I lay for hours in the garden, letting the dandelions seed around me, stupid as a stone. But at night my dreams were extraordinarily vivid and active, as though to compensate for the lethargy of my days, and all concerned obsessively with my childhood: not in a direct way, but I'd dream about those gardens with their lupins and Michaelmas daisies, and aeroplanes would crash on them, or earnest officers from some War Crimes commission would dig up the lawn behind the buddleia and unearth mutilated human remains. It was as though some intricate working-out was going on deep inside me. Ursula came for coffee on the way to an exhibition and, disinhibited and half drunk, perhaps, with all the pregnancy hormones, I talked about our childhood.

'D'you ever think about it? You know—Dad, and the things he did to her?'

We were sitting at the table in my kitchen; I was sitting sideways because I could only just fit between the wall and the table, everything about me lumbering and clumsy.

She looked at me warily, sitting stiffly, something withdrawing in her. She didn't say anything.

I'd have leant towards her and grasped her wrist, but I was pinned down by my swollen stomach, unable to reach out.

'Don't you remember?' I said. 'You can't just not remember.'

I felt a flicker of impatience, the feeling growing in me that there was something I had to face up to before my own child came—and that only she could help me.

Her face was tight, like a closed door. She picked
a loose thread from her sleeve.

'They just had the odd bad patch,' she said. 'It happens. It happens in an awful lot of families.'

I remembered her fear, how she'd pressed the blankets to her eyes and ears. I could see it, quite vivid.

'Some bad patch,' I said.

She didn't say anything.

I felt then how inviolate her reserve was—sleek
and hard as varnish, everything running off it.

I tried again.

'D'you ever feel—I know it's stupid, we were just
kids—but that we could have stopped it? I mean, I
know we couldn't. But d'you ever feel guilty about
it? D'you ever feel ashamed?'

She was glancing around my kitchen as though
planning her escape.

'Ursula, please talk to me. Don't you ever feel
that?'

She cleared her throat.

'You live in your head too much, Ginnie,' she said.
'I always think we were lucky to have such a happy
childhood. I mean, when you look at what some people
go through.'

There were things I could have told her, that I
wanted so much to tell her—the things I'd been thinking, lying amid the dandelions, trying to understand.
How I'd chosen Greg because he seemed so different
from our father, but now I was starting to worry that
the peace he'd seemed to promise was really a kind

of absence—that it wasn't something you could build a marriage on. How sometimes I wondered if half the things I'd done had been a struggle to prove that there's some good in me. How even now I felt such shame because I let Mum down.

But I couldn't say these things to Ursula, who was frowning as she sat at my table, looking as though she wanted to be anywhere but there.

'You mustn't brood,' she said. 'Really, Ginnie, you mustn't. It's bad for the baby.'

CHAPTER 14

It's a dull day by the river, soft, warm for November. We go to the place at the side of the path, the secret place where the branches hang low. More leaves have fallen since last we came here, we have to go further in to be hidden from view. We make love quickly, keeping on most of our clothes.

'D'you have to go straight back now?' I say as I brush the leaves and twigs from his shoulders.

He looks at his watch.

'More or less. Well, I don't have time for a drink, anyway.'

'Perhaps a few moments?'

'OK. A few moments,' he says.

There's a place where I turn off the path, taking him through the scrub between the path and the river. Over the water on Eel Pie Island, the trees are turning gold. The grass here is worn where people have walked, and stone steps lead down to the water.

'There's a beach here,' I say. 'When the tide's right out.'

Years ago I often brought the girls here. We discovered the beach one lazy summer afternoon—a little crescent of bronze sand, littered with black fronds of seaweed, ragged and shiny and plastic-looking, the sand all lightly imprinted by the feet of many birds. But today the tide is coming in; the sand is swallowed up already. We sit on the steps, our feet on the lowest step not covered by the tide. The stone has a pale crust of dry mud. He puts his arm around my waist, pushing his hand between my clothes and my skin, spreading his fingers across my skin. There's a cold smell from the river.

'Talk to me,' he says. 'Tell me what you think about when we make love. Tell me what you like.'

I'm hesitant. I think of his taste, of his warm slide into me, of everything in me opening up to him. But I've never had this kind of conversation.

'I don't know if I can say those things,' I tell him. 'Women are different.' I'm playing for time, taking refuge in generalisation. 'Women are better at saying what they don't like.'

'I'd noticed,' he says, a little rueful and weary, making me smile.

'I could tell you the things I don't like… Anything to do with food—eating strawberries off each other, all that kind of thing. And cross-dressing. I mean, why would anyone choose to dress as a woman, if they don't have to?'

'You don't like being a woman?'

'I'm not sure.'

'You do it well,' he says.

'I've had practice.'

'But surely it's much less boring, isn't it, being a woman? I like women. Women are more interesting.'

I smile. Eva would say, A man who likes women a lot has liked a lot of women.

'Group sex too,' I tell him. 'I've never understood it. I don't see how sex can be communal: wouldn't it lose its charge?'

'So what do you like, Ginnie?' he says.

The tide is rushing in, water clear as air covering the lowest branches of the rosebay willowherb that clings to the banks of the river. I love the way the plant moves under the water, its dance, its sinuousness, the way it seems to be stirred by a secret wind.

'Your mouth. Your hands, the things you do with your hands, the way you move them. The sound of your breathing.'

He has his mouth in my hair.

'OK,' he says. 'Your turn. Ask away.'

'Things you like, then.'

'Oh, all of it really. You know how men are.'

'Tell me.'

'I like to watch you come,' he says.

I curve in to him. I want to make love again.

A houseboat goes by, green-painted with a pattern of roses and a dog stretched out on top. It's all so contradictory here by the river—behind us the path and the shadowy hidden places, and in front this watery thoroughfare where everything can be seen.

There are other things I could ask, because they fill me with a feverish curiosity. How old is your wife—is she very much younger than me? And is she very beautiful, as beautiful as her photograph? How often do you make love with her? Have you had affairs before? How long did they last? And who did you have them with, and exactly how much did you love them? But I don't ask these questions.

A heron takes off from somewhere near, the sound of its wings like someone tearing linen, its plumage the colour of smoke or winter sky. It lands in the willow with branches that fall into the water at the end of Eel Pie Island. We are quiet for a while, watching.

'When I first came here with Molly and Amber,' I tell him, 'we found some mussel shells and an abandoned sandal, and someone had written their name with a stick in the sand.' I think how the waves came rushing up in the wake of the pleasure boats, making the girls shriek with delight and run for the safety of the steps, and with the turbulence came that wonderful brackish smell, the mixture of fresh and salt, the promise of the sea. 'And once we came in the evening, and the water was pink and all these geese and swans were just standing in the shallows.'

'I'd like to hear more about your girls,' he says.

I tell him some of Molly's university stories.

Two swans come over and linger near us, casually

dabbling, their long necks sinuous as snakes, but mud-coloured, not immaculate like their backs or wings. They're so close you can hear their grunting, and the soft shushing sounds their beaks make as they preen their feathers.

'You never talk about Jake,' I say.

He slips his hand out from under my sweater; he still has his arm around me, but not touching my skin.

'Jake's not like other kids,' he says. His voice is tired, heavy.

I think of the photograph, the unsmiling little boy.

'Megan always thought there was something wrong,' he says slowly. 'She thought it for months, she kept on about it. I told her not to worry.'

I wait quietly. I remember the shadow I've seen on him, and the way he looks so sad when he thinks that no one can see.

'I feel dreadful about that now,' he says. 'I should have listened.'

For a while he doesn't say anything. I bite back the urge to ask more.

'They say it's Asperger's,' he says then. 'Like a mild form of autism. He can't read people... Sorry, I'm being really crass—you'd know about these things.'

'Yes. But not from inside, like you do.'

'Everything's very literal,' he says. 'He doesn't get the social rules. Stuff like—if someone says, How are you? they don't really want you to tell them. And nobody likes him, of course. He says the wrong thing and upsets people.'

We're sitting separately now. I'm very aware of the space between us, the way we have edged a little further apart.

'Yes,' I say. I'd like to hold him and comfort him, but I feel I don't have the right.

'I just see him getting everything wrong. It breaks your heart,' he says.

We're silent for a moment, looking out over the water.

'Will you have another child?' I say then.

He shrugs.

'I don't know. Not the way we're going.'

He isn't looking at me now.

'I have this dream,' he says, 'of seeing him kicking a football round the garden with his mates. Except he doesn't have mates.'

'I'm sorry,' I say.

We sit there in the cold, with the sounds of the swans and the tide coming in. Soon the water will reach us.

'Ginnie.' There's a new sound in his voice, urgent, definite. 'I don't want to change or disrupt anything. You know that, don't you?'

'Yes. Of course.'

He turns to me, he has my face in his hands. His hands smell of our love-making.

'Ginnie. Can we do this without anyone getting hurt?'

'If I didn't believe that, I wouldn't be here,' I say: then think, Is that true? Wouldn't I still be here however risky it was? Could I stop myself? My mind shies away from the thought.

He lowers his hands, shakes his head a little.

'There are all these people, all these children,' he says.

'I think... I make it all right with myself,' I tell him, 'by imagining this is another world, a separate world. That when I'm with you, I've entered a different world—and what happens in one world doesn't change anything in the other. That what I do here can't harm them there...'

The water has reached our feet now. We get up and turn to go. I realise that I'm shivering.

'We just have to be very careful,' I say. 'As long as we're careful, everyone will be safe. Won't they?'

There's such a sense of loss when he leaves me, when I drop him off in Sheffield Street and he walks away. As I move through the week I tell myself, With every step I take, I am walking towards the next time.

CHAPTER 15

I have another session with Kyle McConville. He kneels on the floor by the Lego box. He's turned away from me. He builds the room again, the high walls made of Lego, no doors or windows in the room, the adult and the boy.

His face is white as chalk. He still seems very afraid. I think of what Will told me.

'The little boy's safe in the room,' I say. 'The walls are keeping him safe. Nobody's going to harm him.'

He goes on building. His movements seem less abrupt today, his hands moving more fluidly as he snaps the bricks into position.

I choose some window pieces from the box of Lego. I spread them out beside him on the floor.

'Perhaps the boy would like a window in his room,' I say. 'He might like one of these windows. It could go in quite high up. Just a little window.'

He looks at the window pieces for a long, slow moment. I sit there quietly, not looking directly at him. There's silence all around us: you can hear the rooks in the elms, and Kyle's rapid, fluttery breath. His forehead creases in a frown. Then he puts out his hand and picks up one of the window pieces. He slots it into his wall.

'Now the boy's got a window,' I say. 'He can see out a bit if he wants to. He's still quite safe in his room.'

He goes on building. He builds the walls very tall, and he puts on a roof with a chimney. When he's finished, he sits back on his heels and looks at his work for a moment.

When he goes he gives me a small, crooked smile. I know that we're moving forward. One day soon he'll put a door in the wall: and he'll go through the door and face the thing he's afraid of.

Amber has her braces removed.

I'm in the kitchen when she comes back from the orthodontist's appointment. I hear her fling down her bicycle, and her rapid step in the passageway. I can tell she's happy.

She makes an entrance, pushing the door wide, tugging off her helmet so all her hair swings out.

'Well?' she says, and smiles with parted lips.

It's startling. She isn't a girl any more. She has a wide, even, immaculate smile.

'Wow.' I hug her. 'You look beautiful.'

There's a bag of toffees she's bought in celebration—forbidden for two years in case they stuck to her braces. She dumps them on the table: she's eaten half the bag already.

'I've got this retainer, it really hurts.' She thrusts a pink box at me. 'But nobody wears them anyway.'

'That's up to you,' I say.

'Are you sure they're OK?' she says. 'Are you really really sure they're completely even? That there isn't a tiny gap?'

'I'm sure. It's just the most perfect smile,' I say.

She turns to look at herself in the mirror that's shaped like a crescent moon. The mirror is high: she has to stand on tiptoe. She has her head on one side, then the other, she's posing, holding her head at different angles, like a photographer's model. She's thin and her hair is heavy and full where she crimped it last night for a party: she seems top heavy, like a flower, her head a bright lavish blossom on the slenderest stalk.

'Yes,' she says. It's a statement of how things are. She gives a little laugh of pleasure.

She's about to go upstairs. I look at her, her skinny jeans and her long red hair and that smile. I clear my throat.

'Amber—there's something I've wanted to say. If you and this boy you're seeing—you know... I mean, if you're serious...'

She fixes me with a clear stare. Her eyes are a washed blue, like sky after rain.

'What is this, Mum? Are you trying to say, am I on the pill?'

'Well, yes.'

'Mum, for God's sake, what do you think? Of course I am.'

'But you haven't been to the doctor.'

She shrugs. 'We all get our stuff from Oasis,' she says.

It's a clinic where some of the girls I work with go. I picture her sitting in Reception next to Caron Clarkson, whose arms are tattooed with dragons, who has sex in car parks for very small sums of money.

'Is that, well, OK?'

'It's what everyone does, Mum. I'd thought you'd have known.'

'Well, good,' I say. 'As long as you keep yourself safe. As long as you know what you're doing.'

I start to fill the dishwasher. I think of all the books I read when Molly and Amber were younger—books on raising girls with boundless self-esteem and inspiring joyous sexual self-awareness and empowering our daughters to feel at ease in their bodies. This isn't the conversation I'd imagined having.

'Lauren knows some people who have sex in St Dunstan's churchyard,' she says. She's a little self-righteous, as though to say that she'd have nothing to do with such excesses. 'I think that's gross. People should get a room.'

'Amber, if you ever want to bring anyone back here…'

'Thanks, Mum, but we're OK...'

She unwraps a toffee and stuffs it in her mouth. It makes her cheek bulge. She looks like a little girl again.

'Mum, I just can't believe you'd think I'd be that stupid. You know, not to use anything.'

'You wouldn't rather go to our doctor?'

'Mum, I'm fine, OK? How often do I have to tell you, exactly?'

She goes up to her room, leaving the box with the retainers in but taking the toffees.

On Saturday, Eva throws a party—a joint birthday party for Ted, who is fifty, and the twins, who are sixteen. It's at the rowing club.

It's a squat concrete building, unimposing from outside, but on the first floor there's a bar and a dance floor and a balcony with a wide view of the Thames. The place is already full when we get there. There's a band, playing eighties hits with great enthusiasm. We drink, and talk to Ted and Eva's friends. There's a thread of sadness woven through these conversations. Someone's father has Alzheimer's and he can't remember his wife's name, though he can still play the piano: someone's daughter has Down's, and she leaves school in the summer, and what will happen to her then? I think that we are fortunate, Greg and I.

The more extrovert of Eva's friends are already on the dance floor, remembering the moves they used to make, bouncing around with an air of unselfconscious enjoyment, the febrile gorgeousness of disco lights playing across their faces and clothes. I'd like to ask Greg to dance, but I know what he would say. The teenagers—Lauren and Josh's friends, Amber among them—lurk like beautiful moths on the periphery of things. The girls are dressed like Amber in clingy jeans and vest tops, all bones and gleaming golden skin and expectation. I recognise some of them, Jamila, Sofia, Katrine: it's a loose friendship group that Amber is part of. In winter they meet at parties: on summer evenings they like to gather in Stoneleigh Gardens, behind the gasworks, where they gossip and drink from cans and text their friends. Their parents perhaps have brought them tonight but they don't really want to be here yet. They stand with their backs to the dance floor, keen to convey that whatever is happening there is no concern of theirs. Occasionally one of them will weave their way to the bar across the floor between the dancers—shoulders hunched, eyes down, rapid and unsmiling, like someone venturing into enemy territory. Later the parents will go and their party will begin.

When it gets too hot in the bar, we go out onto the balcony. You can smell the cold smell of the river. Everything is black, the sky, the water, the trees on the opposite bank, except where light from the rowing club catches the water just below the balcony, spilling from the tops of the waves the way shine spills from silk. Across the water a single white-painted house glimmers pale. Our music must be loud to them, carrying over the river with unimpeded clarity. There's a scattering of stars and a slice-of-melon moon. You can't see people's faces out here, only the lights from inside that play across them, the careless dancing colours in their glasses of wine and their eyes. After the heat in the bar, the cold silk touch of the river air is wonderful on my skin. We drink silently for a moment, resting our arms on the balustrade. I glance at Greg. His face is blotted out by shadow. I have a sudden giddy sense that I have no connection to him: that he could be anyone. If I said his name, would he turn to me? Once I saw a TV programme about how people cope with urban living: how for each of us there is a group of familiar strangers—those people we recognise but never greet. Sometimes Greg seems like that to me—someone I don't really know, just someone who's waiting on the same rail platform. I look out over the water, feeling the dizziness that's induced by its scarcely perceptible movement, just caught on the edges of vision; as though where you're standing is not as secure as you thought.

I take Greg's arm.

'I'm cold. Let's go back in.'

We refill our glasses and seek out Ted, who is comforting and capacious and tonight is wearing a tie with a pattern of peonies, and we have a soothingly banal conversation about the congestion charge.

We go at half-eleven, leaving Amber to find her own way home. I briefly consider offering to come back later to pick her up—but there's a boy wrapped round her, his fingers pushed proprietorially into the back pocket of her jeans, and I know my offer wouldn't be welcome.

I sleep fitfully, waking repeatedly, listening for her. Just after two o'clock a noise wakes me. I get up and go out onto the landing. There's a smell of cigarette smoke and down in the hall I can see her kicked-off shoes: I breathe the smell in gratefully, and I go back to bed, stretching out luxuriously, knowing I will sleep now.

On Sunday I drive down to Hampshire to see my mother.

I park in the road. The garden is tended, the Michaelmas daisies in flower, purple as smoke and ragged under the front bay window. Her car is parked in the driveway; I see there's a dent in the wing. She hasn't said anything about this. I wait on the doorstep, amid the sounds of my childhood—the whispering shrubbery, the singing of the electricity wires that pass over the back of our garden.

She greets me warmly. She feels thin, more fragile, in my arms, her face a little frayed: but she smells freshly of soap and Blue Grass and her make-up is neat, exact, and her hands well cared-for, her nails palely varnished. She leads me into the sitting room. She's taken the dust sheets off the furniture for me. Everything is orderly—the photos on the mantel-piece, the small shelf of books that marked us out as a middle-class family—though her colours and tulip prints are fading now. The room looks out over the back garden, the plum tree, the stream that is sometimes bright with toxins, the heavy moist hedges hanging over the stream: and I see she has put out food for the birds. All these things reassure me.

I've brought her a novel I thought she might like, and some photos of the girls. She puts the novel to one side.

'I don't read very much nowadays, darling,' she says. 'I seem to lose the thread.'

Only the photographs interest her.

It's cold in the house: heating it adequately always seems extravagant to her, however much Ursula and I assure her that we will pay the bill. When I rang I said I'd take her out for lunch, but she hadn't wanted to go. Now I regret that I didn't persuade her. I'd like to be with her in some place that's cosy and banal, to have a dry sherry and a gammon steak and talk to the waitress about the unseasonal weather and the autumn colours in the Forest: I don't want to be here, in this cold house full of memory.

She brings in tea.

'I didn't make you anything,' she says, apologising for the shop-bought Victoria sponge. 'I don't do much baking nowadays. I seem to get so tired.'

I tell her the cake is delicious: and think of our childhood, when her hands were always busy—mixing her fruit cakes in a vast yellow-glazed bowl, or ironing shirts on a blanket on the kitchen table: Monday was her wash day, and we'd come home from school to the safe, particular smell of almost-scorched linen.

It isn't easy to talk today. Usually she has gossip to tell, about people at church, or her neighbours: but she seems to have run out of stories.

'Ursula said you had a bad spell in church,' I say tentatively.

'Ursula thinks I should go to the doctor.' In her voice there's an edge of impatience at Ursula's insistence. 'She's fixed it up. She says she's going to take me.' She shrugs. 'But what can he do?' she says.

Her gesture reminds me of Amber—a way they both have of shrugging while turning their faces away.

I ask what happened to her car.

'Nothing, darling,' she says. 'Is there anything wrong with my car?' A splinter of hesitation in her voice.

I feel a flicker of panic.

'It looks like something bashed into you.'

'Does it, darling? I could have driven into something. I can't remember exactly.'

Her face is veiled.

As we say goodbye she stands there for a moment, her hands on my arms, her fingers pressing into me.

'Darling, I do so hope things work out well for all of you—Amber's exams and Gregory's book and everything.'

I feel her thin urgent grasp on my arms. I smile and hold her close. I try to push away the meaning of what she's saying. But I know she thinks she may not see me again.

I take a detour on the way home: I drive down to the sea and park for a while on the clifftop, looking across the Solent towards the Isle of Wight. The sea is a cold blue, the island clear. It was an enchanted place to us as children: a place that was always there on the horizon, blue as hyacinths or hidden by rain or absolutely precise with its fields and little woods in the clear, wet, spring sunshine—yet never visited, unknowable. We used to talk about going there; Ursula and I used to beg to be taken to this magical, inaccessible land across the water, and our mother would play along, imagining a picnic on the cliffs, a swim in the sea at Ryde, where the waves would be rougher and more exciting than on our familiar beaches—but somehow it never happened. Now, even as I watch, the island is blurred behind a veil of rain.

Driving back to rejoin the motorway, I have to drive past the gravel pits. It's a road that still makes me uneasy; when I was a child, I was followed once on this road. I was walking back from a piano lesson. I don't know why I didn't have my bicycle—perhaps a puncture I hadn't had time to fix. But I know I was wearing a faded blue cotton frock that I liked, that the sun was warm on the bare skin of my arms, that my music case was heavy with a new volume of Beethoven sonatas that I was very proud of: I carried the case with my arm stiff and straight, so it wouldn't bang on my legs. There was a smell of sun on grass, and the musty, sweaty scent of that ragged yellow-flowered weed that seems to thrive in gravelly soil. Beyond the gravel pits there would be the field with two horses, one black, one chestnut, that would come up to the fence when I passed and that liked to be petted and talked to. I looked forward to the horses. I walked on through the hushed summer afternoon under the arc of the sky.

I became aware that there was a man behind me. He was walking at just my speed, perhaps twenty paces behind. I glanced over my shoulder. He was ordinary-looking, a little taller than me, in his shirt sleeves. Not someone I'd ever seen before. I was afraid, my heart thudding. He didn't gain on me, just stayed there, walking behind me, always keeping his distance. You could see a long way to either side. There were no people, nothing. Lorries were parked at the gravel pit, but nobody was working there today. It was quiet on the road, no sound but the cries of seagulls. The smell of the yellow weed was thick. I thought of the girl whose body was found in a ditch on Southampton Common; I'd read about it in the *Southern Evening Echo*. I wanted to run, but something stopped me: embarrassment, perhaps, and some calculation that he could run faster anyway, and my music case was so heavy, and I didn't want to leave my new sonatas behind.

I came to the crossroads. I heard his quickening footsteps behind me. I knew he was gaining on me. He drew level with me, standing close. I couldn't move, I felt pure terror. He asked me the time, then walked on, overtaking me, going off left beyond the field at the crossroads. As soon as he was out of sight, forgetting the weight of my music case, I ran all the way home. I remember it still so vividly—the footsteps behind you, the sense of something so inevitable, drawing closer, something you couldn't escape from.

CHAPTER 16

I see Will every week—through November, into December. It's cold by the river. When there's no sun, the river is a harsh colour, like metal, with a white skin where it holds the shine of the sky. Some of the trees are bare now; at the sides of the path there are soft dark heaps of leaves. The balsam is dying back and broken, just a few ragged leaves still clinging, with swollen red knots like injuries on the stems. The ground and the trees are sodden and we have to take care or the places where we make love will leave their mark on us, and we'll go back with smears on our clothes from the green velvet algae on the tree trunks, or wet leaves in our hair.

Our timing is wrong. We should be having this love affair in the summer, when it's close and warm and secret here, and pale dust rises from the path where you tread, and flower scents brush against you, the winey sweetness of elder, and the fruit-gum smell of the balsam flowers, which are mauve with a scribble of black and intricate as orchids. Like on the summer afternoons when I came here with the girls, walking the tow path or exploring the islands in the river.

I think of the time we crossed the arched footbridge onto Eel Pie Island. The houses had a shack-like, temporary air, and the gardens were overgrown, with tangled roses with great shaggy heads, spilling out their perfume, and white hollyhocks that brushed against us like pallid fleshy hands. In one garden, baby dolls and Barbies were stuck into the window boxes and beds of earth like flowers, perhaps fifty of them, all naked and their hair stiff with soil and matted. The girls stared at this perverse, witchy planting. Amber went close, intrigued, but Molly was scared.

'That's creepy, Mum,' she said. 'The dolls won't like it.' Her liquorice eyes widening, her hand tightening in mine.

Another time I took them across a different bridge to an island further upstream. It was a summer Sunday morning, with a slight silver haze on the river. There were notices saying that this was Taggs Island and trespassing wasn't allowed, but we just walked on past them; it was one of the few illicit things I'd ever done. It was an island of gardens, of moored houseboats each with its own small plot of lawn and flowerbed, the gardens ornate with pergolas and rockeries, and the houseboats painted the colours of fruit—mandarin, lime, lemon—and one apple-green with a little blue dinghy tied up. It was completely quiet, a world away from the Sunday traffic on the river bank road, no one around but a cat with narrow gold eyes, and an old man sitting in the sun in his porch, who viewed us with suspicion. The island is a horseshoe shape, there was water on every side of you, crimped by the breeze and shimmering. An enchanted place, on that hazy summer morning: though I didn't feel the enchantment was entirely benign. But Amber adored it.

'Could we live here, Mum? Could we? I really really want to.'

'Maybe we could,' I said. 'One day. Who knows?'

'I want to, Mum, I shall live in the little green houseboat. And I shall have a cat and a boat to row in…'

In summer the plants at the sides of the river paths grow as tall as a man, weaving lavish walls of meadowsweet and mallow. There are places off the path where you might be hidden—shadowed scented places, private and enclosed.

But it's winter, and our dreams are all of rooms.

'I'd like to lie down with you,' he says. 'I'd like to stretch out on a bed beside you. To make love to you so slowly on a great big bed.'

We talk about this room where we could meet in secret, but never reach a decision.

'We could go to a hotel perhaps,' he says.

'Yes. I suppose. I don't know…'

I like to think of going to a hotel. I imagine it often.

I picture the delicious embarrassment at Reception, feeling like people from a 1930s movie; it's so like a scene from an old film in my imaginings, that when I picture it, it's in black and white and I'm wearing suede court shoes. I think how I'd try to keep my face sealed, serious—yet knowing I must look flushed, a little apprehensive, thinking for a moment, perhaps, What on earth are we doing? We'd walk up the stairs, not touching, maintaining a decorous space between us: and we'd go in together and close the door. The room would be nondescript, impersonal, with prints of stags on the walls and a red Gideon Bible and little soaps wrapped in cellophane: and we'd make love with such extravagance, relishing all that space and licence, my head flung back over the side of the mattress as he moved his mouth on me, my back stretched out and arched, intensifying everything.

'Could we really do that?' I say. 'Can you book a hotel room just for an hour or two? Do people do that—ordinary people like us? Just take a room?'

'I'm sure they do.'

'But the girl on Reception—I mean, they'd know exactly what you were doing.'

'Of course. It would be good though, wouldn't it?' He pushes my hair away from my eyes: his fingers are warm on my skin. 'But I don't suppose we will…'

I would like him to say, We'll do it—I know just where to go, I've booked the room… Yet at the same time I feel uncertain: if you take a room, you're doing something definite, irrevocable. You're leaving clues, there's a trail for people to find.

Sometimes I think of rooms that are more dream-like, that don't belong to anyone: that we inhabit in a different life that's parallel to this one, that's entirely constructed around this passion we share. A basement room perhaps with muslin curtains blowing at the windows and people passing in the street above us—near enough to hear us, not able to see in. Or an opulent room with a wide white bed and a canopy of some pale crushed apricot fabric: and I lie very still on the mattress under the apricot canopy as he moves his hands across me and eases me apart. It's absolutely vivid when I think about it: I can feel his fingers opening me and the wash of heat over my skin.

I never tell him about these rooms I imagine. We don't talk much when we meet. We just make love, quite quietly, in some hidden place by the river path, then drive to the bar in Sheffield Street, and if he has time we'll have a Coke and a whisky and a snatch of conversation. He might tell me a little about his work, and I love it when he does this, I'm hungry to know about him. It's mostly boredom, he says: but sometimes there's the kick, the thrill, and that's what hooks you. Like when you're doing surveillance, and nothing happens for ages, you're just waiting in the car, then suddenly the call comes, and your coffee goes straight out the window, and you're following this guy, you're on a high for hours...

I tell him I envy him for the directness of what he does, how it somehow seems so real. Whereas in my own work, I deal in representations all the time, in memories and imaginings.

'But you're good at what you do,' he says. 'I can tell that. Your empathy for those kids you work with.'

He runs one finger down the side of my face, his hand so gentle, as though I am some precious thing.

He'd hoped to have moved a bit further up the ranks, he tells me. He applied for the job that Roger Prior has now, in the murder squad.

'To be honest, I knew I didn't have a hope once I heard that Roger was going for it too,' he says. 'He's sharp. You can't get anything past him…'

I sense the disappointment in him—the feeling that life hasn't turned out the way he'd planned. I rest my hand on his. And we leave the bar, and he kisses me as we stand there in the street, a light formal kiss, his lips just brushing my cheek, and we move back into our separate lives, the things we have to do, the people who need us. Till this rhythm starts to seem natural to me, and I come to believe that nothing will be damaged.

C H A P T E R 17

It's parents' evening at Amber's school.

I'm late; the school gym is already a sea of people. There's a faint, residual smell of feet and adolescent sweat, and the air tastes stale, as though it's been breathed a thousand times before. The women are dressed as though for a job interview, smartly lipsticked and jacketed, and most have their husbands with them. I try to quell the familiar pang of envy. Greg has never come to a parents' evening. I used to try and persuade him, but he'd always be reluctant; now, I just handle all the girls' issues on my own. But I've noticed how the teachers view you differently if you're without a man, take you somehow less seriously.

The teachers are sitting at desks arranged down the sides of the hall. We all have bits of paper with our interview times, but nobody keeps to their times and you end up queuing for hours. Every ten minutes someone sets off a school bell that sounds like a fire alarm, to encourage us to move on. I feel a brief instinctive panic every time it sounds. I join the queue for Mrs Russell, Amber's form tutor.

I glance round the hall. Eva is in a queue a few yards away, waiting to see the ICT teacher. She's wearing a classy long black skirt with part of a French poem printed in white round the hem.

The siren sounds and it's my turn.

'I'm Amber's mother.'

'Ah,' says Mrs Russell. She shakes my hand.

I sit down. She has a cup of tea beside her, with a gingernut in the saucer. She takes a sip of tea.

I haven't met her before. She has a pink, flustered face and her purple lipstick clashes with her sweater—as though she doesn't have time to make things match.

'I'm sorry my husband couldn't come,' I say.

'Not to worry,' she says.

She has Amber's marks set out in a book in front of her. I realise I'm craning forward, trying to read them upside down. She looks at her book: there are sharp little vertical lines between her eyes. A familiar apprehension clutches at me. I think of the comments on Amber's most recent report. 'Teaching Amber is like stirring porridge...' 'Amber's efforts are to be commended in a subject for which she has so little aptitude or enthusiasm...'

'Amber does have quite a mixed bunch of marks, I'm afraid,' says Mrs Russell. 'To be honest, we *are* a little concerned.'

I flinch, thinking guiltily of the private tutor I never got round to fixing.

'It's not that she doesn't have ability—quite the reverse,' she says. 'But she doesn't do herself justice. She's so erratic. She needs to get herself organised.'

She has a resonant voice. I remember what Amber said about Academic Mentoring Day, when the girls all have individual interviews with their form tutors. You're in this hall, and everyone's waiting behind you, and Mrs Russell says, like, really loudly, Amber, are you being bullied? and you think, No, but now I will be...

'I know what you mean,' I say carefully.

Her look is severe and concerned, as though she thinks I haven't understood.

'This is a really crucial year for her,' she says. 'It's a very bad time to lose the plot. And unfortunately we don't feel anything's in the bag yet, quite honestly, with her GCSEs. She badly needs a bit of focus.'

I don't know what to say. I have a brief wayward urge to explain about my daughter. How she seems to slip through my fingers like water—yet I always feel her feyness is part of her, the way she's meant to be. How her talent for friendship dazzles and delights me. How when she was little she wanted to fly across the river on the back of a bird.

'I don't think planning's her strong point,' I say. 'You know, thinking things through—thinking into the future. I don't think she connects what she does now with the future—with the rest of her life. I mean, teenagers don't really, do they?'

'Some of them do, Mrs Holmes,' she says rather sternly. 'Some of our girls here are very goal-oriented, I'm happy to say. Of course Amber *is* a very pretty girl: and I feel her social life does rather take precedence over everything.'

'She's quite extrovert, I guess,' I say.

Mrs Russell leans towards me, folding her hands with precision.

'Another thing I feel with Amber—she's quite an impulsive lass. Perhaps a bit of a drama queen?'

'I know what you mean,' I say.

I think of the wild streak in Amber, the way she's sometimes drawn to destructive, extravagant gestures. Once, after she'd fallen out with Lauren, I found her in the bathroom, sobbing and cramming some aspirin into her mouth: and when a boyfriend had dumped her she scratched her arm with some scissors. It was just a little scratch, but it scared me. I don't tell Mrs Russell this.

'I worry too that she's rather distractible,' she goes on. 'Obviously, you'll provide good conditions for her to work in...'

It's a question.

I picture Amber in her room—the whole place shuddering with sound, Amber tugged in so many directions by urgent text messages and friends on Facebook and ominous horoscopes and crucial clothing decisions.

'I hope so. I try to.'

Perhaps I look upset, because she reaches out her hand in a little truncated gesture, as though to reassure me.

'Don't worry too much, Mrs Holmes,' she says. 'With a following wind, she could do very well. I'm just so concerned she won't quite do herself justice. She absolutely needs stability in her life.' And then, embarrassed about what she might be implying, 'Which I'm sure you give her.'

The bell blares again. I have a strong urge to evacuate the building.

She's glancing over my shoulder, at all the couples waiting behind me to see her.

'Just one last thing, Mrs Holmes. D'you know if she's sorted out her work experience yet?'

I feel a pang of guilt. The letter came home weeks ago, along with a reminder that the correct length for hemlines was no more than half an inch above the knee.

'I don't think she has,' I tell her.

She puckers up her purple lips.

'It's the second week in December,' she says. 'She really should have it organised by now. It's that lack of commitment again, you see. I wondered if you or your husband could help with that at all?'

I explain that Amber can't come to my clinic because our work is confidential.

'Your husband perhaps? Now, I'm not sure where he works?'

'At the university. He's a lecturer in medieval Irish literature.'

Her whole face softens. 'How wonderful,' she says. 'So could he fix up something for Amber perhaps?'

'I suggested that, but she didn't seem too keen.'

I remember her actual words—OK, Mum, if you give me a swig of Rohypnol...

'What does she want to do?' says Mrs Russell. 'When she leaves school?'

'She's not at all sure, yet.' In my mind I run through Amber's only expressed ambitions: to become a roads protestor; to release some captive mink into the wild; to be a DJ on Agia Napa.

'Well, time's running out,' says Mrs Russell briskly. 'If the worst comes to the worst, we could probably fix her up with a nursery somewhere. But I do really like the initiative to come from the girls. Organising the placement is very much part of the project...'

I promise her I'll see what I can do.

The interview is over: she's already smiling at the couple behind me. The man has gold cufflinks and an executive air. Mrs Russell greets them warmly.

I weave my way through the milling parents to Eva, who's still waiting for the ICT teacher. I'm so happy to see her.

'Fancy a drink?' I say.

She brightens. 'You bet. Are you through yet?'

'Not really. But I'm thinking of absconding.'

'I've only got one to go, but it could be half an hour,' she says. 'I think I might give it a miss.'

She stands and smoothes down her skirt. The white words ripple.

'Are you sure, Eva? What about Lauren's computer skills?'

She shrugs. 'I'm not too bothered, quite honestly. She seems to know what she's doing. She's been molesting people in chat rooms for years.'

We leave, feeling like truants.

The Cafe Matisse is almost empty. There are candles on the table and, over the sound system, Nina Simone.

Eva orders a Bloody Mary, I have whisky.

We catch up. Josh has just bought an amplifier on eBay that he can't afford and is in big trouble with Ted. And Lauren has alarmed Eva by catching the wrong night-bus home after clubbing with a friend in Leicester Square, and they didn't realise it had turned round and was heading back towards London. They got stranded at Clapham Junction at three in the morning and Ted set off a speed camera rushing to pick them up.

Eva is a laid-back parent; she's always believed in making things easy. When Lauren and Josh were younger, she'd sometimes draw the curtains and turn on the clocks by two hours and tell them it was bedtime—which was, I thought, quite dazzlingly delinquent. She used to think I made things harder for myself, with the absolute rule I had about not smacking my children.

'I've only ever smacked in anger,' she'd say. 'Not

kind of deliberately—in cold blood—I think that's
rather horrible. But if you just lose it and wallop
them—well, so what? They'll live.'

But she really doesn't like the teenage years.

'It freaks me out,' she says now. 'I can't get to
sleep till they're in. I think this is just the worst bit
of parenting—I hate it, it's just so scary...'

We've both heard about a murder on the news—a
girl going home from the cinema, taking the last bus
with just a five minute walk from the bus-stop to her
home. She was attacked there in the street a few yards
from her house by someone with a hammer; and there
was a ring at the door and the mother thought, She's
forgotten her key again, but it was the police to say
they'd found her daughter's body.

'I cried when I read that,' says Eva. 'Your heart
goes out to her. That poor poor woman.'

Her eyes are full. We drink for a while in silence.
My whisky tastes wonderful after the hot stale air
of the gym. There's a single dahlia in a glass on our
table: you can smell its thin peppery scent.

'Lauren's madly in love with some boy again,' she
says then. 'It's the real thing, as usual.'

I smile.

'Still, he *is* rather cute. You've got to admire her
taste.' Her eyes are on me, pensive. She takes a slow
sip of her drink. 'D'you envy them, Ginnie, having
all that in front of them?'

'Sometimes,' I tell her.

'All that exploration, all that sex,' she says. 'All the stuff that seems to have gone for good.'

She looks at me, a look like a question.

'Eva,' I say carefully, 'there are lots of couples who don't have that much sex.'

'It's not that exactly,' she says. 'I mean, we do have a sex life. It's not like when the kids were babies.' She smiles. 'You and I used to have that running joke—remember? "It's nice to know sex is still there, like the Tower of London, and if I get the energy I might revisit it one day…"'

'I remember,' I tell her.

'No—we do quite well really. Once a week or so. It's just—I don't know. There's none of the *charge*. But then of course there wouldn't be. You've got to be real, haven't you? And of course you can't expect it to be like it used to be. It's fine, really. I mean, you know how Ted is. He's a really sweet man. He's so polite I've heard him say thank you to a cash machine…'

There's a sadness to Eva nowadays, a mood she seems to trail round with her, a faint lavender-scent of nostalgia. Throughout our friendship, she's always seemed to have so much of everything, with her earth-motherliness, her assurance about what it means to be a woman, her involved, dependable husband, her splendid curves. But somehow, imperceptibly, she's become rather mournful and full of regret. I wonder when this happened.

'It's fine, really,' she says again. 'There isn't a problem.'

We listen to Nina Simone, that darkly luminous voice, singing about abandonment.

'Sometimes I wonder if we're all like this,' she says quietly. 'Hungry. Hungrier than ever. Is this what happens? Do people just get hungrier?'

'Maybe they do. I don't know.'

She licks the tomato juice off her lips.

'We're much better off than lots of people, Ted and me. I know that. I don't know what I want really,' she says. 'It's desire, I suppose. The thrill. And I know I won't have that again. Not ever. And sometimes I just feel so sad. If I watch something on the TV that's got romance in—you know, *Casablanca*, or something—I can feel like crying for days—just thinking that that's over in my life.'

I'd so love to open up to her, to tell her about Will. I imagine how we'd lean towards each other across the table, our heads almost touching, the candle-flame flickering in our excited breath, how her eyes would gleam and widen.

'Maybe it doesn't have to be like that,' I say tentatively.

She looks at me quizzically. 'I'd never have an affair,' she says. 'Anyway, who'd have me?'

I rest my eyes on her—her wonderful cleavage, her skirt with a French sonnet on.

'Eva, you always look fantastic.'

She shrugs this off. 'The other day I was at the MAC counter,' she says, 'and I glimpsed myself in a mirror, and I thought, There's some mistake here, this isn't really me. That isn't what I look like. I really thought that—that it was a mistake.'

'I hate the lights in that shop,' I say. 'They're quite excessively bright. You can see the most minuscule wrinkle.'

'And my knees are starting to sag,' she says, 'and when I lie on one side everything kind of responds to gravity. If I had an affair, I'd have to do it standing up.' She takes a long slow sip of her drink. 'No, Ginnie, you've got to be real. You just have to live with it, I guess. The hunger...'

The music wraps itself around us, the sadness, the velvet voice.

'Though just sometimes,' she says, 'just sometimes I feel... Like, if there was a bargain, and, if I was willing to sacrifice everything, I could have those feelings again, have all that again... Sometimes I feel I'd do it,' she says. Her voice is faint, misty. She runs her finger round the top of her glass, like you did when you were a teenager, making your glass ring— that moment of effortless magic. I can't work out her expression; I think it might be fear. She takes a deep breath. 'Not really, of course,' she says, and her voice is her own again, brisk, cheerful. 'Not really. Hey, if you're there, God, forget it, OK? I didn't mean it...' She looks across at me. 'Just sometimes,' she says. 'Just for a moment.'

I touch her hand. I don't say anything.

'It's this music,' she says. 'It isn't good for us.'

CHAPTER 18

The river dazzles under the pale blue shine of the sky. There's light everywhere. The turning trees are richly coloured, like the hides of animals, and the hawthorn is bare, its crooked branches an embroidery of spiky cross-stitch branches, and in the place off the path where we go, the leaves seem too thin and fragile to conceal us. I think, What if somebody sees? Then he reaches out his hand to my face and it doesn't seem to matter any more.

There's a crashing in the undergrowth, something lurching towards us.

'Hell,' says Will.

He grabs my jacket and holds it round my shoulders, pulling me close. A labrador hurtles into the space between the bushes, twitchy and alert. Behind him, a woman with crisp white curls walks through the bushes towards us, with confidence, as though there is a path there. She passes, looking away from us, calling her dog. I rest my head on Will's shoulder. I feel embarrassed, ridiculous. I know she must have seen.

'We can't stay here,' says Will. 'You'd better get your clothes on.'

I leave my bra in my bag and just pull on my T-shirt. A twig caught in the fabric scratches my skin.

We stand on the path for a moment. There are dog-walkers and cyclists, and the river is alive with rowing teams, barges, pleasure boats. Out here in the busy brightness, our furtive attempt at love-making seems a crazy chaotic dream.

'It's like the fucking High Street,' says Will.

I sense how the desire has seeped away from him. He's frowning. I know he's going to say that we shouldn't be here, that we need to get back to the car. I can't bear it. I want him so much, the grace of his hands exploring me and the patterns of his quickening breath and the cinnamon scent of his skin.

'What the hell do we do now?' he says.

There's a clatter of geese going over, a ragged V flying upriver. We watch them for a moment, hearing their creaking cries and the rush of their wings.

'We could go on for a bit.' My voice is thin, unsure. 'You know, round the bend in the path.'

'What happens up there?'

'I don't really know. I've never been that far.'

'OK. If you'd like to.'

We walk on—a little apart, not walking like lovers. All conversation eludes me.

I'm sure he will stop and turn. I know exactly how this will happen: how he'll touch my arm and say, You don't mind, do you? Apologetic, knowing he's taking something from me: I can hear his exact intonation. I'm sorry, but I really ought to be getting back now… Each time he draws breath I fear he is going to say this.

The river bends so the path behind is hidden. Suddenly it's quiet. The rowers have passed, there are only ducks on the water, and rubbish circling in an eddy near the river bank, a polystyrene cup like some pale exotic flower. Here, the belt of woodland to the left of us seems thicker and more tangled. A rowan leans across the path, its berries bright as flame.

'Look,' he says.

Ahead of us and to the left, between the trees and the path, there's a little wooden building. It seems broken-down, abandoned. The walls were once white-painted, and the roof is edged with intricate barge boards, jade-green and curled like opening leaves or ferns. You often find this kind of carving on the river bank, as though the river somehow gives licence to extravagance. It was once perhaps a summer house, belonging to a big house that stood higher up the slope, that must now be demolished. We stop for a moment: he moves close to me and slips his hand in mine.

At the side of the house, there are the remains of a garden: a lawn of long grass, and hydrangea bushes with papery dead flowerheads, and a hedge that no longer seems to mark out any boundary, and on a sprawling rose-bush the tattered remnant of a white summer rose. The plants are straggly, neglected for years, the roses half strangled with ivy, but it's as if the place hasn't quite forgotten how to be a garden. I wonder who the people were who tended this garden, who walked here by the river. At the edge of the lawn the wood presses in, with just a narrow gap where a path leads through the trees.

I go to the river. There's a broken jetty that seems to belong with the summer house, and a dinghy, half rotting, tied up with fraying rope. The boat has a name on the prow in peeling letters. *Sweet Bird of Youth*: a flamboyant name for such a little boat. Fallen leaves have massed on the water between the boat and the bank, thickly, like a carpet: so in a moment of carelessness, or of being willingly taken in by the illusion, you might almost step out onto them, believing them to be solid, not just a surface loveliness of yellow and russet and gold.

'I like it here,' I say.

There are windows at the side of the house, with cracked glass. Will goes to look in the window, cupping his hand at the side of his face to shield his eyes from the brightness.

'It's empty,' he says.

The door in the side of the house is green-painted like the barge boards, though the paint is peeling and worn.

Will glances along the path, then unwinds the twist of wire that secures the door.

'Will, for God's sake—we can't just go in,' I say.

'Why ever not?'

'It's trespassing…'

'That isn't a crime,' he says. 'Not if you don't damage anything.'

'But surely—I mean, this must belong to someone, mustn't it?'

'It doesn't look like they're very bothered about it,' he says.

He turns the handle, holds it there, gives the door a quick kick. It shakes and creaks open, with a shower of paint flakes.

He peers in.

'Are you OK with spiders?' he says.

'Kind of.'

He gestures me in.

'But we can't…'

'Ginnie, just look at the state of it. No one's been here for years.'

I follow him through the door.

It's a single room, with bare floorboards and a table against the wall. The corners are hung with vast spiders' webs, like lacy festoons of some worn grey fabric, and there's thick dark dust on the floor and streaks of glimmering birdshit—there must be a missing tile where the birds get in. Things have been left here—a canvas deck-chair folded up, a Coke can, a cigarette lighter thrown down on the floor—but these things are so dusty and long abandoned, they feel like outgrowths of the place, as organic as the ferns that grow up through the floor. There's a rich river smell, of mud and rot and reeds.

The glass in the windows is smeared and cracked, but a lot of light comes in—river light, the random lovely intricacy of sunlight moving on water, so the room seems alive with silvery shiftings and patternings.

He closes the door, turns to face me, leaning back against the door.

'Well,' he says.

He gives me a small smile of triumph, like a man who has just achieved something. His eyes gleam in the river light. I'm standing there in the middle of the floor, looking at him. I stretch out my arms. I feel such excitement, in this enclosed space, with its secrecy, its shut door. Here we can do anything. Here we will not be seen.

He comes towards me and starts again to take off my clothes, heaping them carefully on top of my bag, knowing the dust could mark us and give us away. I pull off his shirt, and see how the river light moves across his body. Here there is a different rhythm: we can be slow, tender. I feel it all so exactly, the cool dank touch of this enclosed air on me, the silky solidness of his cock against my lips, my fingers: and his body pressed against me, its lines and bones and hardness, and the softness of his skin.

He kisses my hair as my breathing slows.

'Did that feel good?' he says. 'It looked as though it felt good.'

But I can't quite speak yet.

He turns me round and bends me across the table and slides into me. He says my name over and over.

Afterwards I ask him to hold me, and we stay like that for a long time.

'I'd like to lie down with you,' he says. 'That would be wonderful. But this floor's so filthy.'

I think how that would feel, to lie stretched out together.

'Perhaps I could find us something to lie on. Perhaps a blanket or something.'

'Could you?' he says.

We brush the dust off one another's clothes. We secure the door again, so it's like it was before. We check along the path, so no one sees us leaving. As though this is a crime we have committed.

We don't talk much as we walk towards the car. My body feels slowed, gentle. I drop him off at Sheffield Street, and go home with the dust of the river house on my knees and the soles of my shoes and his smell all about me; and for hours, if I close my eyes, I can see the river brightness against my eyelids, the dance and dazzle of light. There's a childlike part of me that believes in pattern, in significance; that whispers, If it were all wrong, if we shouldn't be doing this—then why did we find this place—this room full of glimmering light, this place to keep our secret?

CHAPTER 19

On Sunday Max and Clem come to dinner.

Max is first. He's brought me flowers, yellow lilies with speckled hearts, and an expensive Burgundy. In his pale Armani jacket, he seems much younger than his years. He kisses me lingeringly on both sides of my face.

'You're looking well,' he says.

'I'm fine,' I say.

'No, really, Ginnie. There's something different.'

I shrug a little, laughing, afraid he can read something in me.

He has an invitation for me. He's had a call from Dylan, the conductor of the choir we sang in at university. Dylan is planning one of our periodic reunions, at the church in Walsall where he is choir-master, to celebrate his fiftieth birthday in February. I say I'd love to come. I find a vase for the flowers and put them on the dining-room table; their pollen powders my fingers, as though I have dipped them in turmeric.

Clem is wearing one of her vintage outfits, a chiffony anthracite-grey skirt and blue suede boots with fringes, and her hair is tamed by some resinous hair product.

I hug her.

'You look gorgeous,' I say.

'I saw a heron fly over,' she says as she takes off her jacket. 'Making that weird noise they make. You always feel special, don't you, if you see a heron? It must be lovely to live so near the river.'

'It's jolly damp,' says Greg. 'We have awful problems with damp.'

We go into the living room, and Greg pours us drinks. Max sprawls expansively on the sofa. Clem runs her fingers over my patchwork cushions.

'You might have underground water,' says Max. 'Perhaps there's a stream that runs under your house— a tributary going down to the Thames.'

Greg talks with animation about his fears of flooding, and the time the cellar flooded and we had it pumped out and got horribly overcharged.

'There you are then,' says Max. 'Apparently there are all these trapped rivers in London, rivers that have been concreted in, flooding people's cellars and generally causing trouble. I just read this weird thing,' he says. 'In Peter Ackroyd's *London*. They did a study in some hospital and found that most of the people brought in with asthma or allergies lived over underground streams.'

'Well, of course,' says Clem. 'They disturb the magnetic field of the body. Underground water is terribly bad for you.'

Her eyes glint: she knows about these things. Once she showed me how to dowse with rods made from metal coat hangers. She'd straightened the coat hangers out, with a little hook at the end. You held the rods between finger and thumb so they could swivel freely, and you had to walk quite smoothly, like a cat. It happened just as she said it would, the rods swinging out suddenly and precisely to follow the lines of streams below the ground. It was unnerving, feeling the tug of a force that I didn't know was there.

I never told Greg about this: he sees Clem as terribly flaky. Now, he raises his eyebrows slightly.

'They say that where people think they see ghosts,' says Max, 'or anything supernatural, there are usually underground rivers. That they make people feel spooked.'

We go into the dining room. I've lit lots of candles on the mantelpiece in front of my wide gilt-framed mirror; the flames reflect in the glass with a witchy glamour. The walls of the room are a deep jade green; they seem almost black in the candle-light. The scent of Max's lilies brushes against us.

Clem admires the candles. The Burgundy is like velvet on your tongue. We eat melon, then coq au vin, and listen to Miles Davis. Max tells us more about the book about London he's read. He likes to be listened to.

'Some of it was quite gruesome,' he says. 'There used to be these special places along the banks of the river, where they took the bodies of people who were dragged out of the Thames. Suicides or drownings. They called them the dead houses. The bodies were laid on a shelf till the coroner could come.'

Clem shudders.

'Imagine what those places would have been like,' she says.

Greg takes a slow sip of Burgundy.

'It means the Dark River,' he says.

For a moment, the rest of us don't understand what he means.

'The Thames,' he says. 'The word comes from tamesa. It's Sanskrit—the Dark River.'

Clem shakes her head a little.

'All those poor lost people,' she says. 'People who died and maybe nobody missed them.'

For pudding I've made a blackberry pie, with blackberries from the garden and the last of the convent apples. It has a crisp buttery crust, and the filling is sharp and sweet and winey, with a syrup that stains you. We eat and talk about Molly—everyone rather envious, wishing, as people do, that we could do it all again but knowing what we know now: and I talk, perhaps with excessive emotion, about the difficulties involved in parenting teenage girls, and Amber in particular, who has gone to the pub with friends, and should be home by now.

'You worry too much,' says Greg to me.

'He's right, it's what kids are like,' says Max, with the authority of the childless. 'You have to be a bit more laid-back about it.'

'It isn't that easy,' I say.

After the pudding, Greg says would we mind if he went to bed: he has a nine o'clock lecture tomorrow. I see Clem glancing at me as he goes, but she doesn't say anything. There's a kind of easing after Greg has gone. Max lights a cigarette, Clem kicks off her shoes. The lilies glimmer in the candle-light, just a flower-shaped luminescence, their colour all washed away, and the jade-green walls are so dark it's as though we're underwater, under the sea in one of Ursula's paintings, that claustrophobic jewelled world. I can just make out our faces in the mirror: the candle-light is kind to us, making our eyes gleam, showing the shape of our bones. The music has ended, but I like the silence. Almost any music would be wrong now; except perhaps a solitary flute, high and clear and distant, spooling out its bright notes into emptiness.

Clem sips her wine. 'Don't worry about Amber,' she says. 'I'm sure she's being protected.'

Sometimes Clem unnerves me.

'Well,' I say lightly, 'I hope so.'

'No, really,' she says, 'I'm serious.'

There's a little spilled wine on the table. Clem

moves her finger in it, tracing a pattern that no one else can see.

'I heard an angel once,' she says. Her voice is quite matter-of-fact, no question in it.

I glance at Max. I expect a sardonic smile, or at least a deeply sceptical look, a raised eyebrow. But he's listening quietly, blowing out blue smoke.

'It was when all that stuff was happening with Gordon,' she says. 'When it was falling apart.' Her voice quiet, thin, suspended in the stillness. 'I was staying at my mother's, and I woke, and it was dark. I was thinking how could I carry on. I couldn't begin to imagine how I could start all over again—love again, trust anyone again; and I heard this voice in the darkness. Saying the words of a hymn we'd sung when I was a child. "Love divine, all loves excelling…" It wasn't in my head,' she says, as though responding to some protest from Max or from me, though we're just sitting there quietly. 'It was an absolutely clear voice.'

The reflections of the candles float in the dark of the mirror, as though they're floating on water.

'I went to this therapist last year,' she says, 'and I told her about it, and she'd refer to it sometimes. And she'd always say, That angel you thought you heard. But I didn't *think* I heard it: I *heard* it.'

I can hear Max's breathing, and at the window the whisper of the rain.

'"As we grow older, the world becomes stranger,"' he says. 'Who wrote that?'

But Clem and I don't know.

'It was some poet,' he says. 'I think some poet said that.'

'I'm envious,' I say. 'I'd like to hear an angel.'

'Sometimes I think…we're all connected,' says Clem slowly. 'Sometimes I think…' She makes a slight gesture. 'I don't know what I think…' Her voice trails off into silence. 'But it was a wonderful thing. It got me through.'

There's a crash as the front door opens and is flung back. I jump, then feel the relief that always surges through me when Amber is home. We smile, lean back in our chairs, the spell broken.

'There you are then,' says Clem.

Amber comes in, stands uncertainly in the doorway.

'Hi, you guys,' she says.

She smiles, her new wide practised smile. She's just a little shy. She never uses an umbrella, she hates the way the rain runs down her sleeve from the umbrella handle, and the furry trimming of her coat is clumped together and sodden, and her hair is wet, as though she's been dragged through water.

'Was it a good evening?' says Max.

'OK.' She shrugs off her coat. She's a bit disorganised, her movements rather random, from too much Bacardi perhaps. She's wearing tight jeans and a little top, exposing lots of skin. There's glittery varnish on her bitten nails. 'There was this really sad guy,' she says. She twists her mermaid's hair behind an ear. 'He came up to me and it was, like, If I could rearrange the alphabet I'd put U and I together. I gave him a look and he went away. Can I have a drink, Mum?'

'No, sweetheart, I think you've had enough already. Have you eaten?'

She shakes her head.

'There's some coq au vin you could heat up in the kitchen.'

She frowns.

'Mum, you know I don't like to eat animals.' She turns to Max and Clem. 'I try to tell her,' she says, 'about animal cruelty and stuff. But will she listen? I've even brought her leaflets... Yum. Blackberry pie.'

I spoon some out on a coffee saucer for her. She eats greedily. They chat to her as she eats, about school and what subjects she's doing and whether she likes her teachers. Her lips are wet and stained with vivid juice.

'My form tutor, she's always getting at me because I haven't fixed my work experience placement,' she says. 'Like it's this big moral thing.' She's expansive, making the most of her audience. 'I mean, we have war, we have famine, we do these horrible things to animals: what's the big deal about a few days' work experience? She has issues, Mrs Russell.'

'So what's involved?' says Max.

'It's just for a week in December,' I say. 'It shouldn't be that difficult. But I can't take her because of the confidentiality thing, and she's adamant she's not going to Greg's department. Though really I can't see why not…'

'Mum, please don't start all that again,' says Amber sternly.

His eyes rest on her. I see a bud of an idea beginning to form.

'In December?' he says.

She nods.

'We've had students on placement before,' he says. 'They seem to quite enjoy it.'

'You could have *me*,' she says.

He smiles. 'I'm sure we'd be able to work out something. If you'd like that.'

'Please,' she says. 'It would be perfect.'

'Max, are you sure?' I say. 'I mean, it's sweet of you, but you mustn't feel you have to…'

'Absolutely. As long as Amber doesn't mind being a general dogsbody—making the coffee, that sort of thing.'

'She could learn,' I say.

Amber glares at me.

'And you could come to court, of course,' says Max. 'Though I can't guarantee there'll be anything remotely glamorous. Most of the time it's unbelievably boring.'

'No murders?'

'I'm afraid I can't promise a murder.'

'Will I need a suit?' she says.

He shakes his head. 'Just something smartish.'

'Mum could lend me something.' She finishes her

pudding and gives the spoon a comprehensive lick. 'Thanks, Max. You've saved my skin.'

She takes a scrap of envelope and an eyeliner pencil from her handbag and writes her number down for him, with a sketch of a flower next to her name. She hands it across to him with her new, lavish smile.

'Court,' she says, with satisfaction. 'That'll show her.'

She doesn't quite know how to say goodnight. She picks up her coat and gives Max and Clem a slight, self-conscious wave.

'She's so lovely,' says Clem, after she's gone. 'You're so lucky, Ginnie, with your daughters. She's lovely, isn't she, Max?'

'She certainly is,' he says. He tucks the scrap of paper in his pocket.

We hear Amber clatter upstairs, and the shower running. The mood has changed. I would like to talk more about Clem's angel, but I know that the moment has passed. We are more ordinary now.

I make coffee, and we discuss the mayoral election and the inadequacies of the local rail service, then Clem and Max gather their things together and go off into the night.

I go back to the dining room, not wanting to go to bed yet. Amber is asleep now: my home is quiet, just creaking a little like somebody turning over and settling down to sleep. I think of the things we talked about, of the pull of hidden water and the angel that Clem heard; of how as you grow older the world becomes stranger. And I think of making love with Will in the house on the banks of the river: and I wonder how I came to this place—everything fluid, nothing fixed, so different from how I'd imagined it would be.

CHAPTER 20

Amber has her work experience placement in the second week of December. I'm pleased how seriously she takes it. She buys herself a skirt—an item of clothing she didn't previously possess—and a pair of prim, if rather high, court shoes. She borrows some pearl earrings of mine, which I never wear because I think they look too middle-aged on me, but on her they look beguilingly demure.

I go to wake her on the first morning of the placement, but she's up already. In her decorous new clothes, she looks like the secretary in a black and white romantic movie, in the moment of revelation when Cary Grant whips off her glasses and takes the clip out of her hair.

Max arranges for her to spend the day in court. It's a social security fraud case which doesn't sound especially thrilling, but the whole thing fascinates her—the wigs, the bundles of paper tied up in pink ribbon, all the pompousness and drama. She feels a rush of empathy for the defendant.

'The prosecution lawyer gave her a really hard time,' she says. 'This horrible barrister. Can they do that, Mum?'

'They can do what they want,' I say. 'They're just out to get a result. It's what they're there for. They don't care if they upset people.'

'It shouldn't happen. That poor woman. She was only trying to feed her kids,' she says. 'She didn't hurt anybody.'

I remember that certainty—how at sixteen life is so simple and obvious, and you're utterly convinced you know what's right. Though as you get older you become less sure.

At the end of the week Amber decides she's going to be a lawyer. I send Max a bottle of Glenfiddich. He rings to thank me.

'Really, you shouldn't have,' he says. 'It was a pleasure.'

I don't see Will for two weeks over Christmas. We're both with our families. We don't speak or phone.

Molly comes home, bringing an intimidating heap of washing. Greg moves out of her room and rolls out the futon on the dining room floor.

'That won't be very comfortable,' I say. 'You don't have to sleep there.'

My face goes hot when I say this: I'm embarrassed

inviting him back into my bed, as though I'm suggest-
ing something illicit. I think how strange this is.

He shrugs: he says he's got used to sleeping on his
own.

Molly looks different. She seems somehow to have
grown, though she isn't any taller. I gaze at her, loving
to rest my eyes on her, trying to puzzle out what's
changed about her. There are the obvious things. Her
style is cooler, more subtle. She wears her hair down,
not piled up in complicated ways or wrapped all round
itself. She doesn't wear the little spangly tops any
more and she's thrown out the pink eyeshadow. But
something inchoate has changed as well, as though
she has her adult bones now, as though the structure
of her face is more defined.

She's out every evening, catching up with friends
in The Blue Hawaii or Starbucks. She's already planning her summer. 'Is it OK if I don't come on holiday
with you guys next year, Mum? There's this boy I
know—his parents have a house in Crete, near Agios
Nikolaos… You wouldn't mind, Mum, would you?'
When she's at home, she spends hours with Amber in
one of their rooms, playing music and sharing secrets,
and when I go in they stop talking. She's happy to be
home but I know she's moving away from me.

And she's broke, of course. She's terribly sorry—but
could we help her out, just till her next loan cheque
comes? She's had to buy an awful lot of books… Her
eyes are large and liquid as she says this. Greg and I
discuss whether to subsidise her.

'For Chrissake,' he says, 'she's spent a fifth of her money on phone calls.'

'But no one can manage on a student loan,' I tell him. 'Shouldn't we be glad we can help, so she doesn't have to go off and be a strippagram?'

It's Christmas weather, cold and clear. One Saturday we wake to a powdering of snow; the world seems full of light, and there's a line of frozen snow down the side of the trunk of the pear tree, precise, immaculate, like a child's attempt at drawing light and shade. I wonder what it would be like at the river house. The grass that once was mown would be perfect under the snow, untouched except for the delicate stitchery of birds' footprints, smoothed out and perfected, like white velvet. I imagine the quiet of it, and the dance of the light. Though when I glimpse the river from the window of Greg's study, the brown of the water looks soiled against the dazzle of the snow.

By mid-afternoon, it's melting, and the world is full of the drip and glitter and rawness of the thaw. Amber is going out, wearing just her leather jacket over a cotton milkmaid top. Her breath smokes in the open doorway. Her skin is pimpling with cold.

'You can't go out like that,' I say.

'You weren't meant to see,' she says.

At my insistence she puts on a sweater: it has a very low neck.

'Can't you choose a warmer one?' I say.

She shakes her head.

'I did what you said. I put on a sweater,' she says.

'Well, wear your scarf, then.'

'I can't,' she says, shocked, as though I've suggested something obscene. 'I couldn't possibly. Those colours together are *gross*.'

Molly overhears and lends Amber a scarf of her own, a stripy one from Gap.

'Funky,' says Amber. She tries it on and smiles at her reflection.

'I'll kill you if you get anything on it,' says Molly, as an afterthought.

Amber is meeting friends tonight for a Mexican meal: I imagine a major scene, in which Amber hands back the Gap scarf with a chilli salsa stain. So I give the scarf back to Molly, and hunt out a scarf of my own, which Amber seems content with, though it's the exact same shade as the one she rejected. I wonder if all this negotiation was worthwhile, or if I should just have let her shiver.

'Amber,' I call after her. 'Have you got your keys and your phone?'

'Mum, you don't need to go on about it. I never go anywhere without my phone.'

I go to the mall to start the Christmas shopping. There are massive queues in all the shops, and three large animated bears that are switched on every half hour and sing along to Christmas songs. Teenagers sit on the rampart of the fountain in the basement, eating crisps and texting their friends; the turquoise floor of the fountain glints with coins, and a notice says that this is a wishing well, and your money will go to charity. I buy the shots glasses that Molly wants, and some books and CDs for Greg, and a new short skirt for myself, thinking of Will, hoping that he will like it. There are new shops opening for Christmas, candle shops and places selling charity cards; and a shop that looks more permanent, a rather classy sex shop aimed at affluent women. It's enticing, full of silk and mirrors. I wander inside, intrigued to reflect that I might have a use for these things. There are camisoles and thongs in subtle colours, pale like under-ripe fruit or the colours of skin, and satin blindfolds, and lubricants scented with passion-flower, and leather restraints with a trim of blue glass beads. It's all rather lovely, but in the end I walk out again with nothing. It all seems so pale and perfect: you'd have to be so young and unblemished to use or wear these things.

The health food shop is more promising. They have a special Christmas promotion—a free plaid blanket or sports bag if you spend over twenty-five pounds. I shop with enthusiasm—gingko biloba to stave off Alzheimer's, multi-vitamins for the girls, some blackcurrant and ginseng tea because I like the packaging. I am effusively grateful for my gift: the shop assistant, a cool dark girl with a Central European accent, gives me a quizzical look. But in some crazy way, according to some eccentric moral code I have invented, this isn't the same as deliberately buying a blanket: I can pretend to myself that I didn't choose to do this. Yet I still feel troubled with the blanket in my bag, as though it binds the threads of my different lives together, when everything depends on keeping them apart. Then I hear Will saying, I'd like to lie down with you, I'd like that so much, and I feel desire move hotly through me, and I think of spreading this blanket out on the floor of the river house: and just there, walking past the families, the toddlers writhing in their buggies and clutching Rudolf balloons, the bears singing 'White Christmas', I feel a shiver of longing, taking away my breath.

Leaving, I throw a coin into the fountain. I do this surreptitiously—embarrassed, looking over my shoulder in case I'm seen by anyone who knows me. I close my eyes but for a moment I don't know how to articulate my wish: which is for everything to go on being just the way it is. My family, my lover, secret and safe and separate: everything the same.

Greg is in the kitchen when I get back.

'Why the blanket?' he says, as I unpack my shopping.

'They were giving them away in Millennium Foods if you spent over twenty-five pounds… It was either that or a sports bag. I thought it might come in useful.' I hold his eyes; then, remembering I read somewhere that people do that when they lie, I look away. 'I mean, it's quite good quality: and we could use it as a throw on the sofa. I've been thinking for a while that the cover's looking quite tatty…'

He shrugs, bemused at this elaborate explanation.

'I hope you remembered my aloe vera,' he says.

'Hell, I forgot.' Guilt seizes me. 'Oh, Greg, I'm so so sorry.'

'OK, OK,' he says. 'There's no need to go on about it.'

That night I dream about Will. I dream of lying with him on the blanket from Millennium Foods, stretched out on the floor of the river house, feeling the pressure of his body against me, in some enthralled sweet moment after making love. And then the dream changes; I'm not part of the dream now, I'm just an observer, and Will is at home with his family, in a house with elegant tall windows and a round dining table with a white damask cloth and a large jade teapot in the middle of the table. I know it's his house in the dream, though no one is there, just the table set for tea. It's a child's vision of domesticity, really: a fifties family tea with angel cake and currant buns, a picture book children's teatime. I have this dream again and again in these cold, crowded days around Christmas. Sometimes the table is empty, sometimes he sits at the table with his family. Always the quiet house, the perfect family, nothing to do with me.

Eva comes round with her Christmas presents. My house has a hot scent of pastry and spices: my mince pies are from the supermarket, just heating up in the oven, but I always make my own mulled wine, loving its glamorous smells of cloves and brandy, and the citrus peel that leaves its rich oil on my hands.

We sit in my kitchen, which is decorated with juniper

branches cut from the garden and a trail of discreet magenta ribbon. I know that Eva's own decorations will be equally restrained; last year her tree was draped in ice-blue beads. Neither of us really goes for red crêpe paper and glitter: the early years of mothering expose you to enough bright primary colours to last a lifetime. There are carols playing, my favourite CD of Christmas music, the women's voices very high and clear.

Eva bites into a mince pie; a little flour sifts down and powders her sleeve.

'D'you ever miss those Christmases when our kids were little?' she says. 'You know, drowning in waves of ripped-up wrapping paper and someone always went ballistic because they were having some electronic toy, some Roller Blade Sindy or something, and you'd forgotten to get the batteries... D'you miss them?'

'A bit, sometimes. Not very much...'

'I do,' she says. 'I miss them. When you're in the middle of it all, you think that's how it's going to be for ever. Isn't that odd? All those lists and obligations and always so busy and needed... You think it's never going to end,' she says.

She hasn't put on any make-up and I see how pale her lips are, and that there are purple smudges in the skin around her eyes.

'You look so tired,' I say.

She says her school's just been inspected.

'Everyone's stressed out and having tantrums. And the kids aren't too good either,' she says. 'And we had this godawful staff party, as usual, and in Surprise Santa I got a bottle of sake with a lizard in it. Not just a bit of lizard, the whole damn animal.'

I smile and fill up her glass. She wraps a tissue round it because it's too hot to hold.

'God, I'm fed up with teaching. Did I ever tell you?'

'Just possibly.'

'I hate it. The boys who say, Ooh, miss, are you a lesbian, miss? And the smell of the classrooms and the bitching in the staffroom and the endless endless admin…'

'Couldn't you move—do something different?'

She slumps a little, shakes her head. 'I think it's too late to change, quite honestly, Ginnie. And Ted could be made redundant. The ad industry's pretty cruel, they like to cull them at fifty.'

There are women's voices singing a lullaby in Latin: the music is pure, perfect. The sweetness of the wine spreads through me. Eva has her head down, her face in shadow.

'I mean, I only did it because it seemed so convenient when the kids were little—you know, with the long holidays. And you think, Well, I can always change later on. And one day you wake and you think, Well, this is it, I'm stuck here, this is how it's going to be.'

She looks across at me, her face creased, as though she's struggling to articulate something.

'D'you ever feel it's hard to cope with how random

everything is?' she says. 'You know? You make all these little decisions—some of them tiny decisions, very small stuff at the time—and where you are now is the sum of all those decisions. And somehow you've ended up in a place where you can't really change anything.'

Her voice is hesitant, thoughtful. I can only just hear her above the singing.

'You've followed a particular path,' she says, 'and without thinking about it very much, you always imagined you could turn off it—and now you find you can't...'

'I know what you mean,' I say.

We drink our wine and listen to the singing.

'The trouble is,' she says slowly, 'you don't know which the important bits are at the time. Life doesn't come marked up with highlighter pen to show you which are the things that really matter. You know— pay attention now, this bit's important...'

I don't know how to make her happy. I put my hand on her wrist.

'There was this TV programme,' she says, 'about the Potters Bar rail crash. Did you see it?'

I shake my head.

'Christmas can be tough,' I say. 'It gets to people. You'll feel better once it's all over.'

She doesn't seem to hear.

'They had this CCTV footage,' she says, 'all these people running for the train. And they thought they were going to miss it, and they must have been so relieved when they got on, and they all got into the last carriage, and that was the one that was crushed. So you knew what was going to happen to them. That they were all going to die. It was terrible—all these people, thinking it was just an ordinary day.'

I fill up her glass, but there's nothing I can say.

CHAPTER 21

I spread the blanket out on the floor of the river house.

'That's good,' he says.

He reaches out and unbuttons my coat. But as we undress one another, I briefly wish I hadn't brought the blanket. It adds something new and awkward. We can't just fling ourselves down on it, abandoned, like we do in my fantasies, sprawling out on the big wide bed with its vast white softness and its canopy of silk: the floor is hard and we have to lie down with care. Lying, you're so close to the smell of the place, the smell of wet and rot and growing things. I'm suddenly self-conscious. This feels so much less tentative than when we usually make love: you can't pretend it's something that just happens. We lie side by side, with my jacket for a pillow. On my back I feel the cool air from under the door.

'Hey,' he says. He moves a finger down the side of my face. 'What's wrong?'

'Nothing.'

He kisses me.

But then, as he starts to move his hands over me, it changes: I no longer notice the hardness of the floor. It feels so good, stretched out against one another, skin against skin. The rhythm changes, we're slower, everything unhurried, more complete.

'You come on top,' he says. 'I don't want to squash you.'

He enters me, with a sigh.

As we move together, so gently and slowly, I seem to enter a different place: as if I've passed some boundary where you normally stop, and I can't quite tell where I end and he begins.

Afterwards I feel dazed. We lie there for a long time, wrapped around one another. When he gets up, it's still too soon. I could have lain there for ever, his warmth and his smell all round me, his heartbeat against me, everything fluid, merged.

We pull on our clothes. A spider the colour of apricots is crawling on my arm; I feel a surge of tenderness for this tiny creature, and ease it onto the table. I fold up the blanket, folding the dirty side inwards—concealing evidence, like someone who has committed a crime. As soon as I get home I shall put it in the washing machine. He picks small dead leaves out of my hair that have blown in under the door.

We go out into the light, and he secures the catch.

I watch him, his strong dark hands twisting the wire together.

I say, 'That was the best time.'

'The best time we've had?'

'The best time ever.'

He waits for a moment, turned towards me, as though he is surprised. He doesn't say, For me too, and I feel a little thread of embarrassment, like the first time you say, I love you: as though I have given too much away.

I walk away from him. In the patch of ground that once was a garden, there are new shoots, little spears of sharp green. Bulbs—snowdrops perhaps, they're usually first. And the lumps on the red stems of the roses, that in spring will be leaves, are beginning to swell. There's a sense of things starting to happen, of the promise of the earth.

'Look,' I say. 'It all happens so early nowadays. Spring comes so soon.'

He's on the path, waiting for me, wanting to be off.

'Make the most of it,' he says. 'It's all going to stop. When the North Atlantic Conveyor switches off. In twenty years the sea could cool and we'll have another Ice Age.'

I know he wants to go, but I linger there for a moment. I wonder what else will come up here, whether there will be primroses. I hope so. I love primroses, the perfection of their colour, that yellow, pale, intense, like clotted cream.

'Ginnie, I really need to be getting back,' he tells me.

I slip my hand in his. We walk back along the sodden path, stepping round the puddles that hold the grey of the sky.

'D'you ever wonder what it was like?' I say. 'When this place was just built? When people lived here and the garden was cultivated?'

He smiles as though I amuse him.

'Not really,' he says. 'I just think it's amazing it's been left like this so long.'

But I imagine it. Walking back along the river path, in this languorous mood, my mind lazy, wandering. Imagining summer evenings here, when the garden was cultivated and in flower—those heavy blooms on the hydrangeas that start to brown at the edges even before they've fully flowered, and the lawn close-cropped and velvet, softly falling away. I imagine a party up at the house, a jazz band playing. In the shade of the trees on the river bank, everything will be blue. A man and a woman come here, to the boat called *Sweet Bird of Youth*: they have left the party together, they are conspirators, seeking seclusion. She has a long dress of gauzy cloth, a shawl around her shoulders, her skirts flutter mothlike across the shadowy grass. He wears a dinner jacket, his white tie hangs loose, he has a bottle of wine. He holds the boat for her. She takes off her high-heeled shoes, but when she steps in, the boat still rocks unnervingly. She settles on the bench, arranging her silk skirts to keep them out of the dampness in the bottom of the boat, letting her shawl slip from her shoulders so he can see the curve of them: her skin glimmers in the blueness. He pushes out from the jetty, takes up the oars. She trails a white hand in the river, leaving a wake of brightness where her fingers break the surface and the water catches the light. She's looking at him, she loves to look at him, scarcely moving her eyes from his face even when the heron, disturbed by them though they make so little noise, takes to the air with a fierce rush of wings and a cry. There is no sound but the distant music and the dip of the oars and the heron and their breathing. Perhaps she too is escaping from something—from the sameness of things, from everydayness and loss, from the things that cannot be mended: imagining that it could all be different, stepping out into the boat and gliding free, leaving no trail but a wake of broken gold.

The boat moves out of sight in my mind, into the dark around the island: the water is undisturbed, as though they had never been.

When we get to the car, before we drive off, I lean across and brush my lips against his, resting my head on his shoulder for a moment, breathing him in.

'When we don't see each other any more,' I say, keeping my voice light, playful, 'I shall need to know the name of your cologne. And when I'm missing you too much, I shall go to the chemist and smell it.'

He smiles and ruffles my hair. He needs to get to his meeting.

I don't know why I said that.

Amber is in her bedroom, listening to some ferocious music and French manicuring her nails.

I turn her music down. Her wardrobe is open; most of her clothes are in a heap at the bottom, because she hasn't bothered to put them on the hangers.

'Amber, didn't you say you had an essay on *Othello*?'

She waves her fingertips in the air to dry them. There's a thick sweet smell of varnish remover.

'I'll do it later,' she says.

Mrs Russell is in my mind, her rumpled face, her purple lipstick, her thoughts on limit-setting.

'What's wrong with now?' I say.

'I'm really not in the mood, Mum, to be honest,' she says. 'I can't do my best work unless I'm in the mood.'

She twists her hair up into a ponytail, holding her

fingers out straight because of the varnish, then lets it fall. Her hair glints in the light from the window; it has a scent of papaya.

'I'll give you some help if you want,' I tell her.

You aren't really supposed to help them with their coursework, but lots of parents do. Though not always with the results they might have hoped for. Ted, Eva's husband, who's a designer with a prestigious ad agency, once did a storybook for Lauren's Graphics project: the work got given a C.

'We can talk it over, at least,' I tell her. 'Where's your copy of *Othello*?'

She shrugs.

'I can't, like, find it, exactly,' she says, with studied casualness. 'I'm sure it'll turn up. Don't look at me like that, Mum. It must be somewhere around.'

I hunt through the chaos on her desk, but the book isn't there.

'Don't worry, Mum,' she says, brightening. 'I'll go across to Katrine's. We'll do it together, I can use her copy. If you could just run me over...'

She's pulling on her trainers, the wet nails forgotten.

But I know just what will happen at Katrine's: lengthy experiments with Katrine's new eyelash-curlers, and an impassioned debate about skincare.

'I'm sure Dad's got a copy,' I tell her.

'It won't have my notes in.'

'No. But nor will Katrine's.'

I go up to the study. It's empty: Greg must be

downstairs. I go to the window. The colour is all gone from the gardens, everything dark or pale, except where little white narcissi with butter-yellow hearts are flowering far too early at the edges of my lawn. I can see the river down at the end of the road. Starlings swirl in the sky, like leaves in a millpond.

Just for a moment, here in the stillness of his study, I feel how separate his life is, and how far apart we have grown. I wonder if Greg is happy: I wonder if this is the life he would have chosen. Perhaps he wasn't really meant to be a married man. Centuries ago he might have lived in a monastery, following his bliss, drawing dragons with fabulous inks in the margins of a manuscript. I wonder whether like Eva he feels that a lot of little decisions have brought him to some place where he doesn't want to be.

I find the book I need. I'm turning to go when my eye falls on his desk. There's a paragraph of prose with pencil notes at the edges—an extract from his Celtic book. Phrases tug at me, and I remember again what I've forgotten for years, amid my resentment that all these words constantly drew him away from us—the loveliness of this world that he inhabits. It's just a short extract, just a moment that's described. A man called Froech is swimming through the water, carrying a branch covered with berries that he has broken from a rowan tree; a woman called Findabhair watches as he swims. 'And Findabhair used to say afterwards of any beautiful thing which she saw, that she thought it more beautiful to see Froech across the dark pool;

THE RIVER HOUSE 197

the body so white and the hair so lovely, the face so shapely, the eye so blue…' My eyes fill with tears as I read. Perhaps it's because of the rowan tree, and the berries that are like the berries near the river house. The emotion is so strong it shocks me—as though something has been opened up in me, or peeled away.

'I didn't know you were up here.'

He's standing in the doorway.

'Amber had an essay crisis.'

He puts his coffee down on the desk. He frowns at the copy of *Othello* in my hand.

'That's a crap edition,' he says. 'I'm always meaning to throw it out.'

'It'll do. Really. It's fine for what she needs…' I pick up the page of prose. 'I was just reading this,' I tell him.

He looks at me with a slight air of surprise.

'It's Irish,' he says. 'Eighth century, probably.'

'It's beautiful,' I say.

'It's for my anthology,' he says. 'It's going to be a bit of a mish-mash, quite honestly. But Fenella thinks it'll sell.'

I push away the image of Fenella, with her velvet hairbands and limitless self-assurance.

'I was wondering who these people were,' I say. 'With their names I can't pronounce. She's in love with him, isn't she? She must be. That's what it sounds like.'

He looks amused.

'Froech is an elvish king,' he says. 'They live in the sid, the underground kingdom, the otherworld.'

'It's by the river,' I say.

'These writers had a lot of beliefs about the edge of the water,' he says. 'That you could find wisdom there. That it was a rather magical place where anything could happen.'

'But they don't have to be supernatural, do they?' I say. 'You can just read that, and it could be anyone, couldn't it? Just recalling that moment, of something so perfect, of someone seeming so beautiful. Like it's imprinted in her mind for ever. She can always see it.'

He likes me saying this. There's a brightness about him—his eyes, his face—that I haven't seen for ages.

'There are very precise descriptions of people in early Irish writing,' he says. 'They used a lot of colour words. They were interested in exactly what people looked like.'

'I think she must be in love with him,' I say again. 'The way she's looking at him. How she loves to look at him.'

I put the sheet back on his desk, precisely, just where it was.

He's looking at me, puzzled, pleased, as though he's only just really seen me.

'You're looking so pretty nowadays, Ginnie,' he says. 'Have you done something—you know, changed your hair or something?'

'Not really. It's much the same.'

He's studying my face. I feel I need to say more, to be casual, to conceal myself. I suddenly worry that I have given too much away. 'Maybe the girl cut it better than she usually does,' I say.

'I'm sure you've done something,' he says.

He reaches out and puts his hand on the bare skin of my arm.

Just very briefly, something recoils in me. It feels so wrong to me, his touch; it feels like something taboo, something that shouldn't happen. This is an instant thing and I instantly suppress it—but he senses it, of course he does. I stand there, quite still. I try to smile.

He turns away from me. I see how his eyes harden.

He goes to the window, resting his hands on the sill, looking out, looking down to the river.

'The water's very high,' he says.

'Yes,' I say, with too much enthusiasm. 'I've noticed that too. Well, there's been so much rain.'

'We could flood here,' he says. 'You know that, don't you? We're definitely at risk here.'

'It's never flooded before.'

'It's different now,' he says. His head is bowed, he has that creased look, when he seems too old for his years. He looks defeated. I know I should go and put my arm around him, but I don't move.

CHAPTER 23

There's a wet, green smell, and clouds that bulge with rain. Today the path is empty: even the old man who feeds the geese has decided not to come, or taken shelter somewhere, fearing the storm. Even the river seems quiet. I like it like this, when the whole place belongs to us, this dull hushed world, the russet slime of the bracken, the cries of the gulls.

'You haven't got the blanket,' he says.

'It was difficult today,' I tell him. 'Greg was working at home today—I didn't want him to see—to have to explain.'

As we near the river house there's a sound in the bushes along the path like many people whispering, and then the first drops fall.

'Come on,' he says. He grabs my hand, and we run like children, my shoes clumsy on the rutted path. Just as we reach the door the downpour begins, huge heavy drops that kick up the pale earth of the path, and a rattle of rain.

'Good timing,' he says, closing the door.

We laugh; we are lucky.

It's dark in here today, no river light: and cold too. When he's taken off my clothes I pull my coat around my shoulders again. The rain is noisy on the roof. It seems to create a space, a quietness for us, making the river house seem so secret and safe.

'I like that sound.' It's as though he thinks my thought. 'Like being in bed as a child and it was tipping down outside. That kind of safe feeling.'

I put my arms around him, breathing in his smell of smoke and cinnamon. My eyes are half closed, my head on his shoulder. Through the window in front of me I can see the path, the river, the rowan tree, their shapes and colours blending, washing together between my half-closed lids, like a child's painting done with too much water, the red of the berries, the grey of the rain and the river. He slides his fingers inside me. I feel how I open up to him. My back arches a little. He gives a small sigh of pleasure.

Over his shoulder, I see something moving towards me out of the distance; a man running in the rain, along the path towards us: moving straight down my line of sight, between the river and the rowan. He's running fast: his eyes for a moment looking straight towards me. He's wearing office clothes, suit trousers, a shirt, a tie. I think briefly how wet, how cold, he must be. Why would anyone be out in such a storm?

Just before he reaches the river house, he stops. I see him quite clearly: his fair thin hair, full face, the way he chews his lip, his intent expression. He seems for a moment to peer in at the window, as though he is looking for something. For a brief shivery moment I think he may have seen us: that he will burst in on us and find us here, like this, entangled together. But then he turns and walks briskly away, across the overgrown lawn and into the trees.

'Will, I saw someone.' Whispering as though I might be overheard.

'Mmm?' he says vaguely.

'There was someone on the path. I'm worried he saw us.'

A flicker of anxiety crosses his face.

'How far away was he?'

'A few yards.'

'Don't worry,' he says. 'He couldn't have seen in.'

'Are you sure?'

'Of course I'm sure. It's dark in here. You can only see inside if you press right up to the pane.'

'But if he looked really hard? If he was looking for someone?'

'Ginnie, what is this?' He takes my face in his hands. It's not a caress, more the way you might cup a child's face to be sure you had their attention. 'Forget it, for God's sake, darling,' he says. 'We haven't got long.'

He kisses me, as though to start again from the beginning, then he's moving his hand on me. We can still hear the rain, but more gently now, just fingering the roof, and already the sky is brighter. I close my eyes, try to lose myself in this sweetness, that usually makes me shake. But the man I saw is imprinted on my closed lids. Against the blurry river path his image is clear, brief and distinct as a photograph, as he runs between the river and the rowan. His shirt hanging out, the urgency of his running, something about his face. He won't leave me. I feel as I've never felt before with Will—that I have to make it happen. Excitement surges in me then dies away: I never quite get there.

I move his hand away from me.

'I don't think I can come today,' I say.

'Are you sure?'

'It's hard standing up. I've kind of got used to doing it properly. My legs feel too shaky.'

'OK,' he says, with a hint of relief. 'If you're really sure you don't mind.'

He turns me round, pulls my coat off, bends me forward over the table. It's cold without my coat. I wish I'd brought the blanket and we could lie down. If we were lying together, perhaps I could get lost in these feelings, lost in him. I'm too aware of the awkwardness of the position, the edge of the table pressing into my stomach. The sun is breaking through again; there's a harsh square of light from the window on the table in front of me. It's too bright, too searching. Suddenly I see us as though I am looking in on us: and it seems a little preposterous, this hurried, hungry love-making in a neglected room.

He comes quickly, wraps up the condom, starts putting on his clothes.

'Was that OK for you?' he says.

He's never asked that before; there's been no reason to.

'Of course. I really didn't mind… I mean, I still enjoyed it. Next time I'll bring the blanket.'

'So what's the matter?' he says. 'I know that something's the matter.'

The light from the window is shining straight into his face: his eyes are narrowed against the brightness of the light.

'I don't know.' I shake my head. 'It's just that man I saw. Something about him—the way he was running.'

'Ginnie, it was raining. He probably would be running,' he says, with an edge of impatience.

'But people don't usually run. Even when it rains.'

'We ran,' he says. 'Anyway, he was probably a jogger.'

He's buttoning up his shirt. He hasn't held me. I want him to, but it's too late to ask now.

'He wasn't dressed like a jogger.' I'm pulling on my tights, but it's hard to do standing up, I'm struggling to keep my balance. 'It was like he was looking for something. I mean, you read these things in magazines. About people hiring private detectives to check up on their partners, and bugging phones and things…'

I see his expression, one eyebrow raised, amused, a bit exasperated.

'I'm probably being silly,' I say.

'I think so,' he says. 'Just forget it, OK?'

'I'm sorry,' I say. 'That was wonderful, anyway. It always is wonderful. Thank you.' I reach across to kiss him lightly on the lips, but I time it wrong and our mouths clash together abruptly.

Will seems impatient to be gone, to move on to the next thing. I feel how fragile everything is, how easily it can start slipping away from you. I'm angry with this man who came running along the path and disturbed our time together. I wish I'd brought the blanket—then I'd have been lying down and I wouldn't have known he was there.

After I've left Will, I turn my phone back on. There's a message on my voicemail.

'Ginnie, it's me.'

Ursula's voice is higher-pitched, too emphatic.

'God, I hate leaving messages on these things. Anyway, Ginnie, it's to let you know they admitted Mum to hospital this morning. Mary Grayson found her. You know, Mary Grayson next door? I'm afraid Mum had collapsed, Ginnie. Mary went in because she didn't see her yesterday. She's on Bentham Ward at the General. They don't really know what it is yet, they're doing some investigations. Visiting's from three to four, but they said we could go any time.'

I go to see her the next day, driving down to Southampton through a clear afternoon. The road goes through the downs, through a landscape of vast bright fields and gorse with yellow flowers. The motorway is quiet, and I drive at the speed limit almost all the way.

I get there at three o'clock, as I've agreed with Ursula: then waste minutes at the flower stall in the hospital foyer, unable to make up my mind. The daffodils are cheerful, but rather cheap and obvious. The roses suggest my father. The arum lilies seem somehow morbid: I remember a vicar I once knew, who always said they made him think of funerals. I stand there incapacitated: every choice seems wrong. This is ridiculous, I tell myself—to come all this way, to drive so fast, then waste precious minutes struggling with such a trivial decision. I settle for some innocuous tulips, then almost go back to change them.

The nurse at reception on Bentham Ward has flamboyant turquoise eyeshadow and a wide, white smile.

'Your sister's here already,' she says, when I introduce myself. 'She's a poppet, your mother. Really no bother at all.'

I follow her down the ward. We're high up here. Broad windows open onto a vista of rooftops and tower blocks and the dazzle of sun on windows, a cityscape of gleaming towers. A sharp smell of antiseptic catches at my throat.

Ursula is there at the bedside, in a sleek new coat of mahogany leather. She gives me a small, anxious smile. Lying in the bed is a grey, gaunt woman who, just for an instant, I don't recognise. Her face is worn and frayed, the bones sharper, the shadows deeper, as though since I last saw her she has lived through many years.

I'm walking towards her but she doesn't seem to have seen me.

'Look who's here,' says Ursula.

'Mum.' I go to kiss her.

Her cheek is cold. Illness hangs around her, in the sourness of her breath, in the partial, fractured gestures of her hands.

'Ginnie.' She swallows carefully. 'How lovely.'

'I've brought you some flowers,' I tell her.

'They're pretty,' she says, but her mouth twists, as though the words have a bitter taste.

There are vases at the nursing station. I take one,

fill it, arrange the tulips on the locker, glad to have this simple task to preoccupy me. I'm vaguely aware of the groups at other bedsides, the gentle flurry of visitors, the self-consciously bright voices, the gifts of fruit and flowers. At the next bedside, a woman is having trouble with her little girl, who keeps slipping from her quick as a minnow and running around the ward: 'Stop it, Sophie, only *hooligans* do that… No, I'm not laughing, I'm very cross with you…' The child's hair bounces as she runs and light ripples in it: her vivacity is welcome in the quiet of the ward. The air is thick and warm: it presses down.

The nurse with the turquoise eyeshadow comes up to us.

'You're having a busy time, Jacquie. Quite a social whirl. I'll sit you up,' she says.

She adjusts the pillows and props our mother against them. Our mother tries to thank her, but her face contorts in panic, her hand flailing towards her locker as she starts to retch. The nurse grabs a foil bowl from the locker and puts an arm round my mother's back and holds the bowl for her. The little running girl stops and watches with fascination. Our mother's body convulses as she retches into the bowl.

'Never mind,' the nurse says, over and over. 'Never mind.'

She lies our mother down again. She wipes her face and smoothes her hair with her hand. She's embarrassed.

'Oh dear. Not one of my better ideas,' she says.

And then, as she goes, 'She's marvellous. Really no trouble.'

'Sorry,' says our mother as the nurse moves away.

Ursula pats her hand. 'They'll have you right as rain soon,' she says.

We sit there for a while. The light through the wide windows edges across the floor. I hunt in my mind for things to say, but my mind seems wiped clean, as if someone has stolen my memory. Ursula too is quiet. We're stilled, silenced under the blanket of thick, hot, disinfected air.

I've brought photographs of the girls. I hold them in front of my mother, but her face has a veiled look, she doesn't seem able to focus.

'Thanks, Ginnie,' she says. 'I'll look at them properly later.'

Saying this exhausts her. She closes her eyes for a moment. A petal drops from the tulips onto the locker; you can hear the soft thud as it falls. Ursula brushes it into the rubbish bag taped to the side of the locker.

Eventually Ursula catches my eye.

'OK?' she says.

I nod.

'Mum,' she says, 'we're going to leave you to sleep now.'

Our mother murmurs something I can't make out. We kiss her.

Her eyelids flicker extravagantly. She falls asleep with the abruptness of a door closing.

* * *

There's a cafeteria in the entrance hall. It looks out onto a patch of gravel, and beds of those municipal shrubs with shiny dark leaves that always look the same. We buy muffins and coffee from a slow, tired woman who has purple patterned artificial nails. We go to a table by the window, under a sign that says, Please be a helping hand and return your tray. The cafeteria has a half-hearted country-kitchen look, with a rustic beam in the ceiling and a copper kettle and three old books on a shelf. The plastic surface of the table is veined to look like marble, and has a faint smell of dishcloth.

'I didn't think she'd look so ill,' I say.

Ursula sips her coffee. It's hot in the cafeteria but she doesn't take off her coat.

'She's been very odd.' Her voice is hushed, the way you'd speak of something of which you're ashamed. 'I stayed with her one night last week and she got up at three in the morning. She sounded perfectly normal, like she really thought it was time for the day, and she made me get up too and she made a pot of tea and got dressed and put in her curlers, just like a normal morning… Things like that. As though her body clock had packed up. I know it sounds kind of funny.'

'It doesn't sound funny,' I say.

Ursula starts to take the cellophane off her muffin. She does this rather slowly, as though the task is too difficult for her. My coffee has a sour taste, like my mother's breath, as though I've breathed her in.

'Another time she was just standing in the kitchen,' says Ursula, 'and she did this kind of slow-motion faint—just slid very slowly down the side of the cupboard till she was sitting on the floor. Like in a film, when somebody's been shot. It was quite spooky, really.'

She sits there quite still for a moment. There's a menu card on the table—'Look out for our tasty special offer.' She runs a finger absently along the edge of the card.

'Ginnie, what d'you think it is?' she says then. 'It's not a stroke, is it? They thought it was a stroke to start with. I mean, I don't know about brains, but I don't think it's a stroke.'

'It doesn't sound like a stroke,' I say.

I take a bite of my cake, but it's hard to swallow, it sticks to the roof of my mouth.

'Well, at least we know she's in the best possible hands,' says Ursula.

'Yes.'

'Her doctor's really nice. Dr Spence. I think we're very lucky that Mum's got such a good doctor. He told me he came from the Isle of Wight, from Ryde. Isn't that a coincidence?'

'I'm glad he's good,' I say.

We sit quietly for a moment. Around us other people are chewing at food they don't want or staring out of the window. A man in a crisp expensive suit scrunches up his Mars Bar wrapper and sticks it into his polystyrene cup. He has the look of a sleep-walker. I know we must seem the same.

I don't know what to say next. We aren't easy together, Ursula and me. We don't know how to talk to one another. I try to imagine a fluid, comfortable sisterliness, sharing clothes and secrets and doing each other's nails, like Amber and Molly. An ease that would mean you could say anything. Greg and I haven't had sex since four years ago last Christmas… I'm in love with a man I fuck in a house on the river bank… She's dying, isn't she?

Ursula is moving things around on the table—the ketchup bottle, the salt cellar—as though playing chess against an invisible opponent.

'They're going to ring me straight away if there's any change,' she says. 'They've got a brain scan booked. Not till next week though.'

'Shit. Why not straight away?'

'There's a lot of pressure on resources, Dr Spence told me.'

'But can't we do something? Pressurise them— make them do it sooner?'

She shakes her head.

'You know how it is with the NHS,' she says.

'Did he tell you what they're looking for?' I say.

'He didn't,' she says. She raises her cup to her lips: her hand is shaking slightly. I see her Adam's apple move as she swallows. 'He said he wanted to wait to discuss it till he had something definite.'

'Well, I suppose he would.'

'She's had a good life, really,' says Ursula. She looks at me warily, as though afraid I'll say something that cannot be unsaid.

'I guess so,' I say.

She moves on hurriedly, telling me about her latest project, another fairy-tale book—Beauty and the Beast, and The Princess and the Frog, and Hans My Hedgehog.

'They're going to be quite contemporary. I'm planning to do Beauty in Chanel, with a boxy jacket and little white gloves. A bit Jackie O,' she tells me.

'That sounds delicious,' I say.

I puzzle over the contradiction of my sister, this cautious woman with rather thin lips and a garden full of decking, and the fabulous things she imagines into existence, the princesses, the entangled gardens with parakeets and claws.

'There are so many stories like that,' she says. 'The animal groom stories. Where the person the girl falls in love with seems like both a man and an animal. And you don't find out which he really is till you get to the end of the tale. It's weird, isn't it? The way that kind of story just keeps on cropping up? I guess it must mean something.'

'I'm dying to see what you do with them,' I say. Then flinch at my choice of word: but she doesn't seem to notice.

'Mum's so proud of you with all your books,' I tell her.

'And you with your girls,' says Ursula.

We're being so polite and careful: like in the photos from our childhood album, with our candystripe summer dresses and shiny parallel shoes.

'It's so nice Mum knew about Molly getting into Oxford,' she says. 'Before—you know—before all this started happening… They love her on the ward, don't they? They really think she's marvellous. Of course Mum's the perfect patient really. She'd never want to give anyone any trouble.'

CHAPTER 25

I sit with Amber on the sofa, attempting to test her French verbs. It's one of those rituals you go through because it's what a good mother should do, rather than for any result: like making wholemeal sandwiches for children's birthday parties, though you know they'll all be left uneaten on the plate. Amber is struggling, protesting that we have war, we have famine, why do we need all these declensions. She fiddles with the tie in her hair.

It's getting dark, but I don't close the curtains. My room is brightly reflected in the darkening windows— my kelims and velvet cushions in all their jewel colours, the family photos on the piano, the fig in the corner with leaves like wide-splayed hands. There's a rich smell of pork and garlic from the casserole that's simmering in the kitchen. Light from my table-lamps spills across the floor like fallen petals. Our house feels safe, protected, in the warm spilled light: nothing could harm us here.

Amber stretches extravagantly and sighs.

'Mum, I *have* to wash my hair. It's really gross. I can't possibly concentrate when my hair's all greasy.'

I tell her we'll leave it and close the book at *s'asseoir*. Afterwards I shall always remember this, which verb it was.

I turn on the television for the weather forecast, to get some idea what the weather will be on Thursday, when I'm seeing Will, to help me work out what to wear: but it's not quite time for the weather, it's still the local news. I go to the kitchen to see if the casserole is ready. Night is settling over my garden, over the narcissi and the little sunken lawn, but there are rags of light still hanging in the sky. I shall wear my red boots, I think, even if it's raining, and my new short skirt, the one I bought at Christmas. I sometimes worry that Greg might wonder why I only wear skirts on Thursdays. Standing there, I let myself enter my secret world for a moment: imagining the warm pressure of the palm of Will's hand on my thigh.

Amber's shout jolts me.

'Hey, Mum. Come here. Mum! This is *freaky*.'

I go back to the sitting room. Amber is standing quite still, one hand to her hair, as though entranced in the act of taking out her hairband. I stare at the picture on the screen.

It's the car park by the river: our car park, the place where I go with Will. It must have been filmed this afternoon. There are panda cars with flashing lights and forensics experts in baggy suits, and uniformed policemen and women, talking in twos and threes. The path is cordoned off with tape. An ambulance waits: but no one is rushing, there's no urgency, everyone is slowed: they have all the time in the world. You know if you could hear their voices they'd be solemn and subdued. You can tell there's death here. My first thought, quick as a heartbeat, is that something has happened to Will: my mind making some instant crazy connection between this place that we have made our own, and the whisper of fear that's always there, my dread that I might lose him.

'Mum—don't you recognise it?'

I nod; for a moment I can't speak. I stare at the television. Behind the cars and the people, the river is in carnival mood, festive with rowers in striped Lycra and barges painted with roses in blowsy, lipstick colours; but the pennants and flowers and brightness seem all wrong. I have a sense of huge confusion, and a nagging thought that there's something here that I ought to have expected.

'Mum—for God's sake.' There's an edge of impatience to Amber's voice, as though I'm not reacting at all the way she'd hoped. 'It's where we used to go for our river walks, isn't it? You know, when we were little.' And, when I don't say anything, 'You know, where I used to sneak up and give the heron a fright? I used to love those walks. Oh my God, this creeps me out.'

My mouth is so dry it seems to stick together.

'What's happened?'

'They've found someone,' says Amber. 'In the river.'

'Do they know who it is?'

'They've just said it's a woman.'

'Maybe it was suicide.'

'No, it wasn't,' says Amber, very definitely. She has the slightly triumphant look of those who have privileged information.

'She could have jumped off a bridge,' I say. 'It's happened before. The tide can move things for miles.' I try to persuade myself, to make this true. I tell myself that Amber always loves to dramatise. 'Drowning's quite a common form of suicide.'

'Strangling isn't,' says Amber dryly. Her eyes glint, she's relishing the drama of this. 'I don't think she managed to strangle herself somehow. Anyway, Mum, they found her in a rubbish bag.'

Everything in the room around me seems to recede from me, like something seen through thick glass: it's sharp and clear, but very far away.

A woman in a sheepskin coat appears on the screen. She has stiff grey hair and immaculate vowels. Amber grabs the remote, turns up the sound. The woman is saying she lives near the place where they found the body and she won't feel safe till they catch the man who did this. A reporter with blonde expensive hair is nodding with practised empathy.

Amber twists her hairband round her wrist and shakes out her hair, pulling her fingers through it.

'I bet it's the same guy,' she says. 'You know, the one who did that other murder. That girl who got killed so near her home. I bet it's a serial killer.'

'Is that what they're saying?'

'They haven't exactly said it yet. No one's said anything about who did it. But I bet it is. I bet it's that psycho. Mum, don't you think it's weird?'

I tell her yes, I think it's weird, for it to have happened just there. But she shakes her head a little, as though I just don't get it.

'How long ago do they think it—you know— happened?' I ask her.

'They haven't said. They haven't identified her or anything.'

A detective is on the screen now. He has a stern gaze and a bony, hollowed-out face. He talks in the careful, measured way in which we speak of the tragedies of strangers—the composed face, the downward intonation. I wonder if Will knows him. There's the usual warning that women should be wary of going out alone. And then the appeal for witnesses: if you've seen anything odd or suspicious near the place where the body was found—anything at all, no matter how trivial it might seem. There's a number to ring. My body is weighed down. I don't move.

Amber looks at me as though I have disappointed her.

'Honestly, Mum, I thought you'd be more interested.'

She goes to wash her hair.

It's cold in the kitchen. I make a coffee but don't drink it. I sit at the table, clasping my hands round the mug. Light catches in the gluey silver trail of a snail, that traces a random arabesque across my terracotta tiles. Other women don't have snail trails in their kitchens. I ought to be like other people, with their orderly thought-out lives.

I realise that I'm shivering, my body shaking as if this death has touched me in some direct way. I clutch my coffee mug to warm my hands and tell myself that this has nothing to do with me. That the man I saw was just an ordinary stranger, out for a walk by the river, minding his business, caught in a shower of rain. I sift through all the things I know about witnesses and how they can't be relied on, how we can't remember precisely what we saw; we think we remember but really we're recalling details we've imagined. Details that are quite vivid to us—as I now picture the woman who died, whom I have never seen; as this conjured face persists for me, her glazed eyes and that swollen terrible pallor of those who find death by water. This woman I have never seen—yet in my mind she is real.

I tell myself again and again that there was nothing odd about the man I saw on the river path. I've invented details, given it too much significance, because I was there with Will, illicitly and scared of someone seeing us. I've projected the guilt I felt onto this random stranger, seeing *him* as guilty and scared of being seen.

But I don't persuade myself. So I try to recall if anyone else was there that day by the river. I hunt along the path for other people, for someone who could take this responsibility from me. But there was no one: not even the man in the shabby coat who likes to feed the birds. Even the river seemed empty. I remember how glad I was, how it made it all seem safe and perfect and somehow meant to happen—that the river bank was ours alone, that everyone was sheltering from the gathering storm.

I shout to Amber that I'm going down to the corner shop. My mobile is in my pocket.

Outside it's cold: when I pass beneath the street lights, my breath is thick as smoke. The moon shines yellow through a veil of cloud. Halfway to the corner shop, in a pool of shadow where I can scarcely see, I stop and ring Will's number. As I move my hand there's a warning inside me, telling me not to do this, clear and unequivocal. I pay no attention.

'Yes?'

'Will, it's Ginnie,' I say redundantly.

A silence.

'What is it?' he says then. His voice is level, brisk. It's his work voice, not the way he ever talks to me.

'I'm sorry to ring you like this, but I didn't know what else to do...'

In the background I can hear music, and a woman talking; I don't know if this voice is his wife's or on the television. I strain my ears to hear, but the voice is too far away. I try to picture the room where he is, and the home he never talks about. I think of my dream, of that perfect family life I envisioned for him, the damask tablecloth, the table set for tea, the jade teapot. In that moment I see so clearly, how little I know of him and how little of him I possess. As though he's just some dream I had. I hear how he walks away from these sounds, out into a hallway perhaps.

'OK?' he says.

'Will, they've found a body in the river.'

'Yes,' he says.

'Near where—you know, near where we go. When we're together.' It's as though I need to remind him: because just at this moment I don't quite believe in our love affair. I can't imagine that I was ever intimate with this brisk and wary man.

'These things happen,' he says.

'Why I rang—I was thinking about that man—you know, the man I saw on the river path... Whether I should say something—'

He cuts me off.

'Look, we need to talk,' he says. 'But it's not a good time for me right now. Couldn't we speak on Thursday, like we planned?'

'Yes, of course,' I say. 'But I wondered—'

'OK, then,' he says. He switches off his phone.

As I go back through the front door Amber's music blares down at me. A sudden hot rage surges through me.

I go upstairs. The bathroom door is open. There's

a clot of long red hairs in the plughole, and discarded towels and water all over the floor.

I go into her room without knocking. She's sitting on her bed eating a KitKat, talking on her phone. Her hair always has a rich blackish sheen when it's wet. It's hanging everywhere and she hasn't begun to towel it: it's dripping all over her duvet and some school books that are flung down there.

'Amber, I want that music off.' My voice sounds shrill and ugly to me. But I can't stop: anger has its claws in me. 'And no wonder you can never eat your dinner if you're forever stuffing yourself with crap.'

She looks up at me, outraged.

'Mum, for God's sake, I'm on the *phone*.'

I pay no attention.

'And you can just go and deal with that bathroom now. It's a bloody swamp in there.'

'Look, Mum,' she says, 'I'm speaking to Katrine.' She articulates the words patiently, as though to someone rather stupid. 'I'll deal with the bathroom when I've finished. Just cool it, OK?'

I turn to go.

'I'm so sorry,' she says to Katrine in a sibilant stage whisper. 'That was my mum. I think she's had a bad day. I expect it's PMS.'

I go slowly downstairs. The rage has left me, as suddenly as it came. I'm ashamed to have been so angry about wet towels and a KitKat. There are too many things I have done that I ought not to have done.

* * *

I have one of those dreams where you're only half awake, but believe in the dream that you've completely woken. It's raining again, I can hear the sounds of water, and I dream that the river has come into my room. I can smell its brackish smell, the sea salt and the smell of drenched leaves and decay. The river rises above the bed, so my body is partly submerged, and my hands on top of the duvet have the unreal look of the willowherb and balsam when they're gradually covered by the rising tide. I know there are things I should do—that I should pile up sandbags to protect my home and children from the flood: but the water holds me there, I can't move.

The dream changes. The lights come on; this is a dream of daytime, ordinary and banal. I'm in a warehouse—one of those furniture megastores where you go to buy flat pack furniture and insubstantial sofas with abrupt Scandinavian names. I walk down the aisles of the warehouse, between banks of shelves that stretch up to the ceiling, big metal shelves with a lot of space between them; they hold bundles loosely wrapped in cloth, and I see that these are bodies stacked like carpet or rolls of curtain fabric. I know this is one of the dead houses, but I don't feel any fear, just a kind of certainty. All the bodies are turned away, so I can't see their faces. I reach to the two bodies nearest me, and try to turn them over; they're heavy, drenched, it takes all my strength to shift them. Their hair is dripping, as though they've just been pulled from the deep. One of them has tangled hair of that dark colour that red hair goes when it's soaked, as though there's a lot of black in it. With a very great effort, I turn the bodies towards me. They have the faces of my children, just as I knew they would.

CHAPTER 26

I wait in the mirrored bar. I listen to the music and look at my newspaper, though none of it makes sense.

He comes on time. He kisses me. He's just the same as ever. I feel a huge relief.

I drive towards the river house just as I always do. But halfway there I find myself stopping, and pulling in to the kerb.

'What is it?' he says. 'What's the matter?'

'Perhaps we should go somewhere else,' I say.

He strokes my hair, but he's a little impatient.

'There isn't anywhere else to go,' he says. 'We've been into all that.'

'Maybe we could—you know—find a hotel, like we keep saying we will,' I say without conviction. 'Get a room somewhere.'

'There isn't time,' he says. 'I've got to get back by half past two.'

'It just seems weird going back there—after what happened.'

'Bad things happen everywhere,' he says. 'They don't leave anything behind.'

'But what about the police? Maybe there will still be police there.'

'No. They've finished,' he says.

I just sit there for a moment, don't start up the car.

He cups my face in his hands: his skin is very warm. I press my mouth into his palm.

'Ginnie,' he says, 'I really want to make love to you. But we don't have to if you're not sure.'

He pulls me towards him and kisses me.

'I'm sure,' I tell him.

The car park is churned up, and on the path there are tyre-tracks where vehicles wouldn't normally go, but otherwise it is all much as it always was. It's a cold bright day; frost has left its white footprints in the shaded places, and in the sun the grass is heavy and bright with moisture. You can hear people playing football, perhaps on a school playing field, their voices echoey in the stillness, as though the sound bounces off the hard rim of the sky. The swans are close to the river bank. As we pass, one takes off with a great clatter from the still sepia water.

We walk on down the path. There, at the foot of a willow that droops down into the water, someone has left a bunch of flowers in cellophane. The flowers are dying, finished off by the cold. I see him look, but neither of us says anything.

I want to make sure that everything is right between us; I'm longing to explain.

'Will—about Tuesday night—I wanted...'

He turns and puts a finger on my lips.

'Not now,' he says. 'We'll talk about it later.'

At the river house he untwists the wire. It's chilly inside. Even the thin winter sun on the path must have had a bit of warmth in it. The spiders have been busy, their webs forming huge soft festoons across the corners. I feel a shiver of some inchoate emotion— anger, perhaps, and a sense that our secret place has been spoilt.

'Will, I'm not sure...'

He pushes my hair away from my face. I turn a little, so if by mistake I opened my eyes I still couldn't see down the river path.

'You're so jumpy,' he says. 'There's nothing to be frightened of.'

He kisses me, his tongue exploring my mouth.

I've brought the blanket. We lie down. Today I want him on top of me, his warmth and weight and urgency, wanting to hide in him. His body tells me how he loves me. I start to shake as he moves his hand on me.

But as excitement surges through me an image sneaks into my mind. It's whole and complete, as though I'm remembering something I've seen. A man and a woman, naked and anonymous, like an image from pornography. The man is standing behind the woman, he has his hands round her throat, his fingers are pressing into her. It's precise and clear and many-coloured, floating as dream images float, I can't switch it off or get rid of it. I don't know if it excites me: maybe it does, I don't know. It just stays there, till I come: it won't be pushed away.

Afterwards he lies beside me, holding me for a moment.

'There. That was OK, wasn't it?' he says. 'It looked as though it was OK.'

I kiss him. 'I've been in a weird mood. Sorry. I'm just not quite myself.'

He strokes my hair.

'Ginnie, you think too much,' he says.

We walk back past the fleet of swans, and the flowers in their wrap of cellophane, and the boy on Eel Pie Island. As always, just for a second or two, I think that it's a living child. When you're by the river it's hard to tell what's real.

'I've got time for a drink,' he says as we go to the car.

This makes me happy. I always hate it when he leaves too soon. Really, I'd like to spend hours together after making love. I'd like to drowse, our limbs entangled, to watch him as he's sleeping, to see the flickering under his eyelids when he dreams. But I know I can't have that: and a drink is much better than nothing.

We go back to the bar. He has Coke, I have Scotch.

We sit on the terrace, in our coats, though really it's too cold for me. There's a low dazzling sun. He puts his sunglasses on.

His hands rest on the table between us; I look at his hands, at the thin dark hairs on the backs of his fingers, the lilac net of veins inside his wrists. I think how much I love him. I want to reach out, to press his hand between mine again, to drag my finger along the smooth skin inside his arms. I would like to hold on to this moment, to keep it like this for ever: him sitting quietly here with me in the winter garden.

He leans towards me. His expression is unreadable because of the sunglasses.

'Ginnie. I was at home when you rang. You mustn't do that. You mustn't ever ring in the evening, when I could be at home.'

'I won't do it again,' I say. 'I know it's difficult for you. But I was just so worried. About that man I saw. That he was something to do with—you know, what's happened.'

'For God's sake, Ginnie.'

'I mean—what shall we do?'

'What shall *we* do? It's not *us*, Ginnie, it's *you*. I didn't see anything.'

I'm studying his face. But all I can see in his lenses is my own reflection—distorted, like the face of the moon in a children's nursery rhyme.

'But—d'you think I should tell someone?' I say.

'Look,' he says. He's trying to be reasonable, but I

can hear the edge of exasperation in his voice. 'Tell me again what you think you saw.'

'It was a man running.'

'So?'

'It was something about him—I don't know, he made me feel afraid… I had this mad idea that he was looking for us. But maybe it wasn't that. Maybe that wasn't what he was looking for.'

'Ginnie, you saw whatever you saw. But I just don't get why you think this was so significant.'

'It was just a feeling…' My voice tails off; it sounds so flimsy and insubstantial, what I was going to say. I take a slow breath. 'But I've learnt to trust my feelings, in the kind of work I do. Clem and I, we quote this at one another—how someone makes you feel is information…'

He makes a rapid gesture, as if he's flicking something away.

'Listen,' he says. 'She can't have been killed on the river path in broad daylight. Or dumped there, come to that. No one—however deranged—would do that. Not in such an exposed place with all the traffic on the river. It can't have been the man you saw.'

This soothes me, it sounds so reasonable. It's what I want—for him to reassure me—so I can close this door in my head and never open it again. But I have to pursue it a little further, to be completely sure.

'But—mightn't he have gone back to the place where he left her? Perhaps to check her body hadn't come to the surface?'

He shrugs. 'Unlikely,' he says.

'I just want to be certain. To know I've done the right thing.'

'Yeah, well.' He twists his mouth, as though he has a bitter taste. 'It isn't always exactly obvious just what the right thing is.'

If only I hadn't had my eyes open: if only I hadn't seen. But I did see. What you see can hurt you.

We sip our drinks. In the thin clear light, the shadows of our hands on the table are sharp as though cut with a blade. I'm very alert, sensing the anger that's hidden under his words, watching for clues to his mood: as a wife might watch her husband, as my mother used to watch my father, always vigilant. How did this happen? I push the thought away.

There's a scrap of music as someone goes into the bar, a saxophone, indolent, caressing, singing out for a moment, then abruptly silenced with the closing of the door.

'Who was she?' I say. 'The woman who was killed?'

'They don't know yet. You'll see it in the paper, once she's been identified.' He sips his Coke. 'Roger's in charge of the investigation.'

'Roger?' This gives me a cold feeling. 'That's a weird coincidence, isn't it?'

He shrugs.

'Why? It's his kind of case.'

He finishes his Coke and pushes the glass away.

He leans towards me. When he frowns there are hard lines etched around his mouth and his eyes.

'You need to think about what we've got to lose,' he says. 'I mean, it would be a total fucking disaster if this got out.'

'Yes, of course. For me too.'

I know this. I think it often: we have talked about it, promised one another. That what we will seek to do above all is to keep our love affair absolutely secret. But when he says this, my eyes fill up with tears.

Maybe he feels he's been too abrupt.

'Look, you know I love you,' he says.

'I love you too,' I tell him.

He puts his hand on mine.

'You'll just forget all about this?'

I nod.

I think for a moment—What happens to people like us, to secret lovers, at the end of the affair? How do you keep going? You'd be plunged into all that grief, and you'd never be able to show it, ever, ever. What happens then?

'I'd better go. I'm getting late,' he says.

'I could drop you off somewhere.'

'But you haven't finished your drink...'

He gets up, reaches across to kiss me lightly on the lips.

'Don't worry about it,' he says.

I feel a thread of sadness that makes me want to cling. And I wonder if I've been kidding myself, pretending it's all so easy: that I'm so strong and independent, that I can let him go. Have I been lying to myself about this all along?

'Next week?' he says.

'Yes please…'

He smiles at the 'please'.

I watch him go. The melted frost on the grass has a cold glitter. I watch his grace as he walks down the path and out of the winter garden and away from me.

CHAPTER 27

On Saturday afternoon, Greg is working in the university library, and Amber is going shopping with Jamila: there are sequinned ballerina shoes Jamila really *needs*.

'Amber, I could be out later,' I tell her. 'D'you have your keys and your phone?'

'Mum, you ought to know by now,' says Amber, rather wearily. 'I never go anywhere without my phone.'

When she's gone, I call Max and invite myself round.

It's a half-hour drive to Max's house. I pass the high mossy wall that goes round the convent garden, and the Victorian waterworks, where seagulls bob on the reservoir like scraps of discarded paper. There's a funfair at Hampton Court. For much of the way the road goes close to the river. It must have been very pleasant here, before London encroached and heavy traffic started coming through. There are old timbered houses, a Norman church, and an antiquarian book-shop where, years ago, the girls and I spent a leisurely afternoon. It was crammed and disorderly, books overflowing the shelves and heaped on the floor in piles as tall as a child. Baroque motets were playing, and there were tatty sofas covered in rose-red velvet, and everything had its soft grey bloom of dust. The spines of the books cracked when you opened them, a tiny sharp sound like the breaking of tiny bones. The proprietor had an ancient greatcoat and the voice of an Oxford don and a week's worth of stubble; he sat and read in the back room. Through the window behind him you could see a tiny courtyard, enclosed and enchanted, with statuary and vines, the ground grey with the leaves of many autumns, and on a wrought-iron table a candelabrum with burnt-down stubs of candle: you could picture him drinking there on summer evenings. We found many treasures—a *Gulliver's Travels* illustrated by Rackham that I bought for Ursula; an edition of Dante's *Inferno*. I read the first stanza of the Dante to the girls, the lines about finding yourself in a dark wood where the right way was lost, reading in a hushed voice. The pages were roughly cut but thick and edged with gold.

From outside Max's house looks like an ordinary semi, but it's been expensively gutted and modernised. His silver soft-top Mercedes is parked in the street. I ring his bell and wait on his doorstep, between two trim conifers in metal buckets. I can hear the Saturday

sounds, children playing in a garden, the lazy afternoon rhythms of suburban trains.

'Ginnie. How lovely.'

There's a tiny hesitation before he kisses my cheek.
But maybe I'm imagining it. He has a rich male smell,
of sandalwood and leather.

'There's something I need to talk about.'

'You said. Come through.'

His kitchen is gleaming and glamorous, all stain-
less steel and spotlights and complicated controls. He
uses it for fixing drinks and cooking an occasional
Marks and Spencer's ready-meal.

I watch as he pours our whisky. In the unrelenting
afternoon light that comes through his wide windows,
you can see that his hair is flecked with grey, that his
body is getting more solid, gravity pulling hard on
him, his Guernsey sweater just a bit too tight. Still
good-looking though: with elegant hands. I'm sure men
don't have the faintest notion how avidly we watch
their hands—the way they pour a drink or take out
their cufflinks and push up the sleeves of their shirts:
always secretly alert for a grace that might give us
pleasure. And you can guess from his hands that Max
would be a skilful lover.

It could have happened, perhaps, if I had let it.
There was always something between us—a flicker
of sex—though compromised by the fact that I'm an
inch or two taller than him. I remember a moment in
the early days of our friendship, when we were still
students. We were drinking after a concert, all the

others had gone—even Dylan, who always drinks with great commitment—and Max held my eyes a little too long, and remarked that I seemed so up-tight, that I really ought to let go. That moment when everything can change, the man moving in closer, speaking obliquely or in metaphors, casually bringing sex into the conversation or saying he'd really have liked to give you a lift… I've always found that how you respond in that moment is utterly beyond your conscious control: yet a laugh or a slight turning away will close the door for ever. And in my head I was open to a relationship with Max: but I think I laughed a little and shrugged and looked away. All for the best, probably: it could have been a disaster. Max can be pretty heartless. I once spent an intense evening sharing a bottle of Beaujolais with one of his many discarded lovers: he'd dumped her by email, and she'd been devastated by the casual way he'd ended what for her had been the real thing. Not that he doesn't take his love affairs seriously. He views them with a cool detachment, as a practical project worthy of proper study, like choosing and maintaining a stereo system.

Max opens his fridge to get to the ice-box. The fridge is empty except for a bottle of sparkling mineral water. He breaks ice into our glasses.

'Are you OK?' he says, turning back to me. 'You look a bit shaky, Ginnie.'

I tell him about my mother.

Max sympathises. He knows about sick parents:

his own mother has osteoporosis. Max often stays the
weekend with her. I've met her: she's stiff and twisted
as a thorn tree, but sometimes I feel that this worn,
fragile woman is still his safety, his centre: that he'll
commit to a lover only when she's gone.

'But that isn't what I came to talk about,' I say.

'No. I gathered that.'

He gives me my drink and we go through to his living
room, which has leather sofas and CDs alphabetically
arranged. Wide windows open onto the garden, which
is mostly expensively landscaped pebbles. There are
orange tulips in pots. The flowers are sprawling open,
you can see the blue stain at their throats.

I've chosen Max to confide in because I know he
will be secret. He won't condemn me and I'm sure
he'd never tell. Not out of some moral compunction:
not because he'd think it essentially wrong to break a
confidence, just because it would never occur to him
to do so. But now I'm here it's difficult, more difficult
than I thought. My mouth is like blotting paper.

'Max, I'd just like to get your view on something.'

'Yes. You said.'

He has a slight sheen of sweat on his forehead.

'You don't mind?' I ask him.

He makes a quick, vague gesture with the hand that
holds the drink. The ice rattles.

'I don't know what it is,' he says.

He glances across at me. He's sipping his whisky
too rapidly, as if he's anxious at being confided in:

though maybe I'm imagining this, projecting my own anxiety onto him.

I clear my throat.

'There's a woman I know,' I tell him.

A slight smile. 'OK.'

'She has a relationship that's very secret.'

He nods. 'It happens,' he says. He's peering into his whisky.

I'd thought he'd be more intrigued—that he'd tease or cajole me, trying to find out more. But he just waits quietly for me to carry on.

'She's with her friend in a secret place, and nobody knows they're there. And she sees something that perhaps should be reported.'

He's alert now, looking at me: but also in some way more relaxed, as though some tension has fallen from him.

'To the police, you mean?' he says. 'This thing she sees—it's something criminal?'

'Maybe. She doesn't know that. She just thinks it could be. But she'd certainly report it if she hadn't been with this person.'

He nods. There's a glint in his eye—enjoying this game we're playing.

'But if she tells, and it all comes out—people might be hurt?' he says.

I nod. We sit in silence for a moment.

'I wanted to know what might happen if she rang the police. I mean—she could do that anonymously, couldn't she?'

'Yes. Of course. Lots of people do.' He takes a pensive sip of whisky. 'But you'd have to think—your friend would have to think—would she be happy to do that and leave it there—if she really had some information that might affect a criminal prosecution? And presumably that's what she thinks or she wouldn't be so concerned.'

'Yes. She thinks that.'

'She has to ask herself—what will she do if the case goes to court, and they want her to give evidence?'

'They could make her?' I say.

'That depends. The judge could subpoena her. But that's a last resort, of course. The police would try to persuade her, they'd rather she did it voluntarily. Assuming her evidence is crucial to the prosecution case, and she can't know that yet... How I see it, Ginnie—it would be hard to take just one step along that path and leave it there...'

We drink in silence for a moment. I think of the face that haunts me—her glazed eyes, her swollen pallor—the woman pulled from the water. Of the flowers on the river bank.

'Max, look at it another way. What's the *right* thing for this woman to do? If you viewed it in the abstract, as a moral problem. What would be the right thing?'

He shakes his head at me.

'Jesus, Ginnie, if it's moral advice you're after, I'm the very last person in the world you want. You need a philosopher or a priest—not a rather lecherous lawyer.'

'Tell me. Please. What would you do, if it was you?'

'Ginnie, this isn't fair.'

'I'm asking you to tell me.'

He moves his hand, swirling the drink round his glass: the ice makes a percussive sound. He smiles the salacious smile I've expected from the beginning.

'I'd need to know more, really. A few details.'

'No. You know quite enough.'

He says nothing for a moment, sipping his drink.

'I think I'd keep quiet,' he says then. 'You have to be pragmatic. You have to take the long view.'

'But justice matters.'

'Of course. Ginnie, look, you did ask for my opinion. It's not fair to then say it's the wrong opinion when I give it.'

'But maybe this woman owes something to…whoever was the victim of this crime.'

'Maybe.' He's turned away from me, looking out at the garden.

'Wouldn't she just feel guilty all her life if she left it?' I say.

'There are things that are best kept quiet,' he says. 'Maybe I'm wrong. But that's my view on it, Ginnie.'

He turns back to me.

'Look at it this way,' he says. 'What's done is done. Your friend can't undo the bad thing—the crime— whatever it was she saw. A lot of damage is done by people who are sure they're doing the right thing. I think she'd be well advised to be pretty cautious about this: to weigh any good she might do by telling against the hurt she might cause…'

I go to the bathroom before I leave. It's plentifully stocked, unlike his fridge or his kitchen. On the shelf above the basin, there are bottles of shampoo and shower gel in sugary, feminine scents, so there must be some woman who visits. Well, there usually is. He has a picture above the bath, a Japanese erotic print, a man and a woman on a veranda, the moonlight shining through a maple, the leaves of the tree as red as blood and fringed and curled like flowers. The man is behind her, poised to penetrate her: you can see his large pale penis and the intricate folds of her flesh. It's unnerving, the way it's at once so explicit and so decorous: they're still wearing their sprigged kimonos, they have neat elaborate hair.

I stare at my face in the mirror for a moment. In the clear spring light you can see every crease and the greyness under my eyes. I run cool water over my wrists. I feel very alone. He's given me an excuse, a way that leads out of the wood—so why don't I feel more at peace? I realise I hoped for the wrong thing: that I looked for an easy answer, and there isn't one. Nobody can tell me what to do.

Max senses how I feel.

'I haven't been much use, have I?' he says as he takes me out to the door.

'It helps to talk,' I say. 'Thank you.'

He shakes his head a little.

'Obviously, this is just between us,' I tell him.

'Obviously.'

'And thanks again for having Amber.'

'Not at all. She was great to have around,' he says.

'She really enjoyed it,' I tell him.

We finalise our arrangements for the weekend, when we have the choir reunion in Walsall.

'It'll do you the world of good,' he says. 'Get you away from your troubles for a bit. Your poor mother, and your rather adventurous friend…'

We hug, and I walk off between the immaculate conifers.

CHAPTER 28

On Friday evening, Mrs Russell brings round Molly's canvas. It's so big she has to use the school minivan. I see her struggling with it in the street and rush to open the gate. We ease it in through the door and prop it up in the hall.

The figures Molly painted command attention: our mother with her worried air, the lines deeply etched in her face, and our father looming over her, and Ursula and me, with our stripy summer dresses and our conscientious smiles. The acrylic colours sing out in my quiet hall. I think of the autumn evening when we went to the school art exhibition—the day before I met Will. It seems so long ago now.

'There,' says Mrs Russell, with relief. She's pink, she's breathing heavily. 'Mr Bates wanted to say thanks to Molly for letting us keep it so long.'

'Not at all,' I say.

'He was very keen to have it there for our Open

Day. I said I'd bring it round for him.' She lowers her voice a little. 'I thought I could take the opportunity to have a quick word about Amber.'

'Oh.' I feel a surge of anxiety, or maybe shame, expecting a reprimand. 'I think she's in the kitchen.' I gesture Mrs Russell through the hall.

'It was you I wanted to speak to,' she says.

She stands close to me: she smells of fresh deodorant.

I nod.

'I'm happy to say that generally there's been a real improvement,' she says. 'We're very pleased. She seems to be putting in a lot more effort. Several of her teachers have remarked on it. Obviously something you're doing is really working.'

'Well. Good.' My voice is hesitant. I don't think I've done anything.

'So what happened?' she says. 'Did you have a good talk with her?'

'Kind of.' I hunt around in my mind for something to say. 'Well, she did enjoy her work experience. Maybe that helped her get a bit more focused.'

'Excellent,' she says. 'What I wanted to talk about— it's just this issue of getting her work in on time. That's the one area where we don't seem to be getting anywhere. Somehow we're just not getting through. I can't stress how important it is, with her GCSEs coming up.'

'Yes, I do see that.'

She has the flustered look she had on the parents'

evening, as though everything happens too fast for her, and things rush past and she struggles after them, calling for them to stop. 'Coursework has to get there on time, there are no second chances. If we don't get it sent off by the due day, the girl risks not getting a mark. Well, I'm sure you understand.'

'Absolutely.'

'She doesn't seem to listen when I tell her. It just doesn't go in somehow...'

There are sharp little vertical lines between her eyes.

I think how Amber slips away like water between your hands.

'I know what you mean,' I tell her. 'She can be rather vague.'

'I think perhaps we do need to take a firmer line. It's not as though she has no ability—quite the reverse. Well, it's obviously there in the family. Just look at what Molly's achieved.'

She leaves a pause. I think of saying that Molly and Amber aren't meant to be the same.

'Well, yes,' I say.

'Now, Amber's English teacher tells me that her next piece of work is due on March the third. That's the essay on *The Go-Between*. If you could make sure that she hands it in, we'd all be very grateful.'

'I'll talk to her today,' I say. 'And I'll put it in the calendar.'

'It's her future that's at issue here,' she says. 'I hate to see her throwing her chances away.'

* * *

Amber is sitting at the kitchen table poring over the *Evening Standard*. She's changed out of her uniform. She's wearing a T-shirt she bought on her shopping trip with Jamila. It says, 'Boys are stupid: throw rocks at them': the fabric is a fetching petal pink.

'Mrs Russell just came. She brought round Molly's picture.'

She screws up her face without raising her eyes from the newspaper.

'Why Mrs Russell?' she says, in a tight, defensive voice. 'What have I done now?'

'She wanted to check you got your coursework in on time. She was trying to be helpful.'

Amber hasn't put in a hairband today: when she looks at her paper, her face is almost hidden in the warm fall of her hair.

'I can't stand Mrs Russell,' she says. 'Last week she did an assembly. On the Fallopian tubes. It was, like, Ground, swallow me up.'

'Well, anyway. She says your English coursework is due in on March the third. Your *Go-Between* essay.'

'I hate that book,' says Amber.

'Promise me you'll get it in on time,' I tell her.

'Mum, you don't need to go on about it.'

I can't tell if she's taken in a word I've said.

'I'm putting it in the calendar,' I tell her.

'Whatever,' she says.

My calendar is on the wall. It has paintings by Jack Vettriano, men in sharp suits, groomed women in

stiletto heels—my Christmas present from Molly. I
turn the page to March. I'm briefly distracted by the
picture—lovers meeting after an absence, perhaps at
a railway station, in front of a coloured glass window:
he has a lean, worn face and they're wearing fifties
clothes. I write Amber's Coursework in large letters
on March the third.

I turn back to her. She's still deep in her newspaper.

'I wish you'd pay attention when I speak to you,'
I tell her. There's an edge of irritation in my voice.
'Nothing's more crucial than this. It's your whole
future, Amber.'

It's Mrs Russell speaking through me.

She looks up. Her eyes on me are the blue of summer
sky after rain. She shakes her head, but I'm not sure
what she's saying no to.

'They've found out her name,' she says then. 'The
woman in the river. They've found out who she is—I
mean, was.'

There's a lurch in my heart. I wonder if Amber will
see the shock in my face, but she's turned back to the
newspaper. I read it over her shoulder.

It's just a brief piece, placed between a double-glazing
advertisement and a photo of a school presentation.
The headline says: Body Identified in River Murder.
It says she was called Maria Faulkner, and she was
twenty-three. She worked as a care assistant, and
her husband was an estate agent. They'd been married three years, and they lived in Caterham. One

evening she told her husband she was going out for a walk: he rang the police that night, when she hadn't returned.

It feels so different, knowing her name and where she lived: knowing about the people who knew and loved her. It brings her closer.

'I wonder what she looked like,' says Amber. 'They usually have a picture, don't they, with these things? When somebody's died.'

'Maybe they didn't have space to print it.'

'I'd like to know what she looked like.' She looks up at me, perplexed. 'D'you feel kind of curious about it, Mum? Sort of excited? That's how I feel: *excited*. Is it horrible, d'you think, to be so interested?'

'No. Of course not.'

I put my arm round her shoulders. She rests her head against me. I'm comforted by her warmth and the papaya scent of her hair.

'I think I'm horrible,' she says. 'To feel like that. But I can't help it.'

'When something like that happens in a place where we used to go, you're bound to be curious,' I say.

'But *you* aren't, are you?' she says.

'Maybe I just don't show it,' I tell her.

Her eyes rest on me for a moment, wide and cool and clear. Then she looks away from me.

'I keep imagining it,' she says then, her voice hushed. 'Being strangled. What it was like for her.'

I stroke her hair.

'When people get attacked it usually happens very

quickly,' I say. 'I expect it was over so quickly she didn't feel very much.'

She looks up at me. We both know I'm just trying to comfort her. She shakes her head a little.

'She shouldn't have gone there alone,' she says. 'Not in the evening. Not when there's no one around. Anybody would know that, wouldn't they? It can be spooky by the river. D'you remember when we went to Eel Pie Island? And there were all those Barbies in that garden, like they'd just been planted there? That was really freaky.'

'I remember,' I say.

'Taggs Island was lovely, I really wanted to live there,' she says. 'But Eel Pie Island was weird.'

I move away from her, I go to the sink and start to wash some coffee cups.

'There's something creepy about the river,' she says. 'If you called out, no one would hear you.'

'I know what you mean,' I say. I keep my back to her.

'You wouldn't want to be by the river on your own.' She flicks on through her newspaper. 'It's just so sad,' she says. 'I hope they catch him soon.'

I drive to Walsall with Max. We go in my car: on Sunday Max is travelling on to Newcastle by train. I feel organised and efficient: there's a load of washing left to run, and a meal for tonight for both of them, and strict instructions to Amber to get her homework done. Everything I've left behind feels tidy and controlled.

We pass through open countryside under a gentle spring sky. The hedges and fields are already greening with spring. Max and I reminisce a little, and speculate on how big our audience will be—Dylan is rather unworldly and notoriously bad at publicity. Once Max says, 'That friend of yours…' leaving a significant pause, smiling in a knowing way '…did she solve that problem she had?'

'I think so,' I say. I'm relieved he doesn't pursue it.

We're meeting in Dylan's house for an afternoon rehearsal. He greets us with exuberance. He's fey-looking, slim as a boy, with effortless cheekbones, his feyness now just starting to shade over into a stylish gauntness. We wish him Happy Birthday, and thrust our presents of music and alcohol at him, and meet his new partner, Jeremy, a plump and amiable dentist. The others are there already, sixteen of us altogether—local singers from Dylan's choir, and university friends. There are people here I once knew so well—Ivor Browning, and Monica Druce with her diffidence and her shaggy, coppery hair. People with whom I once shared late night coffee and emotional crises; though now our knowledge of one another is limited to a line or two at Christmas, and these reunions every two or three years.

Ivor comes to hug me. He's a GP in Somerset: he lives in a country rectory with Beathe, his wife, and their delectable daughters, who have hair like lint and stripy dungarees. I've stayed with them sometimes, soothed by their sweet and orderly lifestyle; there's a mulberry growing up their wall, and a pony in a paddock, and at night it's perfectly quiet and so dark the stars look huge.

'You're obviously thriving, Ginnie,' he says, kissing me.

'You too,' I say.

But I notice the signs of ageing in him—the lines scored deep in his face, the darkness under his eyes. And I wonder what he really sees in me.

The church where Dylan is choir-master is in a run-down part of the city, next to an outreach centre for drug users. It smells of childhood, of All Saints where my father used to hand out prayerbooks, a smell of dry-rot treatment, mouldy prayerbooks, pollen. In the Lady Chapel, four stone angels stand guard around a tomb—beautiful boys with indolent gestures and great wide intricate wings. There's been a wedding and the flowers are still there, lilies and carnations, now drooping and spilling their petals on the chancel floor.

We gather on the altar steps. We wear black and white, as we always did, these formal clothes, now rarely worn, evoking long-ago college concerts, little snapshots of memory—concerts when I was faint with nerves before Finals, or thrillingly in love with some louche young man whose name I can't now recall. The chancel is lit, the rest of the building in darkness; in the shadow the church seems immense, stretching into infinity, the angels white and poised where light from the chancel falls across them, above us the great ribbed arches pale as bone. Everything is monochrome, except for the fading creams and pinks of the flowers, and the quiet colours of our hands and faces and hair.

We have an audience of one—just a rather decrepit man, presumably from the outreach centre, who sits near the front, with an expectant expression. Max mutters over my shoulder that this has to be a record. The man is unshaven, he has an ill-fitting coat the colour of mud, and several packages with him, all tied up with string with many elaborate knots. But he is our audience, and for this moment we love him.

We sing Palestrina and Shephard. The man listens with an air of careful politeness. Now and then he taps his hand on the pew in time to the music, as though to demonstrate his involvement. We sing well, the music casting its shimmering nets over everything.

Halfway through the programme, the man gets up and gathers his bags together and gives Dylan an apologetic wave. He walks down the aisle and pushes open the door. The outside leaks in for a moment—the tangerine glow of a street light, the shriek of a siren. Then the door slams shut behind him. We are enclosed, apart.

Dylan gestures us into a circle. We sing on through the programme; we sing to one another. Dylan scarcely moves his hand, the slightest gesture holding us together. The music floats up into the night that contains us. We are a circle of light in a sea of darkness. I feel weightless, disembodied; everything seems simple now, this music is the answer, everything is explained.

We end with a Bruckner motet, *Ave Maria*, a slow, hushed prayer. The words in my mouth seem rich in meaning. *Ora pro nobis peccatoribus, Nunc et in hora mortis nostrae.* Pray for us sinners, Now and at the hour of our death. I think of my mother. I think of the woman pulled from the water. I think of my own death.

We come to a quiet close, a long held note. We listen to the echo, and the silence after the echo, a silence alive with remembered sound, as though the music is still happening somewhere above us, way up in the rafters. There's a little collective sigh, something beyond happiness.

Dylan smiles.

'Perhaps an encore?' he says.

We sing it once more, to the silence and the dark.

Pray for us.

Afterwards we go back to Dylan's house, those of us who are staying there—Monica, Max, and Ivor and me—and sit round the table in the dining room. I kick off my shoes; the men loosen their bow ties. I sense that Jeremy has an enviable and generous talent for domesticity: there are daffodils in a white jug, an open fire of applewood, everything gleams. He's made a birthday cake for Dylan; he brings it in, candles ablaze. We sing Happy Birthday in slightly self-conscious harmony. The cake is moist and dark, with lots of brandy in it. Monica has brought some whisky that has a peaty taste.

Dylan has stories of people we used to know; he's an inspired gossip, with an interest in people at once salacious and compassionate. We drink the whisky and listen to his stories. Chris, who used to be an administrator at Kingston University, has become a Buddhist monk and lives a contemplative, celibate life in a monastery in Croydon. Fiona, who was abundantly attractive, and lusted after by all the men in college when she appeared as Eve in a mystery play wearing

only a body stocking and a fig leaf, has fallen in love
with a woman; they have an inventive sex life, involving
copious quantities of strawberries and crème fraîche.
Jenny, who in our college days was our star soprano,
has been diagnosed with multiple sclerosis, and her
husband, an orthopaedic surgeon, has left her for a
younger, healthier woman.

'Let's drink to absent friends,' says Dylan. 'To
Jenny! To Chris! To Fiona!'

In my twenties or thirties, I'd sometimes be envious, hearing other people's stories, their loves and
schemes and successes. As you get older, it changes.
You listen with a new gentleness: because by now we
all have something, some block or burden, something
that defeats us. Everyone has the mist falling over the
land.

The room is mellow, easy, a haze of whisky fumes
and the children's party smell of blown-out candles. I
lick my fingers that taste of marzipan. Monica's hair
glints like metal in the firelight. We lean in closer
around the table, talking of ourselves.

'So, Ginnie,' says Dylan then. 'Still busy with those
girls of yours? Let's have a quick résumé—life, the
universe and everything.'

I tell them about Molly.

'I don't believe it,' says Ivor. 'Molly at university
already.'

Time slips by so quickly: we all agree.

'And Amber's doing her GCSEs. She's really into
clubbing and staying out late. And of course she simply

isn't bothered when I'm worried… Though Max sees a different side of her. Don't you, Max?'

I turn to him. He murmurs agreement.

'She's been doing work experience at Max's office,' I tell them. 'She really enjoyed it, didn't she? She seemed to have a good time.'

Max nods.

'She was excellent,' he says. 'Very conscientious.' He pulls out a pack of cigarettes, pats his trouser pocket to check for his lighter. 'Well, I'll just go out for a smoke, if you'll excuse me.'

He opens the door. I feel the touch of unheated air from the hallway, like a cold hand on my skin.

'It's all fine, really,' I tell them.

I wonder how much the rest of us are hiding, what stories aren't being told.

'To Ginnie!' says Dylan.

'To Dylan!' I say. We drink.

I put my hand on Ivor's arm.

'Ivor, you haven't told us anything.' I think of the last time I visited them: of the delectable daughters on the swing under the apple tree; and Beathe in the kitchen, with a bunch of carrots just pulled, still smelling of the garden, her face flushed and quiet and wise. 'How's Beathe? How's life? Still flourishing?'

He takes a swig of whisky, holding it for a moment in his mouth. The fire shuffles softly.

'I met a woman,' he says.

There's a sudden tension in the room, a little electric charge. No one says anything.

'It was at a medical conference,' he says. 'I fell in love between lunch and the afternoon tea break, watching her. We hadn't even spoken. I mean—can you understand that? That's crazy, isn't it?'

Dylan and Jeremy smile at one another.

'I understand,' I tell him.

Max has come in, but he doesn't sit down, just waits behind my chair.

'I've never felt anything like it,' says Ivor. 'The intensity of it.'

He's staring into his whisky. It's quiet in the room apart from the shift and stir of the fire.

'I've tried to make some kind of sense of it. And I think she may have reminded me of my sister. The same blonde hair that swung across her face... I mean, you're our resident psychologist, Ginnie. Does that make any sense to you?'

I nod, I murmur something.

He pours more whisky, he drinks. For the moment he's disinclined to say more.

Monica tells a story she read in the paper, about a man in East Germany who was taken from his mother and fostered in the West and didn't even have a picture of her; but when he kissed his first girlfriend and ran his hand down her hair, he suddenly knew that his mother too had had long dark hair. We talk for a while about these sexual templates, the patterns that are imprinted in the brain. But we're marking time really, waiting for Ivor to talk again. He raises his head; we are quiet.

'Maybe it was that,' he says. 'I guess it could have been. It was shocking, to fall in love like that.' He takes another long, slow sip of whisky. 'We didn't sleep together though. We didn't have an affair.'

Max sits down heavily at the table, shaking it as he sits. I can feel his gaze moving across me. I keep my head down.

'Why the hell not?' he says.

'I wanted to,' says Ivor. 'I'm sure it would have been wonderful: I know it would have been... Well, wonderful to start with.' He smiles a little: I don't know how much struggle is hidden behind the smile. 'Rather like stepping off a cliff—exhilarating to start with, and then horribly messy.'

Dylan raises his glass.

'To Ivor!'

We drink.

Ivor doesn't drink; he's moving his finger on the shiny surface of the table, as though he's writing words that only he can read.

'D'you ever see her?' I say.

'Sometimes,' he says slowly. His face darkens. He looks old now. 'We have dinner together—once or twice a year... When you're twenty-five, you can make a mess of things. You're got all the time in the world. It doesn't matter when you're twenty-five. But I'm forty-eight, I've got two kids, it's different. When you're forty-eight you can't fuck up,' he says.

CHAPTER 30

I sleep deeply, and wake with my mind like a pressed sheet, the creases smoothed away. I drive Max to the station, then head off home alone, taking my time, wrapping the benevolence of yesterday evening around me. I can still hear the music we sang.

At lunchtime I buy a baguette and a newspaper in a garage, and park beside the road, where amid the litter and the brambles there are primroses: they are the most perfect of yellows, at once so rich and so pale. I open the window. There's a little wind that smells of the changing seasons. The newspaper says that the weather's been far too mild for the season. There have been all sorts of aberrations. Swallows are nesting in Kent, and frogs are mating in Shropshire, and there are bumblebees in Scotland, and all the blossom is coming out too soon. Everything's happening at the wrong time.

When I've finished my lunch, I stay there for ages,

just sitting there. I think of our conversation, of people's troubles. I tell myself I am lucky, that I should cherish what I have. I hear people's voices in my head. Max, calm, pragmatic, when I went to visit him: There are things that are best kept quiet. And Ivor last night, his darkened face, his quiet resolution. I tell myself that what I saw on the river path meant nothing; I gave it a significance it simply didn't warrant, projecting my own guilt onto this passing stranger. It all seems simple and obvious now, the way ahead quite clear.

It's evening when I get back. Greg is hungry already—I suspect that he made himself a rather inadequate lunch. Amber has spent the day with Jamila, wandering around Southall: they had free naan bread and dhal in a gurdwara that had an open day, and signed a petition in Punjabi for somebody not to be executed—they didn't understand it, but they signed it anyway, because people dying generally isn't a good idea; and they went to this shop Jamila knows and they bought some wicked Indian sweets. She hasn't begun her homework. Then I find that the wash I left running on Saturday morning had a tissue in: it's shredded and got into everything, and the wash must all be done again. I make an early dinner, feeling my peacefulness already starting to seep away.

Amber is going to a school disco in a warehouse in Twickenham, where everyone will be dressed in a disco caricature of school uniform. She wears a flamboyantly short skirt, deliberately laddered fishnets, her highest heels and a crumpled school blouse and tie. It's time to go but she isn't ready. She's standing in front of the mirror in the dining room, trying to plait her hair. She's arching her back, reaching behind her head to make a parting, but she can't see what she's doing. She mutters expletives under her breath. I pretend I didn't hear.

'Mum, would you do it for me?' she says then, cajoling. 'If you do it I'll come straight home from school tomorrow and start my *Go-Between* essay. I *promise*.'

I do it for her. She watches intently, to check the plaits are even. I love the feel of her hair as it slips between my fingers, leaving its musk on my skin and its faint papaya scent. I don't often touch her now; it slides away from you so quickly and irrevocably, that easy intimacy of the early years.

'I wish I had perfect hair,' she says. 'Katrine's hair is always perfect…'

'I think you have the loveliest hair,' I tell her.

She shrugs.

'You would say that. You're my *mother*.'

She puts on some candy-pink lipgloss that clashes fabulously with the red of her hair. She smiles at herself in the mirror.

'There,' she says.

I kiss her cheek.

I give her a lift to the party. I don't want her waiting at the bus stop looking like that. Though I probably needn't have worried: it's going to be a big event, and

Twickenham seems full of nubile girls all dressed in similar clothes.

Greg is in his study when I get back. I pour myself some wine and stretch out on the living room sofa, trying to recover this morning's peaceful mood. Too lazy to read, I flick on the television.

I watch a programme on how to make a cottage garden, then something earnest about the Pharaohs. I'm bored, I move through the channels. On BBC1 it's the news—the familiar apparatus of the police press conference, the long bare formal table draped in blue, the microphones, the untouched tumblers of water. It looks like an appeal from the family of a crime victim. My finger is on the remote, I'm about to switch over. Family appeals are always so painful, all that naked emotion; I want to cling to my gentle, grateful mood. But my eye is caught, the world tilts. I feel that startling sense of significance that comes when you see someone from your own familiar world on television—a shock of recognition that comes before you make sense of what you see. Roger Prior is sitting behind the table, wearing a sharply cut jacket, like in the pub on Acton Street when I was there with Will.

'Earlier today,' says the voice-over, 'Sean Faulkner made an appeal for help from the public in solving the murder of his wife, Maria.'

My immediate response is a warm surge of relief. I feel almost that it's a sign that I've made the right decision. People will come forward now, all sorts of other people, all the witnesses. It's nothing to do with me now. The thing I saw will count for nothing, it won't be up to me.

A reporter briefly reiterates the details of the crime. There are shots of the scene by the river, the day they found the body. You can see the vivid sunlight, the rowers, the barge with painted flowers. There are more shots of the room then, the camera panning round the audience, taking in the journalists and all the other people who wait tense and expectant; and moving back to the table, to Roger: his grey hair, grey eyes, composed face: he has a slight frown of concentration, as though he's watching out for something that no one else can see.

The camera slides along the table, seeming to follow Roger's gaze, coming to rest on Sean Faulkner. Sean Faulkner clears his throat and starts to speak.

'There's someone out there who knows the person who did this. He must be somebody's brother, somebody's partner, somebody's son. Maybe a person you know behaved suspiciously or oddly around the time Maria died. I'm appealing for anyone who can help to come forward. Please, please help the police to solve this appalling crime...'

He's urgent, pleading, his voice shaky with grief, very clear in the hushed room. But I scarcely hear the words above the thud of my heart.

'I loved Maria. She was a beautiful woman and I miss her terribly...'

He cries, his face is contorted, anguished—the face

of a man who inhabits some private unguessable hell. But his grief doesn't touch me. As he cries he chews his lower lip, he pushes his blond hair back from his face—and I see him now as I saw him then, the week before they pulled Maria's body from the water: running between the river and the rowan.

CHAPTER 31

I wake and feel the thickness of the dark. It's so quiet in the room without Greg: the space feels hollow and still. I realise how his presence used to soothe me in ways I was unaware of, his slow heavy breathing and the warmth of his body part of the familiar texture of the night.

I lie awake for a long time, wandering the mazes of my mind. Eventually I hear the click of the door, and know that Amber is home. It's the loveliest sound in the world to me. I go out onto the landing.

She's flushed and the plaits are ragged now. A hazy smell of smoke hangs round her.

'I didn't mean to be this late,' she says. Her gestures are vague, she's blurred with tiredness and too many Malibus. She's forming her words with care. 'Me and Lauren lost our cloakroom tickets, so they made us stay till last to check the coats were really ours. You were meant to be asleep.'

'Was it good?'

She yawns.

'It was OK,' she says.

She goes into her room.

I lie down again and wrap the duvet tight around me. The arguments in my head start up again. There's a smooth voice, a voice that can talk its way out of trouble. The voice of sense, of pragmatism. The police had Sean Faulkner in their sights anyway. That's why they got him to make the appeal. They do that, I know, I've read about it somewhere, they get the suspect to face the press, to see if there are clues in his or her behaviour. It's one reason they set up appeals, to see how the suspect reacts under that pressure. They make special videos that show the least flicker of expression, that they can slow down and analyse: Were these real tears? Is this emotion genuine? That's why Roger seemed so intent and focused when I saw him on television. They undoubtedly have something on Sean Faulkner—they don't need my evidence. And anyway, what did I see? A man running along the river path. I'm sure it was him—but what does that add up to? It's near where they used to live. Anyone can go there. It might mean nothing.

I want so very much to believe this voice.

I lie there till I hear the first bird, with a call like a pot being scraped, and light seeps silver round the edges of my curtains. I feel such relief that night is nearly over. I fall uneasily asleep, and dream the dream I had before, about the dead houses and finding my children there.

* * *

The ordinariness of my office in the clear morning light comforts me. There's a wide-open sky and the air is echoey with the calls of rooks. Some hyacinths on my window sill have flowered: the room is sweet with their clingy, insinuating scent.

Clem comes to talk about a case she's finding difficult, one of her anorexic girls. Clem's been trying to get the father involved, but it isn't working well. He sat with his daughter for two hours, urging her to eat, while she slid her hard-boiled egg round her plate and shredded her slice of cucumber into fifty tiny pieces: then he hit her. I admire Clem for taking on these cases: they're terribly hard to treat.

'Ginnie, are you OK?' she says as she closes the file.

'Just tired.'

She frowns at me.

'You look like you might be going down with something.'

'Really, I'm fine,' I tell her.

'Everything's OK, isn't it? You know, with the family?'

Her eyes rest on me, brown and quizzical.

'OK-ish,' I say.

'If you need me, you know where I am,' she says.

Everything seems simpler than in the mazes of the night. I'm sure what I must do now. I need to ring Will, and we will talk and share this and work it out together. I tell myself that he withdrew from me because

270   Margaret Leroy

he was frightened and confused, he wasn't thinking clearly. But I know he'll understand now; when I say it was Sean Faulkner that I saw, he'll know how much this matters. I think of Will's tenderness to me, and I reach out my hand for the phone. But then hesitate, and tell myself I'll wait and call him at lunchtime. I need a little more time to think this through.

I see Katy Croft. She's a diminutive Goth with a spiky collar and boots that are made for kicking and frightened eyes. She cuts herself: she scratches her arms with compasses, and sometimes she'll press ring-pulls from cola cans into her thighs. She's kept this secret for months, even from her family. 'I can't tell people what really is me, what's really inside of me,' she says in a small voice, glancing at me through the curtains of her hair. By the end of the session she's started to meet my gaze and her voice is stronger, and I feel we've made a beginning.

At lunchtime I take out my phone to call Will. But before I can dial, the phone rings, making me jump. It's Ursula.

'Oh, Ginnie, I'm sorry. Are you at work? I'm so sorry if I've bothered you at work…'

There's a gasp in her voice, as though she can't get enough breath.

'It's OK,' I say. 'Really.'

'We went to the hospital this morning. They've got the results of the brain scan,' she says.

'Yes.'

'It's not good news, I'm afraid. They were hoping it was just a bleed.'

'*Just* a bleed?'

'Well, you can survive a bleed apparently. They said they were very sorry but it wasn't a bleed.' Her voice is careful, edging around the words, as though they were sharp and could cut her. 'It's a tumour, Ginnie.'

'Does she know?'

'She doesn't want to know, she hasn't asked,' says Ursula. 'If she asks I'll tell her, but I just feel she doesn't want to know. Like she knows there's something very wrong, she just doesn't want the details. That's OK, isn't it? It just seems wrong to tell her if she doesn't want to know.'

'But can't they operate?'

'She's too old.' Her voice is heavy and tired. 'The tumour's too big. It's nearly half of her brain. They said she'd never survive the operation.'

We're silent for a moment. We don't ask if she should have gone into hospital sooner, if there's something we could have done. But the thought lurks under our words.

'We saw Dr Spence. You know, the one who grew up on the Isle of Wight? He was very nice to us. He took us into his office, Paul and me. He said life has to go on… They've put her on steroids. He said they'll give her a bit of relief for a while. I mean, we suspected something like this, didn't we? We knew it wasn't a stroke. It never sounded like a stroke to me…'

'I'll go tomorrow,' I tell her. 'I'll take the day off and go down.'

'Don't feel you have to, Ginnie. You don't have to drop anything. She's not going to… I mean, it's not going to happen that quickly. It could be several weeks, they said.'

'I'd like to,' I say.

'Well, I'm sure she'd love to see you. But, Ginnie, look, don't tell her anything she doesn't want to know.'

I put down the phone. My mother takes up all my mind. I know I won't ring Will now.

Amber comes straight home from school as she promised, to do her essay. I hear the clatter as she kicks off her shoes and flings down her bag on the floor. She comes into the kitchen. Her hair is crinkled where it was braided; she still smells of smoke from the party. She peers in the fridge, shrugs, goes to the bread basket. She takes out the bread and breaks off a chunk with her hand, though the bread knife is in its usual place on the counter. The ink stains on her fingers have smudged the bread with blue. I bite back the urge to tell her off.

'Amber, there's something you need to know.'

She spins round sharply, as though she expects a reprimand. Her eyes are smeary with last night's mascara, which she hasn't yet wiped off.

'What is it?' she says. 'What have I done now? I came home like we said.'

'It's nothing to do with you,' I tell her. 'Ursula rang about Granny. She's very ill.'

Her eyes widen.

'You mean she's going to die?'

'Sweetheart, she could.' I clear my throat. 'I mean, yes, she will. It's a brain tumour. It's too far gone to operate. Anyway, she's too old.'

'Poor Granny,' she says vaguely. She takes a bite of the bread. 'God, I'm famished. There were only these gross samosas left when I got to the canteen.'

'I'm going down tomorrow.'

'No problem, Mum. I was going round to Lauren's anyway.'

She drifts off upstairs, chewing at the bread. I feel a flicker of irritation.

I start to make a meal, a chicken stew that I can easily reheat when Greg comes home at nine, when the faculty closes. It's a clear, bright evening, light flooding the kitchen, the searching light of spring that shows up any imperfection. I see how smeared my windowpanes are. Everywhere feels dirty, my windows and my kitchen and the inside of my head. I start to cut the vegetables, but I'm clumsy after my sleepless night and I put the knife through my skin. I watch the blood well from my finger, tulip-bright. The pain is almost welcome, a relief from all the turmoil in my head. I have a moment of empathy with girls like Katy who cut themselves.

Amber's music is turned up loud, the whole house seems to shake with it. I can't imagine how she can work like that. Mrs Russell is in my mind: I'm sure you create good conditions for her to work in… I think we need to take a firmer line… My finger throbs.

Eventually I go upstairs. I push her door open without knocking.

The room is in chaos. She's on the floor by the desk, a litter of paper and cardboard cuttings and bread crusts around her. Just by her feet there's a perilously full jar of paint-stained water.

'Amber—what on earth is this?' My voice is shrill. 'You're meant to be doing your essay.'

When I shout she flinches from me as though I have raised my hand to her.

'I was making a card.' She has a tight, hurt voice. 'For Granny. I thought you'd be *pleased*,' she says.

It's made from an old shoe-box. She's punched holes in two squares of cardboard and tied them together with ribbon, like a little book. There's a cut-out bird stuck to the front, a water bird flying, a goose or a swan, like in her childhood nursery-rhyme book, with a tangerine beak and intricate, textured feathers and a wide white sweep of wing. She's made the feathers with shavings of cardboard that she's curled by wrapping them round her pencil.

I can't speak for a moment.

When I don't say anything, she looks at me uncertainly.

'Don't you like it?' she says. 'I thought perhaps it wasn't good enough.'

'It's beautiful,' I say.

'I don't know. You feel it has to be extra good, if someone's as ill as Granny. If somebody's going to die, you can't send them a crap card, can you? And I worried it might fall apart on the way, before she gets it.'

'Sweetheart, I'll make sure it gets to her safely. I'll be so careful, I promise… And Amber, when you've finished…'

'OK, OK. I'll do the essay.' She opens up the card and takes a purple pen and writes a flamboyant greeting. 'But sometimes you've got to think what really matters, Mum.'

I have Amber's card in a padded envelope, and a primrose in a pot. I feel sick with anxiety, walking through the hospital, past its blue walls and trolleys and affable porters and antiseptic smells.

But my mother is sitting up in bed, with lipstick on, and a bed-jacket. She looks so different from last time, her face more vivid, defined. I feel a brief, crazy flicker of hopefulness. She sees me coming and smiles.

'Ginnie. How lovely.'

I kiss her.

'I'm so much better,' she says.

'Well, I can see that.'

'They've put me on these wonderful drugs. Steroids. They make such a difference,' she says.

'That's marvellous,' I say.

She smells of Blue Grass: and I see she has painted her nails. But close to her, touching her, I know how fragile she is, and see that the vividness in her face is an illusion, unreal, like the ruddy outdoor complexion of fever.

The afternoon ward is quiet and full of gluey yellow light. Through the wide windows you can see the shining cityscape, the silver office blocks and towers, all bright and far and silent.

I give my mother Amber's card. She runs her finger along the curled feathers, in a gesture like a caress. She props it up on her locker.

'It's like the ones Molly used to make,' she says. 'Does Molly still do her drawing?'

I tell her about the canvas Molly painted.

'She took it from a photo we had—you and Dad and Ursula and me. It's huge, the school had to send it round in a van…'

A shadow moves across my mother's face.

'I'd have loved to have seen it,' she says.

Her face is tight, dark, her eyes on me, just a whisper of grief in her voice. She's telling me that she knows: that she will never see Molly's picture. Ursula is right: we don't need to tell her anything. She knows what she needs to know.

I put my hand on hers. Her skin is cool, and dry as winter leaves.

'You'd have loved it,' I tell her. 'It was in the garden at Bridlington Road, in front of the forsythia.'

She's entering into this, trying to remember, pushing away the sadness.

'Was it the one your Auntie Carol took?'

'I don't know: it might have been.'

'Was your father wearing that pinstripe shirt?'

'I think so.'

'I remember the one. It's good of your father, that photograph. He wore clothes well,' she says.

'I guess so.'

'He was a good-looking man, your father,' she says.

I shrug. 'Yes,' I say.

She hears my hesitation.

'Now, Ginnie, you mustn't judge your father too harshly.'

I don't say anything. I think she will move on, leave it there, just as Ursula always does. There's a thread of reticence and evasion stitched into everything she says. Things weren't so bad, we mustn't exaggerate, really we were a perfectly normal family... Silence laps at us, a little darkening pool.

'I know that you thought I should just leave him,' she says quietly. Dropping her words like stones into the silence, clear and precise and astonishing. 'You did, didn't you, Ginnie? That's what you thought.'

My heart pounds.

'Maybe,' I say carefully.

'I could see that,' she says. 'Poor Ursula was terrified we'd divorce, and you really wanted us to. Ursula was so frightened of being different—she wanted to fit in more than anything in the world. But you—I always felt that you were impatient with me. That you felt I should have just taken you both and gone.'

'Yes,' I say quietly. 'I did think that.'

The easy rhythms of the ward would soothe you into sleep—the rustle of magazines, the footsteps in the corridor, the clink of cups and murmur of talk where the nurse with the turquoise eyeshadow is bringing round tea. The woman in the next bed snores softly, her head on one side, her face sunk sideways and out of shape, under her sprawl of newspaper. But my mother is alert, intent.

'I thought about it, believe me,' she says. 'I thought about it a lot.'

'I didn't know,' I say.

'It would have been so difficult, Ginnie,' she says. 'We'd have been very hard up. And when you're young, that may not seem so terrible. But I knew what it would be like and I couldn't face it. I felt you'd have a better life if we managed to stay together. And I'd say to myself, well, it doesn't happen very often…'

I don't say anything. I put my hand on hers. Her hands are cold and quiet now: hands that in our childhood were smooth and quick and busy, keeping us fed and clothed and trying to protect us. Stirring the cake mixture in the yellow glazed bowl; ironing shirts on a Monday afternoon, with that hot, safe, delicious smell of almost-scorching fabric. Pushing shut the door.

'It's different today,' she says. 'You can get help with these things. There isn't so much shame. People talk about them. Back then—there was nothing… Though I did try, once, you know, Ginnie.' Defensive, as though she thinks I may blame her. 'I want you to know that.

I tried to get help. We went to this psychiatrist. Dr Ellis. D'you remember? Your Auntie Carol had to pick you up from school.'

I nod. Remembering the afternoon: my mother wearing the blouse with all the little pearl buttons, and tea in Auntie Carol's kitchen—the tinned peach in Carnation that looked like a poached egg and tasted far too sweet.

'Well, he wasn't very sympathetic really, darling. He said I provoked your father. He said I obviously knew what wound your father up. That I made it happen with my provocative behaviour.'

Rage slams into me.

'No, Mum.'

My voice is too loud for the ward. The nurse glances sharply across at me.

But my mother just shrugs.

'Your father was wearing that Burton's suit he had. As you know, he could be very charming. Dr Ellis took a real shine to your father.'

I shake my head. This appals me.

'To give him his due, I think in his saner moments your father knew that wasn't right. It was confusing—we both felt so confused. It's hard when someone says something is true, and you know in your heart it isn't. You don't know what to think then.'

Her face looks tired suddenly, blurred. All her brittle energy has gone. Saying these things has drained away whatever vigour she had.

'I gave up then,' she says. Quietly, so I have to lean

forward to hear. 'I knew there was no one to help me. I just decided—That was my bed, and I had to lie on it... I hope you don't mind me saying all these things. I didn't want to bother Ursula—I know she finds it upsetting.'

I stroke her hand.

'It helps to know,' I tell her. 'What it was like for you, why you did what you did. What you went through.'

We sit there for a moment. Light from the long windows falls across the floor.

'When you're stuck here with nothing to do,' she says, 'these things do prey on your mind. And you think—did I do the right thing? It's difficult to know, sometimes, just what the right thing is. It's hard to be really sure.'

The nurse with the trolley stops by my mother's bed. She smiles her white professional smile, and gives us tea and gingernuts. She lingers for a moment, looking at Amber's card.

'Is that from one of your granddaughters, Jacquie?'

My mother nods.

The nurse picks up the card.

'When I was a kid, we lived by the river,' she says. Her face is suddenly serious. 'You see something and suddenly you're back there. All these years later. Just the smallest thing. It's weird, that, isn't it?' She props the card up on the locker. She switches her bland smile back on. 'Well, ladies, enjoy your tea.'

My mother sips at her tea as the nurse moves away.

'You feel so lonely,' she says then.

At first I think she means here, ill, in hospital.

'Oh, Mum. I'll get down again just as soon as I can. And Ursula comes often, doesn't she?'

'Oh, not here, Ginnie. I'm all right here. I'm very well looked after. You can see how nice the nurses are. No, I meant, when you're in—you know—that situation—that I was in with your father.'

She tries to put her cup down on the locker, but her hands are shaky and uncontrolled, and tea spills into her saucer. I put a tissue between the saucer and cup.

'There's no one to help you, Ginnie, you see. No one to take your side or hear your story. You think you're completely alone... Sorry to go on, darling. I guess this isn't really what you came to hear.'

The journey back is slow, especially once I reach the outskirts of London. There's a race meeting at Kempton Park, and the traffic is stuck for miles. I'm tired and hungry and longing to be home. But when I come to the convent, on impulse I stop the car and go in through the gateway.

There are petunia seedlings on the table today, where in autumn there were apples. A handwritten notice invites passers-by to help themselves to the seedlings: the ink has run in the rain. There's an old Cadbury's biscuit tin for donations. My feet make an obtrusive crunch in the gravel that leads up to the door. I realise I've forgotten to change out of my driving shoes—the ugly, clumpy lace-ups I keep for motorway journeys. I must look as if I'm off on a trek. My body feels clumsy and hot. I don't know if I have any right to do this: I half expect that someone rather stern and holy will come and ask what I'm doing, or explain that this is a private and consecrated place and I really shouldn't be here.

The door is in a conservatory that has white tiles and lots of ferns in wicker pot-holders. Another handwritten notice advises you to ring the door-bell twice. I ring: a woman comes. She seems very down-to-earth for a nun, and unexpectedly stylish, a pashmina draped over her shoulders. She smiles at me through the glass as she unbolts the door.

'I'm sorry to disturb you. I just need to be some-where quiet. I wondered if I could come in and sit for a while. I mean, d'you have a chapel or somewhere?'

She leans towards me a little, as though listening with care. My request sounds weird to me, but she doesn't seem surprised. It enters my mind that people like me come knocking here quite often—apologetic people, tired and puzzled and on a difficult journey, still in their driving shoes.

'I'll show you the way,' she says. She takes me down a corridor.

I hoped for something old, a shadowy sacred space like a cave, with gold-encrusted icons and votive candles that dance in the dark with a secret, numinous glim-mer. But it looks quite unexceptional: contemporary, with too much concrete, and chairs with wicker seats arranged in a semi-circle, some with cushions, perhaps for the older women, and a plain cloth on the altar, and the whole place full of the ordinary light of day. But as soon as I sit there I feel the silence wrap itself around me, a silence that soothes and contains me, as real as an arm round your shoulder or the touch of a hand. There's a faint polleny scent, where the windows are open onto the gardens at the back of the convent; I hear planes going over, and people tending the garden—feet on gravel, raking, the insect drone of a mower. Now and then there are footsteps in the corridor—the pashmina-wearing nun, perhaps, going about her business, doing whatever nuns do. But these things all sound so far away: as though the stillness of this place encompasses and protects me.

I sit there for a long time, like someone who has to come to a decision: though maybe the decision has already been made.

CHAPTER 33

I've kept the number; it's on a scrap of paper in one of the drawers in my apothecary cabinet. I poke around in the drawer, pushing aside the plasticine figures and Molly's vague pink knitting. It doesn't seem to be there. I feel a surge of relief, that perhaps I can postpone this: I have a perfect reason now for leaving it till tomorrow. But then I find it, under a box of fuses.

I take the scrap of paper and go back to the car. Greg and Amber aren't home yet, but I still don't want to make the call from here. I drive round the corner and park in a side street, beside a squat grey church with a poster up that says 'Come 4 A Miracle': the writing is faded and pale. You can hear the distant roar of rush-hour traffic. There's a low sun in a saffron sky, and intricate tree shadows reach across the street. A boy in a fur-trimmed parka is delivering free papers from a fluorescent-green trolley. Two pigeons scuffle, fighting or mating, on the ridge of a roof. A builder with a wheelbarrow moves in and out of a front door, taking cement from a mixer. I see these things acutely, vividly, as if someone has turned up the definition, every detail clear.

My phone is in my hand. I set myself targets. When one of the pigeons moves from that rooftop, I shall do it. When the builder comes back, I shall make the call. The pigeons fly away, the builder reappears in the porch of the house, and still I don't move. And then find myself pressing the keys on my phone, almost without thinking. I watch my hand on the phone, as though this is nothing to do with me. It's the easiest thing in the world, just a little step: as though there isn't a rift here, a crack between before and after.

'Incident room.' A female voice, young, a South London accent.

'There's something I wanted to tell you. About Maria Faulkner.'

'Right,' she says. 'Now, would it be OK if I took your name?'

'I'd rather not give it,' I tell her. 'I hope that's all right.'

'Of course,' she says, but there's a sag in her voice. 'Now, my name's Kim, OK? So if you ever want to ring again, you ask for Kim.' I imagine her bored already, playing with a biro or examining her nails. 'Now, what do you want to tell us?'

'Well, it may be nothing.'

Suddenly I'm full of doubt. Perhaps Will was right,

perhaps it doesn't mean anything. I watch as the builder shovels cement into his wheelbarrow, slowly, as though each shovelful is unutterably heavy: the whole world slowed, but inexorable.

'Could you just tell me?' she says.

I tell her. That I was on the river path, the morning after Maria disappeared, a week before her body was recovered. That there was a man I noticed because he kept on looking around. I feel unreal, as though I'm outside the whole scene, watching myself do this: as though everything around me is a hallucination— the car, the boy with the parka, the flaming saffron sky.

'Then when I saw the TV appeal,' I tell her, 'I recognised the man. Maria's husband was the man I saw.'

'You saw Sean Faulkner's appeal?'

Sudden interest sharpens her voice. I can almost see her, the way she stiffens, everything alert.

'Yes,' I say. 'And I'm sure that he was the man I saw on the river path.'

She wants the date, the time. I give them.

'This is a lead I'm sure we'd want to pursue,' she says. 'And it would be really helpful to us if you felt able to give your name—so we could follow this up in rather more depth.'

'I was with a friend and it's a rather awkward situation,' I tell her.

'I understand,' she says, her voice emollient, soothing. 'I do understand.' I hear the carefulness in her voice, as though I'm a wild animal she's scared will shy away. 'And we do appreciate what you've done in ringing the line today. But if you *were* willing to talk to the investigating officers, we'd be extremely grateful.'

There's a little expectant silence.

I stare down the street. Two girls come roller-skating along the pavement. They're six or seven, wearing cartoon sweatshirts. They're messing about, their long hair swishing, waving their hands around, one of them pushing her ponytail up and over the top of her head, so it flaps on her face like a fringe. They giggle.

'I don't think I could,' I tell her.

'It would all be very relaxed,' she says. 'And they'd see you wherever you chose. Just wherever suited you.'

The girls move on down the pavement, through the woven shadows of trees. The sky is deepening, yellow darkens to bronze. I don't say anything.

'It's really nothing to worry about,' she goes on. 'You could just tell them what you've told me and answer any questions that they might have. I mean, is there anything you'd like to ask about what that might involve?'

'No, not really,' I say.

The girl with the ponytail trips and falls. She lands on her knees, breaking her fall with her hands. She holds onto a garden fence and drags herself to her feet again. Her face is creased with pain, but she's trying not to cry.

'It's entirely up to you,' says the woman, 'and I do understand it's difficult. But as you can imagine we're all so very keen to get justice for Maria.'

It's just a little step. I give my name.

CHAPTER 34

They come at ten in the morning, when Greg is giving a lecture and Amber is safely at school. There are two of them, a woman and a man. I see their shapes through the frosted window in my front door, featureless, darkly dressed, like shadows against the glass. For a moment I think: I could refuse to see them. But I go to open the door.

The woman is blonde and rangy, with long toned limbs and short layered hair. The man is short and solid and smells strongly of some over-sweet hair product. I once had a boyfriend who smelt like that: I'm reminded quickly, irrelevantly, of teenage dates, of fumblings in the back row of a cinema watching Barbra Streisand. They both have briefcases.

'Mrs Holmes?' says the woman. Her lips curve in a smile that doesn't reach her eyes.

'Yes,' I say.

'I'm Detective Sergeant Karen Whittaker, and this

is Detective Constable Ray Jackson. Just call us Karen and Ray.'

'Right,' I say. I take them into my living room. I offer them coffee but they say they're fine.

There's a tender blue sky, light spilling over everything. Out in my garden, there are drifts of pale narcissi in the lawn. A little wind shivers the tiny new leaves of the apple tree. Along the path by the river house it will all be happening now, all the fattening and opening up and reaching out of spring—yellow lacquered celandines glinting among the nettles, and a frail white froth of blossom on the sloe. I long so much to be there.

The woman sits beside me on the sofa, the man on the armchair. The man opens his briefcase and takes out a pen and a notepad, and eases off the elastic band that holds the notepad shut. The woman crosses her elegant legs and looks around her; she's taking in my house, as women do.

'What a beautiful room,' she says.

I feel this is just politeness: that it isn't her kind of thing; my style would be too bohemian for her. And today it looks so scruffy. I cleaned before they came, feeling some subliminal fear that they might charge me with keeping a disorderly house and having illicit snail trails in my kitchen. Yet in the searching spring light that reaches its long fingers everywhere, I see how tatty everything is—my bookshelves that are made from reclaimed church pews, and my patchwork velvet cushions, and all my fringes and unravellings.

The worn, distressed textures I love, that seem so rich in a gentle light, look threadbare in the sunshine. Everything here is lined and fading and old.

The woman looks at the piano, at the framed pictures of my children taken by school photographers and the pictures of family Christmases. Molly at ten, with hair pulled back and soft, dark, liquorice eyes, diffident and earnest. Amber as a toddler, unafraid and gleeful, thrusting bread at pushy geese that come up to her shoulder. The four of us eating Christmas dinner, photographed by Ursula. The latest school shots of the pair of them, Amber with her closed-lip smile before she had her braces off, and both of them with illicit make-up, discreetly applied so the teachers wouldn't see.

'Those are your daughters?' she says.

'Yes,' I tell her.

'What lovely girls,' she says.

She turns back to me and clears her throat and leans a little forward. She pushes a crisp blonde curl behind an ear.

'Right, Mrs Holmes. On Tuesday you rang us and said you had some information that you could give us, about Maria Faulkner?'

My mouth dries. I nod.

'Perhaps we could go right back to the beginning, and hear it in your own words,' she says.

I repeat what I said to the woman on the phone line. The man is writing it down. When I say that I saw the television appeal, and realised that the man

I'd seen looked like Maria's husband, they catch one another's eye—just a tiny look, a flickering.

'OK,' says the woman then, quite impassive. 'Let's take this a step at a time. Now, what date are we talking about? When you saw this person?'

I tell them.

'You seem very sure,' says the man.

'Yes, I'm sure,' I say.

I take a deep breath, like someone flinging themselves into water.

'There's something I need you to know. I was there with a friend. I know the date because we always meet—met—on a Thursday.'

'Right,' says the woman. I see her glance towards the piano and all the family photos, a rapid, darting blue glance, then back again to me. There are justifications I've used—that I loved him so much, that no one would be hurt if we were secret, that my affair was in some way keeping me here, helping me hold my family together. Desire pleads its case with such eloquence. But my arguments dissipate in an instant under this woman's cool blue gaze.

'There are families involved,' I say. 'We're trying to keep it all very quiet. I don't want my husband to know.'

'We understand,' she says. She's soothing, matter-of-fact. Her hands are folded precisely on her lap: she has manicured nails and a platinum wedding ring. I try to tell myself this is nothing to them—just an ordinary affair, an everyday bit of deception. They see this all the time. 'In the circumstances, we do appreciate you coming to us,' she says. 'We'll go through it all quite slowly. So—you're pretty certain you're right about the date?'

'Yes.'

'And you were where on this date?'

'There's a place we go to. You go round a bend in the path, and there's this little house.' The smell of the man's hair gel is making me nauseous. I clasp my hands tight together. 'It's a house that's broken down, just a single room. There's a little quay and a dinghy tied to the quay.' I try to remember it, the crimped light swinging across the ceiling, the thrill of freedom we felt the first time we went there. But all I can see is the spiders' webs and the way the dirt clung to our clothes.

'We know the place,' says the woman.

'We were in there,' I say. 'I mean, I know we shouldn't have been, I know that was trespassing really. But the door wasn't locked and it was just so easy…'

'Don't worry.' The man smiles, indulging me. 'We aren't about to tell you off, Mrs Holmes.'

'And your friend?' says the woman. Her voice is smooth as Vaseline. 'He—this is a he we're talking about?'

I nod.

'He was with you?' she says.

'Yes.'

'And could you tell us exactly what you saw?'

'I could see out of the window. And I saw someone

running along the path—I just thought there was something odd about him. To be honest, I was worried because I thought perhaps he could see us—I thought he could see in.'

A door slams shut upstairs. I flinch, my pulse skitters off. But I know it's nothing, just a stray draught. I must have left a window open in my bedroom; the breeze will have sneaked through the window and slammed my bedroom door.

The woman reaches out and holds a hand an inch above my wrist, in a little gesture of calming.

'Just relax, Mrs Holmes,' she says. 'You seem a bit jumpy. But, trust me, there's nothing to worry about. You said there was something odd about this person?'

'It's hard to pin down. I mean, it was raining—so it wouldn't be odd to be running, would it? It was like he was looking for something. He kept peering round and I thought maybe he was looking for us. I mean, you do read about people hiring private detectives. When I thought about it afterwards, I realised that was paranoid. That it could have been anything.'

'What was he wearing?' says the man.

I see him clearly in my mind, running between the river and the rowan.

'Suit trousers and a shirt and tie. Office clothes, really.'

They glance at one another. In the woman's face there are sudden patches of red.

'And the time of day?'

'One-thirty. We always met at one—it would have been about one-thirty.'

'And you were actually inside this house you describe when you saw him?'

I nod.

'Have you talked about it with your friend?' she says.

'Yes. But he didn't see anything and he doesn't want to speak to you. He has a family too.'

The man leans forward towards me. He's put down his notepad, his elbows are on his knees. He rubs his palms together, like someone separating wheat. His face is focused, intent.

'How can you be so sure he didn't see?'

'I asked him. He told me.'

'But if he was there with you?'

'He had his back to the window. I saw this man over his shoulder.'

It's there in my head, the image: Will and me at the river house, wrapped around one another. I see it quite precisely. But I don't want them to imagine this. I know how I must look to them in the unforgiving spring light that floods in through the window—the lines from my nose to my mouth that seem deeper every morning, the purple stains under my eyes. A middle-aged mistress. Having a last-chance affair.

'You didn't remark on it at the time, or point this man out to your friend?'

'I told him but by then the man had gone.'

'Right, Mrs Holmes. Anything else you'd like to tell us?'

I shake my head.

The woman tucks her hair behind her ear. She has a slight placating smile.

'We wanted to ask if you might be willing to make a statement?' she says.

'What are the implications of that?'

'It could form part of the prosecution case.'

Her voice is gentle, level.

I hear Max's voice in my head: It would be hard to take just one step and leave it there. I don't say anything.

'It would be very helpful to us,' says the woman. She glances again at the piano, at the photographs. 'You have lovely daughters of your own, Mrs Holmes. You know just how vulnerable young people are. I'm sure you'll understand how vital it is that we find the person who killed this young woman…'

The man opens up his briefcase and finds a lined pad and takes my statement down. This seems to take a long time. I read it through and sign. My signature is rather wild: the pen seems alive, as though the paper is slippery, skating over the page.

'Thank you so much,' they say.

I stand. I'm desperate for them to go now.

'I guess you won't need me any more?' I say.

Again that quick, conspiring glance between them. The woman clears her throat.

'It's possible we might need you to come on an

identification parade. We'll obviously have to confer with Roger, our boss.'

Roger: their boss. The little hairs stand up along my arms.

'But that wouldn't be accurate, would it? If I think I might have seen Sean Faulkner on TV?'

'Well, it wouldn't be watertight. But it might still help us,' she says.

'I'd much prefer just to leave it there,' I tell them.

'Really, you mustn't worry,' she says. 'It's absolutely nothing to get concerned about.'

She picks up the briefcase she hasn't opened.

'Mrs Holmes, I can assure you, you did the right thing in coming to us,' she says. 'So—are you still seeing your friend?'

'I'm not sure.'

What kind of woman doesn't know if she's seeing someone?

'Of course, if your friend would like to speak to us,' she says, 'that would be very helpful. After all, a woman has died. But I can see it's difficult.'

She gives me her card.

'Do get in touch if there's anything else you want to say. If you remember anything.'

They shake hands as they leave, and say how grateful they are.

I close the door behind them, lean with my back to it for a moment, breathing deeply. I tell myself it's over—that I did what was right, what I owed to the woman who died: and now it's over. Nothing more will happen: it's such a little thing I saw.

I go into the living room and open the window wide to get rid of the scent of hair gel, so no one could tell that strangers have been here. Down the road someone is mowing a lawn, the first mow of the season. A scent of sap and crushed grass floats in through the window, the promise of summer, the freshest, greenest smell. I drink it in.

There's a creak behind me. My pulse judders. I think it must be Greg—that Greg has come home and heard everything. I spin round.

Amber is there in the doorway.

'My God. Amber. You frightened me. Why are you here?'

She comes straight up to me. Her eyes are huge, like a startled child's.

'They were police, weren't they, Mum?' She's frightened, her voice is high, the words tumbling over one another. 'They had that look. They were so *serious.*'

Panic seizes me. I wonder how much she has heard.

'What's happened, Mum?' she says. 'Has someone died? I heard them say someone had died. Is it Molly, Mum? Just tell me Molly's OK?'

I know then she can't have heard it all. I wrap my arm round her. She's tense and taut as a wire.

'Everything's OK.' I'm trying to be calm, but my

heart is pounding: I wonder if she can feel it as I hold her. 'It's nothing to do with Molly.'

'Everything can't be OK,' she says. 'You look awful.'

'I'm fine,' I tell her. 'But, Amber—you shouldn't be here.'

'It's March the third, Mum.'

I stare at her blankly.

'You wrote it on the calendar,' she says. 'It's my coursework. I came back for my coursework.' She's spelling it out patiently. 'My *Go-Between* essay, Mum. I forgot it and it has to be in today.'

'Does Mrs Russell know you're here?'

She nods. 'I got permission and everything. Jamila wanted to come as well, but Mrs Russell said she reckoned I probably knew my way home by now. You were on at me about it. Don't you remember? You got really stressed about it. I thought you'd be pleased that I bothered. Anyway, for God's sake, tell me, Mum.'

I tell her just the outline of it—that they came to ask me about the murder we saw on the television.

Her eyes are bright with astonishment.

'So why *you* exactly?'

'I went for a walk by the river,' I tell her, 'before they found the body. And I saw this man who looked like the husband who made the appeal. And I thought I should tell the police—you know, just in case it was relevant.'

She stares at me.

'But this is just so random,' she says. 'I mean, I just

don't get it. You didn't say anything, Mum—when we saw it on television, when they found the body. You didn't seem that interested.'

'I only thought of it later,' I say. 'I only realised later it might be useful.'

There's a deep frown stitched to her forehead. It's the face she has when there's something she can't make sense of.

'So you'll have to go to court and everything?' she says.

'I hope not,' I say. 'Look, I'll give you a lift if you like. I could take you to the bus stop.'

'OK,' she says.

But she just stands there, her perplexity written all over her.

'What were you doing there anyway, Mum? When you went for this walk?'

'It was to do with a work problem. A case, a child I was seeing. I wanted to clear my head about a case…'

Her glance is sharp and glittery, like a blade.

'I didn't know you were into that kind of stuff,' she says. 'Going off for walks to think about things.'

CHAPTER 35

I give Amber a lift to the bus.

'Don't forget to hand in your essay,' I tell her. 'After going to all this trouble.'

'I came home, didn't I, Mum?' she says.

But she's still preoccupied. I leave her at the bus stop with a troubled frown on her face.

When I get home, the post has come. I flick through. Offers of credit: a flyer for a book by the Queen of Clean, which will tell me how to get pumpkin stains off my pine table with a little non-gel toothpaste. And then a packet from Molly. As I open it photographs spill out. There's a note inside, in her rounded, studious handwriting.

'Hi all. Just got these back from Jessops. We came to London for Kev's birthday trip—we went on the London Eye. We had the cake in Trafalgar Square but the wind kept blowing out the candles. Hope you're feeling better, Mum! xxxM.'

The pictures show a group of them in a glass bubble
high in the sky, the spring sun shining bright on them.
The girls have stripy scarves, and poised and nonchalant
smiles; the boys, a little self-conscious, are pulling
faces for the camera. Molly's face is flushed, she has
gleaming liquorice eyes. The city is laid below them
like a great embroidered cloth flung out: you can see
the silver trail of the Thames with its many intricate
bridges. I will send these pictures to my mother: I
think how she will love them, how proud she'll be to
show them round the ward. I look for a long time at
these golden lads and girls with the world spread out
at their feet.

I go to the kitchen. The cups that I put out for the
police, for the drink they didn't want, are still waiting on the tray. I make a coffee but I don't drink it.
Everything is much as usual around me, yet it all looks
different—like when you come back from holiday,
and the shapes and sizes of things seem to have subtly
changed. Till I heard Amber there behind me, I still
half believed that I could limit the damage, and keep
it all safe and secret. But I know now that I have to tell
Greg—that I have to talk to him before Amber does.
I'm dizzy with the sense that everything is slipping
beyond my control.

When Greg comes in that evening, he goes straight
up to his study. Amber is at Lauren's, but she could
come back any time. I know I can't postpone this.

He looks up, surprised, as I open his door.

'I was going to come and find you,' he says. 'There's something I want you to see.'

He takes a piece of shiny card out of his briefcase and hands it to me. He looks happy.

'It's the cover for the book,' he says. 'It only came today.'

It's a drawing taken from a Celtic carving, a tangle and twist of budding branches and foliage: you can see the curl of a fern frond, the patternings of leaves. You can't make out where the shapes begin or end, everything is entwined with everything else, nothing separate: it might all be drawn with a single elaborate line. And as you look you begin to see creatures emerging from the foliage, as though, by some enchantment, the plants are also animals: a tendril of ivy writhes like the coils of a dragon, a stag sprouts antlers like the branches of trees.

'It's beautiful,' I tell him.

He misreads the hesitation in me.

'Are you really, really sure?' he says. 'You don't sound convinced. I need an honest opinion.'

'Really. I love it. You can see so much in it.'

'Fenella wanted me to get your response,' he says. 'You're the nearest I've got to your average punter in the bookshop.'

'You can tell her I really like it,' I say.

'You don't think it's too kind of abstract?' he says. 'I mean, they did have some other ideas too. You don't think it would be better to have some diaphanous woman on it?'

'I think it's lovely,' I say. 'Well done.' I hand it back to him.

I think of the passage I read from his anthology, the woman looking at the man called Froech, and how she used to say of any beautiful thing she saw, that she thought it more beautiful to see Froech in the dark pool. I think how that moved me. I don't know the way from here to where I have to get to.

I go to the window, glance down over the gardens. The sun is setting, lavishly red. Cotton-wool clouds soak up the coloured light like a stain. The river dazzles.

'Greg, there's something I need to tell you.'

He's quite still suddenly. A shadow crosses his face. I move on quickly.

'Some police came here today.'

'Police?' He's baffled.

'Has Amber said anything?' I ask him.

'No, I haven't seen her. Why would she anyway?'

'Because she saw them,' I say. 'She'd come back for her coursework. She was worried. I thought she might have mentioned it.'

His expression is strained, as though he's peering at something that's just out of sight.

'Ginnie, could you just tell me what this is all about?'

'They came because I rang them.' Laying the words out before him like little stones, precise and irrevocable. 'It was about that murder—the woman they found in the river.'

'Good God,' he says. 'You mean you saw something?'

I tell him what I told Amber. That I was by the river. That I went off for a walk because I needed to think about a case.

He frowns.

'Why didn't you ring them straight away?' he says.

'I couldn't decide how significant it was. Then I saw the TV appeal and it made me feel I should do something. Because this man I saw—he was like the man on the appeal—her husband. I mean, I can't be sure, of course, but I think that it was him.'

'Well, it's often the partner, isn't it, in these cases? You've always said that.'

'Pretty much.'

'That poor woman,' he says. 'Well, I'm sure you did the right thing.'

'I hope so,' I say.

He's quiet for a moment. He takes off his glasses and puts them down on his desk and rubs his eyes. It's an old man's gesture. He looks tired suddenly. His head is bowed, he isn't looking at me.

I turn to go, breathing a little more easily. I've done what I had to do, I've told him, and nothing has been destroyed.

'You were by the river, you said?' His voice is light, level, as though this is just a casual enquiry. My heart thuds.

'Yes.'

'That's quite a long way to go just for a walk, I'd have thought. From your clinic.'

'I had a bit of time to spare,' I say.

His head is bent, I still can't see his eyes. In a moment of cold, it enters my mind that he suspects me: that he suspected me long before this moment, before I told him these things.

It's quiet between us for a moment. In the stillness you can hear the smallest sounds, the ugly chime of an ice-cream van, a pigeon that startles in the apple tree in the garden, with a sound like something torn.

'I like it there,' I say. 'I used to take the girls there.'

'Yes, I remember,' he says.

'So—anyway—I just wanted to tell you what happened.'

He looks across at me then. In the strange red light of evening, his eyes seem bright, too bright, as though they're full of tears.

'Will it go any further?' he says.

'I hope not. I really hope not.' Cheerful, confident. 'I'm just assuming that's the last I'll hear of it. That it's all over now… I'll leave you to get on, then,' I say, and turn and go.

But I know that nothing is over. Not even this conversation.

CHAPTER 36

I wait at my favourite table by the window. The bar is empty except for the barmaid. Today her hair is tied with velvet ribbon, and she's wiping glasses with a white cloth with a wide green band. Now and then she holds a glass to the light, checking for smears. There's jazz playing. I look out into the garden. It's changed so much since first we came here. The drifts of dark leaves have all been raked from the lawn, and bulbs are coming up in the grass, little slivers and blades of fresh green. But it's pouring with rain, fat silver drops that rattle and bounce on the terrace and wash the topsoil out of the flowerbeds. You couldn't go out in this weather, in a minute you'd be soaked through.

He's late, he has a preoccupied look. He smells of smoke and rain.

'Perhaps we should wait here a little, see if it stops,' I say.

'OK,' he says.

I buy him a drink. We talk about our other lives. I tell him about my mother's scan and diagnosis.

'Poor her,' he says. 'Poor you.'

I ask about Jake. There's a specialist school they're trying to get him into, but it's such a struggle, he says: the council's refusing to provide the funding. He says they're going to fight it all the way.

The rain is easing off now: the sun is shining behind the cloud, so the pale sky has many faint iridescent colours, like a pearl. Soon we will go to the river house.

'Will...' I watch his hand on the table, his long clever fingers curling around his glass. I think how much I love his hands. I know I have to tell him now. But it's hard to drag the words out.

'Will, I saw Sean Faulkner's TV appeal.'

The words in my mouth are solid things.

He looks up sharply.

'He's the husband of the woman they found in the river,' I tell him.

He's sitting quite still.

'I know who Sean Faulkner is,' he says.

'Will, I think he was the man I saw that day on the river path.'

I feel his gaze on me. He doesn't say anything.

'I made that call,' I tell him. I'm looking at his hand, not looking at him. 'To the incident room.'

I make myself look up then.

His eyes are narrowed as though I am his enemy. His silence scares me.

'Jesus,' he says then.

'Will—how could I have done differently? I was trying to do the right thing. I couldn't just leave it—it would have felt so wrong.'

'The whole thing's wrong,' he says. He's leaning forward, speaking in a low voice—as though afraid people might hear, though there's no one near except the barmaid. I can see the red flecks in his eyes. His voice has a knife-edge of anger, but I don't know who he's angry with, whether it's him or me. Perhaps he doesn't know either. 'We shouldn't have been there anyway. We shouldn't have been doing this. None of this should have happened.'

His mood frightens me. For a moment I can't say anything.

'And then?' he says.

I stare at him blankly.

'What happened?' he says, in that hard voice.

'They came to see me. They took a statement,' I tell him. 'There were two of them, Ray and Karen.'

'Christ.'

'Will. I did everything I could to protect you—to protect us. I told them that I couldn't say who I was with.'

'You said that—that you were with someone?'

'They'd have known,' I say. 'They'd have worked it out. They've been around—they know what people are like. I mean, why would I have been in the river house on my own? She isn't stupid, that woman.'

He's looking at me as though I appal him. I can't believe how rapidly we got here. You're so close to someone they feel like part of your body, you move to a single rhythm. Then just a few words and suddenly this coldness—so quickly, so easily—everything undone.

'I had to do it. Please understand, Will. I know it's difficult—'

He interrupts me.

'Who else knows? Does Greg know?'

'I just told him I'd seen something and I'd rung the police. I said I'd been there because I'd gone off for a walk. It seemed OK.'

'Oh yeah?'

'I mean, he didn't say much...'

I hear the doubt in my voice.

I want this to be over now, for him to come to the river house. I hold this in my mind, as though by some magic I can make it happen. By thinking it, imagining it, I can conjure it up. I want to say, Come and make love to me now, but my lips are stiff and it's hard to form the words.

I push my glass away.

'Are you ready?' I ask.

He doesn't move.

'Will, d'you want another drink? Or shall we go now? It looks like the rain's stopping...'

He sits quite still; he's looking intently at his hands.

'I think we should leave it there, don't you?' he says then. 'After all this?'

It's silent between us for a moment. There's a chink as the barmaid puts down a glass on the bar. A sharp little sound, like something breaking.

'OK.' I force myself to smile. 'Next week perhaps?' Trying to sound casual, but my voice thin, frail, suddenly. The world cracking open.

'I'm busy next week,' he says. 'I'll ring you.'

I'm scared to press him. I could say, Is it over between us, then? Are we ever going to see each other again? I swallow down these questions. I don't want to hear his answers to them, don't want to hear the words.

This is how it ends, then, says a voice in my head. You've often wondered: now you know. It ends with this coldness and wariness in his eyes, here in the empty bar with all the mirrors: watched by an indifferent barmaid wiping glasses, the saxophone playing: keeping your face still, trying to hold back your tears.

'I'm running late. I need to go,' he says.

'Will.' I reach out then, put my hand against his, awkwardly. The warmth of his skin astonishes me always. 'Don't just go. Don't just walk out of my life.'

My throat is sore, as though saying this has hurt me.

He gives me a puzzled look: it's as if he's discovered

I'm not the person he thought. I watch as he walks away from me.

But at the door he turns. I can see that the anger has left him. He's hunched, he looks defeated. He comes back to the table. He reaches out and puts his hand on my hair, pushing my hair from my face: it's a brief, tender gesture. Just for a moment, he's the way he used to be.

'Ginnie, I can't cope with this. I'm sorry.'

I know then that it is really over.

After he's gone, I sit in the bar for a long time, with my empty glass in front of me. I sit very still: as you might sit in the absolute silence after a car crash, afraid to move in case part of you is broken.

C H A P T E R 37

That night, and for many nights afterwards, I wake at four, suddenly and crisply, waking into absolute alertness. Immediately I feel the thickness of the dark, and know there is still a lot of night to get through. I lie awake for what seems like hours, then sink into a fragile sleep just as the first birds stir. When I get up in the morning, my back aches as though I have lifted heavy weights in the night.

On Tuesday I wake from another poor night's sleep to an extravagant spring day, my bedroom curtains filling with light as a sail fills with wind. I push back the curtains, looking down into the garden. At the edge of the lawn, where I never mow, there's a tangle of forget-me-nots and white wild strawberry flowers.

The sound of the phone jolts me. People don't usually ring so early in the day. I know what it is before I answer.

'Ginnie, there's some sad news.' Ursula's voice is

slow and formal, but I can hear the shake in it. 'I'm ringing to tell you that Mum died at three o'clock this morning.'

'Yes,' I say. All other words dry up in me. All I can think is that I haven't sent her the photos, the glittery pictures of Molly with London spread out at her feet. I was going to send them and I know she would have loved them, but I left it too late and now she'll never see them. The finality of this shocks me, like something I've only just learnt.

'They told me she died very peacefully,' says Ursula.

'Are you all right?' I say, stupidly.

'All right-ish,' she says, carefully. 'I mean, it's not exactly unexpected… Dr Spence said it's the time of night that people most often die—everything slows down, apparently, all your metabolism.'

'Yes, I've heard that…'

'Her suffering's over now,' she says. 'In a way it's a blessing that she died before it all got worse. I'm thinking next week for the funeral. Wednesday. Would that suit you?'

I tell her yes. We talk about the service. No flowers, of course: she wouldn't want flowers, she always said they were pointless, after you'd gone. We will sing 'Lord of all Hopefulness'. Afterwards, there will be refreshments at the King's Arms next to the church—and am I happy for her to take care of all the arrangements? Yes, of course I am.

'Oh, and bring some boxes,' she says. 'We'll go

on to the house afterwards and you can have a quick look through and see what you'd like to take. Would that be OK? I mean, I'm perfectly happy to do all the clearing. You know, as I'm right on the spot. It makes much more sense than you having to make lots of trips—and with Amber's exams coming up and everything...'

'That would be wonderful, Ursula.'

'It's no problem,' she says. 'Really.'

I go into the kitchen, where Greg is eating soy milk and cornflakes with *The Times* propped up in front of him. A slice of sunlight falls across the floor. I sit down rather heavily at the table.

'Greg, Mum died this morning.'

'Oh, Ginnie, I'm so sorry.'

Everything feels removed from me. I'm standing outside, just watching, as he pushes aside his cereal bowl and gives me his full attention: you can't go on eating after somebody's died.

He reaches out and pats my arm.

'Are you OK?' Like I said to Ursula.

I nod. 'I just feel a bit shocked. Weird, when we knew it had to happen...'

He studies my face, perhaps relieved I'm not crying.

'You seem to be coping with it very well,' he says.

'I don't know.'

'Perhaps it was a good thing it happened before she got any worse,' he says.

'Perhaps. The funeral's next Wednesday.'

'Hell. I've got a meeting,' he says. 'Well, they'll just have to manage without me.'

'Greg, don't feel you have to come if it's awkward.'

'You'll want me there,' he says.

I think of taking Greg and Amber to the funeral—sorting them out some sober clothes, negotiating with Amber about not wearing anything too revealing, finding them someone to talk to at the funeral tea. These simple tasks seem utterly beyond me.

'Look, I don't suppose Amber will want to come anyway,' I tell him. 'I wouldn't expect her to. Funerals are horrible for children. So you could hold the fort here.'

'Well, if you're sure...'

'Really, I'll be fine. We're planning to start on the house afterwards, me and Ursula. There'd be a lot of hanging around for you.'

'If that's really OK,' he says.

'Really. Greg, you can carry on with your breakfast.'

'Thanks,' he says.

He goes back to his cornflakes.

I ring Molly. She's been to a ball at the Union. There were fairy lights and a marquee, and cocktails with cream on called Blowjobs, so all the lads thought it was really funny asking for two Blowjobs, which Molly thought was *so* infantile; and someone said

Prince William was there, but the person who told her was drunk so she still isn't sure. Her voice keeps cracking: she has a heavy cold.

I tell her about her grandmother.

'Poor Granny,' she says. She's sad, but in a detached way. 'I used to love visiting there, when we were little,' she says. It's as though her grandmother was already in the past for her. 'I loved those cakes she made, the ones with the currants in. And the stream with all the colours.'

She breaks off to cough extravagantly.

'Molly, you ought to be in bed.'

'I can't. I've got a Morphology class.'

'Then miss your class and go to bed,' I tell her. 'Tuck yourself up with some Lemsip.'

I hate her being ill when she's so far away.

'But it's Karaoke tonight. And if I miss my class I won't feel able to go to Karaoke...'

'Have you been taking your vitamins?'

'Well...' A little guilty pause. 'Nobody takes their vitamins, Mum. There's this guy I know, and his parents were coming to take him out to dinner, and they'd given him all these vitamins, and he took all the pills the night before so he wouldn't have to lie... Anyway, Mum, are *you* OK?'

'I'm fine, sweetheart.'

'You don't sound it,' she says. 'Really, Mum, you sound terrible.'

Eva takes me out for a drink at the Cafe Rouge. She's wearing leather trousers and a rather unbuttoned silk shirt. We sit at a table by the window with carnations in a glass. The waiter lights our candle. I tell her about my mother.

She puts her hand on my arm, looking at me anxiously.

'Ginnie. You look awful.'

'It doesn't feel real yet,' I say.

'Is Greg doing all the right things?' she says.

'Greg's being fine,' I tell her. 'I mean, he isn't coming to the funeral. But I said he didn't have to.'

Her eyes widen. I see her throat move as she swallows.

'It was my idea,' I say. 'It just seemed easier.'

She's chewing her lip, as if there's something she's trying not to say. She looks into her glass for a moment.

'It's a big one, when your mother dies,' she says then. 'It changes you. To be honest, I didn't really feel like a grown up till my mother died...' She shrugs, she has a slight, wry smile. 'But she didn't like me very much, and I guess that makes a difference.'

'I keep thinking about these photos that Molly sent,' I say. 'I was going to send them on to Mum, I was thinking how much she'd have loved them. I was going to do it tomorrow.'

'It's always in the middle of something,' says Eva. 'Death's always an interruption. There's sure to be something you didn't do or say.'

The carnations have a powdery scent, like the

smell of an expensive woman. The candle falters in the draught that comes in round the window frame.

Eva tells me about her week, trying to entertain me. Lauren went off to this party with a couple of friends, and Eva was doing the transport, and Lauren rang at one o'clock, sounding completely out of it.

'It was a nightmare,' says Eva. 'These poor bloody parents had gone off for an innocent evening out, and got back to find all these kids tanked up on vodka and puking in their bathroom. The police had been called and everything. And Lauren and her mates were rather the worse for wear, and one of them threw up just as we were coming down the A3, and I didn't have any tissues… It was like being caught in the circles of Hell,' she says.

We order more drinks and listen to Art Pepper. I ask about work. It's still a total pain, she tells me, the kids couldn't give a shit and there are all these bloody targets. At the table beside us a lean young man with dreadlocks is talking to a stylish woman who's smoking a Sobranie. The woman must be about our age. Eva watches curiously as the young man talks with animation and the woman leans across the table, staring into his eyes.

'I don't know, Ginnie,' says Eva then. 'Sometimes I think I should do something really drastic. You know, move to the country or something. I keep on cutting these pictures out of the paper. Swap Shop in the *Evening Standard*—all these fetching cottages you could buy with the price of your London rabbit-hutch.

Watermills in Somerset, and cottages in Suffolk with thatch and pink-washed walls.'

'But, Eva, I didn't think you liked the country,' I say.

'I don't,' she says. 'I hate it really. I remember that, in my saner moments. I grew up in the country and mostly it's just so tedious. No one who looks like they've ever eaten an avocado and you can't get a decent coffee. Anyway, we couldn't possibly move till Lauren and Josh have finished school.' She fiddles with her rings, twisting them round on her fingers as though she can't make them comfortable. 'I don't know, Ginnie,' she says again. 'I know I need to change something, I just don't know what to change...'

When we say goodbye, she wraps her arms around me.

'Poor love. You seem so sad,' she says. 'It's hit you hard, hasn't it? I only wish there was something I could do.'

It rains a lot. We wake to the sound of water, its whisper on the gravel and the percussive sound where it overflows the gutters and taps on the lids of the dustbins. It's dim all day, too dark for March, as if somebody's left off the lights. Snails creep up our downstairs windows, sucking stickily at the pane, their shells dark as walnuts or the colour of honey, and frilled, blotched toadstools grow up out of our lawn. There are smudges of mould on my kitchen wall, as though someone has rubbed it with a dirty eraser. I wipe at the mould with Dettol, but I know it'll grow back soon.

The Thames runs high, spilling over the bank in places. Greg anxiously watches the news. There's flooding in Chertsey, higher up the river, and the press is full of warnings. Hundreds of thousands of people will soon be at risk because of rises in sea and river levels. Flash floods will be more frequent, where Victorian drainage systems can't cope with sudden downpours. Houses will become impossible to insure. Whole tracts of cities may have to be demolished to make green corridors to take the water away. Greg reads these predictions with mounting apprehension.

One evening, when the sun is setting after another day of rain, but the clouds have briefly blown away, we walk down to the end of the road together. The river bank here is urban, built-up, orderly: not like the untended places where I used to walk with Will. Here, there are houses and gardens, pruned and trimmed and manicured, and the river path is paved. It's a beautiful evening, the sky all gentle flower colours, rose and lilac and lavender, the river holding the colours of the sky. Pink water laps up onto the path and in places covers it over, though it hasn't reached the road, and geese paddle there, and slow, poised, ponderous swans, and Chinese ducks with flashes of jade in their wings. There are little dinghies moored here, waiting for summer: you can hear the nervous slap of the water against their hulls. Other families have come to enjoy the brief lull in the weather. Children in wellingtons wade and splash through the water, relishing the shifting landscape, the way the edges of things are less defined. Their voices as they call out have that lonely, echoey quality of voices heard across water.

'I've never seen it this high before,' says Greg.

'No. But there's such a slope from here up to our house,' I say. 'Just look how steep the road is. It would take a massive flood for it to reach up there.'

Greg shakes his head.

'The soil's so wet. It can't hold much more water.'

Nothing reassures him. Sometimes I find him in his study, his face to the window, staring out at the river, and when I enter the room he scarcely seems to hear.

Karen Whittaker rings. They're holding an identification parade and they want me to attend.

They send a car to pick me up. The driver is in uniform. He has a mop of sandy hair and an urge to reassure. The parade takes place in a purpose-built suite, he tells me. It's all very carefully planned, there's really no need to get stressed out about it. The building is split into two, the stooges and the baddies come in by a different door. I must trust him, there's just no way I could come face to face with the suspect.

'The only thing I'd say,' he tells me, 'they're a bit

on the grim side to look at, those places. They could do with a vase of flowers.'

I ask where they get the people from. They have lots of guys on their books, he tells me, it's money for old rope if you're kind of normal-looking. You can make quite a bit of money, just for standing there.

I wait in a bleak grey room with the other witnesses, and we drink thin coffee from polystyrene cups. A uniformed police officer talks us through the procedure: the formal language is somehow reassuring. When I'm taken through to the room with the one-way screen and the line-up, I know the man from the river path immediately. I tell the officer his number.

The sandy-haired policeman drives me home. He still has an air of being concerned about me.

'That wasn't too terrible, now, was it, Mrs Holmes?' he says. 'Nothing to get worked up about?'

No, it was fine, I tell him: though I'm with him on the flowers.

'Mind how you go,' he says. 'Don't do anything I wouldn't.'

I'm slowed down, heavy, vague, moving through the rooms of my house like someone wading through water. Sometimes I think about my mother: sometimes I think about Will. I keep going over the last time I saw him, re-enacting our conversation, flinching from his anger and the way he turned away from me. I ask myself over and over: Should I have done what I did?

Perhaps I should have kept quiet and never have made the call. I wonder this obsessively, tracing out these labyrinths of the mind, worn out with uncertainty. At times it enters my mind that Will behaved badly to me. This gives me a hot, shamed feeling—so I tell myself that I understand his fear. I think of the unsmiling little boy in the photograph, and I know exactly why he behaved as he did.

There are times when I ask myself if it would have been better if I had never met him—if I'd never felt his eyes on me and watched as he pushed up his sleeves, showing the pale skin of his wrists and the lilac pattern of veins. Anyone else would say this, surely—Eva, Clem—if I told them. That it would have been so much better if none of this had happened. But I can't make myself feel that: I don't regret what I've done. I just want everything to be the way it was—before I saw Sean Faulkner on the river path.

At times I think of Will with startling vividness. A sudden image of him will come to my mind unbidden, clear and precise as a flashback—the touch of his hand, the remembered scent of his skin. Or there'll be a man ahead of me on the pavement—and something about him will make me think of Will—his short greying hair, or the angle of his shoulders. Though 'think' is the wrong word. Because I see him, feel him, as though he is here with me.

I look at the picture for March on the calendar in my kitchen—the lovers at the railway station. They're meeting again after being parted, they're clinging to one another. Stained light through red glass falls over them. She's kicking up her stiletto heels as she hugs him, and he has brought her flowers in white paper. I want to be the woman in that picture, with her trim little skirt and her flirty shiny shoes and her hair flying everywhere and her lover's arms all round her. I cannot think of any happiness like that happiness: meeting after an absence, held in your lover's arms.

CHAPTER 38

We park our cars in the drive, behind our mother's car.

The grass is long, the lawn littered with shaggy dandelions. Unlived-in, places so quickly start to revert to the wild.

'I'll need to find someone to cut the grass,' says Ursula. 'Before we get the estate agents in.'

She unlocks the back door: she has to push to open it, there's a soft heavy heap of letters and free newspapers inside.

She's wearing a black silk suit she bought specially for the funeral: the fabric is rather beautiful, with a prismatic sheen like oil on water. Now she pulls off the jacket and rolls up the sleeves of her shirt. She heaps the letters on the kitchen table.

'I'll deal with those later,' she says.

There's a list our mother was making flung down on the dresser—tomatoes, kitchen paper—things she was planning to buy when she was taken into hospital. She's briefly present in her so-familiar loopy, liquid writing, in the plans she was making, the things she was going to do. I hand the list to Ursula but we don't say anything. The hymns that I mouthed soundlessly because I had no breath still resonate inside me: I can taste the egg-and-cress sandwiches I didn't want to eat.

'I thought we could just go round and get a sense of what there is,' she says. 'And anything you want you can take now.'

The house has a musty, wet-earth smell: she never heated it properly, however much we urged her to.

'Let's start in the living room,' says Ursula. 'Bring your box.'

The curtains are drawn. Ursula pushes them aside. Long fingers of light reach in. I think of the last time I was here, eating Victoria sponge, our mother flicking through the photographs I'd brought. The stillness in the house is a palpable thing, as though the texture of the air has thickened, changed.

'These are all yours,' says Ursula. She points to the mantelpiece, and the pictures of Molly and Amber.

I pile the photographs up in the box. This taking back of what has been given unnerves me. I have such a strong sense of the transience of everything—how ownership is temporary, and the things you gave, however whole-heartedly, are really only lent: and how mysterious it is that, most of the time, we believe it to be otherwise.

'Do you ever feel life's so precious,' I say, 'and yet
you spend so much of it being cross or impatient, or
longing for something to end, or standing in the queue
in Sainsbury's?'

'I know what you mean,' she says.

The tick of the clock jars in the stillness. Ursula
trails her fingers along the books in the bookshelf—
our father's prize books from school, various novels
our parents had been given: I never saw either of them
reading any of these books.

'Anything else you want?' says Ursula.

I look round at the books, the landscapes on the
walls. It's all too familiar, too full of ghosts, of memory.
I shake my head.

We go to our mother's bedroom. Her lipsticks on
the dressing table, her hairbrush with the grey hairs
caught in the bristles—these things seem to hold out
some promise that you could reach her, touch her.
Ursula opens the wardrobe. It's crammed with clothes,
mostly hanging in plastic bags from the dry cleaners.
A smell of Blue Grass and mothballs brushes against
us. Smelling her scent, I feel grief tug at my sleeve. I
know it's waiting there, just round the corner, biding
its time, waiting to ambush me.

At the bottom of the cupboard, there are heaps of
shoes. She hadn't worn some of them for years, like
the suede court shoes we used to dance around in
when we were children.

'What did she keep it all for?' I say.

'For when it came in useful,' says Ursula dryly. 'It's

what she was brought up to do, wasn't it? People did then—they kept things, they didn't just chuck them, they mended or darned them, they kept them for a rainy day...'

It's hard to breathe in here, as though these things use up all the air.

'Hey,' says Ursula. She points to a round hat box up at the top of the cupboard. 'It must be that pink hat she liked, that she used to wear to church. I might take that myself.'

She moves a chair and climbs on it, reaching out to the hat box.

'It could be good for my fairy-tale book,' she says. 'For Beauty, in Chanel with little white gloves.'

She gets down with the hatbox, opens it. Dust motes float. She takes out the hat and twirls it on one finger. It has an old smell—dust, damp. It's palest pink, made of some ruched frail fabric: but not as pretty as I remembered. It doesn't look elegantly retro, just rather dreary and faded.

'I don't know,' she says, doubt creeping into her voice. 'Maybe it's not quite right.'

She pushes a wisp of hair behind her ear. All her lipstick has worn off: her face looks older, harder. She puts the hat back in the box.

I want this to be over now. I want to be somewhere else, somewhere bright and banal, a shopping centre, a motorway service station, with packets of crisps for sale and rowdy children. Not here in the silence, with the past pressing in.

'We ought to just check the bureau before you go,' says Ursula, as though she's read my thought. 'It'll only take a moment...'

In the dining room, the light bulb has gone, and the only light comes through the narrow glass door that leads into the garden. Outside, you can see where the heavy hedge that overhangs the stream is just coming into leaf. Long grass with daffodils in it laps up to the door: the daffodils are dying back now, their brown-paper leaves creased and bent. There's a swimmy emerald light.

The bureau is closed with a key that is kept in the lock. Ursula opens it up: it's all very tidy, orderly, inside—places for stamps, for pens. She unlocks the top drawer, and takes out a batch of the letters I wrote to our parents from university, neatly held in an elastic band. There are boxes of old photographs. Ursula picks one out, a woman with a tight fifties perm and her skirt pushed out over a stiff net petticoat. She blows the dust away.

'Who on earth are all these people?' she says. 'I mean, d'you know who this is?'

I shake my head.

'All this history that just gets lost,' she says. 'These people we don't know. And now there's no one left to tell us. We could be related to them, and they're just like strangers.'

Underneath, there's a white album tied with ribbon.

'Good God. I'd completely forgotten this,' she says.

She puts the album down on the dining-table and unties the bow.

The photographs are protected by sheets of tissue paper, and a sprig from our mother's wedding bouquet, a flower blue as smoke, is pressed in the front of the album; the flower looks as if it might dissolve in the slightest movement of air. We look through. The tissue whispers and rustles like fallen leaves. Our mother is wearing a suit, a hat with a veil of net, and elaborate formal make-up—thin pencilled-in eyebrows, dark lipstick with a Cupid's bow. There are group pictures, our parents with three bridesmaids in pale satin, and all the relatives with their carefully composed smiles. And then a series of just the two of them, close-ups in front of a rose bed. There's one where he's turned to her, gazing at her, his lips curved in a half-smile of such contentment, gazing at her as though she is infinitely precious.

Ursula touches the picture lightly with her fingertips, a fractured, tentative movement, as though to check that it's real.

'He looks like he can't believe his luck,' she says. Her voice is slow, exhausted. 'He really loved her once, didn't he? He loved her so much. The way he's looking at her. He really loved her.' She closes the album abruptly, pushes it away from her across the shiny surface of the table, as though it could burn her fingers; her face, half in shadow, looks gaunt suddenly. 'What happened? What happens to love, Ginnie?'

She's stricken: her voice is absolutely bleak. She shakes her head, tears spilling.

I put my arms round her. She holds me urgently for a moment, then pulls away and scrubs at her face with a tissue.

She tries to clear her throat.

'You might as well take your own letters back, Ginnie,' she says, thickly. 'If you want them.'

I don't want them, but I can't think what else to do with them. I put them in my box.

But Ursula can't stop crying. 'Shit,' she says. She pushes the tears aside crossly with her hand.

In the drinks cabinet I find the brandy that our mother kept to put in her Christmas cake. I take it to the kitchen and pour it into tumblers that are still in the dishrack, washed by our mother before she went into hospital, still waiting there for someone to put them away. The brandy is cheap and fierce but it warms us. We sit at the formica-top table and drink.

'It's so quiet,' I say. 'Quiet in a different way—not like if the house was just empty for a while because she'd gone out shopping...'

Ursula nods.

'It spooks me, quite honestly,' she says.

She looks crumpled, in spite of her glamorous clothes, all the disarray of grief. I know I must look the same. She takes a long slow sip of brandy. She isn't looking at me.

'D'you ever dream about here?' she says slowly. 'You know, about the house? About childhood?'

The question shocks me. It's as though the brandy or the grief has loosened something in her.

'Yes,' I say. 'Especially when I was pregnant. Dreams of planes crashing on the garden, of awful things being dug up.' I'm careful, I don't want her to stop talking. 'What do you dream of?'

'Not nice dreams…' She's looking away from me, twisting her wedding ring round and round on her finger. 'I dream about the shouting, sometimes,' she says. 'Still. I still dream about it. Isn't that weird? After all this time, all these years. About the shouting and the bad nights, and…you know…all that.'

'But, Ursula, you always hate it if I try to talk about it…'

She looks at me. She has a lucid gaze, green as leaves.

'We all have our ways of coping,' she says. 'Your way is to talk about things. That's not my way, Ginnie.'

I put my hand on her wrist. Her skin is cold. All my life I've wanted for her to see things as I do, but none of that matters now. We stay like that for a moment, then she finishes her brandy and gets up. She gives herself a little shake, like someone coming up out of the sea, shaking cold water from her.

'Can we just look in the shed before you go? I'd rather have you with me. Is that OK?'

'Of course,' I tell her.

We go out into the back garden. The grass seems even longer at the back of the house, washing up to the patio like green water. There's a haze of drifting thistledown, and the stream is a sludgey, viscous purple under the straggling hedge. Inside the shed there's a sweet grass-and-sunlight scent of last year's apples.

From the shelf at the back, Ursula lifts out our mother's old gramophone.

'This might be worth a bit,' she says. 'Don't you think? I bet people collect this kind of thing... Could you bring the records?'

They're 78s, brittle and amazingly heavy, with crumbling cardboard covers in faded pinks and browns. I pick them up and follow her.

She puts the gramophone down on the lawn and opens it up. The crushed grass has a sappy smell.

She looks up at me with a glint of excitement. I suddenly see something quite different in my sister—the part of her that paints hibiscus flowers with petals like fire and glittery snakes creeping through. It enters my mind that I don't really know her at all, that when she's not with me she may be entirely different: admiring in her a bright, brittle courage I didn't know was there.

'Shall we?' she asks me.

'Yes.'

She chooses a record from the pile. Louis Armstrong: After You've Gone. She slips it onto the turntable. She takes a new needle from the little box in the side and puts it into the arm. She winds the handle and moves the silver arm down onto the record. It prickles, fizzes, bursts into fabulous life, singing out through the spring gardens.

Ursula smiles up at me.

'They'll hear it for miles,' she says.

We stand there and listen right through. The reproduction is crackly yet lavish. It's music to dance to, in a backless dress red as flame, with a man who pulls you close, his hand resting lightly on the bare skin just below your shoulder blade: music to make love to. When it comes to an end, the needle settling into the groove in the middle of the record, we stand very still for a moment.

Ursula lets out a little sigh.

'That's that, then,' she says. 'All over.'

'Yes.'

She still doesn't move for a moment. The silence of the garden seems more absolute now. You can taste it on your tongue, this stillness, this absence.

She bends down to pack up the gramophone.

'OK,' she says briskly. 'You're happy for me to see what I can get for it?'

'Sure. It's a lovely thing but I don't suppose we'd play it again.'

I pick up the records and follow her into the house.

She turns to face me.

'OK, then, Ginnie. Take care.'

We hug.

'You're sure you'll be OK? Paul will be there when you get home?'

She nods.

'I'll be fine,' she says.

'Just let me know if there's anything I can do,' I tell her.

I leave her sorting the mail into orderly heaps.

About five miles north of Southampton, quite suddenly, I know I have to stop. I pull off the road and weep, parked by the rundown café, the overflowing rubbish bags, the bicycle that has been dumped there, the tangled bramble flowers: crying and crying for my mother and all that is now past mending—for the photos I never sent her and the things that we never said and whatever happens to love.

CHAPTER 39

The call comes on a Thursday, the day I used to see Will. Outside, the wind is blustering in my garden, and ripping all the blossom from the pear tree.

'Now—am I speaking to Ginnie?'

My pulse skitters off. I don't recognise the number, but the voice reminds me of Will.

'Yes.'

'Ginnie, I'm so sorry to bother you. This is Roger. You remember? Roger Prior. We met in that bar in the autumn.'

'Yes, I remember.'

The wind sneaks in round the ill-fitting door of my kitchen; I feel its cold touch on my skin.

'So, Ginnie, how are you?' His voice is gentle with concern.

I tell him about my mother.

'I'm so sorry,' he says. 'This is terrible timing,

then. You'll have to forgive me.' I'm very aware of his careful courtesy. I remember Will once telling me that you have to be a bit of an actor to be a good detective. 'Ginnie, what I wanted—I'd really like to have a chat with you about this case of ours. Maria Faulkner. I think Karen may have mentioned that I'm leading the investigation, for my sins?'

I swallow hard.

'I thought that was all over,' I tell him. 'I went to the identification parade.'

'I know you did,' he says. 'Well, thank you so much. You've already been extremely helpful, Ginnie. I just wanted to have a talk with you—just quite informally—about where we go from here...'

He waits for me. I don't say anything.

'We could meet anywhere,' he says. 'Any place that you'd be comfortable.'

'I wouldn't be happy with you coming here,' I tell him.

'No. I understand. What I wondered—there's a café in the main road, quite near where you live. Called Markham's—it's got little trees outside. Would that suit you?'

I know the place, I've passed it sometimes. It looks expensive, with white cloths on the tables and trim bay trees in metal tubs flanking the door. It enters my mind that he has chosen our meeting-place with care: that he wants me to be at ease there. The thought chills me.

'I could do later this morning, Ginnie. Perhaps eleven-thirty?'

I have no reason to refuse.

It's stylish, as I expected. There are stripped untreated floorboards, and bunches of lavender on the tables, and black and white photos of lovers on bridges in Paris, and, over the sound system, classical guitar.

He's sitting at a corner table: I guess that he's chosen it so we won't be overheard.

He reaches out and takes my hand. He's just as I remember: the clever self-deprecating smile, the scent of vanilla, the handshake that seems to last a little too long.

'Ginnie. I'm so grateful to you.'

We sit.

'I hope this is OK,' he says. He hands me the menu. 'A coffee? Something to eat?'

I know I am being seduced.

'Just a cappuccino.'

He says he'll have the same.

The waitress has a long red skirt with bits of ribbon hanging from it, and those flat clumpy boots you have to be really beautiful to wear. He's charming to her.

'I'm sorry about your mother,' he says to me.

'Well, she'd been ill, so it wasn't a surprise.'

'It's still a shock, though, isn't it?' he says. 'My father died last year, and I was pretty cut up about it. It's that time of life for us, isn't it? Our kids grow-

ing up, our parents getting frail. And we're the ones
caught in the middle. Keeping it all going.'

He's resting his arm along the back of his chair.
Everything about him says he's so relaxed and casual,
that this is just a friendly conversation without conse-
quence. But his eyes don't leave my face, eyes of an
elusive colour, between grey and green, like the leaves
of olive trees. They narrow as he watches me.

The waitress brings the coffee. It's strong, with bitter-
sweet flecks of chocolate on top. I drink gratefully.

'You've got daughters, haven't you?' he says. 'Karen
said how gorgeous they were—when she saw their
photographs, when she met you.'

I nod. 'Amber's sixteen and Molly's just starting
her degree.'

He smiles, showing his perfect teeth.

'You must be very proud.' He tips sugar into his
coffee. 'My eldest lad just started college too,' he says.
'It's quite a wrench, isn't it? You think you'll be glad
not to have that ghastly music playing, and then you
miss them horribly.'

'Yes,' I say.

He sips his coffee. A little silence falls.

'So, Ginnie. About Maria Faulkner.'

He's like me, in a way: he's someone who watches
people, I can see that. When I put my coffee down so
carefully, trying to keep it steady, yet it still slops into
the saucer, because my hands are shaking: I know he
sees.

'To get straight to the point, Ginnie: your evidence

is important to us. I want to ask if you'd be willing to go a little further for us.'

He waits for my response, those cool grey eyes on me.

'It's difficult,' I say.

'I know it's difficult, Ginnie. But you come across to me as someone who would want to do the right thing. Someone who's very responsible. I think that's why you rang the incident room—because you wanted to do the right thing. Even when it's difficult.'

'Why does it matter? Why is it so important—what I saw?'

He's leaning forward, his hands clasped loosely in front of him on the table: immaculate, a surgeon's hands.

'OK,' he says. 'I'm going to take you into my confidence. Let me tell you how this all fits together—let me tell you the story, Ginnie…'

'Yes. I think you should.'

In spite of everything, I feel a surge of curiosity.

'We've had our suspicions all along. About Sean Faulkner—the man you picked out from the line-up.'

He waits for me to respond. I ask him why.

'Sean Faulkner has a history of violence towards women, and a total failure to take any responsibility for it,' he says. 'You know how these men are. The scum who beat up their wives. The pathetic excuses they make.' A flicker of anger moves across his face. I glimpse the toughness in him that he's seeking to conceal. 'You'll get a man who says, I was drunk, I couldn't help myself. Well, how many guys did he beat up on the way back from the pub, then? But you know about that, don't you? You know about violent men.'

This shakes me. I've attributed such intuitive powers to him, such powers to read me, that I think for a moment that he is talking about my father.

'Through the work you do, Ginnie,' he says, as though responding to my confusion.

'Yes,' I say.

'Sean Faulkner had recently been abusive to a neighbour who—according to Sean, at least—had flirted with Maria. And there were inconsistencies in the story he told. Like—when we went to his house, after he reported Maria's disappearance, he told us he hadn't washed any clothes, but the washing machine had recently been used. But we'd nothing concrete, nothing to link him with the place where Maria's body was found.'

He leaves a small, significant pause. I feel the thud of my heart.

'Where did he kill her?' I say.

'We think he strangled her at home during a row, then put her body in the rubbish bag and drove her to the river.'

'Why there? Why that part of the river?'

'It's where they used to live,' he says. 'When people dump bodies it's always somewhere they know—where they've once lived, or where they were brought up or something. They need to understand the lay of the land... We think he changed into his trunks and trainers and walked out into the river and sank her body. Probably more or less where she was found—there's an eddy near the bank there, we don't think the tide moved her much. I guess he didn't realise the body would come to the surface. The river's a great place to hide a body—but only for a while.'

'And when I saw him?' I say.

'You saw him the morning after he reported her missing. Our theory is that he went back to check that her body was still hidden, that he hadn't left any traces. Maybe he worried he'd left something—a watch, some footprints. That's why he went back in daylight. He claims he was at work then, but he doesn't have an alibi, not for the time you saw him.'

His eyes rest on me, his enigmatic gaze.

'Yours is our only sighting that links him to the place where he dumped her body. And it was just the morning after Maria disappeared.'

The palms of my hands are wet.

'She was twenty-three, Ginnie,' he says quietly. He doesn't say, Just four years older than Molly; but the thought hangs there, in the air between us. 'Twenty-three and one week. Here, let me show you.'

He takes a photograph out of his wallet and places it in front of me: his hands are gentle, as though this image is a fragile, precious thing. It's a colour photo, rather blurred and amateurish, three women in a bar, their drinks on the table before them, the flash reflecting redly in their eyes.

He points to one of them.

'This is Maria,' he tells me.

She has Italian colouring—coppery skin, and crinkly Mediterranean hair, and dark eyes fringed with heavy, curly lashes. She's all dressed up for her evening out, in a strappy top and embroidered jeans, the kind of clothes that Molly or Amber would wear. She has glitter at her wrists and throat, and lipstick of a sweet, ripe red. She's vivid and gleaming, her face all bright with laughter, with an air of surprise about her, as though she looked up suddenly when someone called her name.

I stare at the image of her—her face on the edge of laughter and the soft dark mass of her hair. Tears well in me. I try to hide this, but I know he sees.

'This was at her birthday party, the week before she was killed,' he says. 'She'd been flirting with a neighbour. We think she was killed for flirting.'

He leans towards me, intent.

'Ginnie, I want to ask you to be a witness for us. I'm asking you to help us nail this man.'

I sit there a long time, not looking at him, staring down into my coffee. There are pictures in my mind, clear and precise as flashbacks, as though these are things that have already happened. The pain in Greg's face, all his confusion and bitterness; Molly, puzzled, reproachful; Amber in a wild mood, scratching her arms or cramming her mouth with pills.

Roger waits for me, just sits there patiently. I know he will wait for ever.

'Could I give my evidence anonymously?' I say. 'You know—behind a screen?'

'Ginnie, I wish I could say that I could make that happen for you. But it's up to the judge. And judges *have* done that occasionally, but only in terrorist cases, when there are lives at stake.' He smiles at me a little. 'Which we couldn't really argue in this case.'

I feel ashamed that I asked.

'The person I was with,' I say slowly. 'You know about that, don't you?'

A slight nod.

'I know what you told Karen,' he says cautiously.

'Would I have to say who I was with? Why I was there?'

'It would make your evidence more solid,' he says. 'But of course I quite understand that there are reasons why you might not want to talk about it…'

He's staring down at his hands that are clasped on the table in front of him, as if he's studying his skin for flaws.

'Ginnie, there's something I need to tell you,' he says. Setting the words down carefully in front of me, as though afraid they could hurt me. 'You need to know there are rumours in the office—I mean, people do talk, you know how people are.'

He leaves a silence, for me to ask the question.

My voice is thin, reluctant.

'And what do they say exactly?'

'The rumours are that it was Will Hampden—that you were involved with Will.'

My mouth dries up. I shake my head.

'We just had a drink together. We had a case in common. We were talking about a case.'

I try to think back to that moment in the wine bar, when I first met Roger. Were we sitting too close? Did we have a hungry look when we looked at one another? Roger would have been able to read us: I know that.

'Anyway, Will's a family man,' I tell him. 'I certainly had that impression. I don't imagine… I mean, it wouldn't be like him, surely, to be involved with someone. His family matters too much to him.'

His eyes on me, the slightest knowing smile.

'That's much what he said about you,' he says.

My heart lurches.

'So Will knows this—that this is what people are saying?'

'Ginnie, he works there…' He leans towards me. 'I felt you ought to know.' Gentle, as though he's seeking to protect me.

I don't look at him, though I know his eyes are on me. I would like to be anywhere but here.

'We all have something unsatisfied in us,' he says. 'There's no shame in that, Ginnie.' His voice is very quiet: I can only just hear him above the sound of the guitar. 'Most of us have been there, or somewhere pretty close.'

He sits there for a moment, waiting for me.

'Tell me where you are now,' he says then. 'Tell me what you're thinking.'

'I don't know what's right,' I say.

'I'm no philosopher, Ginnie,' he says. 'That isn't where I'm coming from. I deal with what's in front of me. I'm here to try and get justice for people who've been silenced, and for their families.'

'I know that.'

'A woman has been killed, Ginnie. Doesn't that take precedence over everything?'

'I just need to think my way through this,' I tell him.

'I know you do,' he says. 'I know you're a thoughtful person.' He's relaxed again, as though he has all the time in the world. 'Let me try and tell you where I'm coming from, Ginnie. While you think it through. You know, I'm a romantic, in a way. Hard to believe, perhaps.' He shrugs, with that self-deprecating smile. 'But I'm passionate about our criminal justice system—with all its failings. That we seek to get justice for wrongs done to strangers—isn't that a wonderful thing? That excites me still. That's a hell of an achievement, don't you think? To seek for justice on behalf of strangers…'

His words hang in the silence between us.

'If I do this, people will get hurt,' I say in a small voice.

'Yes,' he says. 'I can't protect you from that. I would if I could but I can't.' And when I don't say anything, 'Think it over, Ginnie.'

He hands me his card, closing my fingers down

over it, in one of those intimate gestures he likes, his smooth, cool skin against me.

He pays. We part on the pavement.

I walk down the road to my car. The wind is stronger now, banging at the awning outside the café. I pass under a blossoming tree, white petals sleeting down. Glancing back, I see how briskly he walks, as though he has made himself late for something important, though when he was talking to me he seemed to have for ever. Maria's image burns into my mind.

I turn. I have to run to catch up with him.

'Roger.'

He turns sharply to face me.

It's hard to talk. The wind keeps pushing my hair into my mouth and I'm out of breath from running. White blossom falls on us.

'I'll do it. I'll go to court. I'll give evidence.'

He puts his hand very lightly on my shoulder; I sense how everything eases in him.

'Thank you,' he says. 'Thank you.'

'There's something else I wanted to say... The person I was with. He didn't see anything. It's stupid, but I just can't remember if that came out in our conversation. He had his back to the path, I know he didn't see.'

'It's OK, Ginnie. You told me already,' he says. He keeps his hand on my shoulder, as though afraid if he lets me go that I will change my mind. 'Now, remember. Any doubts or worries, you ring me. I'll always be happy to hear from you. Any time, it doesn't matter, day or night, just ring.'

CHAPTER 40

I'm sitting at the kitchen table when I hear Greg come through the door. He comes straight into the kitchen. He puts his briefcase down on the table.

'I've got something for you,' he says. He's smiling.

He opens his briefcase.

'Your book,' I say.

I recognise the pattern on the cover, the tangle of branches, the dragons. But now it's richly coloured, blue and purple and green, the colours of forests and seas. There's a fragment of pattern on the spine to catch your eye on a bookshelf. I take all this in at a glance, everything sharp, clear. I wish this hadn't happened today.

He's about to hand it across to me. But he sees my face, pulls back. He puts the book down on the table between us.

'Ginnie. What's going on?' A thread of alarm in his voice.

'Greg, I need to talk to you.' My voice is slow, dull.

He has that wary, beaten look I've noticed before on his face. He sits down heavily at the table. The wind has dropped. It's very quiet.

'Someone rang me today,' I tell him. 'The detective who's leading that murder case. I had to go and talk to him.'

His mouth is set in a hard line.

'You told me that it was all over,' he says. He stares at me. His pupils seem tiny and needle-sharp through the lenses of his glasses.

'They said my evidence was crucial to the case.'

He has his hand in front of his face, as if he's shielding himself from a blow.

There's a moment you can't go back from. Everything will change, with what I am going to say.

'Greg—what I need to tell you... When I said I was there on my own, that was a lie.' My throat is thick, clogged-up. 'I wasn't there on my own. I was with a friend...'

He's just looking at me, not saying anything. I wish he would say something. He makes a little gesture with his hand, as though to ward this off or push it away.

'It shouldn't have happened,' I say, 'and it's over now.'

'Who is it?' he says then. His voice sounds

different—thin, clipped, as though he's forgotten to breathe.

'It isn't anyone you know.'

He's turned away from me.

'It's Max, isn't it?' he says. A knife-edge of anger in his voice now. 'I've often wondered about you and Max. I can't stand the guy. He's so fucking full of himself. I should never have let you go off on those weekends with him. I trusted you, I suppose. I've been a bloody fool…'

'It isn't Max,' I say. 'It's nothing to do with Max.'

He stares; he's trying to take this in.

'Who is it, then?' he says.

'It's someone I knew through work—you've never met him.'

He doesn't say anything for a while. The silence between us is like water rising, as though the room is filling up with it. Behind him on the wall I can see Ursula's picture, the Little Mermaid, diving down through the blue translucent water. I think of Molly when she was little, staring at the picture, her eyes dark and wide-open and troubled. But won't she drown, Mum? So deep down under the sea. Anyone would drown, Mum. Under all that water.

'Do you love him?' he says then.

I had planned to say, 'It was stupid, it didn't mean anything', wanting to find some crumb of comfort for him: but I can't quite say the words.

'I suppose so. Yes. I suppose I did love him… Greg, I'm so sorry. I didn't want to hurt you.'

He raises his eyebrows slightly, as if this doesn't even warrant a reply. He looks different to me, someone I don't recognise: as though saying the things I've said and doing the things I've done has made him into a stranger.

'So exactly how many other people did you tell before me?'

'Only the police—well, I didn't say who it was… I didn't want to tell you,' I say. 'It's over, and I didn't want you to know. I didn't want to hurt you like that. But they're asking me to give evidence. So it's possible some of this might come out in court—you know, why I was there.' I feel so tired now: it's an effort to drag out the words. 'And I didn't want anything to come out in court that you didn't know about me… I didn't want to put you in that position.'

'It's a bit late for that, isn't it?' His voice is hard and dry. 'To worry about what I think?'

'It's a weird time of life for us,' I say. 'So much is changing—Molly going and everything. I know that's no excuse. But I guess it panicked me a bit. There's just this feeling so much is coming to an end.'

He's looking straight at me now, with a quiet, controlled dislike.

'I've wondered, of course,' he says. 'There's this expression you have sometimes. This secret smile. Closed-in. But I'm not a mind-reader, Ginnie. And most of the time I thought you were happy enough. You've seemed so much more relaxed recently, over the past few months. Happier in yourself somehow…

Fuck,' he says. He screws up his face, realising what he's saying. 'So what was wrong with us exactly?' he says.

'It's not like that. It's not that anything's wrong. That isn't why...' What I'm saying isn't true. I think how he moved out of our bed. My voice fades.

'This friend of yours—has he gone to the police too?'

'He didn't see anything.'

'Maybe not. Or maybe that's what he's saying. But has he gone to the police?'

'No.'

'So he's just left you on your own with this thing? This is the person you gave your love to—someone who could do that to you?'

'He's in a difficult position.'

'Ginnie, I don't begin to understand you...'

He stands up and closes his briefcase. His face is composed, but I see that his hands are shaking.

'What I don't get,' he says dryly, 'is why on earth you were by the river anyway. I thought people usually found a proper room somewhere. In a hotel or something. You could at least have behaved like adults.'

He walks out quietly, his briefcase in his hand. But he trips as he goes upstairs. There's a torrent of curses. I hear the raw anger in his voice: I've never heard him swear like this before. The study door slams.

His book is still on the table. I pick it up: it has a new crisp smell. As I flick through it falls open at the dedication. There's a fragment of Celtic pattern, and

below it: For Ginnie, who showed me the meaning
of Findabhair...

I have a feeling like when you're about to weep,
but no tears come.

C H A P T E R 41

I lie awake for hours. My pulse skitters as though I've had too much coffee, a pointless, febrile energy surges through me. I feel as though I will never sleep again.

Eventually I get up. My alarm clock says three o'clock. I push the curtains wide, open the window, hoping to be soothed by the immensity of the night. For once it isn't raining. I breathe in the rich night scents of flowers and earth. There's a moon, almost full, its cold white washing over everything. I glance down into the garden: I can see the palest glimmer from the narcissi under the apple tree, absolutely without colour in the moonlight. I start, seeing somebody there, a dark bundled shape on the bench beneath the tree. It's Greg, in his dressing-gown. It must be cold in the garden, I can feel the chill of the damp air on my skin: but he doesn't move, just sits there. He's hunched over: he looks so old and alone. I'm frightened.

I grab my dressing-gown and go downstairs. He must have heard me opening the door, but he doesn't turn. I haven't put anything on my feet: the grass is drenched with dew.

I walk across to the bench. Once your eyes adjust, you can see a lot in the light of the moon, all the detail of the garden—the heavy, dense mass of the hedge: the silvered leaves of the apple tree, where the moon is caught in the woven nets of its branches. There's a bright scattering of stars. The world feels vast and hollow.

I go to stand by him. He doesn't look at me.

'Greg. How long have you been out here?'

He doesn't reply. Little sounds scratch the edges of the stillness—a siren, the high percussive bark of a fox.

I sit beside him on the bench.

'You ought to come in,' I say. 'You'll get so cold.'

I put my hand on his arm. He tenses at my touch. His quietness frightens me, and the way he doesn't look at me. I see the raw grief in his face. I'm numbed by how much I've hurt him.

'Greg. You can't stay here.'

'I need to think,' he says.

'You need to get some sleep,' I say. 'You can't think if you don't sleep.'

He says nothing.

I feel dizzy out here without walls, under the huge night sky and the spill of silver over everything. I breathe in the chill sweetness of the air.

'Promise me you'll come in soon,' I say. 'Please, Greg.'

'I'll come in when I'm ready,' he says.

My feet hurt with the cold, the hem of my dressing-gown is heavy with wet. I realise I am shivering. I didn't know it got this cold in April.

I go back to bed and lie there not sleeping. Scenes from the past flicker through my mind, with a kind of feverish brilliance. I think of the Burns Night dinner where I met him. Of his elegance in his dinner jacket, and his cufflinks shaped like little fish, and the story he read, its leaps of logic, the way it was stitched quite randomly together like bits of dream: the four companions walking together in a familiar land, and the mist that fell over everything, and when it rose, all the things they knew had vanished, all their flocks and herds and houses—just the four of them in this bright wide emptiness, alone. I can see the look on his face as he thrust the book into my hand, showing me where he'd written his phone number on the title page—an eager, hopeful, hungry look, as if I was something he felt he had to have. I knew then what my life would be like, I thought it was all laid out before me, a path through a clear country. Perhaps I should have listened more carefully to the story he read.

I tell myself that in all this, it's Amber who's most important. That I'll do all I can to keep her life protected and familiar, at least till she leaves home. That this is what really matters. Deciding this, I sleep.

* * *

I wake with a start at eight o'clock. I must have forgotten to set my alarm, or turned it off in the night.

I grab my dressing-gown and go downstairs.

Greg's overnight case is in the hall. He's standing in the kitchen, drinking coffee.

'Greg—what's happening?'

'I need to do some thinking,' he says. 'I need a bit of space to think things through.'

I don't say anything.

'I'm going to stay with Mother—I've just rung her. I'm going over there straight after my afternoon seminar. I can get into work from there, it's really quite straightforward. You can take the Metropolitan Line to Baker Street, and the Bakerloo Line to Wimbledon, and then I'll get a taxi or the overground train…'

He just keeps talking and talking, wanting to postpone the things we need to say.

'But it'll take you ages…'

'I'll manage,' he says.

'And you won't have enough clean shirts—I was going to do a shirt wash today, half your shirts are dirty.'

'Mother can wash them. I'll be all right,' he says.

I take a slow shaky breath.

'How long are you going for?' I say.

'I don't know. I'll ring you.'

'What about Amber? Don't we need to speak to her?'

'I've spoken to Amber,' he says. 'I've explained everything.'

Fear floods me.

'What did you tell her?'

'What had happened. I told her what had happened. What you've done.'

'Shouldn't we have spoken to her together?'

'You were asleep,' he said. 'What was I meant to do exactly? Make her late for school?'

'Greg. What did she say?'

'Not a lot.' He turns away from me.

'She went to school OK? She had her Graphics Mock-GCSE today. Did she take her ruler and her coloured pencils?'

'For God's sake, Ginnie. She's sixteen. I'm sure she can pack her own school bag,' he says.

My body feels insubstantial, as though I'm just a thin shell that could be blown away in a single breath.

'Greg. I'm so, so sorry I hurt you,' I say.

'It's a bit late for that, isn't it?'

He puts his coffee mug down on the drainer.

'D'you mind washing that?' he says. 'I need to be getting off.'

This shocks me, that he feels he has to ask me to wash his coffee cup. It's as though I've torn the whole texture of our life together, the intricate warp and weft of sharing and obligation. Nothing can be assumed any more.

He goes into the hall, puts on his overcoat, picks up his case.

I go to the door with him. It's raining again: the path is sodden. I hear the rain hiss on the gravel.

'Hell. Look at this.' He turns up the collar of his coat. 'Keep an eye on the river level. These things can happen quite suddenly,' he says.

CHAPTER 42

I have a new case, Kevin Parker: he was neglected as a baby, he's missed out on loving of the most basic kind. His teachers are worried because he's been stealing food from the kitchens, as children who've been neglected so often seem to do. You want to tuck him up in a blanket and feed him with cups of cocoa. He does some drawings of people in his family, all with their hands behind their backs and dressed in identical clothes. Then I see Katy Croft. She talks about her self-harming, and the rush of relief it gives her, the way it blanks out all her psychic pain. For the first time she shows me her scars, where she's pressed the ring-pulls of cola cans into her thighs. It astonishes me that she's managed to keep this secret from her parents.

The sky is dark, relentless: the rain shows no sign of stopping. In the secretaries' office, where I go to get a report typed up, they're eating chocolates to celebrate Brigid's birthday and talking about the rain.

'My brother's got a cottage on the bank of the Avon, they've been flooded twice and now he can't get insured...'

'We looked at a house on the flood plain, and Jim was really keen, but I just said, No way...'

'People don't think when they buy those houses, do they? I mean, what can they be thinking of...?'

Brigid has seen a television programme about the flood of 1953, when hundreds of people died. There was a family where the older children escaped from the flood by climbing up in the rafters, but the mother wasn't agile enough, she stayed on the floor with the pram that had the babies in. And she just went on rocking the pram all night, while the water rose above it and the babies were still inside.

When I check my phone I find a text from Amber: she won't be home till nine. I stare at the phone, frustrated. I can't phone her now: the girls are given detention if their mobiles ring in school. I dread the conversation we'll have, but long for it as well: I just want to reassure her that whatever happens with her father and me, her life will carry on in much the same way. We will keep everything safe for her.

Molly rings.

'Mum, are you OK? Just checking.'

I wonder if Amber has spoken to her. But she's always in such a rush in the mornings: she might not have had time.

Molly is tired. She's been up all night writing an essay on Simone de Beauvoir: she kept herself awake with coffee and ginseng. She's just had the tutorial: she's going to bed now.

'It's funny to think of all you guys there, just getting on with your lives without me,' she says. There's poignancy in her voice today, but it might just be tiredness. 'Everything's OK at home, isn't it? I mean, we haven't spoken for a bit. I just wondered...'

I say something vague and reassuring: she seems to accept this, so Amber can't have rung her. I'll talk properly to Molly when we're both feeling stronger.

I need to write up my sessions, but I can't concentrate. I go to the cloakroom and hold my wrists under the water, hoping the shock of the cold will clear my head. The sound of the rain is muffled in here. Pigeons trying to shelter on the outside window sill are blurry, murmuring heaps against the frosted glass.

Clem comes in. She's wearing a rainbow wrap-around skirt and battered cowboy boots. She peers at herself in the mirror.

'Hell. Look at this frizz,' she says. 'And I'm going out for a drink tonight, with this rather tasty probation officer.' She runs her hand through her curls, then lets them fall. 'When the weather's like this I just give up,' she says. 'I come out waving a little white flag of surrender.'

She catches sight of my face in the glass.

'Oh my God, Ginnie, what's happened? You look dreadful.'

'Greg's left.'

She swings round to face me.

'Did I hear that right?' she says.

'He's walked out, Clem.'

'Oh, Ginnie.' Concern surges through her voice.

'It's my fault…'

'For Chrissake. Of course it's not,' she says, briskly. 'Nothing is ever just one person's fault. Not in a marriage. You're a psychologist, Ginnie,' she says, with mock severity. 'You ought to know that.'

'It's something I did, Clem.'

She wraps me in her arms.

'Poor love,' she says.

She's so unperturbed and accepting.

'Clem. You're not surprised, are you?'

She holds me lightly, her hands on my arms. She's looking at me warily. She shakes her head a little.

'Ginnie, you've been so unhappy. He's been shutting you out for years.'

This shocks me.

She looks at her watch.

'Hell. I've got to go, I've got a case conference. I hate to leave you like this,' she says. 'I'll come round tonight. I'll bring a bottle.'

'No, Clem, you've got your probation officer.'

'I'll cancel him,' she says.

'No. You can't do that. Come tomorrow. I'll be fine.'

She leaves me with a light touch on my arm.

There's a team meeting in Peter's office. Everything

seems unreal—too small, too sharp and clear. There's an urgent discussion about filing. The debate is conducted with great passion: everyone's voice seems loud to me. The remains of Brigid's chocolates are passed round, the hard centres that nobody wants. It's all I can do to sit there. I feel a feverish restlessness.

The last child today is Gemma Westerley. We play with clay together, and talk about the things that make her afraid. After she's gone I sit at my desk for a while.

I check my watch. Eva should be out of school by now.

She answers straight away.

'Oh, Ginnie, I'm really suffering. I'm in bed,' she says. 'I've got this evil food-poisoning bug, I ate some dodgy chicken. It's hideous.'

'Eva, how awful.'

'Anyway, how are things with you?' she says with an effort.

'It doesn't matter. Really. It can wait. We'll talk properly when you're better,' I say. 'You poor thing. Is Ted there?'

'He's coming home to look after me. Well, you know how Ted is, he's such a sweetie… Ginnie, if I was a little old lady I honestly think this would have killed me…'

I watch the rain streak down the window. The sky is a startling ultramarine, the wind rips through the branches of the elms. I feel bereft without Eva. I need to talk to somebody.

I think of Max. And immediately it's obvious
that Max will be perfect to talk to. He knows or has
guessed so much about what's happening: he knows
about my affair. I don't know why I didn't think of him
before. I imagine how I'll sink into his leather sofa, a
very large Scotch in my hand: how he will soothe me
with his pragmatic comfort. I feel a surge of affection
for him, remembering how at college we would talk
about almost anything. Max is my safe ground, my
neutral territory. I cling to him in my mind: I know
that Max won't judge me.

I ring his office. His secretary has a wholesome,
pony-club voice.

'I'm afraid Mr Sutton has gone already,' she says.

I decide I shall go to find him. I can't face going
back to my house and sitting there alone.

My car is reluctant to start, which is troubling when
I've recently spent a fortune on the gearbox. Perhaps
the rain has seeped into the engine.

The traffic is heavy on the road to Max's house: a
street has been closed, there are yellow signs warning
of flooding. I drive past Hampton Court, where there
is a funfair, its febrile scarlets and yellows dulled by
the veil of rain.

The road goes by the river for a while, past the
half-timbered houses in the old village. Soon this
road too will be cordoned off: water is lying across
it, in the dip by the antiquarian bookshop, and I see
that there are sandbags at the door of the shop and a

notice in a florid hand that says Shop Closed Due To Flooding. I wonder if the proprietor with the cultured voice and stubble and ancient greatcoat has managed to save his stock. There were all those books heaped everywhere, with their curly old-fashioned fonts, and their thick, soft pages with the dull gold edging, and the way they creaked as you opened them, with a sound like the breaking of many tiny bones. I can't imagine how he must be feeling, with everything at risk now, all the love and work he's invested. I pass the reservoir, where the wind tosses the seagulls around and whips up the water into rapid little waves. At the racecourse, there is a Crystal and Gem Fayre.

I turn off into some quiet streets where blossoming trees are planted in the pavements. I near the cul-de-sac where Max lives. Suddenly doubt seizes me. I've been so stupid, to assume I'd find him here at home, when he could be anywhere. He's probably in some classy bar, all stripped wood and neon, sipping a whisky and soda, laughing with colleagues, beguiling some woman with extravagant flattery: doing the things that unattached people do. But I've come this far through the flooding and the traffic, and it's hard to turn back now. It takes more energy than I have, to admit I should turn round. It's easier just to keep going.

I park about twenty yards from his house in the only available gap. In the front garden near where I've parked there is a huge magnolia: the flowers are going over, the petals loll outwards, flat and purplish, like the tongues of animals. I go to ring his doorbell, hearing it sound in the hollowness of his house, imagining those quiet immaculate spaces. Just as I expected, nobody comes to the door.

I walk slowly back to my car. I tell myself I'll wait for fifteen minutes, and then if he doesn't come I'll go straight home. I adjust my seat backwards, turn on my radio: it's Jazz FM, a female voice, sultry, confiding. I listen, half closing my eyes.

But I'm in luck. I've only been there for a minute or two when Max's silver Mercedes turns into the road. Relief surges through me; I know that Max will help me.

He parks down the other end of the road, where there are residents' parking bays. I turn off the radio, pick up my bag. I'm waiting for him to lock up his car; I'll meet him on the pavement.

He gets out, then turns: he's looking back into his car. I'm too far away to see his face clearly, but I can tell he's laughing, that he's responding to something that has been said: there's someone in the car with him. It must be a woman: I know this from his smile, possessive, intent. I feel foolish. It's what I should have expected. Of course he would have a woman with him. He leans down into the car again, but the windows are made of smoky glass and I can't quite make out his gesture: it's as if he's touching her face or pushing back her hair. Then he straightens again: he's patting his pockets, perhaps trying to find his house keys. I know I should drive away now: I can always ring him later. But I wait for a moment, watching, as his passenger opens her door and stretches her legs and steps out onto the pavement, hitching her battered pink school-bag up onto her shoulder; and Max goes to join her and eases his arm around her, his hand resting lightly, proprietorially, on her hipbone: and she smiles and presses against him, her long red hair hanging down.

S he kicks off her shoes in the hall and bangs back the door to the kitchen. It's somehow a surprise that she's just the same as ever—her fingers darkly smudged from her leaky fountain pen, her tie scrunched up in the pocket of her blazer, her eyes like a washed summer sky.

She tries to shake the rain out of her hair. Drops of water fly from her.

'I'm *drowned*,' she says. 'I hate it when it runs all down your parting and kind of spills on your nose.'

She's pink and shiny and too emphatic—I can tell she's been drinking.

She grabs the towel that's hanging by the sink and wraps it round her hair and starts to dry it. Her drenched hair has a blackish sheen, and the rainwater brings out its sweet papaya scent.

'Amber. I saw you with Max.'

She's suddenly still, tense, her head on one side, her wet hair hanging down.

'Were you following me?' she says.

'No. I just wanted to talk to him. I saw you get out of his car.'

She shrugs, turns away from me, letting her hair drip. She hangs the towel on its peg again, as though she can't handle what I'm saying while she's drying her hair.

'How long has this been going on?' I ask her.

'It's none of your business,' she says.

Her face is tight, like a shut door.

'Oh yes it is. Yes it is my business.' My voice is too loud for the room, but I can't control it. 'How long, Amber? Since that dinner party? Since you did your placement?'

'Maybe,' she says. Her face is set.

'Amber. He's forty-seven,' I say.

'So?'

'He'll use you, Amber. Surely you can see that. A man like Max…' I feel unreal: brittle, cardboard-thin—and so tired it's hard to find words for what seems so glaringly clear. 'A promiscuous middle-aged man, for God's sake.'

Her face darkens.

'Promiscuous is a stupid word,' she says.

'Anyone could see it's a total disaster,' I say. 'Amber—you're *sixteen*.'

She shakes her head wearily.

'For Chrissake, Mum. I thought you liked him, I

thought he was your friend. Why are you saying these horrible things about him?'

'Why didn't you tell me?'

She raises her eyebrows and gives a noisy, melo-dramatic sigh.

'That's kind of obvious, isn't it?'

'You should have told me,' I say.

'I don't get what you're so stressed about, quite honestly,' she says. 'I mean, which is it? Is it because he's forty-seven, or is it because he's your friend?'

I don't reply. Perhaps I don't want to think about this.

'Does Molly know?' I ask her.

She's hesitant, twisting a strand of hair between her fingers; then she nods a little.

'What does she say?'

'She says it's up to me. Like anybody would. Anybody remotely reasonable.'

I see then how much of her, of both of them, is unknown to me. That I'm not the mother I thought I was, a friend to them, someone to share their secrets, someone they could confide in.

She leans on the table opposite me, bending down towards me. Her drenched hair drips on my hands.

'Mum, I can look after myself.' A little conciliatory now, trying to reach me. 'It's not like we're majorly in love or anything. We have a laugh, Mum. What's the problem exactly?'

As she leans towards me I smell the alcohol on her breath.

'You've been drinking.'

'So? I was upset and he took me out for a drink. Is that so terrible? I told him about you and Dad screwing everything up and he took me out for a drink. Look, can I go now?'

I stand up, pushing back my chair.

'I want you to stop seeing him,' I say.

Her eyes blaze. I can feel the charge of her anger: it sparks and glimmers on the air.

'You can't ask me to do that,' she says.

'I'm not asking you, I'm telling you.'

'No,' she says. 'I'm not going to let you mess up my life. You can mess up your own life if you want to but you can't mess up mine.'

'It's over, Amber,' I say.

'No, it's not.' She's taut as a wire. Her eyes are narrowed, hard. 'You can't stop me. You can't dictate to me. I'll do what I want,' she says. 'So how are you going to stop me, exactly? Lock me up or something?'

'I'm going to speak to Max,' I say. 'That's how I'll stop you.'

Her hands are clenched into fists: you can see the white of the bone.

'No,' she says. Her voice is thin, high, wild. 'You have no right to stop me. You have absolutely no right to control my life. I mean, look at you, for Chrissake. Dad did tell me, you know. He told me all about it. How you've been shagging some loser you picked up. For Chrissake, Mum. Did you forget you were married or something? Did it kind of slip your mind?'

There were things I was going to say to her. I had them all planned, these gentle soothing things, telling her everything would be OK: that whatever happened with Greg and me, we would work together to keep life safe for her. But now I can't reach the things I was going to say.

I dig my fingernails into my palms.

'Amber, listen. I know you're angry with me. I know we need to talk. But that's not what this is about. This is about you and what you're doing to yourself.' A sudden dangerous energy flares in me. 'Amber, you need to listen to me. I'm going to stop you seeing Max. I won't allow it. I'm telling you.'

'Fuck that,' she says. Quietly, but clear. 'Fuck you.'

I hit her, hard, on the side of her face. My hand hurting her makes a loud sound. I see the absolute shock in her face, the widening of her eyes. She puts her hand to her face, turns and walks out, her hand cupped over the place where I hit her. The door of her room bangs, so the kitchen dresser shakes; there's the thump of music turned up far too loud.

I sit weakly at the table. The anger seeps away from me. It's an instant, total thing, water into dry ground. I can't remember why it all seemed to matter so much. I see it, hear it, over and over: the shock in her eyes, the sound of my hand on her skin. There's a taste of iron in my mouth, like when you have a tooth out and your mouth fills up with blood.

I'm desperate to say I'm sorry, to hold her. I know this will happen: when we've rowed before, we've always made up soon. But I wait there, giving her time. Like when she had tantrums when she was a toddler, and I'd leave her raging on the floor, and say, Come to me when you feel better; and half an hour later she'd find me, the passion all passed, her face blank and swollen with crying, her eyelashes clotted together as though with too much mascara, her body hot and heavy in my arms.

I wait for twenty minutes. Then I go to her room.

I knock at her door. She doesn't respond but the music is so loud she probably can't hear me. I open the door a little. The room shudders with sound.

'Amber…'

She isn't there.

I turn off the music. She must be in the bathroom—but the bathroom door is open. I call her.

'Amber. I just wanted to say I'm so sorry…'

There's no reply.

'Amber…' My voice is high now. 'Please answer.'

An empty house feels different: the air is flat, dull, there's a deadness to it. I know there's no point in shouting—that she isn't here.

I ring her mobile from the phone in the kitchen, willing her to answer. When I've dialled I'm startled by a sound that briefly I can't make sense of, a shrill phrase of Eminem from her room, her ring tone. Panic surges through me like nausea. I run upstairs. Her phone is flung down in the middle of her duvet.

She must have deliberately left it—Amber, who never goes out without her phone. Suddenly this becomes something different.

Through the side window on the landing, I see that her bike is missing from the alley. Her helmet and her coat are still in the hall. I'm trying to think, to work out what to do, but my fear is a labyrinth I can't find my way through.

I ring Max. It's his voicemail.

'Max, it's Ginnie. Amber's gone missing and she might be coming to you. I need to speak to you. Please ring. *Now*, Max. Just as soon as you get this.'

I ring Katrine. No, sorry, Amber isn't there. Then Lauren, then Jamila. They haven't seen her since school. 'She did seem a bit upset today, though,' says Jamila. Her voice is shaky and unsure. 'She said something had happened at home.' She's embarrassed, saying this to me: but she says it anyway, and I feel a quick, deep gratitude towards her.

I try Greg, but his phone is switched off.

I ring Greg's mother. For ages she doesn't answer. I picture her, in her layers of exquisitely ironed grey linen. I will her to come to the phone.

'It's Ginnie. I wondered if Greg was there.'

'Oh. *Ginnie.*' There's a significant pause. I wonder what Greg has said to her.

'Greg says you're having a bad patch,' she says then, in a careful, emollient tone. 'Everyone has bad patches, Ginnie. The thing is to work through them.'

'I'm ever so sorry, I can't talk properly now, I'm looking for Amber,' I tell her.

She pays no attention.

'Nowadays people think they don't have to work at things,' she says, unhurried but tenacious. 'People expect it all to come so easily. But you have to work at a marriage.'

There's a scream of impatience inside me.

'That's what Jack and I did, we really worked at it. The thing is, Ginnie, promises are to be kept, that's what we all have to remember. And you've got my two lovely granddaughters to think of...'

'That's why I'm ringing. I'm trying to find Amber. Please could you get Greg to ring me when he comes in?'

I finish the call, too abruptly.

I grab my coat. I write a note for Amber and fix it under the knocker on the outside of the door, in case she comes back and doesn't have her keys. 'Gone to find you! Back soon. Lots of love.' But the rain is driving against the door, and the paper is sodden as soon as I've stuck it there: I worry that the words will all be washed away. The wind in the trees in my garden roars like an animal. The gate clicks behind me. I spin round, with a quick warm rush of relief, thinking to see her coming home with an embarrassed shrug and a self-deprecating comment. I half reach out my arms as I turn, I'm desperate to hold her. But there's no one there: it's just the tug and shuffle of the wind.

I go to my car. I don't know where to drive to, just that I need to be out there looking for her. I turn the key in the ignition. Nothing. I try again. Just the strangulated sound of wet spark plugs. I turn the key again and again. The engine screeches briefly but it doesn't start.

I try to make myself think. I sit in the car and flick through the directory on my phone, though my hand is shaking so much I keep on missing the keys. There's no one here who could help me. Clem is busy; Eva is ill. I come to Will's number. I'd intended to delete it but I didn't know how, and I couldn't ask Amber, who is my usual guide to anything technological. I sit there for a moment with my finger over the key.

He answers immediately.

'Will, I know I shouldn't ring you at home—I mean, I know we aren't seeing each other any more—'

He cuts me off, responding at once to something in my voice.

'Ginnie, what's happened?'

'Amber's run away. And I need to look for her but my car won't start and Greg's left and I don't know what to do.'

'What do you mean—run away?'

'We had a row. Her bike's gone but she's left her coat and her phone. I'm frightened, Will.'

'How long ago was this?' he says.

'About half an hour.'

'You've rung her friends? The obvious places?'

'Of course.'

'Where are you?'

'At my house.'

'I don't know your address,' he says.

I briefly notice how strange this is—that we've been so close, yet he doesn't know the most basic things about me. I tell him.

'Give me ten minutes,' he says.

I wait in my car, hunting in my head for places where we could look for her. Branches above me heave and lurch in the wind, and heavy raindrops spatter the windscreen like a fistful of stones. He comes when he said he would, though it seems to take an age. He opens his car door and I get straight in.

I take him in, his keen unsmiling face, the grace of his hands, his urgent gaze. I've lived through this moment so often, thinking how it would be if I saw him, all the passionate, angry, complicated things I'd want to say. They seem to belong in another world. Now I'm just grateful he's here with me.

'Thank you,' I say. 'Was it difficult?'

'I was just coming home, it wasn't a problem. I've told Megan,' he says.

I don't ask what this means—what exactly he has told her.

He puts a hand on my arm. I'm glad of the warmth of his skin. I realise I am shivering.

'Tell me,' he says.

'We had a row,' I say. 'I hit her. I shouldn't have done but I did…'

'Ginnie, don't beat yourself up. It happens.'

'It shouldn't have happened.'

'Was she drunk?' he says.

'Not exactly. Well, a bit. She'd certainly been drinking. She might be a bit disinhibited.'

'Was she upset?'

'She only heard today—that Greg was leaving— and about us and everything…'

His face darkens.

'Has she ever done anything silly—you know, hurt herself?'

It's like he's the psychologist now: and I'm grateful for this, just to let him take over.

'Not really. Well, she took five aspirin once—when she was twelve. And she scratched herself with some scissors when she'd fallen out with a friend. I always try not to get too worked up about these things…'

He doesn't seem reassured.

'Is there anywhere you can think of—places she might go to?'

'There's a park where they meet sometimes in summer—Stoneleigh Gardens. Behind the gasworks.'

'We'll try there first,' he says.

'I'm scared, Will.'

'Ginnie. Lots of kids run off at some time. Almost all of them turn up safe and sound. You know that…'

His voice is controlled and quiet. But I see how fast he drives.

The first road he turns down towards Stoneleigh Gardens is closed because of the flood. He tries the next one. There's a shriek from the tyres as he turns the wheel.

The park seems deserted—just a man walking his dog, moving in and out of the apricot pools of light from the street lamps: he's holding a newspaper over his head to shield himself from the rain. We pass the picnic benches where Amber's group sometimes gather on summer evenings, drinking Coke or smoking or texting their friends, their talk and laughter and vividness drifting across the gardens. Rain hisses on the gravel paths and the grass is black and sodden.

We go back to the car.

'There's a churchyard too, where some of them go,' I tell him, remembering what Amber once said about the gang that Lauren knows. 'St Dunstan's.'

'I know the place,' he says.

As we drive my phone rings. I scrabble in my bag for it. Relief surges through me, the sudden quick certainty that Amber is safely home.

It's Max.

'Ginnie, I know this must come as quite a shock to you…' His voice is rapid, shrill with discomfort. 'But she knows what she's doing, Ginnie, she's very mature for her years. I wouldn't have dreamt of it, you know, if I hadn't been sure she knew what she was doing.'

'Max, it's not that…'

'We didn't want to upset you,' he says, 'that's why we didn't tell you. I said we ought to tell you but she was sure you'd be upset…'

'Max.' I cut him short. 'I just want to know if she's with you, that's all. Just tell me if she's with you.'

'She's not,' he says. He sounds relieved, perhaps because I'm not shouting at him. 'She's not here. She left at half past eight. Look, we can talk about it, Ginnie…'

'She's run off, I can't find her,' I say. 'Please, please, ring if she turns up—ring me the moment she gets there. I just want to know she's safe…'

The churchyard is dreary under the night and the rain. It looks neglected, with heaps of winter leaves drifted against the graves, and the older stones all crooked with their writing worn away. The storm has spilled the vases of flowers that people have left there. Hunched angels with pointy, extravagant wings with intricate feathered edges loom at us out of the night, their stonework smeared with lichen that's rust-red in the torchlight. Clem's angel comes into my mind, the voice she heard in the darkness: and the angels like beautiful boys on the tomb in the Walsall church, and the Ave Maria we sang there, the hymn to Mary. *Ora pro nobis. Pray for us.* There are lamps along the path to the door, you can see there's nobody here.

We sit back in the car; he turns to me. His face is worn and strained.

'Somewhere else,' he says. 'A place that means something to her. Maybe where she used to go when she was a little girl? Somewhere significant.'

'We could drive along the river,' I say. It's all I can think of.

The traffic is still heavy on the road by the river. Across the water you can see the lighted windows of the houseboats moored on Taggs Island, their yellow warmth spilling onto the indigo water. I think of the long-ago morning when we came here—the slight silver haze on the river, the water lapping, full of light, and the apple-green houseboat with its little blue dinghy that Amber had wanted to live in. The river is up to the top of the bank in places, licking at the grass and seeping down to the road.

We drive past the steep span of footbridge that leads onto the island.

'Will.' I grasp his arm. 'There was a bike. Someone left a bike by the bridge.'

He does a swift three-point turn in the road, holding up both lanes of traffic, and drives rapidly back and pulls the car up on the kerb. We get out.

I know at once it's hers: I know the make, the colour, the scratch on the handlebars from the time last year when she came off and sprained her wrist and we spent three hours in Casualty. It's just flung down, not locked, as if she didn't care what happened to it. It's surprising it hasn't been stolen already.

We look across at the island. Behind the houseboats there are no lights, just a dark mass of trees against the dark of the river. Cold passes through me. He puts his hand on my arm.

'She liked this place,' I say. 'We came here once, when she was a child. It was where she wanted to live then.'

He walks fast and the bridge is steep—I only just keep up with him. He waits for me and takes my hand and pulls me after him. At the top of the span, the wind is fierce, slamming into our faces. The river rushes below us. It's not tidal here, but it's whipped and tugged by the wind.

At the other end of the bridge, there are gravel paths to our left and our right. There's a board with a map of the island: Will stops for a moment to look at it. I'm seized by a feverish energy: it's all I can do to stand still.

'We'll go left,' he says. 'That way we can get almost all the way round. The other way there's an inlet.'

The island isn't like it was that long ago summer Sunday, when we came trespassing in the silver morning mist. It's very dark. The light from the windows of the houseboats doesn't reach here. There are occasional patches of thin light from the old-fashioned street lamps dotted along the path. By the light of Will's torch, you can see that most of the island is flooded: water is everywhere, breaking up this horseshoe of land into many little islets, making its way wherever the land is low or there is a cleft or channel, covering over these trim and extravagant gardens with their rockeries and pergolas, eating into everything and messing everything up.

As we pass one of the gardens a man comes out of a summer house with some cushions under his arm, and a deckchair. He stares at us, a little hostile.

'I shouldn't go that way.' He nods his head in the direction of our path. 'It's under water down there. Well, you can see how it is. We're clearing out,' he says.

'We're looking for someone—a girl,' I tell him.

'Sorry.' He shakes his head.

In places the path goes close to the edge of the land: wooden posts are set there, to stop the earth from being eroded away. You can hear the traffic from the road along the river bank, but it seems very distant, cut off from us by the surge and swell of the Thames. The wind blusters in the branches. There's a crack like a rifle-shot where it lashes at a tarpaulin on a boat moored somewhere near. The island is full of the different sounds the water makes, its insistent seep and trickle and drip, and the splash and suck of our feet where we have to walk through the flood.

Will moves his torch around but we can't see her. The beam catches in things, the eyes of an animal, glowing with an oily green light: a string of crystals like glinting tears that hang from the branch of a tree: a makeshift pagoda, paper-thin, with a rusting dragon weather vane. There's a dead duck flung down in a pool of water, its neck stretched out and crooked, in its throat a bite-mark, black and glossy with blood, a flurry of white feathers around it. My chest is tight: it hurts to take in breath.

We come to the far end of the island. A picket gate opens onto a flooded garden that ends in a drop to the river. There's rubbish in the water on the lawn—a wheelbarrow, garden tools. He puts his hand on my arm.

'Look,' he says.

She's standing on the grass at the tip of the island, looking out into the river. She has her back to us. She's separated from us by yards of shallow water. She must have walked through the flood to get there: or else the water has pushed in quickly, cutting her off from such land as there is, from what is left of the island. Here there are no trees: and there's more light, from the head-lamps of the cars on the river road, their beams broken up on the water like shards and splinters of glass. But I can't see her clearly: she's a dark dense shape against the glittery black of the water, her hair sleeked down by the rain, her soaked clothes clinging to her. I sense rather than see that she is shivering violently.

She must have heard us come. She turns a little in our direction, then turns away again. She's absolutely tense, I can tell that, as she stands there looking out over the river. I know the dark mood that drove her out without her phone or raincoat still has her in its grip. I sense the conflict in her—the pull of drama, of the desperate, wild gesture. She seems so small against the rush of the water.

I'm very afraid. I know how easily I could get everything wrong, when it's all so fragile.

'Let me do this,' says Will.

I let him. I wait on the wet grass.

He walks towards her through the water, talking to her; his voice is gentle, careful.

'Amber, it isn't safe, you know you can't stay here.'

I don't know if she can hear him above the sound of the river.

He's shining the torch towards her: she flinches, raises her hand to shield her face. He sees this: he points the torch down so she won't be dazzled.

'Amber, your mother's sorry, she just wants you to be safe.'

I watch, my pulse skittering, as she moves a little nearer to the verge.

He's halfway through the water, walking towards her. But as I watch he staggers and falls. There could be any obstacle there—a rockery, plant pots, anything. The flood is treacherous, concealing everything. He can't walk on that way. He moves off to his right, to the rim of the land, where the ground is banked up and the slippery verge of the lawn is exposed. The grass glistens wet in the torchlight.

He's only a few yards from her now. My heart thuds. She takes another step towards the brink. From where

I'm standing, she seems to be almost leaning over, staring into the river.

'Amber,' he says.

She makes a small, broken movement with her hands, as if she's warning him off or trying to push him away. She says something under her breath: I can't hear what she says, just the tone of it, the despair. I think she is going to throw herself in. I scream out her name.

Will lunges forward to grasp her arm but he doesn't reach her. The momentum of his gesture unbalances him. He slips, sways. The torchlight, zigzagging crazily as his arms flail, catches his face, his look of surprise. He tips over, so easily, with a kind of random grace: sinks down into the perilous dark and the pull and surge of the Thames. The water swallows the torchlight. I can only see the river and the dark. Someone is screaming.

In that instant I feel nothing but a terrible cold clarity: I can't reach him, can't save him. I'm too slow, too old, it's too far, the water's too heavy on me. I'm struggling through the night and the flood, but I know it's too late, it's over.

Amber spins round. I sense the flare of panic in her. Even in the dark I know her face has changed. She's herself again—urgent, present, her fear for him pushing all her wildness away. She flings herself down on the ground, at the brink of the land, stretching down into the river. She's reaching out but I still can't see him at all, just the glitter and surge of the water. With her free hand she clutches at one of the logs that are set there; her hand grips, claw-like, the knuckles are sharp through her skin. I hear the sob on her breath. As I come up closer I see her forearm quiver, as every muscle in her body tightens: and I hear her great shuddery sigh as she reaches and clings to his hand.

CHAPTER 45

I take Amber up to her bedroom. She sits down
heavily on the bed. I sit beside her, holding her
to me. There are ugly, berry-red bruises on her
arm: you can trace out the curve of the edge of the
logs, where she pressed against them as she clung to
Will's hand. She's crying quietly. Her body is loose
and shivery, sinking into me.

'Amber. I'm so sorry I hit you. I shouldn't have
done that.'

'It really hurt.' She blows her nose noisily, scrubs
at her face with a tissue. 'I didn't know you could hit
that hard,' she says. She gives me a small wry smile
through her tears.

I stroke her hair.

'I'm so so sorry,' I say.

'Will Dad be back soon?'

'We'll sort it out. I promise,' I tell her.

'You'll ring him, won't you? I want to speak to him.'

'Sweetheart, of course,' I say. 'But we can do it in the morning. I want you to get some sleep now. You've been a total heroine, but you still need to sleep.'

'OK,' she says. She yawns hugely. She's so tired she can scarcely hold her head up.

I get up to go and fill her hot-water bottle.

'Mum.' She's hesitant. 'That's the man who—you know—isn't it? The man Dad told me about?'

'Yes.'

She looks at me, her level blue gaze. Her forehead is creased in a frown.

'He was trying to rescue me, Mum. That's why he was there with you, wasn't it?'

'Yes.'

'It's complicated, isn't it?' she says.

'Yes,' I say. 'It's complicated. But I think you should get some sleep now.'

I make her a drink of cocoa and put arnica on her bruises and give her half a sleeping pill. There's such an intense pleasure in looking after her and doing all these things.

Will has showered and put on some old clothes of Greg's that I've found for him. The kitchen is full of the childhood smell of wet wool.

'Is she OK?'

'She'll be fine,' I tell him.

I make coffee for both of us, pour sugar and brandy in it. We sit quietly for a while. I sip my coffee greedily. I've put in too much sugar, but the brandy is fiercely warming as it slides into my veins. I still feel the fear, but faintly, echoing in my mind, like a sound that carries on resonating when the source of it has gone.

'Ginnie,' he says slowly then. 'When you told me that Greg was leaving…'

'He's staying with his mother,' I say. 'I told him about us. I had to. I've told Roger I'll go to court, so I had to explain…'

'So what will happen?' he says.

'You mean, with Greg and me?'

He nods.

'I don't know…' And then I realise I do know, that I can see it all. The inevitability of this shocks me, the whole thing spooling out in front of me. 'Well,' I say slowly, 'I think he'll come back in a day or two. His mother's kind of bossy, she likes to give lots of advice. Anyway, all his books are here. And we'll try to make a go of it, and we'll be so careful with one another for a while.' I look down at my hands. There are bruises like Amber's on my palms that I didn't know were there. 'Perhaps for a bit it will be OK—for weeks, months even,' I tell him. 'But in the end we'll part again. With Molly gone and Amber leaving soon, there'll be nothing to hold us together. There just won't be any point to it. I think that's how it will be.'

He listens to me in silence.

'You don't know that,' he says then. 'Anything can happen.'

There's silence between us for a while. The wind has

dropped, and the rain is gentler now, just whispering at the window. The water will still be rising.

'And you and Megan?' I say then.

'We're still together,' he says. 'She knows. I had to tell her. There were rumours in the office. We don't talk about it.'

'And Jake?'

'He's just the same,' he says. He's moving the coffee spoon from one hand to the other, as if he can't work out what to do with it. 'I've applied for a move to Bradford. Megan has family there. She's always wanted to go back. There's a good school for Jake, where they're getting brilliant results with Asperger's kids. We thought we could make a fresh start.'

'Are you happy with that?'

'I think it's for the best,' he says. He's stirring his coffee round and round, he isn't looking at me. 'She's pregnant, Ginnie.'

'Well. That's great, isn't it?'

He doesn't say anything.

I wrap my hands around my coffee cup to warm them.

We hear Amber upstairs going to the bathroom, then her bedroom door click shut. The house creaks and shifts, all the old timbers contracting, like someone settling down or turning over in their sleep.

I look at him surrounded by all my things, my geraniums and the clutter of flowered crockery on my dresser.

'I like having you in my kitchen,' I tell him.

He looks round at the room, as though he's only just noticed it.

'Your house isn't like I imagined it,' he says.

'How did you imagine it?'

'I don't know. Posher, more modern. More kind of expensive.'

I smile. 'I guess it needs some work doing.'

'I like it as it is,' he says. 'All your pictures and plants. I didn't know you grew all these plants.'

I think how little we know about each other. These are things that belong when you first fall in love—going to your lover's house and looking at all the things they own, eager to understand them. Everything we've done has been the wrong way round.

'Ginnie,' he says then, 'I was wrong, when I told you not to make that call. I shouldn't have done that.'

I feel such tenderness for him, that he's said this. I can tell how hard it is for him to say.

He reaches out and puts his hand on mine. We sit like that for a long time.

It's so quiet in my kitchen. You can hear the softest things—Will's breath, the creak of his chair when he shifts a little, the velvet fall of a petal from a flower. I don't want to say anything, don't want to break the silence. As though if I keep completely still, nothing will happen, nothing will change: nobody will leave me. I look at him, drink him in, his greying hair, his dark eyes with the red flecks in them; his skin and mouth and hands. I know that I'm learning him again, imprinting him on my memory. I'm storing these things away inside me and keeping them safe.

'I'm glad I met you,' I say, in the end. 'I'm glad I had that.'

'Even after what happened?'

'Even after everything.'

I can see the river house in my mind. I think of the way I pictured it, the long-ago summer evening, the lovers who step down into the boat and move briefly through the brightness: then off into the shadow, leaving no trail but a wake of broken gold.

He takes his hand away and gulps down the rest of his coffee.

'I really ought to go now.'

'But you hurt your leg. I could drive you…'

He shakes his head.

'I'll manage. You stay here with Amber. She needs you to be here. I'll send the clothes when I've washed them.'

'Perhaps you should go to Casualty—get yourself checked over. Don't they say you should do that if you fall into the Thames?'

'I think I'll just leave it,' he says.

He leans towards me across the table: his eyes holding mine.

'I hope it all works out OK. Whatever you want. You know, with Greg and everything.'

So I know that he is going finally, irrevocably, now.

'Thanks,' I say. 'And for you. Bradford and—the baby.'

He gets up and picks up his bag of wet clothes.

I follow him to the door. My throat hurts with the things that will never be said now. I open the door but he doesn't go for a moment, just stands there looking at me. I press my mouth into his: we kiss for a long time. In the end, he pulls away from me. He has his hands on my shoulders, looking into my eyes.

'Ginnie.'

He says my name as though it is the answer to a question. Then he turns away, and walks off into the night.

I t's cold in the courtroom. Outside in the streets it's a blazing July day, but in here the air-conditioning is icy. Yet my hands still seem to be slippery with sweat. As I hand the Bible back to the usher I see that I have left wet fingerprints on its plastic cover.

The prosecution barrister shuffles his papers and stands. I glance around the court. Sean Faulkner is in the dock at the back of the court, his face without expression; now and then he chews at his lower lip. Over the barrister's shoulder I can see the jury; a woman in the front row sips from a fruit-juice carton. The judge has his chin propped on his hands, and you'd think he was on the edge of sleep, except for the acuteness of his gaze. I look to my left. The public gallery is full. I see Karen and Ray who came to interview me, and Roger leaning forward with an intent look. So many people, all staring straight at me. In the front row of the public gallery, there is a woman about my age who immediately reminds me of the photo of Maria—Italian-looking, black hair pulled back, dark eyes. Her hands in her lap are never still, moving together as though she is wringing out wet linen, the gesture speaking of her unguessable grief. There are lines scored deep in her face. I know that this must be Maria's mother. The courtroom seems to shift and sway around me. I turn back to the barrister.

'You are Virginia Holmes?'

'Yes.'

He's built like a rugby player, with bits of rumpled fair hair poking from under his wig. His voice is ponderous, every consonant clear.

'I believe you are a child psychologist at the Westcotes Clinic. Is that correct?'

'Yes.'

'And how long have you worked there, Mrs Holmes?'

'Fifteen years,' I tell him.

'Now, on February the twelfth, the day after Maria Faulkner disappeared, you were on the bank of the Thames, roughly opposite Eel Pie Island?'

'Yes.'

'Can you tell me what time this was?'

'It was about one-thirty in the afternoon.'

'And you were where exactly?'

'I was in a broken down house on the river bank. The river path goes past it.'

'Were you there on your own, Mrs Holmes?'

'I was there with a friend.'

'Mrs Holmes, could you please tell me exactly what you saw on the river path?'

'I saw a man running along by the river. He stopped a few yards from the house and turned and went off into the trees.'

'Could you describe this man?'

'He was wearing office clothes. He was tall and fair.'

'And there was something about this man that concerned you, was there not?'

'The way he kept looking around. He seemed to be looking for someone. I thought at the time it was odd. When I saw Mr Faulkner make the TV appeal, I realised it was him I'd seen.'

'Can we just spell this out, Mrs Holmes? You saw the defendant, Mr Sean Faulkner, on television, appealing for witnesses to assist the investigation into his wife's murder?'

'Yes.'

'And you recognised Sean Faulkner as the man you saw on February the twelfth on the river path?'

'Yes, I recognised him.'

'Thank you, Mrs Holmes. No more questions, Your Honour.'

The defence barrister stands. He's rather short and round, apple-cheeked, with an affable look. A man who would charm you. He smiles warmly at me. My heart pounds.

'Could I first just ask your age, Mrs Holmes?'

'I'm forty-six.'

'And I believe you are married?'

'Yes.'

'Now, do you and your husband have children?'

'Two daughters.'

'And perhaps you could tell me the ages of your daughters?'

'Nineteen and sixteen.'

He smiles appreciatively at me, as though this is an achievement.

'Thank you.' He leaves a little pause. 'Now, on February the twelfth, you were on the river path opposite Eel Pie Island. You were there with a friend, you say, Mrs Holmes?'

Just the slightest, delicate emphasis on the Mrs.

'Yes.'

'You were in a derelict hut on the river path?'

'Yes.'

'A place you had doubtless chosen because you were in need of privacy?' His voice is glycerine-smooth.

'Yes.'

'Am I correct in assuming that you were there for the purpose of conducting a clandestine affair?'

I feel my face flare red.

'Yes.'

I clasp my hands tight together. My mouth is completely dry.

'Thank you. Now, can I ask why you chose to come

forward, Mrs. Holmes? Why exactly you went to the police with your information?'

'I wanted to help. I felt I should tell the truth about what I'd seen.'

'So, Mrs. Holmes, you would say that generally you are someone who seeks to tell the truth? Someone who values truthfulness?'

'Yes.' I see where he is taking this. I can't go back now. I have to do what I came to do. I bite my tongue to try and moisten my mouth.

A little gap, a little smile.

'But we have already heard, Mrs. Holmes, that you were in this place on the river bank in order to conduct a clandestine affair. Did your husband know where you were on February the twelfth?'

'No, he didn't.'

'Or who you were with?'

'No.

'Did your children know where you were?'

'No.'

He gives his head a sad little shake, as though this is all much to be regretted.

'You lied to your husband and you lied to your children about your affair—so why should this court believe anything you say? Why should we believe you about what you claim to have seen?'

I can hear my heart, its hard dull thuds.

'I know what I saw,' I tell him. 'I'm telling the truth about what I saw.'

He rubs a finger along his jaw, a questioning, perplexed gesture. He has plump fingers, white as dough,
and a glinting signet ring.

'Now, you were in a derelict hut, you say. But how
did you gain access to this hut?'

'We untwisted the wire on the door.'

'So you were in fact trespassing, Mrs Holmes?'

'Maybe. I suppose.'

'You were trespassing. Yes or no?'

'Yes.'

'Thank you. Now, I'd like to take you through the
precise sequence of events, if I may, Mrs Holmes. This
man you saw or thought you saw—was this before or
after you had intercourse?'

The question shocks me. My instinct is to say I
don't remember. But I know he'd use that to invalidate
everything I've said.

'It was before.'

The judge leans forward.

'Mrs Holmes, I'd be grateful if you could speak up
a bit,' he says. 'We can hardly hear you.'

'Yes, I'm sorry,' I say.

'Thank you, Your Honour,' says the barrister. He
rests his fingers lightly together, like somebody praying. 'So, Mrs Holmes, you saw this man who you felt
was involved in some sort of criminal activity—whose
behaviour troubled you, you say—and you then went
on to have sexual intercourse with your lover?'

'Yes.'

He raises his eyebrows very slightly.

'You can't have been so *very* troubled then, can you, Mrs Holmes?'

I don't say anything. I don't know what I can say.

'Now, this affair that you were involved in—would you say this was a passionate relationship?'

'I suppose so.'

He has his head on one side; his voice is sleek, emollient.

'Would you say you were in love with this man?'

My throat is thick.

'Yes, I would,' I say.

'So, Mrs Holmes,' says the barrister, 'you were there to engage in illicit sexual intercourse with this man whom you were passionately in love with. I put it to you that this is a situation in which a woman's powers of observation might be less than acute.' Again that regretful shake of the head. 'You were completely distracted, weren't you? You can't possibly remember with any accuracy what you saw on the river path.'

'I know it was Sean Faulkner I saw,' I say.

He has his head on one side now, with the perplexed air of someone who genuinely seeks to be enlightened.

'There are just one or two other things that puzzle me,' he says. 'Why has the friend you were with not come forward, Mrs Holmes? Presumably if there was something strange to be seen on the river path, he would have seen it also?'

'He had his back to the path. He didn't see.'

'And did you always conduct your liaison on the river bank?'

'Yes.'

'You never went anywhere rather more conventional—a hotel room, for instance?'

'We just went to the river.'

He gives a deep sigh.

'You are a married woman,' he says, 'a woman with two daughters aged nineteen and sixteen. You are a woman who, at an age when many women are contentedly helping out with their grandchildren, conducts an illicit affair in a semi-public place. You like excitement. You're something of a thrill-seeker.'

'No. Not really.'

'Coming to the police was just another thrill, wasn't it? A way of getting attention?'

'No. It wasn't,' I say. But I can scarcely form the words.

He waits for a moment. He straightens up. He's looking sternly at me.

'Mrs Holmes, you were on property where you shouldn't have been, with a man you shouldn't have been with.' There's a new severity in his voice. 'You were about to have sexual intercourse with this man who is not your husband, and you'd lied about this relationship to your husband and your children. Yet you ask this court to believe what you say you saw. You ask us to believe that you can remember clearly a man you'd never seen before, whom you glimpsed for a second or two in the distance, when you were in the embrace of your illicit lover. The river path is a right of way. Anyone can go there. The man you saw could have been anyone. I put it to you that it wasn't Sean Faulkner that you saw.'

I take a deep breath.

'I saw him clearly,' I say again. 'I'm sure it was Mr Faulkner.'

'That will be all, Your Honour.'

The judge nods in my direction.

'Thank you, Mrs Holmes. You are free to stay in court, or to go about your business.'

After the hush of the court, the noise in the street slams in my face. I stand at the top of the white curved steps that lead down to the pavement. I cling to the hand-rail like somebody blind. I feel worn away, hammered thin. I stand there for a long time. People pass on the pavement below me—a worried woman with a baby in a buggy, a boy with his arm round his girlfriend: ordinary people, busy, preoccupied, getting on with their lives. There's a smell of smoke and petrol, but I breathe in gratefully, taking great gulps of air.

After a while, I start to notice the heat of the sun on my arms. I turn my face to the sun. I breathe more deeply. I think, I am free to go. I think, That will be all. I tell myself this, over and over. I am free to go now.

With my hand tight round the rail, I walk carefully down to the street.

* * *

Ten days later, on Saturday, it's in the national press: the jury have reached their verdict. Amber points it out to me. I read it over her shoulder.

'An estate agent who murdered his wife and dumped her body in a river was jailed for life yesterday. Sean Faulkner, 32, strangled his wife Maria at their home in Caterham, and then dumped her body in the Thames. A jury at Kingston Crown Court heard how Sean Faulkner calmly reported the disappearance of his wife from their home in February of this year... The Senior Investigating Officer, Detective Chief Inspector Roger Prior, said after the trial, "This was a ruthless and cruel act, probably motivated by pathological jealousy."'

The report traces out the case against Sean Faulkner, much as Roger told it to me. Detectives were suspicious of him from the start. He claimed he hadn't washed any clothes, but the washing machine had recently been used. Traces of river water were found on his trainers. A witness on the river path saw him returning to the place where Maria's body had been dumped, the morning after the murder and a week before the body was discovered. The jury took six hours to reach their verdict.

'See, Mum, that's you. The witness on the river path,' says Amber.

There's the photo of Maria that Roger showed to me: the print is grainy and blurred.

'So that's what she looked like.' Amber stares at the photo. 'It's weird to see a picture of someone and know they're dead,' she says. 'It's just so hard to believe in.' She runs her finger gently across the photograph. 'She was ever so pretty, wasn't she? I'm glad they got a result.' She looks up at me: her washed blue eyes have a thoughtful look. 'I bet you're glad too, Mum, after being a witness and everything.'

'Yes. I'm glad,' I say.

After lunch Amber goes into town to meet Jamila in Starbucks. I decide I will give my kitchen a comprehensive clean. I scrub away all the smudges of mould from the insides of my cupboards, and wipe my windows with vinegar, and remove a sprouting and rotten potato from underneath the fridge. Then I ring Eva, who last week shocked everyone by telling Ted she thinks they ought to separate. She sounds very tired but otherwise OK. She knows people won't understand, she doesn't expect that they would, she scarcely understands it herself: it was just something that she knew she had to do. We talk for a long time.

Amber is back at three with lots of shopping bags. She comes into the kitchen, and dumps her purchases on the table. It's hot, and she's tied the sleeves of her sweater round her waist. She's wearing a flimsy T-shirt that says Oui in sparkly letters.

'There were these builders,' she says. 'Sometimes

I feel like saying, Would it still be such a lovely day if I was fat and ugly?'

She shows me what she's bought. An ice-lolly maker for Katrine's birthday. A velvet picture-frame. A flippy silky skirt, because Max is taking her to the ballet. She holds it up against her. 'I thought with my black pointy boots—d'you think that would be OK?' I tell her it will look lovely. And she has a book about Hare Krishna, which someone was selling in the street—she isn't going to read it, she just felt sorry for him—and some earrings like liquorice allsorts, and a bunch of freesias in white paper. She's pink and happy: she loves shopping. The freesias are palest green with a delicate purple veining and the room is sweet with their scent.

'You've bought yourself some flowers.'

'I thought…' She nibbles her lip: she's a little embarrassed. 'It seems silly now, but there was this flower stall, and I thought perhaps we could take them to the river. For Maria. Now it's all over. D'you think freesias are OK? The roses were pretty too but I didn't have enough money.'

'I've always loved freesias,' I say.

'Shall we?'

'Yes.'

'We ought to do it now,' she says, 'or they'll go all brown and horrible.'

We drive there through the bright afternoon.

The river path is beautiful in the lavish afternoon

light. In the warm summer wind, the river crinkles like silk, holding the colours of the trees and the sky. Cyclists in Lycra pass us, talking in some language I don't recognise, and then a small helmeted girl, pedalling with great concentration. You can smell the winey sweetness of elder and the fruit-gum scent of balsam, and white dust rises from our feet as we walk. We look across the water to the house on Eel Pie Island and the terracotta boy. As always, just for a moment I think he's a living child.

As we near the place where they found Maria's body you can see there's a woman sitting there, on the grass on the river bank. She's in a black splash of shade, so still that I think for a moment that she too is a statue. It's an odd thing to be doing—perhaps a bit disinhibited: women don't usually sit here all alone on the grass. She turns her head as we approach, and I recognise her at once—the Mediterranean colouring, her hair pulled back, the lines driving deep in her face. It's too late to go back now.

She looks up at me: I know she recognises me. I feel a little afraid. It's her grief that frightens me—and that I am here with my daughter, and she doesn't have hers.

'You were at the trial,' she says. Her voice is quiet and I can only just hear her.

'Yes,' I tell her.

There are many bunches of flowers against the trunk of the willow, their reds and yellows vivid in the sun;

the ink on the cards is clear still, not yet blurred by rain. They've only just been put here. Because of the trial and the verdict, other people, strangers like us or family, have come here, to the place where Maria's death is remembered. I stand by the woman and watch as Amber takes her bunch of freesias and places them carefully there.

She looks back at me uncertainly.

'We didn't put a message on. We should have put a message.'

'They're very pretty,' the woman says to Amber.

Amber bends for a moment, to read all the words on the cards.

The woman turns to me.

'It's strange you're here,' she says. 'Because I wanted to see you. I tried to find you after the trial but I couldn't find you anywhere.'

'I just went home,' I say.

Amber straightens, looks across at us, working out what to do now.

'Mum. I thought I'd go for a walk,' she says, with studied casualness. 'I thought I could look for the heron.'

She goes off down the path.

I sit on the grass beside Maria's mother. In the shade the ground still has a slight dampness to it, in spite of the heat of the day. We're close to the richness of earth and sap, and the mingled scents of the river bank. The wind breathes softly.

'I wanted to find you to thank you,' she says.

'You don't need to thank me,' I tell her. 'Anyone would have done the same.'

'No, I don't think they would have,' she says. 'Not in your situation. He gave you a very tough time. It must have been horrible for you.'

'It wasn't so bad,' I tell her.

'I'm very grateful,' she says.

We sit in silence for a while. A fleet of slow swans passes.

'I come here quite often,' she says then. Talking as though we know each other well. 'I feel nearer to her here. Each time I come, I think I'm going to reach her, to touch her. But of course I can't.'

I don't say anything.

'I blame myself,' she says. She has her head down, she isn't looking at me. 'I saw things happening. There are only so many times you can walk into a wall.'

'You mustn't blame yourself,' I say.

'It's so difficult, with children, to know how far to interfere,' she says. 'They have to lead their own lives. Well, you're a mother. You'll understand... Though if I could do it again, there's so much I would do differently. Everything.'

'Yes,' I say.

'It's sometimes the hardest thing to know what's right,' she says.

A barge glides slowly past us, with pots of begonias on top, and a man at the back holding a striped umbrella. Three geese take off from the water with a great clatter of wings. We gaze out over the river and all the things it carries and contains, its barges, waterbirds, rowing teams, pleasure boats, its litter of tyres and rubbish bags and polystyrene boxes: and its plants that move so sinuously as the water covers them, as though they are stirred by a secret wind.

Amber has come back, and sits on the grass a few yards from us, hugging her knees, tactfully turned away.

'I guess you need to go,' says the woman.

'Yes, we probably should.'

'I'm glad I met you,' she says.

She reaches out both hands and holds my hands for a moment. Her skin is so cold, in spite of the warmth of the day.

'I wish you well,' she says.

We walk back to the car.

'Was that Maria's mother?' says Amber.

'Yes,' I tell her.

'I'm glad we did that,' she says. 'I felt a bit embarrassed, but I'm sure we did the right thing.'

It's hot in the car. We wind the windows down and the breeze comes in, smelling of salt and elderflowers.

Amber takes some jelly sweets out of the pocket of her jeans. They're a disturbing blue colour.

'Amber, those sweets look like they're made from nuclear waste,' I say.

She ignores this.

'Mum,' she says, 'when's Molly coming home?'

'Saturday. It's the end of term. We're bringing all her stuff home.'

'I miss her,' she says.

'I know you do.'

She looks round doubtfully at my car.

'We'll never get all her stuff in here.'

'We'll manage,' I tell her. 'Dad's coming over, we're going in his car.'

'Just like we used to,' she says.

The yearning in her voice hurts me. I put my hand on her arm.

'It's OK, Mum.' She unwraps a sweet and sticks it into her mouth. 'I can live with it,' she says, through the sweet. 'You don't have to worry about me.'

We come to the high brick wall that runs round the grounds of the convent. There are seedlings on the table in the gateway. I pull up at the kerb.

'Honestly, Mum. You and your plants,' says Amber. 'You always have to have something to look after.'

I get out of the car. The handwritten label says that they are Iceland poppies, and you can put donations in the Cadbury's biscuit tin.

I choose a boxful. I shall plant them out in the border under the pear tree: I know just where they can go. In my mind's eye, they're flowering there already: I can see their sooty stamens, the sheen on their petals, the colours so true that you feel they might come off on your hand. Poppies fall quickly, they're such ephemeral things, you can't expect weeks of flowering: but for those few days they're so lovely. And they seed themselves and next year perhaps they'll come up all over the garden.

A sudden huge gratitude washes through me. I open the biscuit tin, and find my purse and tip out all my money. The mist has lifted and the land has changed. But I know I can live here.

Read all about it...

MORE ABOUT THIS BOOK

MORE ABOUT THE AUTHOR

WE RECOMMEND

MIRA

Read all about it…

QUESTIONS FOR YOUR READING GROUP

1. Is Ginnie right to act as she does? In her situation, what would you have done?

2. How does Ginnie's childhood experience shape the decision she makes?

3. What do you think about the way Ginnie has brought up her children? Is she a good mother?

4. Climate change and the fear of climate change are often referred to. What is the significance of this for the story?

5. Mid-life is one of the central themes of *The River House* and Ginnie, Will, Greg, Eva and Max are all in their forties or fifties. Consider the different ways these characters react to being middle-aged.

6. What role does the Thames play in the story? Why do you think the author chose to set her story by the river?

7. One of the characters says, "It's that time of life for us, isn't it? Our kids growing up, our parents getting frail. And we're the ones caught in the middle. Keeping it all going." Is that a situation that you recognise?

8. Why do Ginnie and Ursula have such different memories of the family life they shared as children?

9. At the end of the book, how has Ginnie been changed by the events of the story?

Read all about it...

INSPIRATION

We drive our elder daughter to university for the start of her first term. It's a strange, unnerving day. We leave her—flushed, thrilled, uncertain—in her rather bleak college room. It seems a huge event, the end point of all those years of full-time parenting: because, though of course we'll still be important, I know we won't be her centre of gravity any more. But there's nothing to mark this moment—my child just slips away. And it happens that she's going to my old college and there's so much I recognise—the worn brown carpets, the portraits of stern, prestigious women, the familiar smells of polish and cabbage on the stairs. Nostalgia floods me. It's a little shift in time, taking me straight back to when I was my daughter's age. I remember how sure I was then about everything: how I knew I would get it all sorted—that some day I'd discover what life was all about. Yet here I am, years later, and the thing I thought I was moving towards continues to elude me.

I imagine another woman in this situation— a woman who has been taking shape in my mind—someone whose marriage has largely been held together by the shared project of child-rearing. How might she feel in this moment—leaving her daughter here? Would she be suddenly, painfully, confronted with the fragility of her marriage? And what if she then met a man to whom she felt attracted? Might she amaze herself by opening up to the lure of a new love? As I think through this love affair, I know that for this woman in her forties it will be intensely physical—more so than anything in her life before; and utterly secret, because both she and her lover will be determined to protect their families; and poignant with a sense of transience, of everything flowing so swiftly past her.

Perhaps this is why I chose to set this woman's story by the river. The Thames flows near my house and beside it there's a narrow belt of wild ground. It's a contradictory landscape: beautiful, with herons flying over, and scented in summer with elder that grows as high as your head, but also rather sinister. It's all quite overgrown and I rapidly start feeling nervous if I'm alone there. And there's always that sense of change, of everything moving on. It seemed the perfect setting—a backdrop for a secret meeting of lovers and a place to hide the evidence of a terrible crime.

Read all about it…

AUTHOR BIOGRAPHY

© Nikki Gibbs

Margaret Leroy grew up in the New Forest and studied music at St Hilda's College, Oxford. She has worked as a music therapist, teacher and psychiatric social worker.

Her first book, *Miscarriage*, was published in 1987 and *Aristotle Sludge*, a story for children, was published in 1991. She then wrote two books about women and relationships — *Pleasure: The truth about female sexuality* and *Some Girls Do: Why women do and don't make the first move*. Both were serialised in the *Daily Express*.

For two years she wrote an agony aunt column for *Options* magazine and her articles and short stories have been published in the *Observer*, the *Sunday Express* and the *Mail on Sunday*.

She has written five novels. The first, *Trust*, was televised by ITV1 as *Loving You* and starred Douglas Henshall and Niamh Cusack, reaching an audience of eight million. She has appeared on numerous radio and TV programmes and her books have been translated into ten languages. Margaret is married, has two daughters and lives in Surrey.

Read all about it…

" …the moment your baby falls asleep, you start writing…"

WHY I WRITE…

I wrote constantly as a child—rather fey fantasies. But I was also into music and, from about age twelve, my piano-playing became all-consuming and I stopped writing till I was in my early twenties. I started writing again when I was studying music therapy. A session with an autistic boy went badly wrong and I went home, disconsolate, and started writing poems to comfort myself. After that, I never stopped writing again—though I never wrote any more poems. But I only gave up my day job as a psychiatric social worker after the birth of our younger daughter. I found that writing while looking after small children is difficult, but not impossible, though you do have to be very focused, so that the moment your baby falls asleep, you start writing. That's a great discipline —and perhaps the reason why women who write while bringing up children never seem to get writer's block.

"...the seed
of a
story can
come from
anywhere..."

Q&A ON WRITING

What do you love the most about being a writer?

The most pleasurable part comes some way into writing a book, when I've created a world that I can then re-enter every time I sit down to write—when I know what that world looks like, sounds like, smells like.

Where do you go for inspiration?

The seed of a story can come from anywhere—perhaps a television programme, or something that happened to someone I know, or something that happened to me. In the case of *The River House*, it was a sentence in a newspaper article about a murder committed long ago, where a witness hadn't come forward because she'd been with her illicit lover at the time. I thought that would be an intriguing moral dilemma to explore.

What one piece of advice would you give to a writer wanting to start a career?

Keep notebooks. Make a note of anything that interests you—even a scrap of overheard conversation. That way you'll have a rich source of material to dip into again and again.

Which book do you wish you had written?

I'd love to have written Ursula Le Guin's Earthsea saga. Her sentences are so beautiful and it must be wonderful to create a whole new world and its landscapes, myths and magical creatures.

How did you feel when your first book was signed?

Thrilled and rather scared. Scared because I sold it on the basis of the outline—it was a self-help book, on miscarriage—and I still had to write the book!

Read all about it…

Where do your characters come from and do they ever surprise you as you write?

It's really hard to remember where my characters come from, because once I've created them they seem as real to me as if they've always existed. I think I often start with some small detail that feels right—maybe their hair colour, or the way they talk—and build them from there. And then for my main character I'll create a back story that will make the dilemma she faces in the present day especially poignant for her.

Do you have a favourite character that you've created and what is it you like about that character?

I love writing children and teenagers and in this book I especially enjoyed Amber—for the way she's so full of contradictions, at once wilful and enchanting, as teenage girls so often are.

What kind of research goes into the writing process?

My idea for this book really started to take shape when I decided to set the story on the river path. So I spent a lot of time wandering along by the Thames and watching the way this bit of wild landscape changed through the seasons.

As a mother, how much has your own experience shaped your writing about parenthood?

Being a mother has shaped my writing tremendously. Here, I wanted to write as precisely as I could about mothering teenage children: about the pleasure you take in them as they grow up, which can be a bitter-sweet feeling as they're also growing away from you, and about the way a marriage can change when children leave home.

A WRITER'S LIFE

Paper and pen or straight onto the computer?

I'm a very low-tech person—I use unlined paper and pencil. I don't like working directly onto the keyboard as I need to see my crossings-out.

PC or laptop?

Laptop.

Music or silence?

I crave silence when I'm writing. I hate hammers and electric drills, and I love my noise-reduction headphones.

"…I keep the less creative stuff … for the afternoon…"

Morning or night?

I'm absolutely a morning person. I keep the less creative stuff like typing for the afternoon.

Coffee or tea?

Very strong coffee in little green French-café cups.

Your guilty reading pleasure?

Re-reading *The Lord of the Rings*. It makes me feel guilty because I've read it so often I practically know it by heart.

The first book you loved?

Shadow the Sheepdog by Enid Blyton.

The last book you read?

The Nightmare Years by William Shirer.

Read all about it…

A DAY IN THE LIFE

We live on the edge of town, near the Thames, and sometimes I'm woken by the lovely wild sound of geese flying over. I'm a great believer in breakfast—it's usually bacon and egg. Then I drive my younger daughter, Izzie, to school. My beloved Ford Escort is twenty years old now and I'm always listening out for new and ominous rattles. The traffic is horrible and I arrive back home with a slight sense of triumph that we've survived another rush hour.

I write in bed—which, I'm convinced, is good for creativity, because you're so much more relaxed than when you sit at a desk. Typically I'll be surrounded by a sprawl of paper. I don't mind a bit of untidiness around me—if things look too neat, it means there's nothing going on. My filing system is a pot of coloured paper-clips.

"…I write in bed — which, I'm convinced, is good for creativity…"

What form the writing takes will depend on the stage of the book that I've reached. I start with lots of brainstorming, then I'll put together quite a detailed plot: I can't just head off into my story without knowing where I'm going. Once I've sketched out the plot, I try to get the whole story down very quickly, scarcely looking back at all. Then I'll go through it lots of times, rewriting and developing. This is much the longest stage of writing a book for me and the part I really love. How well I work varies hugely and I try to have simpler tasks like research or typing lined up for those days when the writing doesn't flow. But if it's going well, I'm completely happy.

Lunch is fried rice and vegetables. I always cook the same thing: I'm hopeless at cooking, but my husband, thank goodness, is a brilliant cook, so we don't starve. While I eat, I read, something I

can just dip into, maybe poetry; at the moment
it might be Lavinia Greenlaw or Alice Oswald.
Any work done after lunch is a bonus, and
—perhaps because it's marked the end of my
working day for so long—I tend to switch off
around the time that school ends, even when
no-one needs picking up.

At the end of the afternoon, I see to the
practical stuff—shopping, e-mails, housework.
Fortunately I'm short-sighted so I don't notice
cobwebs. My inspiration for the practical side
of life comes from J.K. Rowling, who was once
asked how she managed to write while bringing
up her daughter single-handed and said she just
didn't do any housework for four years. My husband makes our evening meal and afterwards
I'll probably watch television: after all that writing, I'm hungry for images. I love television and
there have been so many marvellously addictive
series in the past few years—*Prison Break, Inva-
sion, The Wire*. Recently Izzie and I have had a
blissful time watching all seven seasons of *Buffy
the Vampire Slayer*.

Read all about it...

MY TOP TEN BOOKS

A Wizard of Earthsea by Ursula Le Guin
I always go back to the Earthsea books when life
gets difficult, there's something so healing about
the slow, intricate rhythms of Ursula Le Guin's
prose.

The Siege by Helen Dunmore
The siege of Leningrad, told from a female,
domestic perspective. You really live this story
when you read it—you feel the hunger and the
cold.

The Mabinogion
Dream-like Welsh stories, written down in the
Middle Ages, and full of strange transformations.
I love the story of Blodeuedd, a beautiful girl
who is conjured up from the flowers of the oak
and the broom and the meadowsweet.

The English Patient by Michael Ondaatje
It's about a small group of people thrown
together by war, worn down, somehow
surviving. Ondaatje writes so lyrically about
the desert and Renaissance angels and Tuscan
gardens under rain.

The Pillow Book of Sei Shonagon
Musings and jottings and lots of lists from a
court lady in tenth-century Japan. Her writing
is intimate, sensuous and somehow very contemporary.

Rebecca by Daphne du Maurier
An iconic psychological thriller. I've read it lots
of times, but at certain twists in the plot, my
heart still goes racing off.

Housekeeping by Marilynne Robinson
It's the simplest story, about two girls and their
elusive aunt, who reluctantly abandons her life
as a drifter to bring them up. Perhaps the most
wonderfully written book I've ever read.

Read all about it...

The Bloody Chamber by Angela Carter
Adult fairy tales—sexy, savage and gorgeous.

Jonathan Strange and Mr Norrell
by Susanna Clarke
This story of two wizards during the Napoleonic
Wars is my favourite new book of recent years.
When I got to the end—p. 782—I went straight
back to the beginning and read it all again.

The Mahabharata by Jean-Claude Carrière
The script of the film directed by Peter Brook, based
on stories from the Indian epic. It's bloody but very
beautiful. As one of the characters says as he starts to
tell the story, "If you listen carefully, at the end you'll
be someone else."

14

**If you enjoyed *The River House*,
we know you'll love...**

The Perfect Mother by Margaret Leroy

Catriona has the life she's always dreamed of: a loving husband, a delightful step-daughter and her own precious little girl, Daisy.

But when Cat is accused of harming eight-year-old Daisy through Munchausen's Syndrome by Proxy, Cat begins to realise that the life she has now is more fragile than she could ever have imagined.

Before the Storm by Diane Chamberlain

Born with Foetal Alcohol Spectrum Disorder, fifteen-year-old Andy Lockwood is now a hero after helping dozens of children escape a burning church.

Laurel lost Andy once through neglect and is determined to make amends. Yet when Andy is suspected of arson, Laurel must ask herself how well she really knows her son—and how far she'll go to protect him.

"I'VE STRIVEN TO BE THE PERFECT MOTHER, WANTING TO CREATE A PERFECT CHILDHOOD FOR MY CHILD. YET SOMETHING HAS GONE WRONG..."

Catriona has the life she's always dreamed of:
a loving husband, a delightful step-daughter and
her own precious little girl, Daisy.

But when Cat is accused of harming eight-year-old
Daisy through Munchausen's Syndrome by Proxy,
Cat begins to realise that the life she has now is
more fragile than she could ever have imagined.

www.mirabooks.co.uk

A HAUNTED CHILD.
A DESPERATE MOTHER.
AN UNSPEAKABLE TRUTH.

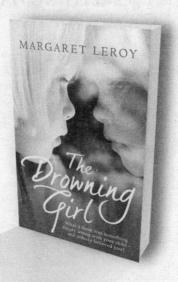

Young single mum Grace is drowning. Her little girl Sylvie is distant and prone to violent tantrums which the psychiatrists blame on Grace. But Grace knows there's more to what's happening to Sylvie.

Travelling from London to the west coast of Ireland, Grace and Sylvie embark on a journey of shocking discovery, changing both their lives forever.

www.mirabooks.co.uk